PRAISE FOR GRAEME HAGUE
AND *MISSING PIECES*!

"Wickedly engrossing."

—*Daily Telegraph*

"Has everything necessary to keep you turning the pages."
—*Sydney Morning Herald*

"A killer ending to keep you gasping!"

—*3-D World*

"I won't be hanging around in big empty buildings at night for a while!"

—*People Magazine* (Australia)

DANGEROUS THOUGHTS

He thought about the fingers in the freezer and about how they were no good now. They weren't good *enough*, that was the point. The entire corpse was useless to him now. The hands, without their fingers, wouldn't be effective. Even the whole arm, with a fingerless hand, struck him as wrong. He needed to get rid of the body and maybe get another one, whole and complete, that gave him more options.

These were ugly, dangerous thoughts growing in the back of his mind. He needed money, which meant he would have to go out and do another job—a good one this time, with plenty of cash to grab. And it might give him an opportunity to play his new game as well. Maybe somebody would get too heroic and force him to pull the trigger, giving him a new corpse and a new *resource*.

Either way, a killing would get him on the front page of the newspaper. He liked that idea.

MISSING PIECES

GRAEME HAGUE

LEISURE BOOKS NEW YORK CITY

A LEISURE BOOK ®

January 2005

Published by

Dorchester Publishing Co., Inc.
200 Madison Avenue
New York, NY 10016

ISBN 0-8439-5482-5

The name "Leisure Books" and the stylized "L" with design are trademarks of Dorchester Publishing Co., Inc.

Printed in the United States of America.

Visit us on the web at www.dorchesterpub.com.

ACKNOWLEDGMENT

For those in the industry, the name Selwa Anthony keeps popping up—especially in my work. However, for this particular novel and the difficult path it traveled between conception and publication, she deserves special recognition and thanks.

ACKNOWLEDGMENT

MISSING
PIECES

Chapter One

Lena Hargreaves had no reason to think today was going to be anything but a normal day. Nothing was particularly different. She was dressed the same as always, looking every bit the professional secretary in a tight skirt and matching business jacket, dark stockings and black shoes, her hair pulled back into a ponytail. Her shoes were high heels, but not stilettos. Her reading glasses, while still fashionable, were also sensible with strong frames and a cord attached so she could hang them around her neck. Lena wore them now as she walked along the corridor towards the company's twenty-first floor reception area. Every time she passed an office she quickly glanced in, ready to nod and smile at whoever was there. The truth was, because of her strong lenses, Lena was hardly able to recognise anyone. Only a blurred figure told her someone was there at all. But she knew the glasses gave her an efficient look, so she kept them on and suffered feeling her way around a world of hazy outlines and fuzzy edges.

Her employers used the entire floor for their offices. Recently they had tried to rent more space on the level above for an archive area. Instead, a room on the highest, thirty-second, floor was offered at a very reasonable rate and they took it. The space was used for storing older files and out-of-date material, so the staff wouldn't waste too much time moving from one area to the other. The management also figured that once you were in the lift, it didn't matter how many floors you travelled. But after the first few weeks staff were quick to disagree with the new system. The "old" files were continually referred to and those who did the trip upstairs complained about forever waiting in the foyer for the elevators. Then, even if it only took a minute to locate the correct file, by the time they returned to the foyer the lift would have been summoned back to another floor, causing a further frustrating delay.

Lena clutched a bunch of files to her chest as she made her way to the elevator. The four lifts were in a small alcove partially hidden from the reception area. With her glasses on, seeing the "up" button was easy—Lena could stand close enough for it to swim into focus. She pressed it and stood back. Waiting, she looked around, trying to pierce the blur of her glasses. No-one was nearby and the receptionist at the desk had her head down, busy. Satisfied nobody was watching, Lena looked up at the numbers above the lift door. They were slightly blurred, but she could read them. After taking a small step backwards, the numbers fuzzed to indistinction and Lena knew she was only kidding herself she could make them out now. With a sigh and another quick search around to make sure no-one was watching, Lena lifted her glasses up to her forehead. After a moment of confusion her eyes focused and the electronic numbers were sharp and clear. She glanced quickly down at the files pressed against her chest, letting them fall backwards so she could read their titles. Even though these were in large, bold type, the lettering was now blurred and indistinct. Lena clicked her tongue in disappointment. It seemed such a shame, her bad eyes, when she had everything else going for her.

A bell pinged announcing the arival of a lift and Lena dropped her glasses back down, but as the doors slid apart she saw it was empty. She stepped inside quickly, suppressing a small shudder as she passed between the doors. Lena hated lifts, starting with a fear of getting caught between the closing doors. Even though she knew they should immediately spring back, they *looked* capable of crushing her and she was always startled when they began to close and she wasn't completely inside.

As the lift began its smooth movement upwards she began to worry about the mechanism itself. Lena's understanding of it was that she was now in a steel box suspended by a slim, vulnerable cable. She had seen too many movies where a lift's occupants were threatened by a fraying, about-to-break cable. Of course, in the movie everybody would get out just in time and the viewers would be treated to a heart-stopping scene of the empty elevator plunging away to destruction down the lift shaft, the severed cable trailing uselessly after it. But Lena could imagine what it would be like to remain trapped inside. She shuddered again and looked uneasily at the walls around her. The lift jerked and she sucked in her breath nervously, but it had only arrived at the top floor. The doors slid apart and she saw the alcove here was empty too.

The top floor was vacant apart from her own company's filing rooms. The decor was still as the builders had left it with bland, inexpensive carpet and pastel paints on the walls. It smelled new with a faint odour of chemicals, paint and adhesives and the air-conditioning to the floor was shut down to conserve energy. The filing room was a short walk down the corridor to an unmarked door. Lena had her own key—in fact lots of people had a key, because so many of the staff needed to come here. As far as she was concerned the security of the place was a joke. It was one of those management areas Lena would soon fix if she was given the authority. She often fantasised about how she would run this or that if she was promoted. She swung the door wide and shoved a small box against it to prevent it automatically closing again.

The filing room was supposed to be a medium-sized conference room. Now it was segregated messily by tall bookshelves, metal filing cabinets and piles of cardboard boxes filled with musty paperwork that Lena was thankful she hadn't needed to delve into yet. The rest of the room was disorganised and hastily labelled with hand-lettered signs taped wherever there was a place. You had to search around until you found the section you needed; only then did you encounter some sort of system. The sole area of any efficiency was a desk near the door where everyone was expected to note down who they were, what files they'd taken, and later cross them off the register on their return trip. Junior clerks were regularly sent up to refile any material left on the desk. Lena was one of the privileged secretaries who didn't have to perform this menial task. She simply dumped her own load for someone else to worry about and used a pencil attached to the register with a piece of string to scratch a line through the files she'd returned. Then she took a slip of paper from her pocket and consulted the list of new files she needed.

Lena didn't like having the filing room door closed when she was in there alone. It was unnaturally quiet compared to the offices downstairs, and there were lots of little niches and spaces where someone could hide. When there was someone else there looking for files, the room became a haven from the work downstairs and you could have a friendly chat or exchange a bit of office gossip. Some of the staff, Lena knew, used the place to sneak a quick forbidden cigarette.

But when you were alone in the room, as she was now, it got a little spooky.

Lena moved nervously through the maze of shelves and cabinets. She knew she was being silly, but couldn't stop herself. The best answer was to find the files as quickly as she could and get the hell out of there. She found herself wishing she'd gotten one of the junior clerks to do this for her. Strictly, she wasn't supposed to do that, because she wasn't senior enough, but a few of the younger male staff members didn't need much coercing when Lena smiled sweetly.

She found the first file soon enough. The second proved harder, and when she went back to the register she saw someone else had already pulled it. Lena made a noise of annoyance to herself for not checking the register against her list. She checked now, and saw the other two files she wanted were still in the room somewhere.

Back among the files Lena heard someone else come into the room. At once relieved to have somebody else with her, and also anxious to make sure it was a staff member she knew and liked, Lena called out.

"Hello? Who's there?"

She tried to sound friendly, rather than anxious. There was no answer.

"Is someone there? It's Lena from accounts here."

Still no-one replied.

Frowning, she made her way back to the register. There was nobody there. Lena dropped her glasses down to the tip of her nose. It made her look ten years older, she knew, but right then she didn't care. The further reaches of the room came into focus and Lena peered anxiously around. It seemed she was still alone.

"Is there somebody in here, or not?" she tried again, torn between feeling silly and frightened.

The room stayed silent.

On an impulse she stepped outside the filing room and stared up the corridor. With her glasses still lowered, she could see one of the lifts had arrived at the floor, the doors open and waiting for whoever summoned it. Either that, or someone had just *exited* the lift.

But Lena, if she was to believe the silence that answered her calls, was still alone on the thirty-second floor.

Maybe it's one of the maintenance people, and they've gone to another part of the floor, she thought, trying to ignore a creeping feeling between her shoulder blades. The noise of the lift arriving must have been what she had heard before.

Suddenly the open lift doors were too inviting for her—and Lena was getting spooked. She'd found one file and that meant it hadn't been a wasted trip. Ignoring writing anything into the register, Lena yanked the door past the cardboard box holding it open. She waited just long enough to hear the latch snicking closed and hurried back along the corridor towards the lifts. Now she found herself hoping the elevator would stay on the floor long enough for her to catch it. Lena stared at the open doors and she walked quickly, willing them to remain that way. It was tempting to break into a trot, but she restrained herself.

The lift doors began to close and she lunged through just in time, causing the doors to spring open again. Her glasses started to slip off the end of her nose and in a practised reflex movement she pushed them fully back on, instantly blurring the world around her. Muttering a startled *"Damn!"* she looked back through the doors. The alcove beyond appeared empty and so did the other corridor leading in the opposite direction. With a sigh of relief Lena stabbed the button marked 21 and leaned back against the rear wall of the elevator. She closed her eyes and took a few deep breaths to calm herself. As usual, the lift doors seemed to take an age to close.

When the elevator began to drop Lena immediately felt safer and began to wonder if she'd been foolish. She quickly decided not to tell anyone about fleeing the filing rooms. Lena opened her eyes and composed herself, becoming the efficient, professional secretary again. Then she saw something on the floor in front of her. It was surprising she hadn't stepped on it as she entered the lift. She screwed her eyes up and tried to focus through the glasses, but it didn't work. She leaned over, peering at the thing, but still couldn't make out what it was. Aware that she had a few seconds before the lift reached her own floor and the doors would open, Lena propped her glasses on the end of her nose and looked over the top of them. The thing on the floor swam into clarity.

It was a severed human finger.

The receptionist on the twenty-first floor heard Lena's muted, horrified scream moments before the elevator arrived with its gay ringing tone. Startled, she looked up to see the doors open and Lena come stumbling out, her face deathly white and her hand clasped firmly over her mouth.

The manila file lay open in the lift behind her, the pages scattered most unprofessionally across the floor.

Chapter Two

Detective Sergeant John Maiden figured he had been at the Rocks police station too long. After seven years he'd had more than his share of arresting the petty criminals, drunks, hookers and junkies who came into the city's central business district in the middle of the night and did what Maiden considered "stupid" things. Stupid robberies of Japanese tourists or stupid assaults on office workers who, in turn, were all too stupid to go home at a reasonable hour. They left their cars in remote parking spots late into the night and then couldn't understand how they got broken into or stolen. Occasionally the criminals would stupidly kill one another, but there was nothing exciting in that for Maiden. Usually, the culprit would be a lover or a best friend and an arrest happened within hours. Either that, or the circumstances of the murder could be so senselessly random and obscure that the casefile got shelved almost straightaway, labelled another instance of one drugged-up poor fool killing another. There wasn't any profit in the Department trying too hard to find a culprit. It usually just wasted a lot of forensic time and taxpapers' money, while detectives like Maiden would have to dig around in the stink of back alleys and question people who hardly knew what their own names were any more. The person the detectives were looking for was probably already on the way to their own death through a drug overdose or an infected needle. The guilty person could just as likely get their own throat cut the next night. It happened, Maiden was sure. Some people seemed to just disappear from the face of the earth.

He sighed and stared out the window at office workers moving along the footpath below. His desk was butted up against the glass, which was tinted grey underneath the stain of God-knew-what smudges of filth. Maiden was convinced the maintenance people never cleaned his window. He couldn't remember anyone ever cleaning the outside, either, which was coated with city smog. He leaned over and pressed his forehead against the cool glass. Maiden was a strong, heavy-set man and the chair groaned in protest. He could see a sea of people streaming along the streets and choking into agitated swarms at the pedestrian crossings. Maiden puzzled over what they were all doing walking the city streets at ten o'clock in the morning, instead of being at their desks and working like he was— they had to be tourists and school groups. He wondered if any of them cared about how this busy, exciting city became something else around midnight and policemen like him were expected to clean it up for them before morning.

Of course they do, he thought wryly. *They know the rules—well, most of them do, anyway. In the middle of the night when they're all safely tucked into their beds Sydney's no different from anywhere else. We might as well be living in damned Los Angeles.*

The glass misted with Maiden's breath and he wiped it away with his finger, carving a neat peephole in the condensation. He spotted a large group of Japanese tourists all dressed in brightly coloured clothes that stuck out in the greys and blacks of everyone else's winter clothing. *Go and see the bloody Opera House,* he told them silently. *Take a million pictures—and don't forget the bloody great Bridge next to it. And the zoo. See if you can get pissed on by a koala.* He snorted a humourless laugh which clouded his peephole again, and sighed and turned away.

Maiden's desk was one of many spread around the room. Some were communal, where police officers shared chairs, phones and the mess. He was lucky to have his own due to his rank and years spent at the station, though that didn't stop people grabbing his telephone the moment his back was turned. He didn't mind. He didn't care about much at all, these days. Lately he had been feeling jaded by work and his life. At least he rarely inflicted his discontentment on others. He figured they were all in the same swamp, with everyone at various stages of enthusiasm. It was no-one's fault but his own that he was still doing the same job, in the same place.

He sipped his coffee and pulled a face at its lukewarm temperature. He'd passed an hour this morning on dull paperwork and was running out of excuses not to check in with his section head, a dour man called Longman, to find out what was in store for him today. Longman, he knew, would be starting to get annoyed.

Another detective, Sayers, who was the same rank as Maiden, flopped down at a desk nearby. He was a small and wiry man, and eternally cheerful. He looked up from a thick pile of papers he'd dropped onto the desk and saw Maiden.

"You see the bulletins from Despatch?" he called above the noise of the bustling room.

"No," Maiden replied, his voice roughened from the coffee and three cigarettes in quick succession on his way to work. He hacked out a cough. "Should I have?"

"That shotgun guy's been out again. This time he hit a drive-through liquor store. He hid himself among all the stacked-up cartons of beer and waited until the place was locked up tight, then sprung the manager as he was counting the money."

Maiden nodded reluctantly and tried to drag up some interest. The spate of recent armed hold-ups, apparently performed by the same person, had been happening outside of his area of operations and was therefore no business of his. But he felt a twinge of jealousy, because someone, somewhere, would be getting their teeth into a decent investigation. Shotgun Man was building up a reputation and getting some attention in the press.

"Well, he seems to do things just a fraction better than your average bandit," Maiden said with a shrug.

"But hey, listen to this. The interesting thing is, this guy was wearing the same clothes and used the same language, but his *physical* description didn't quite match the earlier jobs." Sayers looked at Maiden expectantly, who took the prompting.

"OK, so what's the catch?"

"Seems the manager of the hotel is a bit of gun nut and gave a detailed description of the shotgun. There's a good chance it's the same weapon and the thinking now is it's two guys doing the jobs, taking turns and sharing the risk, and using the same gun."

"The newspapers been told?"

"No, they're definitely trying to keep this bit quiet."

And you're not helping, Maiden thought, but kept it to himself. It would have been pointless. Discussing high-profile crimes was commonplace, anyway. Maiden was feeling twice as annoyed now, hearing the case was taking an intriguing turn. And worse, with this latest robbery there was every chance a taskforce would be formed to track the criminals down, which meant even if it did spill over into Maiden's area, he still wouldn't have anything to do with it. And the chances of him being appointed to any taskforce like that were zero.

His telephone rang, preventing any further conversation. He picked it up with a weary sigh. "Maiden here."

"John, I need you in my office now. Are you finished up?" It was Longman.

The question was a courtesy—Maiden wasn't expected to say he *wasn't* available for any reason. Still, for a moment he was tempted to mention more paperwork and a delay, just to get a dig at Longman.

"Yeah, all done only a minute ago. I'll be right there."

With a nod to Sayers he got up and made his way towards the end of the room to Longman's small office. On the way he brushed past several people and offered a short humourless greeting to each—except for one of the female detectives to whom he gave a smile and got one back in return. Most women found him attractive, despite his rather battered facial features and his thick brown hair which refused to stay in any semblance of neatness. In two months Maiden would turn thirty-nine and, by coincidence, it would be exactly twelve months since his second divorce. Lately, he knew, he hadn't been smiling much.

Longman didn't smile, either, as Maiden pushed into the cramped office.

"There you are," he said looking up briefly. "I've got something here that we've been asked to have a look at."

He handed a report sheet to Maiden, who hadn't bothered to sit down. Maiden quickly scanned the sheet, his eyes blindly running over the standard information until he got to the case description.

"A finger?" he asked, raising his eyebrows. "Is that all?"

"If there was a body and a butcher's knife covered in blood, I'd tell you," Longman said impatiently. "It is just a finger, and that's all I know. Give Crime Scene a call for the details, if there are any. Apparently the Black Widow is handling it. What's her real name?"

"Janet Brown," Maiden told him, biting back anger. Nobody liked Longman because of his constant sarcasm and cynicism, which he had no qualms about using on the people under him. But Longman seemed to enjoy antagonising Maiden in particular. Perhaps because he was the obvious next-in-line for Longman's position and posed a kind of threat. Scanning the sheet again Maiden added, "I've spoken to her on the phone a few times, but I've never met her."

"Well, you'll get to talk to her again. I think you should interview the girl who found the finger, too, so I've asked her to stay put until you get there. Don't keep her waiting long. I don't want you wasting too much time on it—you know how to go through all the motions with this sort of bullshit. I think we'll find it's just some sort of medical-student prank."

Maiden was already acknowledging the instructions, waving the report sheet in the air as he left the office. He went back to his desk and picked up the phone, dialling an internal number connecting him to Crime Scene—the forensic department at the Police Centre in Surry Hills. He heard the click of a switchboard and a female operator asked him briefly, "Which department?"

"I want to speak to Janet Brown."

"Hold the line. I'll have to try and find her."

Aren't you supposed to know where she is? Maiden thought, still feeling annoyed. He tapped the finger of his free hand on the top of his desk. After several minutes he'd only heard the occasional click of the operator confirming he was still waiting, which bugged him even further because it struck him as rudely impersonal.

"I could have bloody *walked* there by now," he finally told the phone. That wasn't true, but the idea of driving over was growing more attractive with every passing second. It would take him about ten minutes to cover the distance to Surry Hills. Maiden figured the trip might put him in a better frame of mind and it wouldn't do any harm to meet Janet Brown in person, seeing he might often be dealing with her. She had been put in charge of her department a year ago and had previously been hidden away in one of the more obscure laboratories. Despite both Maiden and Janet Brown having worked for years for the police force, their paths hadn't crossed. Now Maiden figured it would help being able to put a face to the infamous Black Widow.

She'd earned the nickname quickly and it had spread just as fast. Janet Brown's husband had died a few years before and she was still, apparently, grieving. Everybody said she simply stayed quiet and professional, never encouraging discussion on anything but her work and not bothering with small talk or gossip. Beneath her white laboratory coat she always wore dark clothing. The office grapevine at The Rocks had it she was very good looking, which only added to her mystique.

Maiden decided to drive. "Fuck you, too," he said, hanging up, convinced the operator was keeping him on hold just to piss him off. He stood and took his jacket from the back of the chair. Putting it on, he patted the pockets to make sure his wallet and cigarettes were in place, then he called over to Sayers.

"I've got to go over to Surry Hills for a while, if anyone's looking for me."

Sayers raised a hand and nodded without taking his eyes from the papers in front of him.

Outside, Maiden shivered in the chilly winter air and was already regretting leaving the warmth of his office. But it was too late to turn back now, so he hunched his shoulders against the cold and quickly bundled himself into his car, reaching for the heater straightaway before he even started the motor.

The reception area of the Police Centre was manned by someone he didn't recognise, so Maiden had to identify himself before he was allowed to enter the restricted areas. He made his way downstairs to the basement level and went slowly along the line of offices, hoping to see someone he knew. He didn't, and ended up knocking softly on the door of a room where a woman, dressed in a white coat, was bent over some papers on her desk. She looked up at him through lightweight spectacles.

"Yes?" she asked gently.

Maiden was always polite and soft-spoken when dealing with women, especially pretty ones. "I'm looking for Janet Brown, but I don't know what she looks like. I've only spoken to her on the telephone."

"I'm Janet Brown."

Maiden was taken aback. She was a lot younger than he had expected, perhaps in her late thirties at the most. And the stories were true. She was very attractive, despite the fact she was making no attempts to be so. Janet Brown was wearing only minimal make-up and had her dark hair pulled back from her face into a thick ponytail. She had fine features and large brown eyes. The laboratory coat made her figure almost shapeless, but from the way she sat and the set of her shoulders he would have bet his mortgage she was slim.

"I'm told you're the one I have to speak to about a finger," he said, recovering.

"Ah," she nodded, rising from her chair and letting Maiden see he was right about her figure. "Our missing finger—well," she corrected herself, "the rest of the body is what's missing, really. I suppose you want to see it?"

"I suppose I'd better. What can you tell me about it?"

She was coming around her desk and stopped in midstride. "Not a lot. It's only a finger, after all," she said, looking at him steadily. It took Maiden a moment to realise she wasn't being smart, but rather honest.

"No, it's not a lot to go on," he said, close to an apology, before he realised how stupid that would be.

She moved on, brushing past him into the corridor. Maiden caught a scent of her perfume and was surprised she was wearing any. It didn't fit with the lack of make-up and sensible clothing. He followed her down the hallway into a large open area with many strange-looking medical instruments and devices fitted to high benches. Most of them were being used by technicians, all of whom ignored Maiden and his escort as they travelled through the room. Brown pushed her way through a pair of wide swinging doors, and Maiden had to reach forward quickly to stop them closing in his face. On the other side he found himself in a smaller room lined with shelves filled with all manner of bottles, jars, tins and plastic containers, each labelled with an unpronounceable chemical name.

Brown was at a large refrigerator with double stainless-steel doors. She pulled one open with effort. Maiden wondered if he should have offered to help, then decided she wouldn't appreciate it. He could see the refrigerator contained more strange liquids and concoctions in their labelled bottles. Brown plucked something out from among them and backed away, shutting the door with a metallic clunk. She held a large, clear, zip-top plastic bag towards Maiden, who automatically took it. The severed finger lay nestled at the bottom of the bag. The bloodied end had turned brown and there was a glimmer of bone showing.

"Well, it's definitely a finger," Maiden said after a few seconds, trying to sound casual.

"Today is your lucky day," she said mildly. "I used it as a subject for some students, otherwise you might not have had any results for a few days. It's not exactly high priority."

Maiden managed a grateful nod.

Brown went on in clipped sentences, "OK, it's the forefinger, or index finger, of a right hand. Blood type was A positive and the owner was Caucasian. Since the last time he or she washed their hands they had read a newspaper. The ink was easy to pick up. Apart from that, there's nothing much to tell. There's the usual scalp particles under the nail from head scratching and such, but that's all. It's difficult to put together a picture of the entire human being just from one finger," she finished with a shrug and watched him.

Maiden held the bag closer and studied the finger some more. Now he noticed a black stain of ink where someone had taken a print for identification. He didn't ask the obvious question there. If the print had given them the identity of the finger's owner he would have been told by now. "'He' or 'she'?" he asked, glancing at her a moment. "You can't tell if it belongs to a male or female?"

"I can say the fingernail hasn't recently been shaped or manicured, which means it most likely comes from a man, but not necessarily. It's soft, too. No callouses or scars to suggest manual labour, but then again if it *did*, it doesn't mean it has to be male. You'll find women workers on any building site now. The softness only tells us the owner probably wasn't a manual labourer of some kind."

"Do you know if they were dead when the finger was removed?"

"No . . . Well," Brown changed her mind, "they certainly hadn't been dead for some time. They could have been dead up to six hours previous to the finger being cut off and I wouldn't be able to tell the difference."

"OK. Can you tell if this person cut their own finger off?"

Brown frowned at him before her look changed to one of concentration. "I never thought about that, but now that you ask, I'd say no. There's no way of telling."

"My boss, Longman, thinks it's a prank by some medical students."

"Maybe," she said non-committally.

"It could be, couldn't it?" he asked, still staring thoughtfully at the finger and not expecting her to reply. "Some medical student might have snipped this off a no-name cadaver they'd been cutting to pieces for a lesson, stuck it in their pocket and thrown it into that lift as a sick joke. Pretty fucking stupid, if you ask me," he added, forgetting himself for the moment. Brown didn't comment. "On the other hand, someone might have been abducted, killed and cut into little bits by some maniac and we've stumbled across one of the pieces."

Brown said quietly, "Or, as you suggested, somebody cut their own finger off and left it behind for someone to find, too. But who would do that?"

Maiden let out a humourless laugh. "Believe me, this town is full of insane and stupid people who are quite capable of the twisted logic of lopping off one of their own fingers as a protest or something. It's not beyond the bounds of possibility." He handed the plastic bag back to her and nodded his thanks.

"So, shall I keep it?" she asked turning towards the refrigerator.

"You'd better, for a few days at least. In fact, I'll give you a call when we've reached all the dead ends and you can destroy it. Can you hold on to it until then?"

"No problem. Is there anything else I can help you with? Otherwise, I've got a lot of work and I was late getting in this morning. Even after all this time I can't get used to commuting." She slammed the refrigerator door closed.

Maiden was suddenly tempted to invite her for a coffee in the staff canteen, but stopped himself. "No, thanks. Could you lead me back out of this place?"

"Certainly," she said with a brief small smile. It transformed her face and Maiden could see she was truly beautiful. "Follow me," she nodded towards the door. Then her back was turned and she was guiding him through the journey back to her office. Brown didn't stop until she was outside her door where she paused, facing him, and said simply, "Goodbye."

"Thanks again," Maiden said. He made to walk away, but stopped as he remembered something. "Oh, I forgot to ask you—any idea how old the finger's owner would be?"

Brown looked at him in her steady no-nonsense way, but surprised him once more by sounding hesitant when she spoke. Up until then she'd replied to his questions confidently and quickly, even when admitting to not knowing an answer. "Well, I'd say a young man—or I'd better say a young *adult*, to be safe. Older than a teenager, at least."

Maiden had a fleeting impression she was looking for a chance to keep a discussion going, but didn't know how. Perhaps he should ask her out for coffee.

But the moment was lost and Maiden didn't know how to get it back. "Hey, that's close enough for me," he said, smiling. It occurred to him he'd smiled more in the last ten minutes than he had for the whole week. She nodded and with a small wave disappeared into her office.

His next trip was to the office block where the finger had been found. Stepping out of the Surry Hills station into the car park, Maiden discovered it was raining, a heavy drizzle which would soak him quickly. Cursing, he ducked back against the building and decided to wait for a minute, rather than dashing to his car. He took the opportunity to light up a cigarette. Beyond the open gates of the car park he could see that umbrellas had blossomed everywhere, making it doubly hazardous to walk on the footpath with everyone ducking and weaving to avoid each other. Watching the people hurrying by, Maiden was struck by a thought. *What would any of these people do, if they found a chopped-off finger in their lift this morning? Every day is the same for most of them. Same job, same office, same routine, then all of a sudden—presto! You've got an amputated finger lying between your feet.* Maiden leaned against the wall and let his eyes follow some of the pedestrians as they passed the gate. None of them knew they were being watched, or if they did, didn't show it. Most kept their eyes down, minding their steps on the wet pavement. *Most of you'd probably shit yourselves with fright,* he decided.

Two uniformed policemen emerged from the door behind him and quickly retreated from the rain, squeezing under the cover beside Maiden.

"Much happening?" he asked them, feeling obliged to be friendly by their closeness.

"Nothing new," one of them replied, hunching his shoulders, then added, "That shotgun guy is all the rage at the moment. He's got everyone twitchy."

The other policeman offered, "There's a chance it might be two people, using the same method. Maybe even sharing the same weapon."

Maiden made a grunt of interest, but didn't say anything. He wondered if these men knew their information through official channels or by hearsay. If it was the latter, he thought wearily, it would be in the newspapers the next day, too—if not that afternoon—and the small advantage would be gone. Worse, it could cause a spate of copycat robberies and the one clue that would let the investigators sort one from the other was useless. Suddenly he couldn't be bothered waiting any more. With a nod at the men he tossed his cigarette into a puddle and hurried out into the rain towards his car.

Maiden parked in a loading zone directly in front of the office block. He trotted at a dignified pace through the rain into the lower foyer and consulted the directory of companies in the building. Taking a small pad out of his pocket he made a note of the building's managing company. At the same time he checked his reflection in the glass. Maiden wished he'd worn an overcoat. The rain had left dark, ugly spots on his suit. Running his fingers through his hair didn't help much, either. Shrugging, he headed for the lifts. On the ride up he found himself thinking again about how the average person might react to seeing a severed finger on the floor—he might even be in the very elevator it happened.

On the twenty-first floor he strode out of the lift and went straight to the receptionist. He showed his identification and asked to see Lena Hargreaves.

"She's in the lunchroom," the receptionist told him,

adding accusingly, "She's very upset. She wanted to go home."

Maiden immediately wanted to tell her that Lena only found a *finger* for Christ's sake—not a headless corpse. He took a breath and calmed himself, saying instead, "Yes, I know. But it is a lot easier and more helpful if we can ask her a few questions here, where she found it. She can point a few things out."

"Someone's already done all that."

"That was with a uniformed policeman, not a detective. Which way to the lunchroom?" he asked, cutting off another comment.

"Down the corridor. It's the last room on the right. You'd better knock first."

Maiden deferred to his rising temper by not bothering to thank her and ignoring the advice. He headed for the corridor, feeling the girl's eyes on his back. Down the hallway he saw a man come out of a room. Something about him stirred Maiden's curiosity and he watched him carefully as they squeezed past each other. The man kept his head down and muttered an apology.

The lunchroom consisted of a bare formica table surrounded by a small refrigerator, electric stove and microwave, and a row of cupboards. Lena sat alone at the table staring moodily down at a cup of tea which, Maiden could see, had the whitish scum of having turned cold.

"Hello, Lena. I'm Detective Maiden." He sat down opposite her. "Who was that just leaving? Someone who works here?"

She looked up at him mournfully with red-rimmed eyes in a pale face. If she hadn't been so pretty, Maiden would have been moved to the same mild disgust he'd felt talking to the receptionist. *These people,* he thought, *reacting as if they'd all been in a damned airport massacre. No doubt they'll be calling in an army of bloody counsellors next.*

"Can I go home after this?" she asked immediately. "Do I have to talk to anyone else?"

"No, and this won't take long." He gestured at the doorway, "Who did you say that was?"

Lena sniffed. "A journalist. I can't remember which paper."

Maiden swallowed a curse. It wasn't really a problem. He just didn't like journalists. "What did you tell him?"

"Everything I know. They're going to pay me. There's nothing wrong with that, is there?" She looked bitterly defensive. "I mean, I should get some sort of compensation really, shouldn't I? At least the newspaper will give me some money."

"Most likely," Maiden said dryly. "Just tell me what happened this morning."

She sighed wearily. "It's easy—no big deal. I went up to the filing rooms we have on the top floor, and when I got the lift to come back down there it was. There was this *finger* on the floor." Lena shuddered and made a noise.

"OK," Maiden said impatiently. "Is that all you can tell me?"

She nodded.

Maiden stayed silent. He was already thinking Longman was wasting everyone's time—his in particular. There was nothing here warranting a visit from a detective. He'd just travelled through the city, got rained on and been annoyed by a receptionist, all for little more than a five-second reply to his questioning. He could have got the same result over the telephone. Better still, the report sheet from the patrol car that responded to the call would have been good enough. It told him the same things.

Maiden rubbed at his eyes a moment and told himself he really should work at things a bit harder. His apathy was getting to be a habit. "Look, OK. But for the record, you definitely didn't see anybody suspicious nearby? No-one was following you, hoping for a chance to give you a scare?"

"Well, I don't think so . . ." Lena said, with a helpless shrug.

Maiden smelt a problem. "You don't seem certain. Why?"

Lena thought about telling Maiden how she thought someone was in the room with her. But it would only complicate matters and stop her getting home. Shaking her head, she said instead, "It's just that those filing rooms are so *spooky* at the best of times. It's easy to get a fright, what with the rest of the floor being vacant and everything."

"Did you tell the police officers this? Did you get a fright?"

"No, not really—it seemed a bit silly. Now I wish I hadn't said anything to you, either."

Maiden persisted against his better judgement. He wanted to get out, too. "Are you *sure* you didn't get a scare this morning? Did something spook you? Something we should know about?"

Lena hesitated and hung her head.

Maiden leaned closer and spoke impatiently again. "Lena, I'm not going to laugh at you or think you're silly. The best way is for you to tell me everything, get it out of your system, then we can both go home."

She was nodding jerkily and pulled a small handkerchief from her sleeve. She dabbed at her nose. "I—I did think there was somebody else up there with me, but when I called out no-one answered. *That* scared me a bit. There was a noise, but when I called out again and still no-one answered, I thought it must have been the lift arriving at the floor."

"The lift came up to your floor? The same one you found the finger in?"

"When I saw it with the doors open, I thought it was a good opportunity to get out of there. I was getting frightened." She sniffed again.

A concerned face appeared at the door and looked in, but Maiden gave it such a glare that it disappeared quickly.

"And you didn't see anyone? Not even a shadow or some movement you thought *might* have been someone?"

"No, no-one."

"But someone must have pressed the button to bring the lift up."

"No, they could send it up from somewhere else by pressing the button for the thirty-second floor and stepping out again."

"Of course," Maiden said, annoyed with himself. "Lena, I want you to show me exactly which lift it was and this filing room, and that will be all. Can we do that?"

She nodded again and got shakily to her feet. He followed her out of the lunchroom. As they walked into the foyer and stood waiting for the lift, Maiden could again feel the receptionist's hostile stare. He ignored it. It took several minutes of the wrong lifts arriving on their floor, with Maiden leaning inside them to send them away to different levels again, before they finally managed to summon the correct lift to their floor. When they got into the lift she tried to show him the exact spot the finger had been. This told him nothing. The responding uniformed police hadn't bothered to mark the floor, and he wasn't surprised. Maiden was the only one regarding this case with any seriousness at the moment and even that was beginning to wane fast. He noticed Lena was nervous and asked her why. As she explained her fear about being trapped in a falling lift he tried to listen sympathetically, but privately thought she was being stupidly paranoid.

The filing room showed him nothing, too. Maiden had been there for less than a minute before he began to feel a growing conviction he was getting nowhere. Longman's theory of the sick practical joke was looking good. Somebody had tossed the finger into the lift, pressed the button for the thirty-second floor because it gave them the most time to get away, and Lena Hargreaves had been the undeserving, innocent recipient of the prank. That was it.

Five minutes later Maiden was driving back towards The Rocks. It was raining much harder now, so he had to carefully pick his way through the traffic. He grumbled to himself about the weather and impatiently used his sleeve to wipe at the misting windscreen. The visit to Lena Hargreaves had been a waste of time and now he was going to get wet again running from his car to the police station entrance.

Back at his desk he filled out his own report sheet on the matter and filed it as an investigation completed. Later, Longman asked him for a quick rundown on what had happened and Maiden told him, putting heavy emphasis on Longman's own theory of the medical student prank idea. It wasn't that he wanted to agree with his superior, it was just the easiest and quickest way to get him off his back.

After that, Maiden didn't expect to hear anything about the amputated finger again.

Chapter Three

He waited in the large walk-in wardrobe, the darkness close around him, the smell of cockroach baits and moth-balls unnoticed as he concentrated all his attention on his hearing. He heard them come in. First, the quiet tinkling of the key being inserted into the motel room's main door followed by the snick of it closing and being locked. There were hushed adult voices murmuring nice things and the occasional soft female giggle. He could hear everything: the sucking noise of the refrigerator door; the opening of a bottle; the clinking of the glasses being touched in a salute; gentle music playing.

But these weren't the sounds he was waiting for.

He flinched momentarily at the sound of another door opening, dreading a sudden flood of light revealing him, but it was to the bathroom nearby. He relaxed again. The sounds of a male urinating into a toilet bowl filtered through the wall. An unlovely, unromantic sound, consid-ering what was going to happen soon in the bedroom. The toilet flushed, quickly followed by the tap running and someone brushing their teeth.

He wasn't listening for these, either.

There were a few minutes of silence, but he could picture what was going on. They would be undressing each other, kissing and caressing as the clothes dropped to the floor. He heard the faint squeak of the inner-spring mattress as they fell to the bed. Now their bodies would be entwined, their hands and fingers searching while they softly groaned their pleasure to each other. He listened hard now. His moment was coming. The groans became more urgent, louder and clearer over the music. There was the briefest pause and the sound of a lightswitch being snapped off, before the moans of ecstasy came again. The woman began calling the same thing over and over again.

He slowly opened the wardrobe door.

The room was in complete darkness—but not for him. He had been in the blacked-out wardrobe for hours and the chinks of light coming through the closed curtains were enough for him to see everything clearly. But with the bedside lamp just turned off the people on the bed were as good as blind.

The woman was on all fours with her face turned to one side and pressed into the pillow. The man had entered her from behind and was thrusting himself hard against her buttocks while he held her in place with hands grasping her hips. The bed was rocking with their movement. The woman was calling for him not to orgasm yet; to keep going. The man's face was a mask of near-pain, his eyes closed, as he laboured to maintain the driving rhythm between her legs and not lose control of himself.

It was easy to step up to the bed, close behind him.

His hands grasped the male lover around the neck and hauled him backwards, the man's penis flipping out of the woman. The choking hold was viciously effective, crushing the larynx, so he couldn't make a sound. The shock of pain, too, took away most of his strength. Still, the man fought, but his attacker was much stronger and adept at keeping him off-balance. At the same time the naked man was kept suspended above the bed, so the flailing arms and legs were muted by the blankets and mattress.

The woman rolled quickly onto her back and moved up against the headboard, her legs spread wide. Silently she reached out and turned on the bedside lamp. Her eyes grew wide at what she saw and her breathing came in short, sharp gasps. One of her hands slipped down between her legs and she stimulated herself. Within moments she was writhing and jerking like the dying man in front of her, and letting out renewed groans of pleasure. She became still and contented, her eyes dreamy, even before her lover stopped his own spasmodic thrashing and went limp, hanging from the vice-like grip like a rag doll.

They took him into the bathroom. The woman, still naked, followed after getting some things from her bag. He listened to her instructions, easily supporting the corpse's weight while still being able to hold the limp arm over the sink. She had a knife and used it to cut away at the skin and sinew at the wrist. Blood dripped into the basin and they were careful to make sure it didn't fall anywhere else, although with the tiled floor it didn't really matter, as long as they cleaned it up. Quickly, all the flesh and muscle was pared away from the carpus joints, revealing the pale bone. She looked at it, making a decision, then told him what to do. Holding the body by circling the waist with one arm, he was free to grip and use a wrenching motion to tear the hand away, the joints and bones crackling, the last ligaments stretching and snapping. He let it drop into the basin where it lay palm up, the fingers curled slightly, with more blood seeping from the raw wound.

She brought a large plastic bag into the bathroom and they bundled the body into it. Only then did she wrap a thin gown around herself and, after peering through the curtains for some time to make sure no-one was outside, turned off the bedside lamp again and opened the front door. Their car was backed right up to the doorway. It was a large vehicle with a spacious boot. The body fitted easily and was transferred from the room to the car's boot in a matter of seconds.

They packed quickly after that, the severed hand going into its own special place. After a careful check that nothing was left behind in the motel room they drove slowly away.

The drive to the mountains took under two hours, with the traffic at that time of night thin and the intersection lights kind. Then there was the long and difficult trek through the bush, the corpse slung in a fireman's lift over his shoulder while she led the way with a small torch. There was a particular place they knew, where the path went along the top of a deep and treacherous gully. A waist-high fence made it safe. It also made it perfect for disposing of corpses.

With a final burst of strength he lifted the plastic bag over his head and threw it into the gully. The body travelled several metres before it brushed against the trees below, then plummeted through thick growth with a ripping sound. She tried to follow its progress with the torch, but couldn't. They heard the corpse sliding and falling for what seemed an age. The plant life at the bottom was high and wide leafed, and hidden in shadow for most of the day. As long as the body reached the bottom, everything would be OK. The last one was. She'd come back in the daytime to make sure. It had completely disappeared into the undergrowth.

By the time they got back to their own place it was close to dawn. A grey light washed the street as they went through the front door. She was feeling too elated to sleep and wanted to give him his reward.

When she gave it to him he made more noise—of pleasure and delight now—than he had when he'd killed a man with his bare hands for her.

Chapter Four

Longman called Maiden into his office and the detective expected the normal daily briefing. Instead, Longman was looking especially grim.

"Remember that business last week about the finger?" Longman held up a report sheet, but purposely kept it out of Maiden's reach.

"What about it?" Maiden sensed trouble. "I told you what I did. There's nothing else to be done."

"This time it's an entire hand, chopped off at the wrist. With a bloody message written on it."

"Shit."

" 'Shit' is right," Longman said wryly. "And it's a different hand—a different *person*. The finger belonged to a right hand. This hand is from the right and also intact."

"Same lift?" Maiden asked, trying to get his mind working. "What's the message?"

"It's a lift again, but another building." Now Longman handed over the report sheet. "Read the message for yourself—if it *is* a message. It might be the name of a song or a book. Who knows? You'd better treat this one a little more seriously than you did the last time. Don't just gloss over it."

Maiden glared at Longman, who dropped his head to other paperwork in front of him. "Then you'd better not assign any other crap to me while I do it," he said, his voice tight with anger.

"Whatever it takes," Longman dismissed him with a wave. "But don't make a bloody taskforce effort out of it, either."

Pressing down his anger Maiden went back to his desk and took out his notebook. For a moment he was worried he'd thrown out the relevant page, then he found the name of the property management company for the office tower Lena Hargreaves worked in. He looked up their phone number and put a call through, asking for a listing of all the companies in that building and getting them to fax it through to him immediately. The fax came within ten minutes. He made several photocopies, then faxed one of them elsewhere. By the time he returned to his desk he knew the fax would have been read. He picked up the telephone and called Missing Persons. He asked to be put through to a field officer.

"Yeah, John Maiden here at The Rocks," Maiden said abruptly. "I need a cross-reference between a fax I sent you a few minutes ago and any missing persons reports lodged within the last seven days." He listened to the response and frowned. "Yes, I *know* you're busy and everyone has to wait their turn, but this shouldn't take long and it's bloody important." He listened some more and sighed at what he heard. "OK, I'll wait for ten minutes, as long as you're sure it'll *be* ten minutes. I can't be sitting here waiting for an hour, OK?" He managed to stop himself slamming the phone down. He was feeling unexpectedly nervous.

The answer took fifteen minutes and Maiden was beginning to get nasty. But by the time he'd put the phone down he felt nothing except a cold feeling that something bad had finally landed in his lap. Oddly, he wasn't sure if he wanted it.

An employee in the same building as Lena Hargreaves had been reported missing two days before. A junior clerk named Robert House who worked for a debt collection agency. He hadn't been home or shown up for work for over a week. Finally, his flatmate had put in a Missing Persons report. The disappearance was described as out of character and completely unexpected. No-one knew where he was or what condition he could be in, except that he was considered a mature, healthy individual with no history of illicit drug-taking or medical problems. In other words, he wasn't a latent diabetic or epileptic who could be sick and wandering the streets.

Maiden was already willing to guess one thing about Mr. Robert House.

Wherever he was, healthy or not, he would be missing a finger.

Chapter Five

They gave Maiden an assistant, a detective constable called Martin Creane. Creane was recently out of the Academy. He regarded the seasoned detective senior sergeant with a sort of awe, as if Maiden was some veteran marine sergeant who had stormed every beach in the Pacific against the Japanese and lived to tell the tale. At first Maiden was annoyed that he now had to account for someone else's movements as well as his own, but soon changed his mind. The investigation might need a lot of tedious footwork and he could at least pass most of it off to Creane.

Maiden signed out an unmarked car with a radio and told Creane to drive. The office block they were heading for was close, but it had been raining all morning and he wanted transport close by, if need be. He watched Creane driving as they weaved through the traffic. He was young to Maiden's eyes, perhaps twenty-three or twenty-four years old and was well built in an athletic way. Creane sported a modern haircut which fell within the rules, but would still be regarded as fashionable. Maiden remembered the days when the strict hair regulations of the force always made them stand out in a crowd as police, making it impossible to walk into a bar for a quiet drink without putting half the clientele on edge.

Creane was driving slowly, looking for a place to park.

"There," said Maiden, pointing.

"It's a loading zone. That OK?"

"Of course it's OK. This is a fucking police car, for Christ's sake."

"Sorry."

Maiden sighed. He'd have to behave better around the inexperienced Creane. But he didn't apologise directly, instead saying gruffly while he tapped his finger on the official sticker on the windscreen, "In theory they can give you a ticket, but if any parking inspector writes one out with that thing staring him in the face, feel free to track the bastard down and arrest him for something—anything. You'll be doing the city a favour by removing one bloody idiot from the system." Creane was nodding quickly and Maiden frowned at him. "Don't they tell you this sort of stuff before they let you out on the streets?"

"I graduated from my year with the third highest marks, but I'm damned if I can remember half of what they taught me," Creane told him, concentrating on reverse-parking the car.

Reluctantly impressed by his honesty, Maiden let out a grunt of laughter then said, "Well, don't forget. A stupid question is always preferable to a stupid mistake."

"I'll remember that."

An amputated hand, complete with a possible message, rated more seriously than a finger. This time the patrol officers who responded to the call had shut down the elevator and sealed it off, leaving the hand exactly as it had been found. Again, it had been discovered by a secretary, but this time it was a short middle-aged woman who quickly recovered from her initial shock and had now gone back to her work. She'd left instructions where the police could find her.

On the building's ground floor foyer there was an "Out of Service" sign on one of the elevators. It took Maiden a moment to figure that the lift must have been stopped and sealed on the floor where the hand was first found. That was good. Much better than having it on the ground floor where there would be more passing traffic and nosey, interfering people asking questions.

"Twelfth floor?" Creane asked.

"Yes, but you can meet me up there." Maiden pointed at the registry of businesses mounted on the wall. "I want you to visit each and every one of them and ask for the names of any employees who haven't turned up for work today. Ask them especially if they called in and *said* they'd be away, or if they just didn't show up."

Maiden was walking to the elevators as he talked, Creane following him. He pressed the button at the same time a lift arrived. He waited for its sole occupant to leave, then leaned on the open door to keep it there while he kept talking. "Start on the ground floor. And look for people who haven't been to work for a couple of days already." Creane was searching his jacket for a notebook as he listened intently. "If I finish up on the twelfth floor before I see you, I'll start doing the same thing from the top floor down and we'll run across each other somewhere." Maiden thought about this for a moment. "When we overlap, head for the ground foyer. Otherwise we might chase each other's tails in these lifts all day." He stepped inside the lift and pressed the 12 button. There was an awkward moment while they waited for the doors to close and the two men looked at each other with nothing to say. Creane waved briefly and turned away.

The twelfth floor had two uniformed constables standing, looking bored, in the lift alcove. They stood straighter on seeing Maiden. One of the elevators had bright yellow tape criss-crossing the closed doors with "No Entry by Order of the Police Department" written on it. Maiden introduced himself briefly and gestured at the lift.

"What's happened?"

"Photographs have been taken. Forensic had a look at the buttons for prints, but said it's next to impossible. The buttons are indented so much you have to use the tip of your finger, which isn't enough. Some of them are almost clean. Most of the last people to press them must have been wearing gloves."

"It's cold enough," the second policeman offered.

Maiden nodded his agreement and said, "Can we open it?"

"This floor's got one of the controlling stations for the lifts. The maintenance guy stopped the elevator and locked the doors closed, like we asked, but then the officious little prick wouldn't let us have the key. You'll have to go into that office there and ask the girl to page him back here."

Maiden frowned. "Great, a caretaker with an attitude problem. Do it, will you?" He turned to the other policeman. "Do you need a break? Grab a bite to eat or drink."

The constable nodded gratefully.

Maiden and the remaining constable exchanged idle talk for a few minutes while they waited for the caretaker. After a while, because he was taking so long, Maiden began thinking of making some enquiries about any absent employees on that floor, but then one of the elevators arrived and a short, dirty-looking man in stained khaki clothes stepped out.

"I can't keep coming up here for you guys every five seconds. How long will you be?" the caretaker said bluntly.

Maiden suppressed a flare of anger. "I'm Detective Senior Sergeant Maiden and I'm in charge of this investigation. I want you to unlock the lift."

The caretaker brushed passed him, pulling a bunch of

keys from his belt as he did. He went to a glass-fronted panel and used a key. Operating some switches he muttered, "I should have put the bloody thing in the trash myself. Would've saved a lot of trouble."

Maiden said evenly, "OK, so you're a fucking hero. Just open the lift, all right?"

The caretaker put on a sulky expression and kept fiddling. A moment later the elevator doors jerked, but were held closed by the tape. The constable quickly moved forward, ran a key through the plastic and the doors slid apart. Maiden stepped carefully inside and dropped down to his haunches. The constable stayed outside, but the caretaker pushed past and inserted a key into the panel inside the lift. He bent and stared at the amputated hand over Maiden's shoulder.

"Looks ugly, don't it?"

Maiden ignored him. The hand lay palm upwards, with the fingers curled slightly. Aside from the amputation wound itself, it looked unmarked. He called over his shoulder to the constable, "I'm the last one, aren't I? No-one else is coming?"

"We're only waiting for you, sir."

Now Maiden turned to look at him past the caretaker and noticed a small lens on the ceiling. "Hey, this thing's got security cameras! Has anyone checked the tapes?"

"Yes, I did it myself. Whoever it was used an umbrella," the constable told him dryly, expecting Maiden's reaction.

"They used what?" Maiden frowned at him.

"They used an umbrella. Opened the damned thing as they got inside the lift. After it's opened, all you can see is a grey nothing, because cameras are black and white." The constable had a tinge of admiration in his voice.

Maiden sighed. "OK, so they're smart bastards." He had to admit it was a simple solution and with the current weather, someone carrying an umbrella wouldn't be noticed at all. He took a pen from his pocket and used it to flip the hand over. It was surprisingly heavy and needed two attempts.

On the back of the hand in blue ink, below the knuckles was written, "Money isn't everything."

The caretaker crowded closer and whispered, "Do you think he's dead?"

"What?" Maiden was thinking furiously.

"Do you think it comes from a dead person—like somebody's cut someone up?"

"I can't discuss it," Maiden said shortly. He felt no desire to be friendly and added warningly, "And if anybody from the newspapers comes sniffing around, don't start putting those sort of bloody ideas into their heads, OK?"

Maiden closed his eyes and tried to put the caretaker's inane questions out of his mind. He needed to work out the basic facts before he worried about anything fanciful. First of all, Longman was right. The writing wasn't necessarily a message. Lots of people wrote things on their hands to remind themselves and the words might have been there before the hand was amputated. Dismissing the message for the moment, Maiden considered that whoever dropped the severed hand in the lift probably wouldn't have waited for another elevator to make their escape—if they hadn't simply tossed it in on the ground floor in the first place. They would have used the stairs, to be safe. He looked up at the caretaker. "Where's the fire stairs?"

"Just outside the lifts, over there."

"Show me."

As the caretaker led the way out of the elevator Maiden paused and asked the constable, "Did Forensic leave you a kit?" The constable pointed at a vinyl carry-all sitting in a nearby corner. "I've seen enough. Bag it, will you, and take it down to Surry Hills. Make sure you give it to Janet Brown and tell her I said so. There was a related case last week," Maiden added in explanation.

The caretaker took him to a wide doorway outside the lift alcove. The door had "Stairs" written in bright red lettering. Maiden opened it and looked through. It was a normal cement stairwell with a steel handrail. A litter of cigarette butts and the odour of smoke told the story this was where smokers sneaked the occasional cigarette. Apart from that, nothing unusual struck Maiden.

He heard a shout coming from the alcove and he hurriedly pulled back.

The constable was crouched next to the vinyl carry-all. He had a disposable glove on one hand and was holding an empty evidence bag in the other. "Hey, is that lift going anywhere?" he was asking urgently.

The lift doors were closed, revealing the yellow tape again.

To answer him, the illuminated numbers above the door began falling. Maiden ran to the button and, even though he knew it was too late, stabbed at it several times. With a frustrated snarl he turned on the caretaker.

"You bloody idiot! I only wanted the doors unlocked!"

"You—you said unlock the lift," the caretaker blustered back.

"Don't be stupid!" Maiden stared at him. "Well, don't just stand there! Can we stop it?"

"I can turn it off, but it won't stop until it gets to the right floor."

Maiden threw his hands up in the air. "For Christ's *sake*! Where's it going?"

"How the hell would I know?"

"Will the doors open?"

"Of course."

"*Damn* it!" Maiden quickly rubbed a hand over his face. Through his fingers he could see the caretaker still waiting in front of him. "Jesus Christ, go and *stop* the bloody lift, you fool!"

Half-frightened and angry at the way Maiden was speaking to him, the caretaker flinched, then rushed over and fumbled with the control panel again. They all anxiously watched which floor the elevator stopped at. The glowing numbers flashed until they came to the number "2," and stopped.

"We'd better get down there—no, don't wait for another lift," Maiden snapped at the constable, who was reaching for the button. Maiden headed for the stairs and the others followed.

Their urgent footsteps clattered noisily off the concrete as they rushed downwards. Leading the way, Maiden felt the younger and fitter policeman breathing down his neck. A door slammed somewhere below them—no doubt one of the smokers making a hurried exit at the sound of their descent. Most of all, Maiden feared he would hear the sound of a distant scream, telling him someone had rediscovered the hand.

Someone else has already found it, he told himself, thinking past the concentration of effort he needed to keep descending the stairs at this pace. He was out of breath and his knees were getting weak. *The lift was already at the floor, before we started to move. Unless they're blind as a bat, they've already seen it.*

He nearly over-ran the small landing for the second floor. It was the constable who snatched at a door handle, calling, "Here, sir!" just as Maiden was moving down the next set of stairs. He reversed himself and went through the door, which the constable was holding open for him. The caretaker was much slower and had dropped back several flights. Maiden could hear his keys jangling somewhere above. He didn't wait for him. The policemen emerged from the stairs which were in an identical position to the twelfth floor, but the decor was different, confusing Maiden for a moment. A company logo was painted along the entire wall opposite the stairwell door. He got his bearings and turned to the lift alcove.

Maiden breathed a long sigh of relief when the first person he saw was Creane, standing with his foot jammed in the doorway to the lift. Next to him was a pale-looking man dressed in a suit several sizes too big for him. The man was talking animatedly to Creane, who kept holding up a calming hand and nodding. The younger detective glanced over his shoulder at the noise of Maiden's arrival, then quickly turned his attention back.

Maiden came up behind them. "Everything under control?" he asked tightly.

"This gentleman has just had a nasty fright," Creane told him calmly. "This is Mr. William Watson."

"I'm sorry, Mr. Watson," Maiden said, extending his hand. Watson shook it briefly, a vacant expression on his face. Maiden explained, "Someone turned the elevator back on by mistake." At that moment the caretaker came through the door. He was out of breath too, and looked flustered. Creane saw Maiden's angry eyes slide in the caretaker's direction for a moment and understood.

Watson was speaking rapidly. "I heard about this . . . this hand. Someone told me, but I still got a shock, before I managed to put two and two together. Or is this another one?"

"No, Mr. Watson, it's the same one. The elevator was turned back on too soon," Creane repeated smoothly. "It's lucky for us someone with your presence of mind called the lift."

"Yes—yes, I suppose so."

The caretaker was looking inside the lift, as if making sure it was the right one. "*He* told me to unlock the lift," he called halfheartedly. Before anyone could answer he disappeared inside. There was a jingling of keys as he disabled the elevator. Maiden turned to the constable, who was trying not to puff too obviously.

"For Christ's sake, go and get your kit, bag the damned thing and get it out of here before it goes for another ride."

The constable was already nodding, pulling the bag and gloves from the pocket where he'd stuffed them during the run down the stairs.

* * *

Maiden went back to the twelfth floor and interviewed the woman who had found the hand. She seemed to take some pride in not being too shocked about the whole affair. She explained she had simply called the lift to travel to the ground floor and go out for a bite of breakfast. At first she'd thought the hand was a prank and almost picked it up for a closer inspection. Then she'd caught a whiff of decaying flesh and realised it was real.

"I felt a bit sick for a moment," she admitted. "But I knew it wasn't going to leap up and attack me, was it? Someone must have left it there for a sick joke, right? Well, more fool them. I'm not easily shocked," she added proudly.

"Good for you," Maiden said, trying to sound impressed and failing. "That's exactly what some prankster doesn't want to hear. If the joke doesn't work, maybe they won't be tempted to do it again." He added casually, "You don't happen to remember where the lift came from?"

"Came from?"

"Did it come down from one of the floors above you, or up from the ground?"

She opened her mouth to reply, but stopped herself. "Actually, no," she admitted. "I can't be certain at all. I wasn't watching."

"That's a pity." Maiden was disappointed.

"Will it be in the newspapers? That I wasn't shocked, I mean."

Maiden was tucking his notebook away absently, his mind already on other things. "I'm sorry, but I don't know if it'll make the papers at all."

"How will they know I wasn't shocked and not play the trick again?"

It took him a moment to understand and frowned, annoyed. "Well, perhaps it'll get a small mention, just for that purpose," he said. Then added curtly, "I really must go.

Thanks for all your help. We'll be in contact if there's anything else."

Maiden stopped at the company's reception and asked about absent employees. A quick check revealed only one male clerk was away that day, and he had called in to advance his holidays by a week because his pregnant wife was threatening to deliver prematurely.

"Did you take the call?" Maiden asked the receptionist.

"Yes, and I passed on the message straightaway."

Against his better judgement he said, "Do you think he sounded . . . well, all right? He wasn't too stressed or anything?"

"He sounded really stressed, but he's been that way since the day she got pregnant," she added, killing Maiden's flare of interest. He thanked her, asked that she tell Creane when he arrived to keep working upwards, then took the elevator to the top floor.

The two detectives crossed over on the fifteenth floor. Maiden took the elevator back to the ground, but although the foyer was small and he did several circuits, he couldn't see Creane anywhere. He stood in the centre of the polished marble floor and cursed quietly, thinking maybe he should go out and check the car. Creane appeared at the main doors nursing two polystyrene cups of coffee. He saw Maiden looking at him, so he headed straight for one of the low lounge chairs that were scattered around the room.

"I took a guess and got it white with two."

"Good guess," Maiden muttered, sitting down. The chairs were very soft and his knees came up level with his chest. It was uncomfortable. With the first sip of coffee his annoyance disappeared. He needed it. They began comparing notes.

The building had twenty-nine floors, all of them occupied. With no-one absent there was usually a total of four hundred and ninety-three workers, not counting the caretaker and cleaners who worked for the property management company itself. Today, thirty-one people were not at work for a variety of reasons ranging from sickness to attending business affairs elsewhere. Of those people who had called in ill, all of them, it seemed, demonstrated a certain amount of stress. But as Creane pointed out, very few people were ever comfortable about calling their place of employment to say they wouldn't be coming in—especially if they weren't genuinely sick, which was often the case.

Creane, like Maiden, had asked every company on each level to try and re-establish contact with everyone who was away. "In some cases, it's nearly impossible," he said. "One guy's at a business seminar on one of the resort islands off the Gold Coast. His secretary doubts he'll be sober for days and says he's probably out on a yacht in the middle of the Pacific somewhere."

"Lucky for some," Maiden growled. He had been told similar stories.

"So, what do we do next?"

"Keep hassling them, but at a guess we're just going to have to wait for some of these people to reappear—or to *not* appear, as the case may be."

"Or wait for another piece of a corpse to turn up."

Maiden pointed a finger at him, saying mildly, "We don't know that the owners of these pieces are dead. Don't assume too much."

"OK, but what will we find next, if anything? The other hand? A foot?"

"I don't know, but anything bigger than a hand or foot and *I'll* assume some poor bastard's dead," Maiden said, frowning.

Creane took a sip of his coffee. "I just hope it's one of my days off when somebody finds an entire head."

Maiden had to hurriedly swallow. "For Christ's sake, don't say things like that!"

"Well it's a natural progression, isn't it?"

"Maybe, but it's too early to say. We might not see anything else at all. This might be the end of it." Maiden didn't sound hopeful and Creane could hear it.

"It might be just the beginning, too."

Maiden was silent for a while. "Cheerful bastard, aren't you?" he said eventually. "Anyway, I wonder what's the point?"

"It scared the hell out of that guy, Watson, that's for sure. Maybe that's the idea. I heard this funny sort of squeak when I was quizzing this cute receptionist. I turned around to look at the lifts and Watson was kind of swooning and holding his mouth. For a moment I thought the same as him—that he'd found another one. Then somehow I just *knew* what had happened and I rushed over real quick. He looked like he'd seen a ghost. It sure scared the hell out of him."

"Makes sense—that someone's trying to scare people. Nothing else does." Maiden paused and let out a growl of anger. "Bloody lucky you were on that floor," he conceded. "Fucking idiot caretaker. I could've punched the prick if I'd had the chance."

Creane kept his face straight and didn't comment. Instead, he said, "Perhaps they're meant as a warning?"

"Maybe, but if the writing isn't just a coincidence, the message doesn't really sound like a warning."

"What if it's meant to be like a prophetic, biblical thing—you know, like 'repent all sinners' or something? 'Money isn't everything' is sort of like that."

Maiden grunted doubtfully. "Yeah—OK, it's possible."

After another thoughtful silence Creane asked, "By the way, what would you prefer I call you?"

"Call me?"

"Like, Detective Maiden, Mr. Maiden, sir, or what?"

Maiden considered it, half amused and grateful that Creane was offering him the respect. "Call me John, but not in front of the other junior detectives. I don't want them to get the wrong idea."

"Wouldn't dream of it," Creane grinned, but hid it by

finishing his coffee. He looked around for a rubbish bin or ashtray to dump the empty cup, but there was nothing, so with an apologetic shrug he put it down on a nearby table. "Where to now?"

Maiden dropped his own cup without a moment's thought. It bounced and fell onto its side, spilling out droplets of coffee onto the glass surface. He didn't notice and with an effort he stood up from the deep lounge. "Come and meet Janet Brown," he said.

Chapter Six

Maiden leaned familiarly into Janet Brown's office and asked, "Have you had a chance to look at it?"

She looked up from the papers on her desk and regarded him over the top of her glasses. "Yes, but not for very long. I didn't need very long, anyway." She gestured for him to come in. "I take it you don't need to see it yourself this time?"

"I saw it on site."

"At several different locations, I hear."

Maiden looked wry. "I didn't think it would take long for *that* story to get around. I should've strangled that bloody caretaker. Who told you?"

"Now, that would be telling, wouldn't it? Good policemen protect their informers, isn't that how it works?"

"I can't wait for Longman to tell me about it," Maiden muttered. "He's going to have a field day." He waved a hand at Creane, who stood awkwardly at the door. "This is Detective Constable Martin Creane. He's been assigned to give me a hand with the investigation."

"No pun intended, I hope," Brown said, rising from her chair and extending her hand. Creane shook it, obviously taken aback by her good looks. "I only have one spare chair, but you can probably steal one from next door."

"I'm fine standing," he said. "If that's OK."

Brown's mind had already moved on to business. She shuffled through the papers on her desk, located some handwritten notes and sat silently reading them for a moment. The two detectives waited patiently.

"Nothing much different from the finger—I still have it, by the way," she added, glancing at Maiden.

"Keep it. We've got a missing person file now involving the same building. It doesn't look good."

She nodded and started summarising her notes aloud. "It's a Caucasian again—a different person, obviously. The finger belonged to a right hand, and this is a right hand intact. And again, judging from the lack of manicuring on all fingernails, plus the presence of considerable body hair I'm confidently guessing it belonged to a male. Same blood type, but it's common. The fingerprints aren't registered on our records. I have no idea whether the hand was amputated before or after death, or if death even occurred. The ink in the writing is nothing special and the pen could be from many manufacturers. There's only one detail which may or may not mean anything . . ." She paused to make sure she had their full attention. "I'd say this hand was cut off, not chopped with a cleaver or sawn off with a toothed blade. Most of the muscle and ligaments were cut through with a sharp edge before the hand was pulled off at the wrist."

"The bones were ripped out of their sockets?" Maiden asked.

"There aren't any sockets to speak of, really. It's not like a shoulder or hip, which can be dislocated. The wrist is held together by a complex group of muscles and ligaments and once these are cut away the hand would almost fall off. In this instance it came very close to that stage. The few ligaments that were actually torn by force, rather than cut, probably only indicate a lack of finesse or simply impatience on the part of the person doing the work."

Maiden raised his eyebrows. "Are you suggesting this was done by someone with some medical knowledge?"

"Not at all. Anyone who's carved the leg or wing off a cooked chicken has experienced cutting through flesh until only the joint itself offers any resistance to separating. An intelligent, if untrained, person might think it the obvious way to remove a human limb, too. I'm really only telling you this person used a very sharp knife, not an axe or a cleaver."

"OK," Maiden said, frowning with thought. Creane was looking slightly pale. He wasn't sure he would be able to chew on a chicken drumstick with his usual relish ever again.

"I guess it doesn't dismiss your medical student theory. It might even strengthen it a little," Brown suggested and added dryly, "though I'd have to suggest they'll fail surgery."

Maiden ignored the black humour. "Perhaps. But really, we haven't been told anything new at all, despite the fact we have an entire hand this time."

Creane cleared his throat nervously. "Ah, Mrs. Brown, if whoever left behind this hand *had* first chopped the index finger off and today we found the fingerless hand, how hard would it be to establish it came from the same person as the finger? Considering the blood type was the same."

Brown thought for a moment. "Not hard at all. While each fingerprint is unique, there are still too many similarities between the fingers of the same hand. We'd pick it up almost straightaway."

"You're thinking the opposite really, aren't you?" Maiden told Creane. "You're saying that *because* we've now been presented with a complete right hand, whoever is doing this is deliberately and clearly pointing out it comes from a different person than the finger. They didn't want to allow the slightest element of doubt about how many victims there are by using the left hand."

"Maybe," Creane shrugged, flattered Maiden was interested in his opinions at all. "It could be totally unintended. We're still only assuming both incidents were carried out by the same person."

Maiden dismissed this with a grunt, saying, "Too much coincidence."

"I can't tell you anything more," Brown said apologetically. "But I have a message for you."

"For me?" Maiden raised his eyebrows.

"Robin Bercoutte wants you to drop in and see him in his office at your convenience. He said to keep it confidential, if possible."

"Maybe you've been fired already," Creane murmured, only half-joking. Bercoutte was a Division Head, part of the police hierarchy that detectives like Maiden rarely saw. Maiden was on nodding terms with him, mainly through the longevity of his service, but had hardly ever spoken directly to him.

Maiden grumbled, "Either that, or Longman's got me busted back to constable. Maybe they've heard about the damned lift episode already. I'll go and see him now and get it out of the way." He stood, considering, then turned to Creane. "Martin, I want you to pull that missing person file on Robert House—the guy we think might own the finger. Try and track down his flatmate—at work or whatever, and quiz him a little harder. Give him a scare, if you like. You never know what you might beat out of the bushes. I'll catch a lift to College Street, see what's up Bercoutte's nose, then I'll start telephoning the people we spoke to this morning about how many absentees they've managed to re-establish contact with already."

"You'll do that back at The Rocks?"

"If I've still got a job."

Creane looked apologetic. "I was only kidding, you know."

"Yeah, so am I."

Creane thanked Janet Brown and left. Maiden tried to find his own words of goodbye, but before he could think of anything to say, Brown rubbed at her eyes wearily and said, "It's time for my morning cup of coffee, I think."

"It's nearly lunchtime," he reminded her with a small smile.

"Today's one of those days I'll mix the two together."

On an impulse Maiden asked, "Mind if I join you? I'd like to get fired on a full stomach."

Brown hesitated only a moment. "Sure, you're more than welcome. But I don't go to the staff canteen here. Every five seconds someone comes up and asks me something about work. It's not my idea of a break."

"Where do you go?"

"I'll show you."

She took him to a small cafeteria only a minute's walk from the Police Centre. Brown guided him to a booth near the back of the room. Maiden was slightly uncomfortable fitting his frame between the bench seat and the table, but he didn't complain.

"So, what's the big attraction to this place?" he asked.

"The service," she said. "It's quick, the food's great and I don't have to move from this spot. They take your order and bring everything to you. I hate having to queue up and slide those damned trays along the servery. I always spill my coffee."

"I know what you mean." They were interrupted by a waitress who took their order. Both of them had large mugs of coffee, Maiden adding a toasted sandwich and Brown a wholemeal salad roll.

"Now I'm in trouble," he said with a smile as the waitress left. "If you don't want to talk about work, what can we talk about? I can't remember when I ever spent time with someone who didn't want to talk shop."

"It's only *my* work I don't want to hear about," she said, cupping her chin and looking at him with that steady, honest stare that he now found slightly disconcerting. "I really don't get to hear much about what you people do. I'd like to know."

Maiden was taken by surprise and needed a moment to form his answer. "Well, to be honest we mostly do a lot of boring, tedious legwork and deal with some of the worst people in the world." He stopped, realising how that must sound. "Look, I know that sounds pretty bad, but I don't mind admitting I long ago lost any sympathy I ever had for criminals, even if they're just hookers and drug addicts. The social workers keep trying to tell us they're victims of society and we should pity them, but most of 'em still have enough functioning brain cells to beat up elderly people for a couple of dollars, or to hold up the corner store for next to nothing and end up shooting some poor bastard in panic. And when we drag them in, they're full of demands for lawyers and phone calls and every damned thing else that TV shows have taught them." Maiden stopped, embarrassed about his small speech. He shrugged and stared down at the table, then abruptly asked, "Do you mind if I smoke?"

"No, I'll join you in fact."

"I wouldn't pick you as a smoker," he said, glad of the change of subject. Pulling a packet from his pocket, he offered it to her. She took one, leaning towards him over the table to reach his lighter. Falling back to her seat she speared a plume of smoke towards the ceiling.

"I keep trying to give up, but my nerves won't let me. Does that make me one of your worthless addicted junkies?"

"Not unless I am, too. Look, maybe I . . . ah, just need a break," he said, not sure if she was teasing or really offended.

"So, how often do you get to work on something more exciting, like now? This business with the finger and the hand is looking like it could become big, right? You said there's a missing person file involved now."

"It's getting serious all right," he nodded. "That's why I've got to get on top of these companies we dealt with today. See if they've got any staff who are proving hard to get hold of. If we end up with someone actually missing from that building too, then I might have to press the panic button."

"What happens then? Will they take the case off you?"

"I hope not, but if it suddenly turns into a full-blown manhunt, then I guess a taskforce might be formed." He shrugged, as if it didn't matter to him, but of course it did. "They might tell my boss, Longman, to take personal charge. That would be worse."

"They should leave you alone to get on with the job. Someone with your experience will achieve a hell of a lot more than some taskforce running around like headless chickens. Taskforces are always full of keen young detectives who flood my department with tonnes of pointless work."

Maiden wasn't so certain he agreed, but he appreciated her support for him. "You never know. If it builds slowly, I might get to stay in charge of things."

They were interrupted again, this time by the arrival of their coffees and snacks. They fell into small talk about Maiden's years in the force and the mutual acquaintances they shared.

"You've been away for a while, I hear," he ventured carefully. He tried to catch any adverse reaction, but Brown's face remained almost blank as she stared at him over the rim of her cup.

"Actually, I've been back about twelve months," she said, adding simply, "I had a couple of bad years where I needed a lot of extended leave without pay—that sort of thing. You'll know I lost my husband. That, and a few other circumstances afterwards, made me reorganise my entire life." She shrugged, as if it wasn't so important. "I always wanted to stay at work and I know now that the decision was a good one. I need to keep busy—not to mention the money."

She spoke matter-of-factly without a hint of expecting sympathy. Still, Maiden felt awkward and murmured, "I'm sorry to hear that."

"It's life," she said flatly and shrugged again. "I guess that's why they call me the Black Widow. I don't mind."

Now Maiden felt twice as bad. "You know about that?" he asked.

"Of course." She laughed quietly at his discomfort. It struck Maiden as not a happy laugh. He could hear strands of her tragic few years woven through it.

"Hey, you're not supposed to even smile, or so the story goes," he told her.

She made a gesture with her fingers and became businesslike. "I try to keep a distance. It makes things easier."

"Then what are you doing here?" he smiled.

"You're an exception, because you're not stationed at Surry Hills. I would never do this with someone in my own department."

"I suppose I should feel honoured, then."

"I must admit it makes a nice change to sit here and have a chat with someone. Normally I stare into space and have forensic science rushing around inside my head. I might as well stick to the staff canteen anyway, I suppose. Oh, and don't try and offer to pay for my food, by the way. It'll get me mad and spoil things. For some reason men always seem compelled to pay for a female's meal in these situations. I hate it."

"The thought hadn't crossed my mind at all," he lied. He'd been just about to suggest it.

"Good. Anyway, I've told you a few of my secrets. What about yourself? I see you don't wear a wedding ring."

Automatically the barriers came up in Maiden's mind, but for once he ignored them. "Married and a messy divorce," he said carefully. "Twice, as a matter of fact. And

I've discovered I'm not very good at being single again. I wasn't very good at it in the first place."

"I know what you mean," she said wistfully. "Sometimes I think about going out and meeting new people—men, I suppose—but I know I'd feel clumsy and stupid. Besides, in my heart I don't want to do it. It's still too soon," she added, her voice turning hard.

"These things take time and only you know when you're ready to make a change," he said, surprising himself once more. Usually he would steer well clear of anybody else's problems and offering advice.

"So they tell me," she replied, her tone telling him the subject was now closed. It caused a brief silence.

Maiden pushed his plate and mug to one side. "I'd better go and find out what Bercoutte wants before I do anything else about these bits and pieces of people in lifts. I might be wasting my time on something I'm not working on any more."

"Do you really think you've been taken off the case?" she asked, watching him stand.

"To be honest, I wouldn't have a bloody clue what he wants. Can I walk you back to the station?"

She shook her head. "I've got another five minutes or so. I'll stay here a while longer and have another cigarette. Maybe another coffee, if the waitress comes by quickly."

Maiden was disappointed he was leaving her behind and for a moment was tempted to sit down again. He wasn't sure he'd be welcome. Instead he said, "I'll see if I can grab one and send her your way as I go out."

"Thanks."

He said goodbye and turned away from the booth, but he had only taken a few steps before she called out, stopping him.

"Let me know what happens with Bercoutte. I'll be taking another look at the—at those things at work. I'd like to know who I'll be working with, if it's not you."

"Sure. I'll give you a call later in the day." He waved this time and went to the check-out. As he paid Maiden explained that his companion was hoping for another quick cup of coffee. The waitress behind the till nodded and said she would go straightaway. Maiden realised he felt pleased at having done this small favour for Janet Brown and that, in turn, made him frown.

All he'd done was have a coffee with her and he was thinking and acting like a kid.

Watching him leave the café, Brown wore a thoughtful expression. On first impression she liked Maiden. That was the sort of feeling she hadn't had for a long time and she wasn't sure it was welcome. Her life was just beginning to pull itself back on track and she didn't need any complications. Still, it wouldn't do any harm to be extra helpful towards John Maiden's investigation. It might give her the chance to get to know him a little better—and at least she liked that idea.

Bercoutte's office was in the College Street police headquarters and on a floor that was often host to press conferences and television interviews, so more attention was paid to keeping it clean and neat. As he stepped from the lift Maiden felt like some sort of interloper or someone staying in a class of hotel normally beyond their means. The corridors were hushed and most of the office doors closed. All the sounds of a busy department were muted.

He found the right door and went straight in. Bercoutte had a small reception area with a secretary who had worked in the force for some years and knew Maiden well.

"Hello, John," she smiled at him from where she sat at a computer terminal. "Mr. Bercoutte told me you should be dropping by. I'll let him know you're here." She leaned towards a telephone.

"Hi, Mary. I don't suppose you can give me any hints why he wants to see me?" Maiden asked quickly, but she already had the handset pressed to her ear and, still smiling, shook her head. She spoke briefly and hung up.

"Go right in. He's alone."

Maiden went through the door behind her into Bercoutte's office. It was a large room with full-length tinted windows flooding the place with blue-coloured sunlight. The overhead fluorescents were turned on, but weren't making any impression. Bercoutte sat behind a wide timbered desk covered with papers stacked into orderly piles. His balding head was bent to something in front of him, but he looked up the moment Maiden entered and stood, extending his hand. He was a short man who would have barely satisfied the entry requirements of thirty years earlier, when he joined up. The desk dwarfed him. His physical size hadn't affected his ambition. Bercoutte now held a senior position with considerable power.

"Good to see you, John," he said, ending the handshake and gesturing to a vacant chair. "How are things?"

"Fairly hectic, as usual," Maiden replied, uncomfortable with the familiarity. He didn't know Bercoutte that well— certainly not well enough to exchange pleasantries.

"Nothing changes," Bercoutte chuckled. "God knows I often wish I was still there, though. I miss getting out into the streets."

I'll bet, Maiden thought, keeping his face blank.

Bercoutte leaned back in his chair and regarded Maiden thoughtfully.

"Straight to business, if you don't mind, John."

"Sure." Maiden shrugged slightly.

"How well do you get along with Eric Longman?"

Here it is, Maiden thought, instantly bitter. *I don't hide my opinion of Longman and now they're going to use it as an excuse to move me along, probably to some godforsaken posting. This will be Longman's doing, too.*

He kept his face impassive and said, "We don't socialise

at all, but we seem to have a—good, I suppose—working relationship."

"I've heard otherwise."

"Well, we have our moments to be sure, but I'd have to say I'm not alone. Longman can be a little . . . difficult."

"And what do you think of his work?"

This was definitely getting onto thin ice. Discussing his relationship with Longman was dangerous enough and possibly damaging to his career, but to give a personal criticism of how the man did his job was inviting disaster, whether it was asked for or not.

Bercoutte saw his hesitation and understood. "Look, John. This is strictly between ourselves, right? You've been in that department now for what—six, seven years? You're a respected and experienced detective and I'm asking your opinion because I believe you're in the best position to inform me what's going on."

Maiden almost winced at the word "inform" and the connotations it had for policemen. He wanted to stay on the right side of the line, but he had the feeling Bercoutte might drag him over it to get what he wanted, anyway. He stayed wary and defensive.

"Well, like I said, Longman and I have had our differences," he said carefully, "and we've been known to get pretty heated about things. But I honestly believe that none of it has ever had any effect on my work or how I tackle any job. I still do it to the best of my ability." *There! Now kick me in the teeth and tell me I'm getting transferred anyway. Enough of this "How's it really going?" crap, for Christ's sake.*

"It's not your ability that's come into question, John."

This was the last thing Maiden had expected and it startled him. He managed an uncertain, "Oh, I see," and waited for Bercoutte to explain.

"Longman's job would have been yours a few years ago, but you got tangled in a divorce and the powers-that-be decided you weren't on the ball enough to handle the extra workload. Damned if you didn't do it again—a year ago, wasn't it? But no-one was particularly interested in you at that time, so not too much damage was done. What about now? Has your personal life stabilised?"

Maiden's mind was whirling as he tried to readjust his thinking. "Marriage doesn't seem to agree with me," he said briskly.

"That doesn't answer my question."

"Legally, my divorce is a year old. I haven't spoken to Tracey for over twice that long. I talk to my first wife more often, as a matter of fact. We check up on each other now and again." Maiden shrugged again. "Funny, really." At Bercoutte's steady, questioning look he became more serious. "I believe I have all those aspects of my personal life pretty well sorted out. There's nothing else to go wrong, really."

A small voice rebelled inside Maiden's head. *What the hell has my personal life got to do with how I do the job? Why can't they mind their own fucking business?* But the interview with Bercoutte had suddenly become an important opportunity and Maiden wasn't about to jeopardise it with any emotional outbursts.

"Well, I'm glad to hear it, for our sake as well as your own." Bercoutte paused.

Maiden took the chance. "Am I to understand you're offering me Longman's position?"

"Sort of," Bercoutte nodded as he put down the cup. "OK, this is what we're thinking. We recognise there's a morale problem growing in your section and all the fingers appear to point in one direction. The best solution seems to be giving Eric an option that, in the best interests of everyone, he should accept. But of course he's quite within his rights to argue the toss, and if the union decides to champion his cause he might even win some sort of reprieve. Nobody in this building would like to see that, but these things can happen. Then again, Longman might grab the chance with both hands." Bercoutte mentioned a position in the department and Maiden immediately recognised it for what it was. It was the sort of job where people close to retirement were put out to pasture for their remaining time in the force. It was also where undesirable, but unremovable, "lifers" could be tucked out of harm's way.

"And what do you expect me to do now?" Maiden asked.

"Obviously, keep this to yourself. And when we do make a move on Longman, no mention of your name as a successor will be made. Just make sure you're ready, when the time comes."

"OK."

This felt unreal to Maiden. Promotions among the upper echelons of the police force were usually well orchestrated and came as no surprise to anyone. Sometimes more than one person would be eligible for a vacant position, but it was always made clear who, exactly, was in the running. The type of underhand manoeuvring that Bercoutte was suggesting was rare and showed Maiden how concerned they were about Longman making trouble. Especially if the union decided there was an issue to be raised.

"Are you tied up with anything important at the moment?"

Maiden was about to quickly reply, "No," but stopped himself. Instead, he gave Bercoutte a concise description of the case involving the severed limbs. "There's a possibility it might get very nasty," he finished. "We're trying to track down all the missing employees from the second building now."

"Someone mentioned it to me earlier today," Bercoutte said, absently. "In the face of things, it might be good if you're involved in something heavy. It'll keep you out of circulation when Longman begins to smell a rat. I'll make sure he doesn't try to take it off you."

"It'll keep me busy, whether I like it or not."

"Good. Then I'll be in touch." He reached out to shake hands again. It was a dismissal and Maiden rose to make his escape. As he reached the door, Bercoutte spoke again.

The moment reminded Maiden of leaving Janet Brown in the café and he had to force himself to listen to Bercoutte's parting words.

"And John—about this severed hand thing?"

Maiden turned to see Bercoutte still with the polite smile and casual tone, but there was a glint of authority in his eyes that wasn't to be denied. He said, "That's what I'm going back to work on now."

"I know. Just don't blow it, OK? I might have some trouble giving Longman's job to someone with a recent failure marked on their card, understand me?"

"Loud and clear," Maiden replied calmly, but feeling a fresh flash of annoyance. He swung around and got himself through the door before Bercoutte could see it.

Jesus, he thought angrily, walking through the reception area and not hearing Mary's cheerful goodbye. *The last seven years don't matter a damn if you screw up in the last seven days! The system is well and truly fucked.*

Creane met him at his desk an hour later. Maiden had spent the time in a frustrating exercise of calling the morning's companies and trying to find out if any of their employees were proving difficult to contact. Of course, most of them had disappeared from the face of the earth and it was obvious Maiden wasn't going to get any useful results for several days. Anyone taking a deliberate sickie wasn't going to own up to it and would stay out of sight. The only success was with those employees who were on business trips. The good health of each had been confirmed one way or another, even if some of them hadn't been directly contacted.

"Did you have any luck?" he asked Creane, who perched himself wearily on the edge of Maiden's desk.

"This flatmate is squeaky clean. You mentioned scaring him a little? The poor bastard nearly shat himself when I told him who I was, anyway. He couldn't tell me anything new. According to him, Robert House did everything normal, wasn't acting strange in any way, didn't have a new girlfriend or boyfriend, or anything. I took a chance and went back to the offices and tried to check out what he was wearing on the last day he showed up for work. We got lucky there in one way. It seems Mr. House was a habitual dresser when it came to work. Like, he only had one suit which his fellow staffers reckon he must have dry-cleaned nearly to death, and one pair of matching shoes—"

"Any chance he upset someone too much?" Maiden interrupted. "He was a debt collector, right?"

"Yeah, but he was the soft approach man. The guy to handle little old ladies, that sort of thing. The company sends around some other heavies to anyone who might cause trouble."

"But it's still a possibility, right? He might have got unlucky."

"Well, that's what I was getting to. I called up his flatmate again and asked him to check for the clothing. That's a bingo, because it's there. In fact, his friend now thinks that Robert's Mr. Smooth gear is missing, so it stands to reason that he got home from work, made himself beautiful and went out again on the town. His flatmate thinks that's a little strange, because they hardly went out without each other."

"So now you're going to tell me they're gay and this is a jealousy thing."

"No, judging by the flatmate and what I heard at the office, these two are serious nerds who go out on the town and dream. The closest they ever get to women is buying a pizza or sharing an elevator. They get drunk and pretend they have a great time. Then they go home and wank in separate bedrooms."

"So why'd he shit himself when you knocked on the door?"

"Just a policeman thing, I'd guess."

"Worth a call to Narcotics? See if they want to pay them a visit?

"Honestly, John, I think you'd be wasting their time. The worst drug these guys swallow is Tylenol."

Maiden sighed and scratched the back of his head. When he looked up again Creane was holding out something to him. Squinting at it, he asked, "What's that?"

"The mouse from Robert's personal computer. Perfect for a right index fingerprint."

"Very clever. Get Forensics to compare it to the finger Janet Brown has in her fridge."

"I thought you'd think so," Creane said cockily, then lowered his voice. "What did Bercoutte want?"

"Nothing much. Just a bit of support and said he'd keep Longman off our backs. Let us get on with the job."

Creane frowned. "I'm surprised he's got the time to be interested."

"Well, there's a lesson for you. Never be surprised at who might be taking an interest in you. Not in this job, that's for sure."

"Actually, that's lesson number two," Creane grinned.

"Yeah? What was lesson number one?"

"The bit about stupid questions being better than stupid mistakes."

"Christ, do you listen to everything I say?"

"Religiously."

Chapter Seven

The two men lived in a one-bedroom flat on the eighth floor of a high-rise. Other, taller high-rises were close by, crowding around like thugs harassing a victim, shadowing the windows of their flat at all times of the day and making the rooms dark and depressing.

Neither of the men was clean-living. The sour odour of an overflowing rubbish bin filled the air. Empty pizza boxes were piled high in one corner. Everywhere there were makeshift ashtrays with butts spilling out among crushed beer cans and splayed-out magazines, the nude girls on the covers smiling up uncaringly through the mess. Against one wall was a narrow mattress where the younger man, Howard, slept. He didn't bother with sheets and the cotton fabric covering the foam had a brown smudge down the centre where he lay. Blankets were piled at one end.

His companion, Decker, at twenty-four years of age was older by three years and the leader. He was a role model for Howard, who blatantly imitated his mentor with a close crewcut, the same blue singlets, black jeans with black boots, and had started his own collection of tattoos down each arm. Decker accepted Howard's idolisation as a sign he was doing something right—somebody thought he was worth imitating. Both men had the hard, cruel faces of youths who had known no life except surviving a mean existence, but while Decker was wiry and lean, Howard was much bigger with a naturally strong build. People always noticed his hands, which were oddly large even for his muscled arms.

Decker was sitting in the only seat, a brown vinyl beanbag. Behind him a portable black-and-white television muttered a midday talk show. The reception was poor to the point that the figures were almost beyond recognition and ghosting badly. The sound occasionally fuzzed out. Decker was watching Howard, who squatted on the floor in the middle of the room and counted a collection of crushed banknotes and gold coins.

"Four hundred and twenty-one dollars," he announced, disappointed. "What did I say last time?"

"Four hundred and thirteen, you dumb shit. You haven't come up with the same answer twice."

"It's just over four hundred, that's close enough."

"Then why do you keep counting it?"

"Because I can't believe that's all I got."

"*We* got, pal," Decker immediately told him, growling.

"Yeah, yeah, I know."

"Are you sure you looked under the cash drawer?"

"How many times have I got to fucking tell you? I looked there. It was empty."

"It was a drive-in liquor store, for Christ's sake. There should have been bloody thousands."

"Well, they must have cleared out the till early on."

"It was probably in a paper bag, right under your fucking nose."

Howard jerked his head around to stare at Decker. His

eyes took on a peculiar empty look, but his body was trembling with anger. His finger shook as he raised it to point at Decker's face. "Get off my back, you arsehole," he whispered. "I did everything you told me—I did it *right*. It's not my fault the money was gone."

Decker leaned forward to push his face menacingly at Howard. "And you back *off*, Howard. You start giving me a hard time and you're out of this partnership. I don't need you, remember? I'm doing you a favour."

Decker stared him down until Howard lowered his eyes, but he noted it was getting harder. He was losing control of Howard, slowly but surely. *The little bastard's as mad as a meat axe, most of the time. He's getting more balls, too. One day he'll turn on me and he won't back down. Maybe the time's coming when we have to go our separate ways.*

The idea was attractive in many ways except one. Decker had been grooming Howard to take the risks and it was just starting to come together. His protégé had no qualms about armed hold-ups. Howard didn't understand the subtle differences between robbing someone with a knife, a concealed weapon or a loaded shotgun in the face. If you got caught, the prison sentences could vary in a big way. A judge could throw the book at you. But Howard didn't know that using the shotgun could cost him an extra ten years of his life in jail. So Decker manipulated Howard to do the dirty work for him. He might even be able to pin the earlier jobs he'd done himself on Howard, if it came to that. They were a similar build and height and always wore the balaclava. No-one noticed a few centimetres difference in physique when they had a twelve-gauge shotgun stuck up their nose.

Howard had bent his head to the money again, mumbling to himself.

"What'd you say?"

"I said I don't need you, either. I got my own ideas. I got my own things going for me."

"Who? You and that crazy slut—what's her name? Fiona? She's so pissed and stoned she doesn't know what time of day it is! The only thing she knows is how to take *you* for a ride, pal."

"You leave her alone!" Howard hissed at him. "She's smarter than the both of us put together. She was a nurse once, before she got screwed by the fucking world, that's all."

"*She* got screwed?" Decker laughed cruelly. "Taking more drugs than her fucking patients, right? And by the way, have you been screwed by her yet?" He looked at Howard and pretended to be disappointed for him, clicking his tongue, before shaking his head. "No, and you never will, you stupid sucker. You can buy that bitch drinks and give her smokes until the day you die, but she'll never spread her legs." He laughed again. "You're right—she's too smart for that. Too smart for you, too."

Fiona was a once-attractive woman who Howard had met at a local hotel. The ravages of alcohol and drugs had left her ugly and ill-tempered, although she couldn't have been more than thirty years old. She was tolerated in the bar as long as she didn't harass any of the other customers for free drinks or drugs. Only Howard sought her out, lured by her femininity—she was the only woman he knew. Fiona was known to solicit sex in the alleys too, but she was wise enough not to go so far with Howard. He was more valuable the way he was, mildly infatuated and blind to her faults.

Sulking, Howard started counting the money again. Decker knew he'd pushed his flatmate too far already and that just watching Howard would annoy him, so he reached out for a week-old newspaper and spread it on his knees. He'd already read everything in it that interested him—mainly the article on page four about their own hold-up. Still, he scanned it again and couldn't resist another comment.

"It says here the bandit got away with 'several thousand dollars,'" he said, looking pointedly at Howard over the paper.

"That's crap and you know it. Why do they say that sort of shit?"

Decker suddenly tired of the mindgame. "Insurance," he said, wearily. "They say we took thousands, so they can rip off the insurance company."

Howard held his hand out. "Let me see."

"You've already seen it."

"Well, I want to see it *again*, for fuck's sake. You just did!" Howard suddenly leaned over and snatched the paper from Decker's grasp. Decker threw up his hands in surrender, then feigned exhaustion, clasping his hands behind his head and closing his eyes. Howard smoothed the newspaper out in front of him and read the article. A minute later, with a snort of disgust, he slapped the paper closed. He glanced over his shoulder and saw Decker wasn't taking any notice, so he deepened his sulking and stared moodily at the front page. A headline caught his eye and he read the small article beneath it.

"Shit, look at this," he said, redirecting his anger.

Decker slowly opened his eyes and looked at him. "Now what?"

"We're the hottest act in town and get on page fucking four, while somebody finds a finger in a lift and rates the front page. Why the hell is that?"

"Suits me fine."

"What's that supposed to mean?"

"It means I don't want to be some Bonnie and Clyde. The less newspaper space the better. The cops aren't under so much pressure and we won't get any fucking heroes messing up our jobs."

"Well, shit, we should still be on the front page."

"Forget it."

"A *finger*, for Christ's sake. Shit, we could do better than that!"

"I said, forget it!"

Howard got louder. "Hey—and I'm getting fucking sick of you telling me what to do!"

Now Decker pointed at him. "That's tough, because that's the way it's going to be, Howard! I've got all the plans and I know how they're going to work. I'm doing all the thinking and you're the one who's doing all the *doing*, you hear me? Don't you forget that. You're the gun, pal, and I pull your fucking trigger, all right?"

Decker didn't want to try another staring competition, so he tried deliberately turning away from Howard, ignoring him and closing his eyes again. He heard Howard get up, but he didn't look straightaway. He opened his eyes in time to see Howard disappearing into the bedroom.

"Hey! What the hell are you going into my room for?"

There was no answer. There was a cache of all sorts of things in there that Howard liked, such as more pornographic magazines and a small bag of marijuana. Decker thought about calling him out again, then figured that maybe a joint would settle Howard down. Still, he didn't like him going into the bedroom without asking and it grated on his temper. He heard Howard returning and quickly closed his eyes again, pretending he didn't really care, but there was a strange silence that Decker couldn't handle for long. He opened his eyes once more and looked towards the bedroom door.

Howard was standing in the doorway. Cradled under one arm was the shotgun. With his other hand he awkwardly held a pillow folded over the muzzle. He stared down at Decker, who at first didn't understand what the pillow was for.

"Howard, if you think you're going out half-cocked to do a job on your own, you'd better start thinking—" Then Decker saw the blank look in Howard's eyes again and that he was shaking with rage. "Hey fuck—what do you think you're doing? For Christ's sake, there's no need to get—"

The barrel rose and pointed directly at him.

"Jesus fucking *Christ*, Howard! *No!*"

Howard pulled the trigger. The gunshot wasn't very muffled, perhaps just enough to raise doubts in anyone who heard it. At that moment Howard didn't particularly care. Small pieces of foam exploded outwards from the pillow in a shower. The shotgun cartridge was heavy buckshot and most of the lead pieces slammed into Decker's head and chest. Two entered his heart, killing him instantly. Some buckshot sliced through the vinyl of the beanbag, and the white polystyrene beans burst out in a spray. Decker made a few grunting noises and jerked spasmodically twice, although he was already dead, then went still. His head tipped back and he stared sightlessly at the ceiling. A wound just below his hairline bled into his scalp, seeping through the close-cropped hair.

The white beans continued to pour out onto the floor.

Howard stared at the corpse for a long time, then said quietly, "You're wrong, Decker. *I'm* pulling the fucking trigger, *pal.*"

For the first time Howard realised he was shaking and he looked down in surprise at his hands clasped around the weapon. The trembling had started with his raw, uncontrollable anger. Now it was more from reaction—but there was no remorse. Only the slowing of the adrenalin in his system, bringing him down. Decker's chest was a pulped mass of gore, the blood pooling in the wound. It was threatening to make a real mess and Howard realised he had to do something fast. He dropped the shotgun carelessly and stooped to snatch up one of the blankets from the mattress. He balled it up and, pressing it against Decker's shredded singlet, waited for a long minute, counting the seconds in a whisper to himself. He then pulled the blanket back and inspected Decker's chest. The rug was acrylic and most of the blood, rather than soaking in, had slicked over the surface.

"Fuck, fuck, fuck . . ." Howard muttered, regretting

everything except killing his partner. The blood was going to make a mess—a stain that the police would find if they came looking. The noise of the gunshot might have attracted some attention too, and Howard belatedly cocked his head to one side and listened for the sound of approaching sirens, the way it always happened on television. And he was *upstairs*, for Christ's sake! What the hell was he going to do with the body?

Then a strange thing happened inside his mind. It was as if everything suddenly became too much and he shut down. Howard simply wanted to sit down and close his eyes for a while.

So he did just that.

An unknown amount of time passed. When Howard opened his eyes again nothing had changed, but he didn't feel so stressed about everything either. He saw the blood from the chest wound soaking into Decker's jeans and Howard wondered if he should take them off him. They were a good pair of jeans, after all. But the thought of disrobing his friend made him think of some sick sexual ritual like you saw in late-night movies and he wasn't sure he wanted to do that. The newspaper caught his eye and he considered using it to clean up some of the blood. He knew the paper would absorb it better than the blanket and it made him remember the article about someone finding a finger in a lift.

I can do better than that, now, he thought, looking at the body in a new light. They had a large machete which they were originally going to use for the hold-ups, until Decker had bought the shotgun from a petty thief he knew. *I could be on the front fucking page every day of the week now, if I wanted. How many fingers has he got? Decker won't give a shit.*

This last thought brought a burst of laughter. It was like being able to push Decker around and that felt good.

Howard felt he had something—a *resource*—that would get him all the attention he wanted. He wasn't quite sure how to use it, but the thought of provoking a news item in the paper every day was like a drug to him. It gave him a sense of power, of being important.

He dragged Decker's corpse into the bedroom and dumped it on the bed. The body had a strange, deadweight feeling Howard wasn't expecting and at one stage he collapsed in a fit of giggles when he got tangled in the limbs. It all seemed so funny. He covered the corpse with a sheet.

What wasn't so funny were the white polystyrene beans that had spilled everywhere. Howard quickly lost his good humour as the beans billowed and wafted in all directions. At first he tried stuffing them back into the hole in the bag, but more seemed to come out than go in. He found an unused garbage bag and began painstakingly scooping them into that. It was hard enough keeping the bag open, and he could only put small handfuls in at a time. The lumps of beans that were stuck together with congealed blood were easier to handle, and Howard took care to find all of those. By the time most of the bloodied beans were in the garbage bag, the remainder had scattered all over the room. At this stage Howard gave up. He told himself he would finish it later, but of course he never would.

Besides, he was eager to figure out something he could do to better the front page article.

They didn't possess a cutting board, but the two kitchen chairs had wooden seats and backs, so he carried one into the bedroom and placed it close to the bed. He took the machete down from the cupboard where he'd got the shotgun. Next he grabbed one of Decker's arms and pulled it across to the chair, spreading the hand out so the fingers were splayed. It looked like Decker was reaching out from the bed to the chair. Holding the limb in place with one hand, Howard hefted the knife in the other and considered where would be the best place to strike. He wanted to take off all the fingers. He had a vague notion that dropping a number of them somewhere public was one step ahead of just a single finger being found. After a moment he shrugged and decided to simply give it his best try.

"Take this, you know-all fucker," he grinned at Decker's dead face.

Six months earlier, Howard had been a street kid going bad. Then he became an armed robber. Now he was a killer, and he was pleasantly surprised to find he was going to enjoy this part of it, too. What he was about to do didn't worry him at all. He realised how much he'd hated Decker's authority and unkind remarks about his intelligence and ability.

He brought the machete down in a short stroke. The new blade cut easily into the flesh of the first two fingers, but didn't sever the bone. Howard felt it jar against the solidness. He hit it harder on the second try and didn't quite cut into the same spot, but this time the index finger came away. The second was only hanging by a thread. Blood was pooling on the chair and threatening to run off onto the floor, so Howard went back to the main room, retrieved the newspaper and spread it beneath the seat. It was easy to finish the job on the second finger. The thumb proved a simple task, too. The last two fingers needed the machete to strike at a different angle and, with the first attempt, Howard missed completely, cutting into the back of the hand. He cursed and took more time with his aim. When he finished, those two stumps were ragged and messier than the first ones. All the fingers, he saw, weren't as cleanly cut as he'd wanted or imagined they could be.

After flopping the body over so he could do the other hand, Howard fared little better on this one. The savaged ends of the fingers made them look like curled-up pieces of meat. He pushed back his disappointment, telling himself you *could* see they were fingers and that's all that mattered. He pushed the mutilated hands back under the sheet, made sure the corpse was covered and picked up the fingers, cradling them in one hand against his stomach.

Near the kitchen sink he found a plastic shopping bag and he put them into this. He opened the small refrigerator and inspected the interior. There was a stench of rotting food coming from somewhere to the rear of the shelves so the freezer compartment seemed a better idea. Howard had to shove the plastic bag past a maw of thick ice guarding the icebox. Finally, he bundled the bloody newspaper from beside the bed into the same garbage bag as the polystyrene beans. He tied the top tightly and put the bag next to the pile of empty pizza boxes.

Howard felt a sense of having done a good job. All the loose ends, as Decker would have called them, were taken care of. It was worth going down to the local bar, having a few beers and maybe getting into a game of pool. He might even find Fiona somewhere. They could talk over their plans again—they were definitely different now, without Decker. Without Decker he had four hundred dollars all to himself and didn't have to justify spending it to anyone.

That felt good, too.

Chapter Eight

The next day Howard woke up feeling hung-over and hungry. He lay on his filthy mattress and tried to recall the previous twenty-four hours. It came back to him easily. He felt no regrets—only a sense of freedom. It was like he'd started a new chapter in his life and the end had well and truly justified the means. In fact, his biggest worry was the amount of money he'd spent at the hotel drinking. It was nearly two hundred dollars, as he'd got into shots of top-shelf spirits and liqueurs, and had shouted a dozen drinks to perfect strangers after defeating them at the pool table. Fiona had got drunk too, and Howard came closer than ever, but she changed her mind at the last moment and slipped away when he wasn't looking. She'd been impressed by Howard's plans, though. Impressed like hell.

Howard decided he needed a burger and a milkshake for breakfast and crawled off the mattress and stood up. He was still fully dressed, including his boots. He often slept that way. Checking he still had plenty of notes in his pocket he went to the door, but paused as he grabbed the handle. There was a bad smell in the air that was different from the usual sour odours of the room.

"Fuck it," he mumbled to himself, glancing towards the bedroom door. He hadn't thought about this. But first things had to come first and his stomach was roiling in protest. He needed a good feed, then he could think about things more clearly.

Outside, the morning sunshine made him squint. He walked with his head down, so people coming towards him would have to get out of his way. He wanted a cigarette, more because that was an important part of his image, but he'd left his packet of rolling tobacco in the bar. He shrugged, figuring that with his new freedom and wealth he could afford a packet of tailor-mades. He didn't care what brand.

The nearest store was a small supermarket with a café in front. It was run by Vietnamese and Howard hated that, but they made good food and were cheap. Howard hated gooks, chinks, blacks and every goddamned thing else who wasn't white and working class. Howard often fantasised about joining the Nazi party, but he wasn't sure Sydney even had one. They seemed to be everywhere in America, if you believed the television. Thinking about this as he walked into the café area, Howard wondered if he could steal enough money to get him to America—to New York or somewhere like that where'd they'd be bound to have a Nazi party.

He ordered his burger and milkshake. When the wizened owner turned to the sizzling hotplate Howard quietly took a newspaper from the pile in front of him and sat down at a plastic table near the window. There was no-one else eating in the café. He stared down at the front page and imagined his own photograph there, like a "wanted" poster. *It would be the greatest*, he thought. The reality was a photograph of a prominent politician holding an angry hand towards the camera. Howard tried reading the article, but it didn't make any sense to him. It said something about the politician manipulating banks to bring down companies that were in competition to his own. It was another, completely foreign, world to Howard. He turned the page.

Now he was looking at a beautiful girl in a white bikini, holding a small puppy against her breasts. Howard stared at the model and tried to imagine what it would be like to sleep with a girl like that. The thought made him hold his breath and caused a stirring in his groin. He'd only had one sexual encounter with the opposite sex, and that had been with a cheerless prostitute who'd ordered him around more than Decker, telling him to clean up and wear a condom. Worse, she had laughed at Howard as he struggled to put the prophylactic on properly. The bored, professional way she rejuvenated his erection, then lay on her back and put him inside her had been so passionless and uncaring Howard had to fight down a sudden urge to hurt her badly. When it was all over—and that had been embarrassingly quickly—he'd got dressed and made sure he had his wallet. Then he'd begun to mindlessly and loudly abuse her, although Howard wasn't certain himself what she had done wrong. Only that a special moment in his life hadn't turned out anything like he'd dreamed it should and it had to be the girl's fault. It wasn't long before she'd started screaming back at him to get out and he heard heavy footsteps coming along the hall. Howard fled, squeezing past an enormous security man and was lucky not to get a blow to the back of his head on his way.

A call from the café owner brought Howard back to the real world. His burger was ready. He retrieved it and the milkshake from the counter and pushed the newspaper to the opposite side of the table to make room. Now, as he ate, he could only read the lower half of the pages.

On the bottom of page three was a short "stop press" piece about someone finding an amputated hand in a lift somewhere in the central business area. It compared the find to a similar episode a week earlier, when a secretary discovered a severed finger. The newspaper promised more details in the next issue.

Howard stopped chewing. Anger filled his mind, coming out of nowhere.

"*Fuck* it!" he snarled loudly, startling the owner and a customer who had just walked through the door. Howard was glaring at the article, the print blurring in front of his eyes. When he focused again he found himself staring at the burger in his hand. Blindly he threw it, splattering it against the window.

The owner called out half-heartedly, "Hey! What do you think you're doing—"

"Shut the fuck up," Howard yelled, standing up and tipping his chair over. With a wild sweep of his hand he knocked the milkshake aside in a burst of white liquid. "*Fuck* it!" He was nearly screaming, prompting the customer to flee. Howard grabbed the edge of the table and flipped it, scattering the newspaper and dripping milk, and then stalked towards the door. The owner tried another weak protest, but Howard silenced him as he passed, jabbing his finger.

"You shut the fuck up! I'm going to be getting you! You and all your fucking kind!" He punched the glass of the open door as he left, cracking it.

The walk back to his flat was a complete blank. The streets and people of Waterloo flowed past him unseen and some of the passers-by even stared at him curiously—something Howard would normally challenge right back with a fearsome glare. All he could think about was the careful effort he'd made to cut off Decker's fingers—and now they were useless. Someone had gone one step better. He bumped into several people, some of whom complained or cursed at him, but Howard didn't notice.

It was only in the safety and security of his own home

that his anger started to abate and he began to think coherently, if not rationally.

"I was going to do something like that," he muttered aloud, dropping onto the remaining kitchen chair and holding his head in his hands. "*I* was going to do something like that, the bastards. I should have cut off his fucking hand!" He closed his eyes and waited for some guidance to come to him, but that had always been Decker's job, and Decker was lying dead in the bedroom.

Howard stayed like that a long time, watching the blackness of his eyelids swirl uselessly in front of him. Eventually the despair subsided a little.

"I *still* can," Howard suddenly told himself. "I can do *something*."

He thought about the fingers in the freezer and about how they were no good now. They weren't good *enough*, that was the point. Howard stood up and went to the fridge, digging the plastic bag out of the ice. The fingers were hard. He took them into the bathroom and dropped them one by one into the toilet. After the first four he flushed it and saw them disappear satisfactorily. He put in the rest, but flushed the toilet too soon, before the cistern had a chance to fill. It scared him for a moment, seeing the fingers still there after the water finished briefly cascading, then he realised what was wrong and waited impatiently for the hissing of the valve to stop. The next flush worked. Howard thought about disposing of Decker's entire body down the toilet, hacking it into small enough pieces. But it seemed like a big job.

Decker's entire corpse was useless to him now. The hands, without their fingers, wouldn't be effective. Even the whole arm, with a fingerless hand, struck Howard as wrong. He needed to get rid of the body and maybe get another one, whole and complete, that gave him more options.

These were the ugly, dangerous thoughts growing in the back of Howard's mind. He needed money, which meant he would have to go out and do another job—a good one this time, with plenty of cash to grab. And it might give him an opportunity to play his new game as well. Maybe somebody would get too heroic and force Howard to pull the trigger, giving him a new corpse and a new *resource*.

Either way, a killing would get him on the front page of the newspaper. Howard liked that idea.

Late that night a private contractor drove the forks of his garbage truck into the big industrial bin behind the high-rises. He hit the button to lift it over the cab and empty the contents into the compactor behind. The driver had the windows shut tight and the heater on full blast. This part of town frightened the hell out of him, even though he didn't carry any cash and the hoodlums around here probably knew that. The trouble was, driving these back streets, you never knew when you might disturb a drug deal going down or something, and suddenly you were in deep trouble. So he kept the doors locked, the windows rolled up tight, and watched where he was driving.

He was also supposed to watch a mirror mounted so he could keep an eye on what came out of the bins. He didn't bother very often—there wasn't much he could do about it, if he saw something wrong. He wasn't going to go crawling in the back to retrieve some kid's bicycle or whatever they expected him to do. The mirror was usually coated in filth, making it difficult to see, anyway. However, he watched it now out of boredom and there was a floodlight nearby which silhouetted the dropping garbage in an interesting way.

He had a fleeting glimpse of something crossing the gap between the bin and the truck. Something strange and yet familiar. It made his heart go cold.

He wondered what to do.

He took the easy way out and quickly decided to finish

his rounds and go to the landfill site like he always did. Push whatever it was out the back with all the rest of the garbage.

Let somebody else find it, if they ever did.

Chapter Nine

At the same time a second missing person was confirmed, Robert House was established as the owner of the severed finger. A good fingerprint was found on the computer mouse and it matched. Maiden wasn't surprised. He'd been expecting it. The only thing it didn't tell him yet was whether House was still alive, although he doubted it. Maiden dismissed completely the possibility that House had taken off his own finger. The worst alternative, from Maiden's point of view, was that House had been abducted and his finger amputated and dropped in the lift as some sort of message while he was still kept alive. If that were the case Maiden had to accept they would be dealing with a very sick person indeed. For that reason, and for House's sake, Maiden quietly hoped the young man was already dead. Especially as the criminal didn't seem concerned with cutting off just fingers.

They already had a hand, now.

The hand belonged to a man called Peter Dawes. Again, it had been a flatmate who raised the alarm, prompted by the constant calls coming from Dawes's office, that in turn was being pressured by Maiden. Dawes hadn't come home one night and his flatmate, Tom Fischer, assumed he had gotten lucky. The second night of no homecoming rated as a sexual achievement of some note, but the third with its accompanying phone calls from Dawes's work, a computer software company, couldn't be ignored. From that point it had been simple to pull a fingerprint from Dawes's desk and match it with the hand.

Maiden and Creane went to visit Fischer in the early afternoon. He and Dawes lived in a two-bedroom upmarket townhouse in Neutral Bay. As the policemen climbed the steep driveway Creane pointed out a glimpse of the harbour through the trees, glinting in a patch of weak sunshine. Maiden pulled a wry face and commented that the "harbour view" was probably worth an extra fifty dollars a week in rent. Both of them were speculating that this could be a case of high living and youthful indulgence. Creane made a note to check if the rent was up-to-date.

Fischer opened the door cautiously and peered out. Maiden, who was in front, saw there was someone else inside the flat. "Detective Senior Sergeant John Maiden from The Rocks police station." He held up his open wallet briefly, then flipped it closed and in the same movement jerked it at Creane behind him. "This is Detective Constable Martin Creane. Are you Tom Fischer?"

"That's right."

"We'd like to talk to you, Mr. Fischer. About the missing person report you called in. Can we come inside?"

"Two policemen already came this morning. I told them everything." Fischer didn't sound friendly.

Maiden's suspicions were growing. "Is everything all right, Mr. Fischer? We'd just like to ask you some more questions."

"I'm fine. Shit, all right. Come on in." Fischer walked away from them into the flat. He was a squat, well-muscled man with a close-cropped head and jutting features. The front door opened directly into the living area. The curtains were drawn and the light dim. The place was clean and well furnished. The smell of marijuana hit Maiden immediately and he gave Creane a knowing look over his shoulder. An attractive girl was perched on the table, her legs swinging. She watched with hard eyes as they came in. She had long blonde hair and wore a large T-shirt which only just reached her thighs. Maiden tried to be casual, while Creane stared openly at her, taking in her looks and good legs.

"And who are you, miss?" Maiden asked gruffly.

"Jennifer Musgrave," she said nonchalantly. When Maiden looked expectantly at her, she just stared straight back.

"OK, and do you live here, Jennifer?"

"No, I'm just visiting." She was trying to be cool, but her eyes kept sliding towards Fischer for support. As Maiden's sight adjusted to the gloom, he saw they were bloodshot. He waited again and this time she added, "Tom and I are going out together, you know?"

"Did you stay here last night?"

"Yes."

"What about the night before?"

"Yeah, too."

Fischer made an attempt to sound offended. "Hey, guys, this is about Peter, right? Not us."

"That's right, Tom," Maiden said smoothly, turning to him. "When was the last time you saw him or spoke to him?"

"When he left for work Tuesday morning."

"And you haven't heard a thing from him since?"

"No, nothing."

"That's three nights in a row. Does he usually stay out that long? . . . Has he done it before?"

"No, not really."

"Not *really*?" Maiden stared at him. Creane, who was wandering casually around the room looking at things, paused and did the same.

"Well, I figured he might have had a bit of luck with a girl, you know. So I wasn't too worried."

"Is he good with the girls?"

Maiden saw Fischer glance at his girlfriend. Fischer said, "He's a bit shy, normally."

Maiden's voice got a little harder. "So, for Peter to suddenly score three nights with a woman was probably a bit farfetched?"

"I guess so. That's why I called the police," Fischer said defensively.

"This morning, I know. Do you work, Tom?"

"Sure, at a photographic shop. I run the processing unit."

"Why aren't you at work today?"

"I felt a bit sick this morning, so I called in."

Maiden looked pointedly at the girl and exchanged a glance with Creane.

She spoke up unexpectedly. "OK, so it's been good to have the place to ourselves for a while. Is that a crime?"

Maiden pretended to be pleased for them. "Is that right? So while your flatmate might be in some type of trouble, you two figure to get in a few days playing mothers and fathers, before you tell anybody something's wrong."

"Hey, the guy's an adult, OK? Do you want someone calling the police every time a guy doesn't come home at night?" Fischer said hotly, before realising what Maiden had said. "So, what do you mean—in trouble? Is Peter in jail?"

"Would you explain to these caring people what's been happening, Martin?" Maiden asked Creane pleasantly. "You've got all your notes."

Creane looked startled for a moment, then cleared his throat nervously. "Right. Ah, I'm afraid you might find this a little upsetting," he warned them awkwardly. He pulled a notebook from his pocket and consulted some pages, although he didn't really need to. "The day before yesterday someone found a severed human hand in a lift in the central business district—"

"Yeah, I read about that," Fischer interrupted. But he didn't like the way this was going. The girl's eyes had become worried. Creane started to feel sorry for them. Maiden was casually picking around the flat now.

Creane went on, "Did you notice that it was found in the same office block Peter works in?"

"I don't think it said that."

"It didn't," Maiden said shortly, frowning at Creane.

"I must be thinking of a police report, not the newspaper article—"

"For Christ's sake, Martin. Tell them," Maiden growled impatiently.

Creane went on hurriedly, "Well, we've identified the hand as belonging to Peter Dawes. Through fingerprinting, that is," he added, angry at Maiden for pushing him.

Fischer swore in shock and fell back into a lounge suite. He sat there, staring into space. A moment later the girl burst into tears and jumped down from the table. She disappeared through a door, slamming it behind her. Maiden wandered over and picked up something she had been sitting on. It was a plastic bag half-filled with a green, leafy substance. Without saying anything he gently put it back down. Fischer was struggling for words.

"So—Peter's been killed?"

Creane waited for Maiden to reply and when the silence grew too long answered himself. "To be accurate, we've only got his amputated hand and under normal circumstances the loss of a hand shouldn't be fatal. We can't say for certain that Peter is dead, but the evidence and circumstances suggest there's been a homicide and the hand is some way of leaving a message."

"Under normal circumstances? What the hell would be normal circumstances?"

"Exactly, Mr. Fischer," Maiden said, coming closer.

"That's what Martin just explained. It's possible your friend is still alive, but we doubt it. Now, we need you to answer these questions so we can find out who did this. Are you sure he went out that night?"

"Of course I'm sure! He's not here, is he?"

"OK, let me put it this way. Are you sure he came home, got changed and *then* went out? There's no chance that whatever happened to him, happened on the way home from his work?"

"No, there was a note."

"Did the police take it with them?" Maiden half-directed this question at Creane, who should have known, but Fischer answered.

"They didn't think it was worth anything."

This annoyed Maiden, but he stayed calm. "Do you still have it?"

"It's on the fridge, under the chocolate magnet."

Fischer didn't move from his seat, so Creane went over. He found a creased piece of paper among several bill reminders and a shopping list. He read it before passing it to Maiden. It simply said that Dawes was going out and Fischer shouldn't worry about making a meal for both of them. Maiden read it too, then put it on the table next to the marijuana.

"Is that normal, too?" he asked, nodding down at it.

"I hardly ever smoke. I've had that for ages—in fact, I was going to get rid of it."

"The *note*, Mr. Fischer."

"Ah, he often leaves a note of some kind, because we share a lot of the cooking. But going out on a Tuesday night is a bit unusual."

"Is there somewhere he normally goes?" Creane asked.

"Well, there's a few places we used to all go together, but lately there's been a bit of a problem with Jenny, if you know what I mean. Pete's sort of got a thing about her too, now, and it's been making things a little difficult."

Maiden let out a theatrical sigh. "OK, so tell Detective Creane here all the places you hang out on a normal night. Don't leave any out, understand? I don't care if they're gay bars, illegal gambling joints or God knows where else. Give us them all."

Fischer gave him a list, then Maiden asked for a good guess on what Dawes may have been wearing. This led to a brief visit into Dawes's bedroom where Fischer decided a favourite shirt appeared to be missing. "And jeans," he added, confidently. "Peter always wears jeans when he wants to impress somebody. If he's wearing that shirt, he'll be in jeans, too."

Maiden said, "Are you two still friends? Or has your little love triangle got out of hand?"

Fischer looked angry. "Excuse us all for being human, all right?" He stared at Maiden, who looked back impassively, waiting for an answer. Fischer relented, but spoke harshly. "Yeah, we're still friends, but it's been a little hard. Can you understand that?"

"I do it all the time—how about you?" Maiden turned innocently to Creane.

"I—ah, I'm too young," Creane said, uncomfortably.

Maiden nodded and abruptly announced they were going, leaving Creane to thank Fischer. Creane was surprised to see Maiden ignore the bag of drugs on the table, walking straight past it to the front door. The detectives didn't speak to each other until they were in the car. Creane looked expectantly at Maiden, waiting to be told where they were going next.

"Back to The Rocks," Maiden told him, hunching down in his seat.

Creane didn't start the car. "Can I say something?"

"Sure you can." Maiden closed his eyes.

"Can you warn me next time? When you're going to do the good-cop, bad-cop act, I mean."

Maiden frowned, but didn't open his eyes. "What act?"

"You were going rough on that guy, so I figured you were trying to intimidate him and I was supposed to be Mr. Nice. It's a pretty standard procedure, isn't it?"

"Not for me. That's how I question everyone. What the hell are you going to achieve by being nice? You'll only give 'em the impression they can keep their mouths shut without getting into too much trouble."

Creane thought about this for a moment. "Right," he said, uncertainly. "So, what about the drugs? What are we supposed to do about that?"

Now Maiden opened one eye to squint at him sideways. "Don't be stupid. I'm not going to bust a girl that good-looking. What sort of a policeman are you?" When Creane stared at him, Maiden added patiently, "Actually, I think it might be a good idea to give Mr. Fischer and his girlfriend a bit more rope to see if they manage to hang themselves with it. They didn't seem that upset to hear their friend might be dead, am I right?"

"I thought *she* was. But I didn't take Fischer for being a sensitive kind of guy."

Maiden wasn't listening. He had closed his eyes again and was apparently trying to nap, so Creane sighed and shook his head, then leaned forward to start the car.

Back at the station Maiden sent Creane in search of coffee and sandwiches and sat down at his desk. He wasn't exactly sure what he hoped to achieve next. Beginning a written report confirming he was getting nowhere wouldn't do him much good, either.

The choice was taken out of his hands within seconds of him sitting down. The telephone rang. It was Longman.

"Maiden, you're supposed to be at a press conference in about five damn minutes. What are you doing there?"

"I'm *what?*"

"The media's getting far too interested to let them figure

things out for themselves, so the boss called a press conference, which means you're it. You'd better get to College
Street now."

"Why the hell didn't someone tell me earlier about—"

"Don't tell me your problems, Maiden. I've got enough
of my own."

The phone went dead.

You bastard, Maiden glared at the phone. *You've done
this deliberately, which means you probably know more about
having to hang onto your job than Bercoutte realises. Someone's whispering in your ear, too.* The more Maiden thought
about it, the more he became convinced he was right. And
Longman had called him "Maiden," when even at his
worst he always referred to Maiden as "John." The only
good thing Maiden could see right now was that Longman
had tipped his hand. At least now he knew to be even
more careful.

"A fucking *press* conference," he muttered to himself,
getting to his feet. He spotted Sayers at his desk and called
out. "Hey, do me a favour? When Martin gets back, tell him
to get to the fifth floor of College Street in a hurry. I've got
a press conference and he's got most of the facts and figures in his bloody notebook."

"*You've* got a press conference?"

Maiden was trying to get his jacket on. "Yeah, and don't
laugh. I'm not impressed."

"You'd better brush your hair and clean your teeth."

"Get stuffed. If Martin's not here in two minutes, go
looking for him, will you? I really need him. I'll try and
stall for a while down there."

Stepping out of the lift on the fifth floor of College Street
station Maiden was met by a senior uniformed sergeant
called Overman. Overman was the station Media Officer,
dealing with any inquiries from the general public. He was
also responsible for co-ordinating public relations exer-
cises with people such as charity groups and fund-raising

committees, which was why he rated a nice office on that floor. And because he was there and always impeccably dressed in proper uniform, he got the added job of organising the press conferences and shepherding the right people in the right directions.

He knew Maiden well. He stepped forward cradling a clipboard on one arm. "There you are, John. I was just about to send out a search party."

"I only found out about this damn thing five minutes ago."

Overman looked surprised for a moment. "Well, don't panic. This is only a small job with about six or so newspapers, though if they give it enough space and headlines the next one will probably attract a bit of television. How's it going, anyway? Any luck?" He started to guide Maiden slowly along the hallway.

"Not really. If anything, it's starting to look pretty bad. It's a safe bet we've got two corpses on our hands out there somewhere."

"Two?" Overman looked puzzled. "Well, anyway, that's a bastard—no real progress, I mean. They'll be back for more and making the whole thing bigger than bloody Ben Hur when you tell them it's a probable double homicide."

They stopped outside a doorway. "I'm surprised they're that interested at all," Maiden said, automatically running his fingers through his hair and straightening his jacket. "It must have been the amputated hand that's got the ghouls sniffing for blood. We haven't mentioned the missing persons connection yet. I was hoping it would sneak past without too much fuss."

"You've got to be kidding. Besides, somebody would have worked it out soon enough—one finger and one hand makes two bodies at least. That's the sort of news they're looking for. You're here to clean up the details."

"Thanks a bloody lot."

"No problem. Now, have you done this before?"

"Seen plenty, but I've never done one."

"It's the usual set-up. You sit at the main table and answer as much as you like, or nothing at all, if that's the way you want to do it. There's a list there for you of the things Bercoutte doesn't want you to mention, which isn't much. The stenographer's name is Judy and her husband's got about twenty kilos on you, so don't get any ideas," Overman finished with a grin.

"Very funny. Where will you be?"

"In there with you, but standing at the door."

"My offsider, a kid called Martin Creane, is supposed to be on his way here. Let him in, OK?"

"Sure. Take it easy, John. Most of these reporters are only here because they've got nothing else better to do. They're juniors who'll get replaced when you start talking homicide." With that Overman put a hand on Maiden's shoulder and steered him through the door.

It was one of the smaller conference rooms. In the main area padded chairs were scattered randomly, while at the rear there were several tables for those who needed them. Everything focused towards a raised stage where a single long table sat with a jug of water and glasses, a microphone and the stenographer—who was more a recorder than a stenographer, operating the tape machine connected to the microphone and noting down the journalists' questions if she thought they didn't make it to the tape.

Maiden went nervously to the stage, nodded to the stenographer as he sat down, then faced the reporters looking expectantly at him. There were seven, all male, and bunched together so he could only see the faces of those in the front. There was a chorus of clicks as miniature tape recorders were turned on.

"My name is Detective Senior Sergeant John Maiden," he said clearly. "Please feel free to ask any questions you want, though don't complain if I choose not to answer some. I'll do my best to answer everything, but obviously there's some things we'd like to keep to ourselves for the moment. I'll ask you to speak loud and clearly, so Judy here has an easy time."

The questions began, most of them confirming the facts behind the finding of the severed finger, then similar queries about the hand. Maiden could tell by the intensity of the reporters that they, too, sensed this was the beginning of something big. He thought to himself that Overman was probably right. If there wasn't some sort of break in the investigation soon and the pressure kept building, the next press conference would probably be three times as large and he would have his back against the wall.

Someone asked from the back, "Is it your opinion, Detective, that with these two separate incidents we have two separate homicides here?"

"Technically speaking, someone could survive even the forceful amputation of a finger or a hand, but being realistic I would say two homicides is more likely and the severed limbs were removed from the corpses."

"So we're talking about a double murderer, even a psychopath?"

Maiden hesitated. He realised they were looking at him expectantly and replied slowly, "That is a possibility, given the evidence. However, with a lack of any real victims the opposite is still possible, too. The identified owners of these human pieces may still be alive and obviously suffering from the amputations. We could be looking at a double abduction. There is also the *third* possibility . . ." he paused, to make them listen harder. "That the second instance was a copycat crime inspired by the media coverage of the severed finger. Some newspapers sensationalised it on the front pages."

Maiden waited for someone to deny their newspaper's culpability or stand up for the rights of the press, but no-one seemed concerned. The same reporter then asked,

"So, you have a missing person file connected with each of the office blocks involved. Have you identified the victims?"

"Fingerprinting has established identities, that's all." Maiden was about to reply further when the proceedings were interrupted by Creane sidling through the door. Maiden gave him an angry look, but Creane already appeared anxious enough.

Again, it was the same reporter who asked the next question. Maiden focused on his face now, deciding it might be one he needed to remember. He sounded like he was capable of causing trouble.

"Detective Maiden, what about the corpse they found at the landfill site this morning? Is there any connection with this investigation? My sources tell me it had all its fingers removed."

Maiden was stunned. He turned to Creane, because he had nowhere else to look, and saw the younger detective was trying every subtle body-language sign to get Maiden's attention. Just as the silence was becoming condemning, Maiden managed to say, "Ah, Detective Constable Creane has been looking into that for me, but as you can see he's only just arrived. If you'll excuse me a moment—"

Maiden put his hand over the microphone and gestured for Creane to come closer. Creane quickly slid into a chair next to him and they put their heads together, talking in urgent whispers.

"What the fuck are they talking about?" Maiden hissed.

"I stumbled across it downstairs. It was coming to us through the normal channels they reckon, but everyone else already knows about it."

"Someone's playing bloody games in this place," Maiden said savagely. "What do we know, and what can we tell these clowns?"

Creane told him in clipped, rushed sentences, "They

found the body this morning at the city landfill site. One of the scavenging crew—you know, the guys who look for bottles and things for recycling—thought the dead man's boots were a good score until he found out the owner was still attached to them. The victim's about mid-twenties, looks tough and copped a shotgun in the chest. And yes, his fingers are missing. All of them. There's a team sifting through the site now looking for them, but the body has been buried and bulldozed a couple of times and might have been found miles away from where it was originally dumped."

"How long has he been dead?"

"I could only get hearsay, because I knew I had to get to you here fast, but the word is he's fresh—real fresh. Certainly not more than two days."

Some coughing from his small audience reminded Maiden they were waiting. He straightened up and moved closer to the microphone. "I'm sorry gentlemen, but Detective Creane hasn't told me anything new I can give you." Maiden took a mental punt and added, "I'll confirm there was a corpse found at the landfill site, but I cannot confirm about the missing fingers—"

There was a babble of protest and Maiden held up his hand to silence them. Over the noise, he said. "*Apparently* that is the condition in which the victim was discovered, but I haven't got an official sanction to confirm it. So you may publish that information as unconfirmed, because I know I won't be able to stop you anyway. If you care to wait a while I might be able to get the full story. But it might take some time." Maiden stood up, signalling an end. "That's all, thank you. Anyone waiting for more will hear from Sergeant Overman."

Two people shouted last questions, but Maiden ignored them and strode from the room with Creane on his heels. Overman followed them outside and Maiden jerked his head at the sergeant, telling him to join them in a small kitchen opposite. He closed the door and the three men were bunched close. There was a smell of sweet cold coffee which had been spilled on the benchtops.

"Did you know about this bloody corpse at the landfill site?" Maiden asked Overman angrily. He already knew the answer, remembering the puzzlement in Overman's eyes when Maiden said they probably had two corpses on their hands—two, not three, as Overman knew.

"I heard about it," Overman snapped back. "I expected *you* already knew and you were keeping your mouth shut. You're the investigating officer, aren't you?"

Maiden sighed, deflated, and ran his hand through his hair. "Yeah, yeah, that's right, but you'd think I was the prime suspect with the amount of information I'm being given." He looked sideways at Creane and muttered "Longman" under his breath.

On turning back to meet Overman's eyes he said, "But it's not your problem. Now, do you need me to get an official confirmation on these missing fingers? Or can you do that yourself?"

Overman put on a wry grin. "No-one's waiting for your official confirmation, John. The next newspaper editions will have one corpse, completely fingerless, whether you confirm it or not. Nothing short of telling them the information was absolutely wrong would stop that, and even that mightn't do it."

"I'll call that a lesson learned," Maiden said and turned to Creane. "So, where's this bloody corpse?"

"I don't know. That's a detail I'd left until now, too."

"Then let's go and find out."

Maiden nodded his thanks to Overman and they left the small kitchen. A secretary walking past was startled to see three men emerge from behind the closed door. As Overman went his separate way, Maiden whispered hoarsely into Creane's ear, "All right, we'll try and avoid Longman altogether. If you need his OK to do anything—like sign out a car or get a photographer, anything—tell me and we'll work out a way to steer around the bastard."

Back at his desk with Creane, Maiden called Janet Brown. She answered straightaway.

"Janet, this is John Maiden."

"Hello, John," she replied easily. "Have you still got a job or did Bercoutte fire you?"

Maiden realised he hadn't spoken to her since their shared coffee break and felt guilty. "Sorry, I said I'd call, didn't I? . . . No, I'm still in it up to my neck and things are getting worse. Look, can you tell me anything about this body they found at the rubbish dump? Like where the damn thing is now would be a help."

"It's at the central morgue. I sent one of my assistants down to have a look. He should be back any minute."

"You didn't check it out yourself?" Maiden asked, before he could stop himself.

Her voice turned cool. "Crime Scene hasn't been officially asked to examine the body. I sent someone down there just in case. Normally, we've got better things to do than look over corpses that have been buried under wet garbage for a day or more. He's not going to tell us anything other than what half of Sydney had for dinner last week."

"Apparently he's had his fingers removed."

"That's not an uncommon method of concealing a victim's identity."

"There's also a chance they were removed by whoever amputated the finger in your laboratory down there."

"I consider my assistant is more than capable of making an evaluation about that. I'll let you know as soon as I can. If you want to know sooner, you could try formally approaching Crime Scene to examine the corpse for a forensic report—"

"No, it's all right," Maiden said tightly.

"Then I'll be in touch, John." She was dismissing him and Maiden felt one of his characteristic flares of anger coming. He thanked her tersely and hung up.

"As usual, we'll have to go and have a look for ourselves," he growled at Creane as he stood from his desk.

The drive to the morgue was only short, but it gave Maiden a chance to bounce some ideas off Creane.

"So, what have we worked out so far, Martin?"

Creane had been daydreaming as he drove, watching the city slide by. He jumped guiltily and forced himself to concentrate. "OK . . . ah, well, we've got a finger in one lift and a hand in another. Different buildings. Each human piece has been identified and connected with a person who's been declared missing."

Maiden was nodding impatiently. "Yeah, all right. What about these missing people?"

"One's a nerd and the other isn't far off, at a guess."

"Not exactly policespeak, but I know what you mean. And?"

"They both went out on the town and didn't come back."

"Now you're starting to think along the right track."

Creane frowned in concentration and he drove almost absently. "Well, the *way* they went out was sort of out-of-character. Normally they went out with their friends, but in both these cases they went out alone—and on an unusual night of the week," he added quickly.

"So, Martin. What would cause you to drop everything on a week night, get dressed in your best clothes, and head for the bright lights?"

"Me? A girl," Creane said without hesitation, but his voice faded as he realised what Maiden was getting at. "Hell, you're not saying this is being done by a girl?"

"No, I'm thinking some *sort* of girl could be being used as a bait. From that point on we have a choice of transvestites, active homosexuals in drag, active *hetero*sexuals in drag, a real woman with a very nasty chip on her shoulder—take your choice."

"It can't be a woman," Creane said confidently. "Not unless she knows some martial arts or something like that to overpower these young guys."

"I want to agree," Maiden nodded. "Except a concealed weapon brought out at the right moment would do the trick."

Creane was silent for a moment. "This is getting more confusing every day."

"Tell me about it. Listen, we keep these ideas to ourselves, right? With Longman playing games I want to keep him as much in the dark as I can."

Creane gave a small shrug. "Sure."

At the morgue the body was laid out on a central table with a black plastic sheet drawn over it. The attendant was a short, unexpectedly cheerful man called Wilson. He led the detectives over to the corpse, then made them wait while he retrieved a file from an adjoining room. The air was tainted with the odours of chemicals and disinfectants. When he returned, Wilson looked surprised Maiden and Creane hadn't bothered to pull back the black sheet themselves. Without ceremony he dragged it down to the corpse's upper thighs. Maiden gazed at Decker's remains dispassionately, but Creane uttered a groan of discomfort, turned his head aside and backed away a few steps, before quickly putting on a brave face and returning.

"As you can see, we haven't cleaned him up at all," Wilson stated matter-of-factly, consulting the file. "We probably could, though. Forensics finished with him about half an hour ago. We took the clothes off for that, and photographs were taken on site. No-one will touch an autopsy until he's got clean skin."

"It's pretty obvious what killed him," Creane said thickly, looking at the chest wound.

"Not necessarily," Wilson said, glancing up from the file. "That gunshot wound could be a deliberate attempt to conceal the real cause of death."

Maiden briefly turned his eyes to the ceiling. He gestured at the ragged stumps on one hand, "Any of the fingers been found yet?"

"We haven't heard. You would before us, probably."

Maiden grunted. "And you haven't been given even a tentative identity? No dental records?"

"No. Same story. You'd get any information first." Wilson nodded at the corpse. "But I doubt this guy's ever been to a dentist in his life."

"You'd be surprised what you might be told before me," Maiden muttered. He stared at the dead man's face. "I'll want to get some head-and-shoulders shots to distribute around the place, so you can clean him up, but don't cut him until we take the pictures. I'll have a photographer down here ASAP. This guy doesn't look like a choir boy to me and I'm betting he's seen the inside of a lock-up more than once. Someone might recognise him." Wilson nodded, taking a pen from his top pocket and awkwardly scratching a note on the file. "What was he wearing?" Maiden added.

"Black jeans, dark blue singlet and black boots. Want to see them?"

"No," Maiden shook his head once. He pointed at the corpse's genitals and said to Creane, "He's still got his dick, which almost certainly rules out the missing fingers as a mutilation thing. If somebody wants to cut up a body for fun, they always go for the dick and balls, too."

"So, you're sure the fingers are so we can't identify him?" Creane said, tearing his eyes away from the dead penis and suppressing a small shudder.

"You'd think so." Maiden frowned and looked again at the corpse's face. "But you know, for some reason this guy doesn't strike me as the sort of person who's got fingerprints we'd really give a shit about. He might be a petty crook, for sure. Maybe even someone a bit higher up the food chain, but I can't see him as someone that damned important. He's too young, for starters."

"Maybe someone *thought* he was important enough to keep anonymous and chopped them off just in case?"

"That makes more sense," Maiden nodded, pleased at Creane's thinking. He turned away abruptly. "Do that clean-up for me, will you?" he asked Wilson. "I'm going back to The Rocks now and I'll arrange a photographer to come down here right away."

Wilson hardly had time to acknowledge this before Maiden pushed past him and headed for the door. Caught by surprise, Creane briefly thanked the morgue attendant and hurried after Maiden.

"Do you think there's a connection with our case?" Creane asked, moving alongside Maiden and matching his stride along the wide corridor.

"My gut feelings say no. Did you see how the fingers had been hacked off? The one back at Crime Scene was a comparatively neat amputation. But we can't afford to dismiss this guy totally, either. We'd better eliminate him as a part of our investigation as soon as we can and palm the bloody thing off to somebody else quick. I don't want to be fooling around with any more corpses than we have to."

"So you really think those two missing guys are dead?"

"Between you and me, I reckon if they're not now, they will be before we get to them," Maiden said grimly. "Let's get back to the office. You can finish the paperwork while I make a few calls."

"I thought that as the senior investigating officer, you were supposed to do the paperwork."

"Not as long as I can tell you to do it for me."

The afternoon turned into a grind. Longman stuck to his agreement not to assign anything else to Maiden, but that didn't affect the work he already had on hand. Most of it had been neglected over the past few days and while Maiden tackled it back at The Rocks, Creane squeezed onto a corner of his desk and laboured over reports for both of them.

At an opportune moment Creane pulled out the list of nightclubs Peter Dawes was supposed to prefer and waved it at Maiden.

"What are we going to do with this?"

Maiden looked up. "OK, we've got the security card photo from his job to flash around, but it's a shit picture and I doubt anyone could recognise him from it even if they cared." He stopped and pulled a face. "And at the moment his loving, caring flatmates are much stronger suspects in my mind, anyway."

"But we have to make the effort, right?"

"That's right, we do."

Creane looked at the list and said carefully, "There's only six places here. I can do them myself this evening, if you like."

"Are you trying to say I shouldn't go along?"

"I think you might hate the places. These aren't sleazy dives, John. They're high-tech dance clubs with very loud music you're gonna hate. Rap and house music, that sort of thing."

"Rap and what?"

"See? Besides, you're too old. Everyone will know who and what you are."

"OK." Maiden held his hand up in surrender. It hadn't taken much, because he didn't want to do it. He felt tired and wanted to get a little drunk at home and sleep like the dead. "Can you get someone to go with you? I don't want you to do it on your own, in case you stir something up."

"Give me a few calls."

It only took Creane one telephone call to track down a willing friend, a junior detective assigned to one of the large suburban divisions.

"No problem," he told Maiden, hanging up. "We'll get it done and go on to make a night of it," he added.

"Don't come to work tomorrow sick from too much piss," Maiden growled, knowing he should be grateful, but unable to bring himself to say so.

Chapter Ten

Maiden ended up having a few drinks himself with a colleague in a bar nearby. Primarily he wanted to avoid the traffic until rush hour passed. He spent several hours at the bar, drinking carefully because he wanted to drive, and the two men enjoyed a bitch session where they complained about cases, Longman, the system, wages and anything else that came to mind. By the time he stepped outside it was dark and a mist of rain was falling.

Maiden had a long-standing arrangement with a company who had more allotted parking spaces under their building than they needed. He bought the company's managing director a bottle of good Scotch every month in return for parking his Ford. The parking arrangement was a bit too convenient and the detective suspected the day would come when he was asked a small "favour" on the strength of it, but he didn't let it worry him.

His Ford was something he regarded with pride and was the only thing he'd been determined to keep from his last marriage. It was an ex-pursuit car he had bought cheaply at the government auctions. Since then he had spent nearly as much again on alloy wheels and wide tyres, some pin-striping to break up the white paintwork, and a great deal on converting the standard interior into plush comfort. He didn't care about the running expenses of the eight-cylinder motor; it let him twist and sprint through the traffic and Maiden liked that. Living in Annandale and travelling to and from work gave him plenty of opportunity to do it with a satisfying blast along the freeway system thrown in. But tonight he drove slowly, wary of the windscreen smeared with water and spray thrown up from the wet roads.

As much as he wanted to get home and relax, Maiden couldn't ignore the fact he needed to do some shopping. Normally he would nearly starve himself rather than do the tiresome chore of pushing a trolley around a supermarket, but that morning he had run out of coffee and had resorted to a box of tissues for toilet paper.

He pulled up outside a small supermarket near his townhouse. The prices were high, he knew, but it was convenient and less stressful than a shopping centre, and he could park right in front. It was raining more heavily and traffic splashed past as Maiden quickly got out of the car and ran, crouched over, under the awning of the store.

Inside it was warm and musty and filled with the smell of the goods on the shelves. White fluorescent strip lights lit everything harshly. Maiden could see only a few people picking their way through the aisles. The check-out girl had her nose buried in a trashy novel, and didn't look up as Maiden extracted a trolley from the racks with a noisy clatter. He started at one end of the store and looked at everything, dropping what he chose carelessly into the trolley. He didn't bother budgeting or going for items that were on special. At the refrigerators he grabbed packets of bacon and ham—things he could fry up in a hurry. Further on he chose a variety of green vegetables, even though he invariably left them to rot in the bottom of his fridge. The only strict ingredients in Maiden's diet were coffee and a daily vitamin tablet. While he was scanning the choices of coffee, deciding whether he should try a new brand, he sensed someone come up behind him.

A woman's voice said, "Don't bother with the decaffeinated. The chemicals they use in the process will do you more harm than the coffee."

Surprised, Maiden turned around. Janet Brown was standing behind a trolley next to him. She wore a small, amused smile.

"Hello," he said, momentarily flustered. "What are you doing here?"

"Same as you, from the looks of it. The terrible household things I don't normally have time to do."

"Do you live around here? I haven't seen you here before."

"I just moved into a small house about five minutes away. It's costing me a fortune to rent, but it feels a lot better than the flat I was in before."

Maiden noticed she was still dressed well and suspected Brown, too, was doing this on her way home from work. Thinking of her job reminded him of the last time he'd called her. "I probably owe you an apology," he said. "I was a little short-tempered on the phone today."

"Were you?" She tilted her head to one side and regarded him quizzically. "I didn't notice."

Maiden was puzzled. He was sure Brown had taken offence at the way he'd spoken to her. "Remember I was a bit surprised you didn't go down to the morgue yourself? I shouldn't be telling you how to do your job."

"Oh, that." She shrugged. "I forget about that sort of thing the moment I hang up the phone. I get it all day, so I make sure I don't let it worry me."

"Well, still, I shouldn't have done it. Next time we have a coffee I *will* pay the tab, as an apology." Maiden thought that sounded weak and hated himself for it.

She nodded at the shelves behind him. "Instead of poisoning yourself with that stuff, I've got the real thing back home. The house is a mess, but would you like to come back for a cup?"

Maiden wasn't expecting this and it showed on his face.

She laughed and said, "I don't always invite strange men back to my house. I have an ulterior motive, of course. I've decided I don't like where the movers put the refrigerator. With a bit of help I think I can move it."

Maiden looked down at the contents of his trolley. "Well, sure. I've nearly finished here, I think. I just need to grab a few frozen things and that's it."

"Great. I won't be long either. Where are you parked?"

"Right out the front, the white Ford."

"OK, let's meet at your car. Mine's just over the road. You can follow me home."

Brown moved away through the aisles. By the time Maiden was putting his things through the check-out, she was at the far end of the store. Outside, he put the groceries into the boot of his car. Rain dripped down from the shop's awning onto the back of his neck, making him curse. Slamming the boot closed he quickly got back under cover and pulled out his cigarettes, cupping his hands around the lighter to protect the flame from the fine spray blowing in the air.

Brown took another five minutes, coming out as he flicked the butt towards the gutter. He offered to load her groceries into the back seat of his car, rather than carry them through the rain to her own. She accepted and as they packed the car she explained how to get to her house, in case he lost her in the rain.

She ran across the road to her dark blue Toyota and they both had to wait some time for the traffic to clear so Brown could pull away from the kerb and Maiden U-turn into position behind her. Then it was only a five-minute journey into a narrow street and to a small brick semi with a neat garden. Maiden's car only just fitted into the driveway, hanging out onto the footpath.

He ignored the shopping bags, ducking out of the car to

join Brown on the tiny porch. He became aware of how close he needed to stand behind her, huddling together away from the rain dripping from the porch roof, while she struggled to fit a key in the door.

She said over her shoulder, "We might have that coffee first and see if the rain eases off long enough to unload the shopping. Do you mind—or are you in a hurry?"

"No, no hurry. A coffee sounds good."

The door swung open and with a relieved sigh Brown went inside, feeling for the lightswitch. Maiden followed close behind, blinking as she moved ahead flicking on lights. They were in a hallway with two doors on either side and one at the end. Brown gestured to her left.

"Lounge room here, and we're heading for the kitchen. The bathroom is the one at the end and these others are the bedrooms. There's only two."

The door to the lounge was open and Maiden glanced in as he passed. The reflected light from the hallway showed him a comfortable room furnished with two lounges and accompanying coffee tables, a television with a video and a large portable stereo beside it on the floor. The room had a fireplace, but a small electric heater sat in front of the blackened bricks.

The kitchen was freshly painted in white and everything was spotlessly clean. The sink was clear and a tiny wooden table with two chairs looked highly polished.

"I thought you said this place was a mess," Maiden said.

"You know, people always say that."

"You seem to have moved in all right."

"I don't own that much these days. It doesn't take long." Brown busied herself at the sink, filling a coffee percolator.

"Where were you hoping to put the fridge?"

She pointed. It was only a matter of less than a metre and Maiden easily moved the refrigerator without her help.

"There you are, a five-second job," he said, rearranging the power cord.

"Thanks a lot. Do you still want coffee?"

"Sure." Maiden leaned towards the windows over the sink and looked outside. "I might rescue your shopping now, while you make it. Who knows what the rain's going to do—it might get heavier."

He made several trips to his car. After one he saw Brown had taken a cake from one of the bags and was cutting it onto a plate. He placed the rest of the plastic bags on a benchtop.

"I bought this especially," she said. "Let's move into the lounge."

Maiden took one of the mugs and followed her back along the hallway. The light in the lounge room was softer and she bent down to flick on the heater. They sat on separate lounges and Brown immediately kicked her shoes off with an appreciative groan. The informality made Maiden feel at ease.

"A nice little house," he said, nodding at his surroundings.

"'Little' is the word, but it does the job. What about you? Where do you live?"

He described his home, and the conversation turned to the relative merits of living in flats, townhouses and houses. They didn't touch on the subject of why, as two mature-age adults, they were each living alone instead of with spouses and families as might be expected. Neither wanted to pick over the bones of their lives. They didn't discuss their work either. Maiden had a feeling that the way his investigation was unfolding, he'd have plenty of opportunities to do that other times. As the time passed pleasantly he began to feel more comfortable and became torn between wanting to leave before he got *too* comfortable, and staying as long as he could to avoid his own cheerless home.

Brown watched him finish the last bite of his cake. "Would you like something more substantial to eat? I can whip something up quickly."

Maiden hesitated. "No," he said, finally. "It's tempting,

but I'd better get home. I've still got my own groceries in the boot and I think I need an early night."

Brown shrugged. "It wouldn't be a problem . . . but whatever you like. Seeing as you live so close and we're both on our own, you should come over for dinner one night. It would make a nice change to cook for more than one person."

Again, Maiden was surprised, but this time he managed not to show it. "I'd like that," he said, sincerely. "I must admit, I often get sick of my own company."

"We'll have to work out a night that suits us both."

Maiden finished his coffee and reluctantly stood. "I'd better get going."

"OK. Thanks for moving the fridge for me."

"It was nothing. Thanks for the real coffee."

Brown followed him to the door. Standing on the porch and hunching his shoulders in anticipation of the cold rain after the warmth of the lounge, he turned and looked at her standing in the open doorway. In her stockinged feet she appeared much more attractive than the severe, business-like professional he was used to. Maiden felt a sudden, strong attraction and had to say something—anything.

"I'll try to call you tomorrow. There's some things I'd like to know. Maybe we can figure out a night for dinner at the same time."

"Make it in the morning. I have some trainees coming through in the afternoon."

"OK. And thanks again for the coffee."

"Goodnight, John. I'm going to close this door. It's chilly."

He waved briefly and ran out to his car. By the time he was sitting in the driver's seat the front door had closed and the hallway light switched off. He sat lost in thought for a moment, then backed the car out of the driveway.

Maiden's townhouse proved as cold and dismal as he had feared. He quickly put his shopping away, turned the reverse-cycle air-conditioning to "warm" and "maximum" to heat the rooms fast and settled in front of the television with a scotch and ice in his hand.

But the programme on the screen hardly registered in his mind. Instead, he found his mind going back to the little house he'd just left. He was thinking of doing this with Janet Brown beside him, together on one of her lounges. His imagination replaced the electric heater with a crackling log fire in the fireplace.

"You dream too much, John Maiden," he muttered to himself, taking a sip of his Scotch. But the image wouldn't go away.

Chapter Eleven

Greg Howlett could feed a hundred dollars into a poker machine and the money would be gone before he knew he'd lost it. He rarely won anything worth putting back in his wallet—just the frequent small winnings which sustained his playing time and kept him believing. He had won over a hundred dollars several times, but the true equation had the machines well in front. The habit was starting to eat into his savings now and the time would come when his wife would notice if he wasn't careful.

He had found one way of compensating for his losses. Howlett worked for a large accounting firm in the middle of the city. They'd recently introduced a system where employees logged on to the computer network first thing in the morning and logged off as the final act of the day. The management called it an "efficiency evaluation," but everyone knew it was really a way of checking exactly who was putting in the hours and who wasn't. Most had already worked out ways to cheat, the simplest being to have a friend log on or off for you and hope none of the bosses came looking for you in the flesh.

Howlett put the system to a better use.

He left the office at the same time as everyone else, slipping away without logging off at all, then he would go to his favourite bar and "lucky" poker machine. After playing for a few hours he would return to the office and, using his keys, log off the computer and call the extra time overtime. He didn't care that, because the hours would be charged out, someone would have to pay for his services somewhere along the line. He figured anyone who could afford a separate accounting firm could certainly pay a few extra dollars and may even get some peace of mind believing he was diligently working on their ledgers late into the evening. They were getting their money's worth, one way or another.

Tonight he had overstayed his time at the bar. A couple of early wins on the poker machine buoyed him, promising that a big jackpot might be in the offing. Instead, he had eventually lost his winnings and gone on to spend twice as much as usual trying to recover. Finally he ran out of money and was forced to head for home. But first, he had to log off the computers.

It was dark as he slipped into the narrow alleyway between the tall buildings. The alley led to a security door for which all trusted employees had a plastic card, encoded to allow entry only to a small elevator alcove on the ground floor, then the employee's own floor. Howlett cursed as he saw the twenty-four hour light in the small alcove had been smashed again. It was a regular event, almost a contest between the vandals and the security people to provide a light that couldn't be broken. Without it, the place was particularly dark and he hated that. To his left was a set of stairs leading down to the company car park underneath. A steel mesh gate locked him out now, as it was after six o'-clock, and he would have to take the internal elevator down. His car was down there, a privilege given to Howlett because of the extra "overtime" he was working, while one of the senior partners was on holiday. Such devotion to the company didn't go unnoticed, he was told.

The card caused a soft beep as he swiped it through the electronic lock. At the same moment Howlett thought he heard a scuffling sound coming from the base of the stairwell and he jerked around to stare nervously into the shadows.

"Hello?" he called, an unexpected tremor in his voice. There was no answer. He jumped, startled, as the security door in front of him clicked and unlocked and hurriedly he pushed his way through.

Inside the building he didn't feel any less nervous. The place had a completely different atmosphere in the evenings, closed up with only security lighting which threw deep shadows. Without any people around it had a creepy, empty feeling, as if it had been hurriedly abandoned for some dreadful reason. This was always the worst part of his small fraud, even though he knew that theoretically he was now safely locked *inside* the office block.

The floor of the foyer was polished marble and his footsteps echoed eerily. A lift was patiently waiting, the doors open, and Howlett stepped quickly inside. He swiped his card in the electronic lock and selected his floor.

When the doors reopened Howlett heard the soft whine of a vacuum cleaner, but it was coming from the direction of the toilets and away from his destination. It made him feel easier, knowing he was not completely alone, and his hand was steady as he unlocked the glass double doors in front of the receptionist's desk. Now he moved easily through the warren of offices to his workstation, confident once more that his deception would go smoothly. He didn't bother flicking on the overhead flourescents, logging off the computer took only moments. However, when his monitor flared to life at the first touch of a key Howlett noticed it was only minutes before 9:00 p.m. He decided to wait until the hour ticked over. Most people would work that way, he thought.

In the glare of the computer monitor he noticed an unfamiliar slip of paper on his desk. He picked it up and held it close to the screen, using the light to read by. It was a handwritten message from Tysonne, one of the partners.

> *Greg,*
> *I dropped by to discuss something with you, knowing you were still in the office, but I couldn't find you. I'll be here until 7:00 p.m. Can you come by for a few minutes?*

It was signed and had "6:30 p.m." scrawled under the signature.

"Oh shit," Howlett muttered, feeling his stomach swoop.

He leaned back against his desk. "Shit, shit, *shit*," he repeated. How many times had Tysonne come back to see if he had returned? Was he still in his office now? This caused a moment of panic, before Howlett remembered the glass doors had been locked. It only made him feel slightly better. Tysonne could have left the offices himself only minutes before. He couldn't log off now. His only option was to say he'd completely forgotten to do it at five o'-clock—a minor indiscretion, considering he was a company favourite at the moment. But Tysonne was a suspicious bastard at the best of times. Howlett knew the possibility of his cheating would certainly occur to the partner and that would put him in a bad situation. His scheme for getting extra pay had to stop straightaway. It would be best if he laid low for a while, but he couldn't suddenly stop doing overtime either—that might make Tysonne twice as suspicious. In fact, the only thing he *could* do was work some extra hours to prove he was really doing it.

"Damn it!" he grated, pushing away from the desk and heading for the door. "Damn it to hell and back."

Howlett's mind kept turning over the possibilities as he left the office and re-entered the lift, the imagined terrors of the empty building momentarily forgotten in his anxiety. No matter which way he looked at it, he was trapped. The dilemma made him want to go and have another drink, but all his money was gone and he couldn't be bothered going to an automatic teller. Besides, he was late enough.

The lift doors opened to reveal the dark basement car park. The lack of light made Howlett hesitate for a moment, his foot hovering over the lip of the lift, but worrying over his job and the fake overtime being found out overrode all his other thoughts and fears.

"For Christ's sake, things couldn't be worse," he told himself, wryly. He set out into the gloom, unconsciously hunching his shoulders against the dark.

The car park was lit by rows of fluorescent lights caged in wire mesh. Some of them were broken, creating areas of shadow, and Howlett's car was under one of these. During working hours the garage held over fifty cars, but now there were only three. Howlett's was the furthest away and as he strode quickly over the concrete he wondered who owned the other vehicles. *People who are in a better damn position than I am*, he thought, hanging his head and beginning to feel acutely sorry for himself. He had approached his car from the passenger side and as he walked around the boot he felt in his jacket pocket for the keys.

He stopped with a sudden rush of cold fear as the driver's side of the car came into view. Hunkered down in the shadow, hiding below the line of the windows, was a large and menacing shape. A pair of eyes looked up at him.

"What the hell are you—?" Howlett began.

That was all Howlett managed before he was headbutted fiercely in the solar plexus, driving all the breath from him. A black mist of pain obscured his sight and he felt himself falling, but a fierce throttling grip around his neck caught him before he landed. His spine was wrenched by his own weight, causing a lancing agony in his back. He felt himself shoved hard against his car, the roof edge digging into his shoulder blades. Instinctively, he tried to claw at the thumbs pressing into his throat, but couldn't make any impression. Within his terror and pain Howlett understood he was going to be killed and fought as hard as he could, but quickly weakened by a lack of oxygen his struggles became little more than squirming. A hot breath was washing over his face.

It was the last thing Howlett's senses registered.

When Howlett was dead, she carefully emerged from the deeper shadows next to the wall, carrying a small plastic shopping bag. He hardly noticed her as he concentrated on his task. It took him a moment to search Howlett's body for the car keys, then to choose the right one to open the boot. While she looked on, glancing frequently towards the car park entry and the stairwell, he awkwardly folded Howlett's body feet-first into the cramped space. A silver blade glinted in the light. A tiny torch flicked on and the blade cut away the sleeve of the jacket, then the shirt beneath it. Peeling the cloth back, the white flesh of Howlett's shoulder was exposed.

"I told you, remember?" she whispered, when he seemed to hesitate. "You have to do this part." After a moment he nodded and bent over the boot.

He worked clumsily, slashing inexpertly at the skin and often sawing with the knife. She murmured advice as she held the torch steady, but wasn't sure if he heard her, he was so absorbed. Blood ran freely, pooling in the bottom of the boot. The gore of muscle tissue looked a deeper red in the torch's orange glow. The task became more difficult as he needed to cut through flesh on the underside of the body without pulling Howlett any further out of the boot than was needed. At one stage she ducked under the car to make sure no blood was escaping the car onto the concrete below.

"Why don't you try pulling it apart now," she told him, finally. He tried and the upper arm came easily away from the socket, the bone a slightly yellow colour in the torchlight. Several strands of muscle clung on stubbornly. He sliced through them, the remaining sinews snapping back. As he went to lift the severed arm out of the car, she stopped him with a sharp hiss.

From her bag she took a heavy-duty black garbage bag and made him drop the limb into it, holding the top open for him and making sure they didn't drip blood over the lip of the car's boot. She tied off the bag and dropped it on the concrete.

"Get his wallet," she said, annoyed that she hadn't thought of this before. It proved to be in Howlett's back trouser pocket, difficult to retrieve, but luckily free of any blood. She rifled through it, peering in the torchlight, and took out his security card. The moment she had it, she turned the torch off, tossed the wallet back into the boot and closed the lid, killing the boot light. She took the keys from the lock.

"Hide where you were before. I'll be back in a moment." Without a word he did exactly as she told him.

The arm was surprisingly heavy, stretching the plastic as she carried it to the elevator. The electronic lock worked perfectly, the device not caring who held the plastic card. She had used this sort of card before, in a previous life. She would have preferred to take the lift to the top floor, but the card would only allow her access to Howlett's own level. Once the doors opened she pressed the emergency button to stall it, then gently eased the severed arm out of the bag onto the floor of the lift, watching carefully that she didn't splash blood onto herself. Satisfied, she bundled the plastic bag into a tight ball and looked around for the fire exit stairs. A minute later she was back in the car park.

She put the empty bag in the boot, not giving the mutilated corpse a second glance. Her companion watched silently. Then the two of them got into the car, the woman at the wheel, and casually drove out of the car park. That was really the last moment of risk—the possibility of someone recognising the vehicle and seeing a stranger driving it. Once again the electronic security card did its work, triggering the garage door and letting them out.

* * *

She dropped him off home first. It was better that way. The drive to the airport took forty-five minutes. The parking ticket dispenser for the long-term section was automatic and no-one saw her enter. She placed the ticket correctly on the dashboard and before she closed the door, she tucked the keys under the front seat. On the walk to the terminal she passed a rubbish bin and used the opportunity to peel off the black woollen gloves she'd been wearing for what seemed like hours now and push them deep under the trash. Nobody saw her do it.

She slipped into the back seat of the first available taxi.

"No luggage?" the driver asked in a heavy accent, eyeing her in the rear-view mirror.

"No," she said shortly. "I've been seeing somebody off."

Then she gave him an address, speaking in a tone which plainly indicated she wasn't interested in any more conversation.

Chapter Twelve

Maiden padded around his kitchen in the early morning, a towel wrapped about his waist, while he cooked a breakfast of bacon and eggs. The previous day had been another waste of time. As he absently flipped the bacon he thought about telling Longman his investigation into a double homicide was seriously stalling through a lack of evidence and leads. There was simply nothing left for them to do except go over old ground once again.

The phone rang. It was the Despatch duty sergeant at the station. As Maiden listened to the efficient voice on the other end his face turned grim. The sergeant finished by saying, "I thought you might want to go straight there, sir. Before you came into the station."

"Damn—yeah, you're right." Maiden took a breath and turned his brain on. His worst fear—that the body parts would progressively get bigger—appeared to have been realised. He got some more details, scribbling them awkwardly on a pad with the telephone held with his hunched shoulder. "OK, look. I've got a detective constable called

Martin Creane helping me with these. Can you get his number from the lists and give him a call, too? Tell him to meet me at the scene and get a message to the guys already there to leave everything alone."

This last demand was almost unnecessary, but Maiden didn't want to leave anything to chance. The sergeant agreed and hung up. Maiden stood still, staring moodily at the frying bacon. His immediate reaction was to rush to the crime scene, but he calmed himself. *It's not going anywhere, and this might be the only decent feed I get all day.*

Thoughts of severed arms didn't spoil his appetite, but as soon as the last morsel was off his plate his earlier calm deserted him and he dumped the dishes unrinsed into the sink. He hurried towards the stairs and his bedroom to get dressed. The phone ringing again stopped him. It was the sergeant, saying he couldn't contact Creane. Maiden told him to leave messages everywhere he thought worthwhile for Creane to meet him at the crime scene.

The morning rush-hour traffic had Maiden wishing, not for the first time, that he had a detachable blue light he could stick on the roof. It was a minor compensation when, arriving at the building housing Greg Howlett's accountancy company, there was a small fleet of police-marked vehicles forming a temporary parking area at the expense of a traffic lane, causing its own jam of commuters. Maiden didn't lose time finding somewhere to park. When he swung his car into a space, a uniformed constable immediately moved towards him, but Maiden had his ID ready. The constable gave him a wave and turned away.

This time there were policemen everywhere. There was also a television crew milling about in the foyer, looking for someone who might give them something worth taping. Maiden made a point of avoiding their gaze and moved towards the lifts. It was obvious which one wasn't in use. Its doors were taped closed and a plastic chain was rigged in front of it. Two policemen stood guard. They were watching the television crew suspiciously. Maiden flashed his badge at them.

"Still on the same floor?" he asked, in case it had been moved for security. He pressed the button summoning one of the other lifts.

"Yeah, eighteen," one of the constables replied.

"Have those television guys tried to get up there?"

"Twice now. I'm running out of excuses to stop them."

"Just tell 'em I said. That's a good enough excuse. I suppose there's a crowd up there already?"

"Forensics, photographers, plain-clothes—it's a lot of people to fit in one elevator," the constable said with a humourless grin.

"I can imagine it," Maiden muttered. The lift announced its arrival, the doors opened and a crowd of people squeezed out. Most of them glanced towards the policemen as they passed. Maiden could imagine the gossip and speculation flying around the building on this morning. With a nod at the constable he stepped into the lift. Several people joined him for the trip up, but there were only two men left when the doors opened on level eighteen. The two men craned their necks to look at the commotion as Maiden pushed past them. He turned to give them a glare and they quickly shrank back.

A crowd filled the foyer of the accountancy firm. Looking small and bewildered, a receptionist sat at her desk and stared at everyone. As Maiden watched her the telephone rang and she absently picked it up. He saw Creane talking to a photographer laden with several cameras. He pushed his way through and tapped Creane on the shoulder.

"I couldn't get here any sooner. The damned traffic had me trapped," he complained in a low voice. "What's happened? We've got ourselves a whole arm this time, that's all I know."

"Have a look, first."

Creane led him to the elevator. Its doors were open, but someone had had the sense to strategically place some office partitioning screens to block the view from passers-by. No-one was actually inside the lift at that moment and the severed arm lay in the centre of the floor. A large stain of blood spread out from the ragged stump and there were splotches all over the cloth of the jacket sleeve and what they could see of the white shirt cuff. Maiden got down on his haunches and studied it closely.

"Whoever did it didn't bother taking the clothes off. They just hacked through jacket, shirt and arm in one go. Were they in a hurry?"

"Maybe."

Maiden looked at the ring on the victim's hand. "This guy was married."

"We've got a strong probable identification," Creane said, making Maiden look up in surprise. "A guy called Greg Howlett. He didn't get home last night and he hasn't shown up for work this morning or called in sick. He was supposed to be in these offices last night doing some overtime, but one of his bosses tried to find him around six-thirty without any luck. They've got a system with their computers which says Howlett was supposed to be still in the building. So I put him at the top of the list and I let the forensics take a print from the hand. It's got a distinctive whorl that almost gives us a visual match straightaway from some we took at his desk. Forensics won't say for certain without a laboratory confirmation, but one of the guys here reckons you could bet your mortgage on it. They'll be doing fibres from the jacket and such too, just to make sure."

"A bit of a head start on this one," Maiden said, rising. "I suppose we should be thankful for small mercies."

"You couldn't say this bloke was shown much mercy."

"No," Maiden said absently. "Have you interviewed any of the other staff to get a profile on Howlett?"

"Not yet. I've only talked to his boss. His name's Tysonne. He's the guy standing over there next to the receptionist."

"I'll go and talk to him now. Tell Forensics I've seen enough. If everyone else is happy, we can start cleaning up the scene. Then I want you to have a chat with the rest of the staff."

Something in Maiden's manner made Creane ask, "A chat? Am I looking for something in particular?"

"If this guy was happily married, it might punch a hole in our theory about the victims going out on a bad date. Either that, or it gives us a new style of approaching the victims, which we haven't a bloody clue about. Without spreading too much drama, see if you can find out if Mr. Howlett could have been lured away by another woman. Ask some of the prettier girls in the company if Howlett's ever come on strong to them." Maiden paused and added, "That reminds me—did you have any luck out on the town? Checking those nightclubs?"

Creane shook his head absently. "Waste of bloody time. No-one wanted to talk to us about anything. You'd think it was a drug raid." He dismissed it with a shrug, his mind still on the present. "If Howlett wasn't tempted away by a woman, then there's a chance he was kidnapped, killed and mutilated right here in the building or somewhere very close . . . and within a short space of time without any sexual come-on or luring him away to a bar. That's different to the others—" He stopped and frowned. "Jesus, does that mean we might have the *rest* of Howlett still in the building somewhere?"

"Now you're thinking," Maiden said grimly.

Creane stared at one of the uniformed constables. "Are you going to tell them to start searching?"

"Not just yet, but I can't see any way of avoiding it. You start with the staff. I'll come and find you when I've finished."

Leaving a worried Creane, Maiden walked casually over

to Tysonne, who was anxiously watching the proceedings. Tysonne was a tall, dour-looking man, with a thin build and a face to match. He was pale with shock and looked down over a pair of reading glasses at Maiden as the detective introduced himself.

"Mr. Tysonne, can you explain to me what happened last night and this morning?"

Tysonne looked towards Creane, the glance plainly suggesting he was going to repeat himself and he didn't like it, but he began without comment. "This morning I came to work at the usual time. Often I'm first into the office. When I stepped out of the elevator I noticed the other lift was here on this floor and that something had been left behind in it. It looked so unusual I went for a closer inspection and that's when I discovered the . . . ah, arm." His Adam's apple bobbed up and down nervously. "It gave me quite a scare, I can tell you. Of course, I called the police."

"As simple as that? Nothing else? No matter how trivial it may seem, Mr. Tysonne."

"I—I had to be sick in the rest room, if that makes a difference."

"Not really," Maiden said dryly. "What about last night? You told Detective Creane that a Mr. Howlett seems to have gone missing."

Tysonne's eyes slid reluctantly towards the elevator, where camera flashes were now going off. "I tried to find Greg about six-thirty last night, but he wasn't anywhere. We have a log-in, log-out system with our computers and I could see Greg hadn't logged off, so in theory he was still working somewhere, but I never found him."

"How often did you look?"

"Three times. The last was at eight-thirty, just before I left the office."

"Is there a chance he simply didn't log off the computer and went home without doing it?"

"It's possible. There's nothing to prevent that happening, though we've tried to train our staff to be reliable in this.

Greg is particularly dependable, because of the overtime he's been putting in lately."

"Mr. Howlett worked a lot of overtime?"

Tysonne nodded. "So much that we've let him use Mr. Todd's parking bay in the basement. Mr. Todd's on long-service leave." The accountant blinked, seeing that Maiden was staring at him with barely-concealed annoyance.

"Are you telling me his car could be parked downstairs? Have you told anyone else?"

"I didn't think of it before—"

"Was it there last night, when you left for home?"

"My wife picked me up out the front. I didn't go into the basement."

"What about this morning? Did you notice it then?"

Through his shock and confusion Tysonne was finally getting angry at Maiden's tone. "I don't *use* the car park, Detective Maiden. I thought you understood that."

"OK . . ." Maiden nodded more to himself, uncaring who he might be upsetting. "OK, let's do a quick trip downstairs to check." He went to move away, but stopped when he saw Tysonne hesitating. "Is there a problem?"

"I don't know what sort of car Greg drives."

Maiden reined in his impatience. "But it's got to be in the correct parking spot, right?"

Tysonne gave a small shrug. "It's supposed to be."

The receptionist had been listening. She interrupted, "I think it's a brown Commodore. We should have the registration number here for the insurance, if Mr. Todd did everything properly."

Maiden gave her a grateful smile, which pointedly didn't include Tysonne. "It would be a big help."

She was already quickly punching keys on her computer. After a moment she clicked her tongue with satisfaction and scribbled something on a notepad, tearing the page off and handing it to Maiden. "It is a Commodore, but it doesn't mention the colour here. That's the registration number."

"Thank you." He turned to Tysonne. "Can you come with me? I may have some more questions." Tysonne didn't looked pleased, but he nodded. Maiden caught the eye of a nearby constable and told him, "The victim might still have a car parked in the basement. I'm going down to have a look. If anybody wants me, I shouldn't be long."

Maiden and Tysonne travelled alone in the elevator. The only words the two exchanged were when Tysonne described the security system. The lift stopped at the foyer and Tysonne stepped out. Puzzled, Maiden followed him to the after-hours security door. "If he left the building, this is where he'd come back in," Tysonne explained.

Maiden was staring at the electronic lock outside the door. "How does this work?"

"Same as the lift. Just about every employee has a card which will open the lock."

"Does it need a number?"

"No, you just swipe the card."

"And that will give you access to the entire building?"

To demonstrate Tysonne pulled the door open a fraction. "Now you can get in any time without a card, but at six o'clock the security takes over and you need your card. It doesn't give you access to the entire building, though. Just this alcove for the lift. Mine, for instance, gets me through this door and instructs the elevators to let me out on our floor only. Anyone who works for our company is the same. It's a very good system, really."

Maiden's mind was working furiously. "Show me the car park."

Five minutes later they had checked every parking bay under the office block. Howlett's car was nowhere to be seen. The bay where it was supposed to be was conspicuously empty. Maiden carefully inspected the concrete, but there was nothing he could see except oil stains.

"OK," he said to Tysonne. "Let's get back upstairs."

Tysonne was getting annoyed at being led around. "What do you think?" he asked, impatiently.

"I don't know what to think at the moment," Maiden said, giving him a blank look. In fact, he had several possibilities whirling through his imagination, but he wasn't about to discuss them with Tysonne.

Back on the eighteenth floor, Maiden gave Tysonne a curt nod of thanks, then briefly checked the details of Howlett's car registration with the receptionist and got one of the constables to radio through the vehicle description with a request for a full search and alert. "Tell them anyone who stumbles over it is to approach with caution," he added. "Even if it looks empty. There might be a forensic situation we don't want fucked up by some hamfisted rookie."

The constable's face remained impassive as he passed on the information, expecting Maiden would stay to make sure he got the message correct, but Maiden was already looking for Creane, who saw him first and hurried over. Maiden gestured for him to follow him back into the lift, where he silently studied the control panel.

"Well? Are we going to search the building?" Creane asked impatiently.

Maiden hesitated for a moment. "No—not with the whole cavalry, anyway. We'll send a team around with the standard procedure."

"You don't think the rest of this guy's still here?"

Maiden had a niggling suspicion triggered by what he had seen in the basement. Now he drew Creane over to a quiet corner of the foyer. He lowered his voice. "Howlett should have a car parked in the basement, but it's gone. If you need to get into this building after hours, you have to use a side door and a security card. The card will also only give you access to this floor through the elevators, OK?"

Creane nodded, listening intently.

Maiden jerked his thumb at the open elevator. "On the other occasions the lifts with the amputated bits have been left to travel up and down like normal until some poor bastard gets to have their day ruined, but this time the lift is emergency-stopped on this floor. I think whoever did *that* used Howlett's card to operate the elevator, because maybe they didn't have a choice of floors. "Which also means that unless they hid in the building all day and attacked here, they must have used his card to work the security system and get back inside, too."

"You're saying the arm came *back* into the building? So Howlett was killed and mutilated outside somewhere?"

"It explains the lack of mess and the elevator business. They must have got him in the car park."

"They could have used another card to get in. Killed him somewhere on this floor, locked the lift with the arm in it and escaped down the fire stairs."

"That's the point, Martin. It would have to be someone who works on this floor, or someone with access to a card to this level—and I think that's all a bit too close to home. It would make it too easy for us, too. There can only be a limited number of cards issued." Maiden was shaking his head thoughtfully. "No, at some stage of the game Howlett—alive or not—and his security card were outside the building or at least in the car park." Maiden pointed at the floor. "He *left* this place. Only his arm came back. I'll be bloody surprised if we don't find his car and his remains in the same place."

"So, why did he go out? He must have intended to come back, or he would have logged off the computers."

"OK, so why would *you* go out?"

Creane considered this. "A bite to eat? A drink?"

Maiden watched another of the company's employees press the button for a lift, being careful not to go near any police. "You know, call me lazy and getting old, but I don't think I could be bothered with all the rigmarole of elevators, side doors and security cards just to get a snack. I'd juice up on the coffee machine and biscuits, and wait until I got home where the wife's probably got something warm in the oven."

Creane gave him a look. "You just want me to suggest he

had a better reason for leaving his desk for a while, like maybe a woman waiting for him downstairs. That *might* give us the link we're looking for to the other two."

"Yeah, I guess I do."

"It's only a long-shot theory with the first two victims as it is."

"I know, but it's the only one I've got."

Creane glanced towards the stopped elevator, as if he could see the severed arm with its wedding ring through the screens and press of people. "But this guy was married. You said yourself it might punch a hole in that idea."

Maiden shrugged this off. "I should have known better, Martin. So what if he was married?" He leaned closer. "I'll tell you, a large percentage of the overtime worked in this city last night involved the rampant dicks of married, unfaithful business executives. 'Working back at the office' is the oldest excuse in the book."

"I've only talked to a few of the girls here, but none of them was willing to say Howlett was the kind to fool around on his wife."

"Well, sexual harassment in the office is a pretty hot subject these days. Maybe he didn't do anything here—but doing something *outside* the building is a different thing altogether."

"OK, I'll keep asking around," Creane said, without much hope.

"This could be a lucky break," Maiden told him. "If he went out to meet someone in a bar or an eatery somewhere, I'll bet he didn't go too far or expect to stay too long. He intended to come back soon, if that computer log-on nonsense holds any weight, otherwise he would have signed off, right? We'll need a canvass of this immediate area. Visit every joint that's still open after, say, six-thirty."

Creane gave him a wry look and risked some sarcasm. "So, you want to search the building for a body, a couple of city blocks for an immoral woman, and the whole town for

Howlett's Commodore. Have you informed Longman you need the entire police force at your disposal?"

"Fuck Longman. I'll go right around him and let him burst into tears without me."

"I'll believe that when I see it," Creane said, moving away.

Chapter Thirteen

Howard was running out of money and he hated that idea. He didn't need much to live on. The flat belonged to a friend of Decker's who was currently serving ten years for three counts of armed robbery. There was no telephone. But Howard's day-to-day living was expensive, because he bought so much alcohol and fast food.

All of a sudden he didn't have any twenty-dollar bills in his battered wallet. Last time this happened, he convinced Decker to do a risky, unplanned hold-up at a twenty-four hour chemist. It had been hardly worth the chances they took. The cash register had only held enough to give them two weeks and little more. Now Howard would have to do something similar. At least this time, he told himself, he would choose his target more carefully and there would be a decent amount of money to be taken. Howard believed he could do anything—if he had enough money. It was a lack of funds that had stopped him looking for Fiona in the last few days too, and that was worrying him. Fiona was his friend and he wanted to be with her, but he would look bad if he was broke.

The shotgun had been a favourite object of Decker's, lovingly maintained and cleaned. Howard didn't hold any such sentiments, so he decided to saw off the long barrel to just short of the stock. Concealing the gun had always been a problem and this was an obvious solution. Until now, Decker had always opposed it. Of course, Decker's opinion didn't matter any more.

In an effort to save money Howard bought only the hacksaw blades. Holding on to a blade while he laboriously sawed through the tough steel was difficult. His fingers cramped up and he needed to rest often. The job seemed to take forever. He'd picked up a six-pack from a bottle shop, using the purchase to inspect the place as a potential job. Decker had always said no, because it was too close to home and in a busy part of the street. Howard, after another close look, had to grudgingly agree. The guy behind the counter had even given him a nod of greeting as he'd walked in, acknowledging that Howard came in regularly. That wasn't good.

There were only two beers left, turning warm on the floor beside him, when the last resistance to the blade snapped away and the end piece of the barrel dropped to the floor. Howard had been determined not to try breaking through the final steel, in case he bent the barrel with his effort. Grimly satisfied with his work he aimed the weapon at a speck on the wall and dry-fired. The hammer fell with a decisive click. He had no way of knowing how good his aim was, but it didn't matter. A shotgun with a short barrel needed little aiming. Now the gun would fit easily into a canvas bag he owned and he could carry it on public transport.

On previous jobs Decker had first stolen, then driven, a vehicle to the crime, dumping the car afterwards at the first opportunity. Now Howard had a problem, because his knowledge of stealing cars was minimal. It meant that any jobs he did by himself he would have to flee on foot.

He ripped another beer from the plastic packaging, glugged down a good part of it and looked down at the shotgun. He didn't notice the sour stink of the flat around him or the odours coming from his own body. He rarely bathed or washed his clothes. In the past Decker had to threaten Howard to get any effort at hygiene out of him. There was no-one to bother him about such things now.

He came to a decision and settled on a small petrol station he and Decker had been considering for some time that they could hit just for emergencies like this. Decker had been clever like that—using time and the petrol in stolen cars to look for easy targets. It reduced the risks, planning that way. The petrol station was run down and suffering from the competition created by the large automated roadhouses. But these small businesses, Howard figured, still sold a lot of petrol and this one stayed open until midnight. Better still, it backed onto a railway marshalling yard, an ideal place for Howard to run into the darkness where no vehicles could follow. It would be a simple job. He would wait until half an hour before closing. No later, because that might see a lazy employee lock away the cash early in anticipation of a quick getaway homewards. Howard would make sure nobody was queuing for petrol, step through the door and demand that the lights on the pumps be turned off so any traffic would think the place was already closed. Then he would have more time without having to watch his back to get all the money, which might involve some heavy-handed persuasion of the staff, because these places always had extra cash hidden away somewhere and he might have to force someone to tell him where it was. Once he had everything, he would step over the back fence and disappear among the railway tracks. It would be that easy.

However, if perhaps the proprietor of the petrol station tried something foolish and Howard was forced to shoot him, he wasn't going to waste the opportunity. If an employee was discovered at the scene not only dead, but with some even uglier thing done to them, it would be another sensation. A newspaper sensation that might trigger a manhunt.

A *manhunt*. It was a word Howard had rediscovered two nights before, coming suddenly clear out of the television's snowy picture like a message from beyond. It conjured up all kinds of exciting images for Howard, who imagined himself living the high life and going on a rampage across the country. Wining, dining, fucking and stealing his way to the front page of every newspaper in every town, until he finally went down in a hail of bullets. He would have one hell of a car, busting through roadblocks, and always be one step ahead of the police until the inevitable end. Dying a martyr's death appealed to Howard. And he wouldn't be a criminal, but an outlaw. There was a difference.

The fantasy was a strong one, blocking out the reality of his squalid existence—the filth and sour smells, his lack of education or any real innate intelligence. Worst of all, it ignored the evil in his make-up that wouldn't baulk at killing and cutting up another human being, just to cause a sensation.

Howard was on the road to a violent self-destruction. And he didn't care who he took with him.

Vicki Colonel was the girl of Howard's dreams—though neither knew the other existed. She had long blonde hair, a beautiful face with startling blue eyes and a centrefold figure. Eighteen years old and coyly shy, despite the attention her good looks brought, Vicki was at the crossroads of her youth, torn between career opportunities or furthering her studies. She had already wasted over six months since leaving school the previous year and there was an invitation to accompany a girlfriend on an extended overseas trip. She still had a month to decide and in the meantime wanted to earn some straightforward cash in case she went. Right now, in the dismal chill of the petrol station, a trip to the European summer looked very attractive. An uncle who knew the value of having a pretty girl on the premises offered her work at his garage. It wasn't long before the male clientele began to get more regular, with familiar faces eagerly looking out for Vicki as they came in to pay. It was deliberately sexist, immoral and everything else modern society frowned upon, but it worked and Vicki's uncle wasn't about to find his conscience in a hurry. She sold too much petrol.

She was even, incidentally, good at her job.

Vicki wasn't supposed to work late into the night—and certainly never on her own. But her uncle knew she wanted as much money as she could get and offered a secret trade-off. In return for a significantly increased hourly rate, Vicki would work at the garage until closing time on some nights and not tell her parents she was alone. In return her uncle got to do all manner of things at his sportsman's club, like play darts, pool and gamble on the greyhounds. Everything was supposed to work smoothly, as long as he reappeared at the petrol station to help Vicki close up.

This had happened four times now, and each time Vicki found she was scared in the garage alone and regretted the deal. Occasional visits from a private security patrol car only gave her scant minutes of feeling safe. Worse still, after the first two nights by herself her uncle didn't show to shut up the garage. She should have realised his instructions on how it should be done "just in case" had more deliberate intentions.

Tonight, she had decided, would be the last time. The money was good, but Vicki could do without the wrenching apprehension that came with each car arriving at the pumps. She panicked that every new customer might be someone bad—someone she wouldn't be able to deal with on her own. This evening had so far been quiet, but this made it harder, because there wasn't the comforting thought that anything threatening could be interrupted by more customers.

Vicki sat behind an old wooden counter, trying to concentrate on a crossword puzzle in a television magazine. Most of the questions were about characters in popular soap operas, something Vicki had no interest in, but she kept going anyway. There was a portable black-and-white television on a bench behind her, but the only shows on offer were sporting re-runs or *The Late Show With David Letterman*, which she hated.

Her head bent to the page, Vicki tried to shut out the world around her. She had already grown accustomed to the smells of oil and grease which pervaded everything. The timber of the counter was blackened by years of oil stains. The linoleum floor was the same. A small voice in her head guiltily hoped there would be no more customers that night, but that was unlikely. The driveway bell would ring soon. She glanced at the clock, which was shaped like a spark plug. There was little more than half an hour to go before closing. In twenty minutes she could start putting away the racks of oils, cleaners and petrol additives from the concrete apron. That would effectively fill the last minutes of her shift. The cash in the till went into a tiny safe in the floor behind the counter. It was covered first by a small trapdoor and then a mat. Vicki didn't think it was a particularly smart place for it, but her uncle claimed there was more risk putting cash into the late-night deposit boxes, where criminals were known to lie in wait.

She was chewing the end of her pencil, forcing herself to ponder a question in the crossword, when a flicker of movement at the door caught her eye. Normally customers announced themselves by pulling noisily into the driveway, but sometimes people came in unexpectedly. Vicki looked up expecting someone with a fuel can or perhaps a customer wanting to buy cigarettes.

What she saw made her heart stop and her blood run cold.

A man dressed in black, with a full balaclava over his head, stood inside the doorway. In one hand he held a canvas bag, in the other a short gun of some kind. At the moment it was pointed at the floor. Through her jolt of fear Vicki was aware her presence had thrown the bandit momentarily.

"Who the fuck are you?" he asked, his voice muffled by the balaclava.

Vicki felt frozen to the spot, unable to even stand up from the stool she was perched on. Her throat locked with fear, then she managed to choke out, "I—I work here."

There was a long moment of silence, then the gun swung slowly up to point at her face. It took all of Vicki's willpower not to scream.

"Open the till," he said. "And no tricks."

The night hadn't gone well for Howard. First of all, catching a bus to this part of Sydney and at this time of night hadn't been easy. He'd had to wait for forty minutes at a major terminal, and being dressed in black with a suspicious-looking canvas bag at his feet had been nerve-wracking. The bag only contained the machete, the shotgun and a roll of thick adhesive tape he and Decker had used in the past for binding victims. When he picked up the bag, it seemed to bulge in all the right places to announce he had a gun in it.

He felt better riding on the bus, until he realised he'd missed the stop. This was after staring anxiously out the window for familiar landmarks, only to see them sliding past as the bus picked up speed. He pressed the red button desperately, but the driver assumed it was an early call for the next stop and didn't even bother glancing in his mirror.

The bus didn't service every stop on the road either, and passed several of the distinctive orange posts before halting at a row of shelters.

Cursing, Howard pushed impatiently through the middle doors and set off at a brisk pace back along the footpath. The bright headlights of the oncoming traffic made him squint and he put his head down. It had been his intention to spend at least half an hour watching the garage from a distance, checking there would be no unwelcome surprises. Now he was going to be pushing to get there in time. He couldn't afford to be late. Howard knew it was common for late-night employees to spin-lock combination safes with the day's takings and to have no knowledge of the opening combination. He had to do the job before that happened.

He was out of breath and angry when the lights of the garage finally came into view. His nerves began to tighten. He crossed to the opposite side of the road, looking for a spot where he could pull on the balaclava. The petrol station looked deserted as he passed. He couldn't see anyone manning the place, but guessed they would be inside. There were no customers.

He came to a garden with tall, thick hedges at the front, grown to keep out traffic noise. Howard jumped a small gate and found himself in a neat garden belonging to a brick house. The curtains were drawn, but lights were on inside. He recognised the flicker of a television. Belatedly, Howard silently prayed there would be no yapping guard dog and he stayed motionless for a moment, listening. Nothing happened. He pulled the balaclava from his bag and put it on. Despite the chilly night Howard was hot after the fast walk from the bus stop, and the woollen balaclava felt prickly and uncomfortable against his sweating face. Then he realised he would have to walk the short distance along the footpath back to the garage in full view of the traffic. God knew what might happen if some driver saw the balaclava and had a mobile phone to warn the police.

Annoyed, he tore the balaclava off his head again. He would have to put it back on somewhere in the shadows of the garage itself.

Things didn't get better. Howard still wanted to observe the garage for a while—even if just long enough to see one customer get served so he might see who he would be up against. But no cars obliged. He couldn't see through the hedge, so he had to keep popping his head above or around it like some Jack-in-the-box. It made him feel stupid, and he was aware how bad it might appear to passers-by, should he be caught in the headlights.

This would never have happened to Decker. The idea intruded into his mind. *And Fiona would laugh herself stupid at me*. Angrily, Howard pushed the thoughts away. He didn't need Decker and Fiona wasn't there. He could do this all on his own. He looked at his watch in the lights of the next passing car. It was time to go to work.

Gripping the balaclava in his free hand Howard jumped the gate again. This time he let one of his boots drag and it snagged on top of the steel frame, rattling the gate against its lock. Instantly a small dog inside the house began barking noisily.

"*Fuck* it!" Howard snarled under his breath, hurrying away. Now what was he going to do? That house was probably owned by old people, who would panic at the slightest sound and call the police. Should he keep going?

A mixture of emotions made up his mind. The first was simple greed, because he had grown used to spending money as he wished without Decker complaining. He wanted to keep doing that, but he was close to being broke. He needed a cash injection fast. There was laziness too, as he looked for the easiest solution. It might have been prudent and clever to abandon the job now, with the risks and odds piling up against him, but he would need more effort to find another target on another night and hit it.

Greater in his mind was fear of being a failure—of not living up to the reputation that only Howard recognised. If he walked away now, he would almost hear Decker's ghost laughing at him.

"Fuck him," Howard whispered. "Fuck them all."

He moved quickly along the footpath, unconsciously turning his face away from the headlights now. He re-crossed the road just before the garage and stepped onto the edge of the concrete driveway, moving around outside the bright lights until he came to the building itself, and pressed his back against the wall. He felt wound up to his maximum, trembling and breathing in short, shallow gasps. Howard was always like this before a job. In the darkness he fumbled the balaclava back over his head, struggling to position the holes over his eyes. Then he took the shotgun out of the canvas bag, hearing the barrel clink against the blade of the machete. He cocked the gun and held it ready.

Now Howard felt good. Invincible. Ready for anything.

Except seeing Vicki Colonel.

He stepped through the front door expecting to start the usual fear and panic in his victims, a reaction that was often followed by sly evaluations about how serious and dangerous he was. Howard knew that once they got over the initial shock, the people he threatened always thought, *Will he pull the trigger? Can he be scared away?*

What he saw instead was a beautiful girl staring at him with wide frightened eyes.

Vicki's beauty and innocence radiated without her realising it. Even now, when she was frightened to death, she looked like a lovely startled animal more than a terrified human being. Howard was right to be confused about what she was doing in a run-down petrol station in the middle of the night. It wasn't surprising that his first reaction was an inane question.

Vicki didn't hesitate. With shaking fingers she stabbed at the cash register until the tray slid open. She started pulling the notes out, then stopped and looked at Howard helplessly. He edged forward and tossed the bag onto the counter in front of her. It made her flinch.

"Put it in there," he snapped. As she began stuffing the money into the bag he looked around nervously and asked, "Where's the boss?"

"He's not here," Vicki said, keeping her eyes down to the bag. The machete inside only scared her more.

"Don't lie! You can't be here on your own."

"I—I am. He had to go out. He'll be back in a little while. Very soon, actually."

Howard stared nervously at the connecting door to the workshop. "Is he in there?"

"No—I told you. Here's not here."

"If you're lying and he walks through that door, I'm going to shoot him."

"He's not *here*!" Vicki was trying to put coins in the bag now. Some were spilling from her trembling fingers and clattering noisily on the counter.

"Where's the rest?"

"No-one else works here at night."

"The rest of the *money*, you stupid bitch."

Vicki looked at him dumbly. She knew what he meant now, but for the life of her she couldn't remember where there was any more money. The canvas bag held much less than a day's takings, but all the money was there. Fear was robbing Vicki of her capacity to think straight. The answer grudgingly came through the panic. Her uncle had done a run to the bank late in the afternoon, just in case exactly what was happening now occurred and the garage lost everything. But would he believe her?

"There isn't any," she said, in a frightened whisper.

"*What?*"

"Honest, there isn't any more. Uncle John went to the bank this afternoon and took most of it with him."

Something in her voice and the simple explanation told

Howard she wasn't lying, but he couldn't let it go at that. He darted forward and with one hand pulled the bag towards him, opening it. He stared incredulously at the money inside, momentarily ignoring Vicki, who shrank back to the shelves behind her. With him so close, she could smell his unwashed stench.

He looked up, glaring at her now. "You've got to be fucking kidding! There must be more money than this!"

"There isn't," she shook her head meekly. "There never is at night, in case—" She stopped herself, but too late.

"In case someone like me comes along, right?" he snarled, making her flinch again. With a sudden movement he let go of the bag and swept his hand along the nearest shelf, sending a cascade of bottles, tins and automotive goods crashing to the floor. Then he stopped and stood absolutely still, his head bowed and arms loose at his sides, the shotgun drooping as he stared unblinking at the floor. Howard was breathing in ragged, troubled gasps. Vicki watched him with terrified eyes.

"Where's the safe?" he asked in an ominous voice, without looking at her.

"In the floor here, but it's empty. That money was supposed to go in it."

"Show me."

He walked slowly around to the end of the counter. Vicki was acutely aware of his eyes on her tight-fitting jeans as she bent to the floor and pulled the mat away. She faced him as she lifted the trapdoor and hoped he wouldn't look down the front of her shirt.

"You're good looking," he said, sending a thrill of fear through her. "Pretty."

Not knowing what to reply, she stayed quiet until the small safe was open. She gestured for him to see it was empty.

"See?"

He leaned forward to look. All Vicki could see were his

eyes, sunken within the balaclava. To her, they seemed to be glittering with madness.

After a moment Howard whispered to himself, "I don't fucking believe it."

"I—I'm sorry," she said.

The eyes snapped to her. "You're what? You're *sorry*? What the hell do you mean—you're sorry?"

Vicki stood frozen, then shrugged, tears coming to her eyes. "You know, I meant—"

Howard was on the edge of breaking down, but the moment was disturbed by the sound of a car door closing. Moving jerkily, he stepped sideways so he could see the garage driveway. Vicki almost collapsed at her knees with relief.

Somebody must have pulled up at the petrol pumps.

"Jesus, it's the bloody *cops*!" Howard hissed, shaken. Vicki was so heartened she risked stepping far enough to look for herself and saw Howard was wrong. It was the security company's patrol car. One of the men was casually approaching the office door. Another could be seen waiting in the car.

Howard checked the shotgun.

Vicki realised what he might do. "God, *no*! Please don't do anything—"

"Mind your own fucking business."

"Why shoot him? Can't you just go out the back door? I'll tell them you've been gone for ages."

"Don't be stupid." Howard grabbed the canvas bag and threaded his arm through the handles so he could carry it on his shoulder. He pressed himself further out of sight from the door.

"Please!" Vicki didn't intend to cry out so loud or try to warn the security guard at the risk of her own safety, but her plea carried out to him. His step faltered to a halt and he regarded the office door suspiciously.

"Hello?" the guard called carefully. "Vicki, is that you? Are you OK?"

"You *bitch*!" Howard hissed at her. He whirled away from the wall and grabbed the front of her shirt, pulling her close. "You stupid *fucking* bitch!" As he stared into her face his eyes glazed over as he tried to figure out what to do.

To Vicki, the blank expression was all the more terrifying.

Howard soon recovered, the life coming back to his eyes like someone coming out of a daydream. "Where's the back door? Show me, or I'll blow your fucking face off." The shotgun was waving below her chin. Howard's sour smell and foul breath filled her nostrils.

"I didn't mean to—"

"Where's the *back door*?"

"Through there," she jerked her head at the connecting door to the workshop. But instead of leaving her and fleeing that way, Howard dragged her with him towards the door. Both of them stumbled in the darkness over the hydraulic lifts and workshop junk, before Howard thrust Vicki head first at the door.

"Open it."

She was crying now, and began fiddling clumsily with the deadlock and a chain. From beyond the door a low rumbling could be heard, but Howard either didn't notice it or didn't care.

"Come on, damn you! Open the fucking door!"

"I'm *trying*."

A voice floated in to them from the office. "Vicki, are you in there? Are you OK? It's Geoff."

The guard was standing in the doorway and clearly silhouetted as he looked into the dark workshop. Vicki saw Howard raise the shotgun again from the corner of her eye and she pushed herself against him, forcing it down.

She screamed out, *"Get out! He's got a gun!"* Then felt a fist hit her on the temple and the darkness blossomed with coloured splotches as she dropped to her knees. Dimly she heard Howard curse her.

The security guard reacted instantly, throwing himself

backwards, away from the doorway. They heard him yell out and run from the office.

Howard dragged her upright. "Open the fucking *door*, I told you." She had managed to unlock it before he hit her. Sobbing, and fighting a dizzy pain in her head, Vicki now wrenched it open. The rumbling noise from outside increased tenfold and Howard stared out in disbelief. He uttered, "What the *hell*—"

A long freight train was passing the rear of the garage. In one direction the leading engines were moving away from Howard faster than he could run. In the other, freight cars appeared from out of the darkness without a break. Howard's escape route was cut off.

"Shit, what am I going to—" Howard grated between his teeth, watching the passing freight cars. In frustration he ripped his balaclava off, as if it would help him see better and perhaps the train would be gone. Of course, it wasn't, and he groaned angrily. He held Vicki again, once more by a handful of her shirt so she couldn't pull away from him. Between the garage wall and the railway yard fence was a narrow strip of ragged long grass. Glinting in the faint light were years' worth of discarded oil containers and bottles. One end of the gap was blocked by larger oil drums, but the other was clear.

"This way," Howard told her, pulling Vicki through the door. She protested weakly, but he ignored her. They both stumbled on the rubbish hidden in the grass. Finally clear of the building, they came to an area where the garage parked cars being serviced. It was vacant except for a solitary vehicle.

"Who owns this?" he asked her, holding them both close to the wall and jerking on her shirt to speed a reply.

"It's mine," she gasped, shocked by the cruelty in his face. A part of her wished he'd kept the balaclava on. Then, with horror, Vicki realised she'd made a mistake.

"It's yours? You can drive? Where's the keys?"

"Back—back in the office."

"Fuck it! We're going to have to go back and get them."
He glared at her accusingly.

"Oh *please*, can't you just run from here? They won't
catch you—"

"Shut *up!*"

He dragged her back along the rear of the building. In
the doorway he could see both security guards silhouetted
against the office lights.

"Freeze, you bastards!" Howard yelled, scaring them.
They had just decided Howard and his captive had gone.
"Don't move, or this girl is going to get hurt real bad."

One of them called, "Hey, why don't you just let her go,
and we'll leave you alone. You can go and keep the
money."

"How stupid do you think I am? I want you two to step
inside here." The guards exchanged glances, so in a near-
scream Howard added, "Fucking *now,* or I'll kill her, I
swear!"

Reluctantly they moved into the workshop. One called,
"We've radioed the police. They'll be here any minute.
You'll be a lot better off if you dropped the gun now and
let the girl go."

Howard was confused—he still didn't realise these
were security guards, not police. Still, it didn't alter his
plans. He yanked Vicki close and hissed in her face.
"We're going into the office and you're going to find your
keys *real* fast, OK? Then you're going to take me for a little drive. If you do everything as I say, you won't get hurt,
all right?"

Vicki nodded in the darkness, then let out a squeal as he
pushed her roughly towards the office door. He kept the
gun against the small of her back. "Back up to the other
wall," he snarled at the guards, who did this without taking
their eyes off him. Howard told them with clipped, nervous words, "We're getting out of here and *don't* think

about following us, hear me? If I think you're trying to follow us, I'll cut this bitch to pieces like I did the others, understand? Have you read it in the newspapers? Well, that's
me. Don't fuck with me, or this girl is going to get chopped
up like the rest, OK? I'll leave her fingers at your fucking
front door."

A guard was holding up a calming hand. "Hey, just take
it easy. There's no need for anyone to get hurt."

Howard was ignoring him, standing in the doorway to
the office and pushing Vicki through. "You find the damn
keys and don't think about doing anything stupid. I don't
need you on the end of the barrel to shoot you dead, understand?"

Vicki dropped to her knees and scrabbled frantically under the counter for her bag. Finding it, she tore it open and
produced the car keys. She held them up for Howard to
see.

"Good girl," he said with a nasty smile. "Let's go."

As Vicki moved past him back into the workshop Howard
gripped her upper arm. Vicki felt revolted by the contact.
They again made the hazardous trip across the dark workshop to the rear door. Here, Howard waved the shotgun at
the two guards. "Don't follow us, remember? I meant what I
said." He didn't wait for an answer, shoving Vicki ahead of
him out the door.

Seconds later they were at her car, a small white Mazda.
Howard made her unlock his passenger door first, then
watched both Vicki and the garage for the security guards
as she made her way to the driver's side. He got in at the
same time as she did, the shotgun nestled in his lap and
pointed straight at her.

"Drive normally out of here, OK? No spinning tyres to
attract attention. Then follow my instructions."

Vicki nodded miserably and started the car. She had the
presence of mind to put her foot flat to the floor in an attempt to flood the carburettor, but the engine burst imme-

diately to life instead. Howard kept the gun on her, but he was watching the garage. As the Mazda pulled away and approached the road he could see the guards making their way back into the office. "Get going, for Christ's sake," he snapped at her. The car lurched as Vicki dumped the clutch too hard, then they were speeding up the road. In the distance Howard saw flashing blue lights approaching fast.

"Take the first turn off—*any* bloody turn off. Get off this road."

Vicki swung the car wildly into a small side road.

"Put the lights on high beam. I'm looking for something."

She had expected a high-speed escape along the highways to get as far away from the garage as possible, but Howard made her twist and turn through the narrow streets.

They hadn't covered much distance when he suddenly yelled, "Stop! Stop here!" He peered out the window at a block of flats with rows of carports. "Go in here and park in the furthest empty carport," he told her. She did this and turned off the motor as he instructed.

Everything was suddenly dark and quiet. She found the silence frightening. Howard's body odour filled the car, making her feel ill.

"Put the seat back until you're lying down," he said. Fearing what was about to happen, Vicki nearly began screaming, but she controlled herself and fumbled with the seat adjustments. Howard did the same. The two of them lay side by side in the darkness, staring up at the roof lining of the Mazda. They looked like two lovers unsure of what to do next. Vicki could hear Howard's breathing. It was coming in short, excited gasps. There was an impossible silence and Vicki had a new urge to fill it by screaming again and again. She had visions of waking out of this nightmare and finding her fingers just bloodied stumps.

She kept clenching her hands, telling herself it wasn't happening. Her fingers were still there.

She jumped nervously when Howard finally spoke.

"So, have you got a boyfriend?"

Chapter Fourteen

Maiden's phone rang shrilly, cutting through his sleep. He opened his eyes reluctantly and looked at the illuminated clock beside his bed. It was just before one o'clock in the morning. He had been drinking too heavily, sitting in front of the television and feeling morose and unwanted. The urge to sleep had come through the alcohol, more than any weariness, but it had still taken a while. Now it was even harder to wake up. He fumbled the phone from its cradle and put it to his ear without raising his head from the pillow. He knew who it would be.

"This is the Despatch desk, Detective Senior Sargeant Maiden."

"No kidding? This had better be good."

"There was another armed hold-up tonight involving a shotgun. A small petrol station in Penrith."

"Penrith? What the hell has that to do with me?"

"The guy ended up kidnapping a young woman to help him escape. Two security guards disturbed him, so he used her as a shield. One of the last things he told them was . . ." The sergeant paused and there was a rustle of paper. Maiden knew he would be reading directly from a report. "He would cut the girl to pieces like he did the others. He claimed he was the guy in the newspapers and he would leave the girl's fingers on the security guard's front door. That's why it got it a reference through to The Rocks and yourself, sir."

Maiden was waking up fast, sitting up in bed and rubbing the sleep from his eyes with one hand.

"Where is he now? Is he still using the girl as a hostage?"

"There isn't a situation at the moment, detective. He got away and took the girl with him. There's been no sightings by patrols and no contact about any ransom or anything."

"How the hell did that happen? Didn't the security guys put a call through? How far away was the response unit?"

"Within a minute of the escape, but they lost him."

"Bloody great!" Maiden took a moment to think. "What's happening on the scene now?"

"There's still interviews going on with the garage owner—it took a while to find him. He was in a club down the road. The security guards are still there too, but I'd say things are winding up by now."

Maiden looked again at the clock and did some calculations. "Tell them to stay put. I want to come out and ask them a few things myself. I'll be there in about forty-five minutes."

The sergeant sounded doubtful. "They'll have to wait around. Penrith CIB probably want them at the station for statements."

"I don't give a shit! The damned paperwork can wait. We've got a hostage situation here, haven't we? What do they want to do—go home for a cup of tea?"

"I'll pass on your request, sir." The sergeant hung up. Maiden sprang out of bed too quickly and had to fight off a moment of dizziness. As he got dressed he reflected on the sergeant's use of the word "request." It was true the hold-up might have a connection to Maiden's investigation because of the bandit's reference to cutting up the girl, but the sergeant's call was still little more than a courtesy and Maiden had no real authority to dictate what happened at the crime scene or to throw his weight around at the Penrith CIB. His request might be ignored and the witnesses taken away for signed statements. However, what was more likely was that they wouldn't give him a moment more than his forty-five minutes to get there. He had to hurry.

Going down the stairs Maiden realised his dizziness was more than just getting up too quickly. He must still have a fair amount of Scotch swilling around his system, too. He shouldn't be driving anywhere.

Detouring to the kitchen, he grabbed a large mug, half-filled it with hot water from the tap, and heaped three teaspoons of coffee into it. The acrid too-strong smell wasn't appealing, but he screwed up his face and sipped several times, letting the coffee wash around his mouth. With his free hand he found his car keys, cigarettes and wallet, put them in his jacket pockets, then nursed the coffee mug as he walked out of the townhouse and got into his car.

The garage was a confusion of parked police cars with their flashing blue lights, lines of marked tape stopping access from the road and a television unit just as gaudily painted with fluorescent stripes to add even more colour. Maiden parked his Ford as close to the scene as he could. After the heated warmth of the drive over, stepping out of the car was a chilly slap to his face. Maiden didn't mind. He needed it.

It was easy to spot the security company's car. The guards were leaning against the bonnet, looking bored and talking between themselves. Maiden began to head straight for them before he remembered he was working outside his own turf. He looked for a detective and spotted a younger man dressed in jeans and a tracksuit top, talking to someone who would have to be the garage owner. Maiden went over, interrupted and introduced himself to the other policeman.

"Thanks for hanging around," he added, gruffly.

The detective, named Bennett, shrugged slightly. "I'm not going to bed in a hurry, but I've run out of reasons to hold the witnesses here."

"I'll be as quick as I can. I'd like to talk to the security people first, and then the owner. I assume this is him?"

"This is Mr. John Truemanne. He's the owner of the garage, but he wasn't actually here when the crime was committed." Bennett only just kept a disapproving tone from his voice. Truemanne pointedly looked away from the two detectives.

"So I'm told," Maiden nodded. "Any news from the patrols?"

"No. The bandit took the girl's car, but made her drive. It's a white Mazda sedan, so there's a million of 'em on the road, not to mention just as many Fords, Toyotas and everything else that look exactly the bloody same. We've got the registration number, that's the only good news."

Maiden sympathised with a shake of his head and left them to it, then went back to the security guards. He identified himself, shook hands with them both formally, and asked them to tell him what happened. It didn't take long and there was a silence while Maiden considered the story.

"You're sure it was a shotgun?" he asked, finally.

"Ninety-nine per cent," answered one of the guards. "I couldn't guess what make. It was too dark."

"Fair enough, as long as you're sure it was a shotgun," Maiden said with an absent nod, "But sawn off? Makes it different from the guy that's been operating over the last few months."

The other guard offered, "Otherwise it's the same. He walked into the job, he wore the same black clothes and face mask, and it *was* a shotgun. Maybe it's the same guy with a modified weapon."

Some security companies had full disclosure on crime details, especially when they involved break-and-enters and armed holdups, because it was conceivable their patrols might encounter the same criminals. Maiden had a certain amount of disdain for these men with their pseudo uniforms and marked patrol cars. Now he tried hard not to show it.

"Taking a hostage isn't his usual MO either," he grunted. "Are you certain about the 'cutting her up' bit? It's very important."

"No doubt about it. Said he was the guy in the newspapers." The guard paused, then said carefully, "You know, taking the girl with him might have been a spur of the moment thing."

"What do you mean?"

The two security men exchanged a knowing look. "That girl Vicki is a real stunner. I mean, like Miss Universe material. Maybe he took a shine to her on the spot. She's too good looking to be here late at night on her own." He jerked his head at her uncle in the distance, who was still looking ashamed and uneasy next to Bennett. "That guy's a bloody fool, leaving a girl like that on her own. We don't even normally patrol here—we just fuel up here and started checking on her regularly, just as a favour, you know?"

"You might be right, then." Maiden grudgingly conceded these men had good intentions, even if they still reminded him of highway patrolmen in a Hollywood movie. "Thanks for trying, anyway." He gestured goodbye and began to walk away, but the security man stopped him with a call.

"Hey, I forgot something. He smelled bad."

Maiden turned around. "He what?"

"He smelled bad, like he hadn't had a bath in ages. We went into the office directly after he ran and you could still smell him. He *stank*. This guy doesn't own any soap."

"OK, thanks," Maiden said, moving on. "I'll pass that on to Detective Bennett." He went back towards the other detective, but as he drew close he fixed the garage owner with an angry glare. Maiden's anger was genuine at the sight of Truemanne trying his best to appear innocent. The comment about the bandit's hygiene was forgotten momentarily as Maiden confronted Truemanne, who looked back at him fearfully.

"Mr. Truemanne, can you explain to me what possessed you to leave a young girl alone here tonight? Where were you?"

Truemanne flinched at his tone and looked towards Bennett for help. Bennett didn't offer any sympathy, his expression just as hard as Maiden's. "Detective Maiden is part of an on-going investigation involving several missing persons. There's a chance of a connection here. You should answer all his questions."

Truemanne tried to sound outraged. "My niece has been kidnapped by a madman, for God's sake! Do you think I wanted that?"

"Where *were* you, Mr. Truemanne?"

After a tense moment Truemanne dropped his eyes. "At my club. It's only about ten minutes down the road—hey, I didn't just leave her here, all right? Vicki told me she could look after the place on her own."

Maiden didn't take his stare off him. "And how many times have you gone down to your club and left Vicki alone? How long do you stay there?"

Truemanne shrugged. "I've only done it once or twice, and not for long."

"So, if I go down there and ask the bar staff how often you frequent the place, is that what they're going to tell me?"

Truemanne closed his eyes wearily. "OK, OK, I've been going down there quite a lot lately. But Vicki's an adult and she's been handling this place OK. She may be my niece, but she still works for me, right? I should be able to treat her like any other employee."

Maiden made a disgusted noise and pulled back. He motioned for Bennett to join him. "Have you been in contact with the girl's parents yet?" he asked quietly.

"No, that's something I want to do myself. I should have been over there by now. To be honest, you're the one who's holding me up."

Maiden conceded the blame with a quick nod. "Are you aware Vicki is apparently very attractive? The security guys couldn't say enough about her."

Bennett frowned. "No, I was assuming she was exactly the opposite, otherwise this dickhead uncle wouldn't have left her alone to look after the garage. His description of her was bland." He shot a glare at Truemanne. "Are you thinking this shotgun guy has been watching Truemanne leave her alone, picking himself a pattern?"

"Could be. If it's the same bandit who's been doing these other armed hold-ups, it'll be the first evidence of any surveillance behaviour, as far as I know. I haven't had anything to do with that investigation before. I'm here because of the threat to cut the girl to pieces."

"That's turned into a nasty business in town," Bennett said.

"If this is the guy, the girl's good looks might be her only chance of staying alive, but God knows what else he'll do to her because of them." Maiden stopped and let out an exasperated sigh. He thought about going home and rejected it, despite the hour. "Look, thanks. Damn it, there's not so much I can do. I'm going to head back to The Rocks and stay there. Can you let me know the moment anything develops?"

"They could be anywhere by now, so it's been made city-wide. It would be better to get your own despatch to listen out for you, but I'll try to get a message to you anyhow, if I hear anything."

"I'd appreciate it," Maiden said.

Maiden considered that a few hours sleep would do him more harm than good at this stage, so he decided to go back to the station. Then he realised he needed clothes for the next day and stopped home to pick up a clean suit, shirt and tie. He resisted the urge to stay, as he'd told Bennett he would be at work. At the same time he didn't believe he would hear anything positive for a while. Either by luck or good planning the bandit and his hostage slipped through the police net hastily thrown around the area of the garage. Now it only remained to see how or where Vicki Colonel reappeared.

Perhaps as a prize offered for ransom—or maybe as another murder victim.

The first thing he noticed back at The Rocks was another pile of never-ending routine paperwork waiting for him on his desk. Maiden figured now was as good a time as any to try dealing with it. At this time of night the offices were comparatively deserted. The nightshift detectives were out on the streets or elsewhere in the building processing arrests made during the night. Only occasionally was there some movement between the desks bringing a nod of greeting to Maiden, who wasn't a close friend of any of them. He worked almost undisturbed.

However, it wasn't long before the paperwork slipped from his mind and he dropped his pen, staring into space and thinking.

He tried to convince himself the garage kidnapper and the person leaving pieces of victims in elevators were two different people. The armed bandit's threat of cutting the girl "like he did the others" smacked of a throw-away line inspired by reading the newspapers. More importantly, it required a certain amount of planning and finesse to drop a severed human limb on the floor of an elevator somewhere in the CBD. Especially when the body part belonged to someone you had recently abducted and murdered. The whole make-up of a person who could do that didn't seem to match the traits of a man who, armed with a sawn-off shotgun, walks into a small garage, steals money at gunpoint and kidnaps a young girl when he is cornered.

Unless he was part of a partnership—with another person who was of a completely different character. It would explain why the garage hold-up was done alone. The partner didn't want anything to do with that sort of crime.

"No, it's two different cases," Maiden muttered to himself. "It's *got* to be, unless some bastard's a complete bloody schizophrenic." He thought about contacting Bennett, but immediately decided against it. He would hear from him if there was anything worth knowing. He bent his head to the paperwork again, running his eyes across the papers without really absorbing the information in front of him. Maiden was more tired than he'd realised, so eventually he left his desk and found an empty interview room with a sagging couch. He lay on his back, his legs dangling off the end. It was uncomfortable, but better than nothing. Maiden only wanted to nap anyway. Instead, he fell into a deep sleep.

He was woken by Martin Creane, who shoved Maiden's shoulder gently with the toe of his shoe. His hands were full with two mugs of coffee. Bright sunshine was coming through the slats of a Venetian blind.

"Wake up. It's breakfast time."

Maiden reacted violently, sat bolt upright, then just as quickly put a hand to his forehead and let out a groan. "God damn! What time is it? I didn't want to fall asleep."

"What's wrong with your own bed? Did you wet it?"

Maiden scowled at him from between his splayed fingers. "You are getting too damned cocky and familiar for a junior detective."

Creane wasn't worried by Maiden's bad temper. "And you're supposed to be setting an example. Finding you homeless and hungover isn't exactly encouraging. Do you want this coffee or not?"

Maiden grumbled his thanks and took the mug. "Some of us are devoted to the job twenty-four hours a day," he said, raising the coffee to his lips. He grimaced at the first taste, then said, "I got called out in the middle of the night."

"I know. What happened?" Creane made himself comfortable on the interviewer's wooden chair.

Maiden settled himself with a few more sips of coffee. Searching around for his cigarettes he winced at the aches in his joints and muscles. He remembered where he was and the no-smoking rules, then decided he would get away with it in the interview room anyway. Sometimes interviewees were invited to smoke as a means of relaxing them.

"Hell of a breakfast," Creane said, looking at the cigarette.

"Non-fattening," Maiden mumbled, lighting up and taking a deep, appreciative draw. He closed his eyes as he exhaled slowly and opened them again to look at Creane. "We had some fun and games last night." He recounted what had happened, re-examining the facts as he spoke. "That's all I know," he ended. "I guess someone would have woken me if anything new came up. Bennett said he would let me know, and I told Despatch to keep their ears open for me, too."

"There's nothing new, then," Creane said. "The updates still have the bandit, the girl and the car all missing. Looks like he got clean away."

Maiden made a noise to say the news didn't surprise him.

"Do you think he's our boy?" Creane asked, already guessing the answer—Maiden wasn't upset enough to be thinking they'd missed a big break in their own investigation.

"I don't think so. I can't convince myself that someone smart enough to give us a merry chase with these butchered bodies is stupid enough to hold up a shitty petrol station with a sawn-off shotgun, all for the sake of a few dollars." But Maiden didn't sound certain at all. "Christ, I don't bloody know."

"OK," Creane said. "What about the guy we found at the rubbish dump? The one without his fingers? Maybe the bandit's talking about that mutilation."

Maiden hadn't thought about that. "Possibly, but I doubt it. It only made a few newspapers and we asked them to withold the missing fingers bit. As far as I know, they all complied. So when he yelled about being the guy in the newspapers, he must have been referring to our case."

Creane looked thoughtful, then brightened. "Anyway, I've got some good progress for you on the Greg Howlett case. It came in with the nightshift guys and I picked it out on my way through."

Maiden accepted the change of subject with a nod as he suddenly succumbed to a yawn. "I'm glad someone's making some bloody progress."

"This is good stuff. Remember the system where Howlett was supposed to log off the computer system when he finished his overtime? That's why his boss believed he was still in the building, because Howlett hadn't signed off the computer, right?" Maiden nodded again, but he was only half-listening, still mulling over the events of the night. Creane went on, "Well, it seems our Mr. Howlett was in the habit of not only *not* signing off, but of *not* being in the building either. Guess where he was?"

Maiden growled, "I'm not in the mood to play games, Martin."

Creane's cheerfulness wasn't dampened. "Howlett was gambling. Not only that night, but *every* night, it seems. Same bar, same poker machine mostly, if someone didn't beat him to it. The nightshift team has solid confirmation Howlett was in his usual place playing the poker machines until nearly nine o'clock on the night he disappeared."

Now Maiden gave Creane his full attention. "Explain that to me again."

"Listen, it worked like this: Howlett stays behind at the office to do overtime, but as soon as everybody's out of the building he nips down to his favourite poker machine and blows up to a hundred bucks on gambling and a few drinks. When he runs out of money he goes back to the office, *then* signs off the computer and calls it overtime, get it?" Creane spread his hands. "He's a trusted employee and good enough at his job to make it look like he's doing the extra hours. No-one questions anything, although he must have been pushing his luck by now. Hell, he's probably trying to pay for the gambling with the overtime. He might even have been caught out by that Tysonne guy this time, if our psycho hadn't nutted him beforehand . . ." Creane paused for breath. "Look, whatever. He's a real regular at the bar, knows the barmaids by name and vice versa. So like I said, there's rock-solid confirmation from the bar staff that Howlett was in there as usual, and left about the usual time."

Maiden considered this. "So now we've got his movements until somewhere around nine o'clock?"

"At least. We were all too wrapped up in Tysonne telling us Howlett was *supposed* to be in the building somewhere at six-thirty, when he tried to find him, because of the computer log-out system. We assumed Howlett, the diligent worker, was picked off any time after that." Creane leaned forward intently and lowered his voice. "Now we know he was usually out of the office by then and at the poker machines. I reckon he came back to sign off as usual after his gambling session and *that's* when our killer struck."

Maiden quickly added for him, "And like I said—they got him outside somewhere, probably in the car park. Then they chopped the poor bastard's arm off and used his security card to get inside the building and leave the arm in the lift."

"They even had his car keys and the car itself to get rid of the rest of him."

The two men looked at each other, grimly satisfied with their theory.

Maiden said, "We've got to find that car."

Creane looked sly. "Don't tell anyone you've dismissed any connection between this case and last night's kidnapping. Tell them finding Howlett's Commodore might lead to the girl, too, and you'll have a lot of policemen looking hard for our sake, as well."

Maiden let out a bark of laughter. "You're not just a pretty face, Martin." He lapsed into thought again, his face grim. "I think we'd better pay a more serious visit to Mr. Fischer and his girlfriend, too. Find out what they reckon they were doing during those hours when we can't account for Howlett. There's not much motive, but maybe they got a taste for—"

The door opened and a detective put his head around the corner. "John? There you are. The shit's hitting the fan. The early-morning news bulletins have all covered the garage hold-up without an official police statement and Longman's screaming—your name mainly, because the media's got hold of the guy's threat to cut the girl up, which Longman says makes it a part of *your* investigation."

"What? Hold on a second." Maiden held up his hand. "What the hell are you talking about?"

"You've got a press conference at nine o'clock at College Street. This time you're going to be real famous," the detective added with a smirk. "Apparently the television news teams are fighting for parking space all around the block." He disappeared before Maiden could answer.

"Christ, that's all I need right now," Maiden moaned, rubbing at his face.

"And you look like shit, too," Creane told him, grinning.

"Thanks for your bloody help." Maiden got up and pushed past Creane to the door. He went back to his desk, acknowledging greetings from other detectives with a wave as he moved through the room. He picked up the phone and with his free hand rummaged among papers for a telephone listing. Creane, casually following him, came up and sat on the edge of the desk.

"I need a picture of the girl," Maiden told him without looking up. "Where's Penrith's number . . . here." He stabbed at the phone and waited impatiently for the connection. A long conversation followed, Maiden establishing who he was and what he wanted. His face brightened when he was put through to Detective Bennett, who was still working trying to co-ordinate a search for Vicki Colonel's car.

"I need a photograph of the girl," he explained to Bennett. "Did you get a recent one from the parents? I've got a press conference in forty minutes and there's going to be television. If I can get her picture broadcast and give them your number as a hotline, you might get some results." He listened for a moment, nodding. "Yeah—I know, you might have to stick it in someone's hand and get them to drive it over here pronto, but I reckon it's worth it. OK? Thanks a lot." He hung up and stared at the desk, thinking what he needed to do next.

"What are you going to wear?" Creane asked, looking at Maiden's jeans and jumper.

Maiden looked around expectantly, then swore as he saw the change of clothes that had been on the back of his chair now lay crumpled on the floor.

"Give them to me," Creane said.

"What?"

"Give me your suit. You want that on national television? There's a cleaners on the next block. I'll run down and try to get it pressed."

Maiden picked it up and handed it over. "Thanks," he muttered, awkward with Creane's concern. "I appreciate it."

"No problem." Creane walked away, the suit slung over his arm.

Maiden's phone rang. He picked it up and put the receiver to his ear warily, expecting Longman's acid tones. Instead, it was Janet Brown.

"I figured you'd be at work early today," she said.

"I haven't been home," he complained, pleased at her familiarity.

"Are you too busy to hear about the severed arm?"

"To be honest, can you keep it brief? I'm doing a press conference at nine and I haven't got a damned clue what I'm supposed to tell them. I need to work on it."

"Just read the morning papers and confirm everything you can. Refuse to comment on the rest."

Maiden was taken aback. It was a good idea. Most of the newspapers had night rounds reporters who did nothing but check the hospitals, morgues and police despatches for newsworthy material to put in the morning editions. With the armed hold-up and kidnapping occurring just after midnight, it would easily have made the printing presses. "I might just do that," he said. "What can you tell me about the arm?"

"Identification of Howlett is confirmed, but that's not really news. Pathology-wise, we're in the same boat as the others, although I would suggest we can assume the victim was dead or sedated when the arm was cut off. Someone couldn't remove an entire arm from a living, conscious human without more mess. There's no injuries that might indicate the victim had a chance to resist or attempt to squirm away. A sharp blade was used and the placement of all the cuts suggests there was no struggle during the amputation. The interesting thing I thought you might want to know was the presence of automotive grease and rubber on the sleeve of the jacket."

"Automotive rubber? You mean a tyre?"

"No, a softer compound more like a door or a window seal, they tell me."

"Or a boot seal," Maiden said grimly. "That makes more sense. We haven't found Howlett's car yet. When we do, I have a feeling we'll find the rest of Mr. Howlett, too."

There was a silence on the other end, then Brown said, "That part of your work can't be very much fun."

"No, not often."

"This business is keeping you busy. I doubt I'll ever get a chance to cook us that dinner—to repay you for moving my refrigerator."

"Hey, you don't have to repay me," Maiden said, feeling his heart skip a beat at the thought of an evening with Janet Brown. "But that dinner is still a good idea." He paused and decided to take the plunge. "Look, there's a nice Indian joint not far from that local supermarket where we bumped into each other. How would you like to meet me for a meal there tonight? It's short notice and I can't even guarantee I'll be there right now, I know . . ." He fell silent, feeling it was a mistake.

Brown sounded hesitant. "I know the one you mean . . . Well—I suppose by the time I get home tonight it's going to have been a long day. The last thing I'll feel like is cooking. It's probably a good idea for me to have a definite time to get out of this place for once. I spend too much time here as it is." She went silent, thinking about the offer. Maiden didn't dare to say anything. She said, suddenly, "OK, why not? What time?"

"I'll book for eight o'clock. If I have any problems I'll call to let you know."

"Fine. I'll fax you a copy of this forensic report. And good luck with your press conference."

"Thanks. I'll take your advice and grab a paper."

He hung up, feeling pleased. The phone rang again immediately. This time it was Longman, ruining Maiden's moment of happiness.

"Are you prepared for the press conference?" Longman asked, hardly concealing a trace of animosity.

"It's late notice, but I'll cope," Maiden replied, then couldn't resist adding, "like the last time."

"If it was up to me, we'd have a decent taskforce on this case by now. I hope you'll have the good sense to speak out, when things get too much for you."

What do you mean—when? Maiden thought savagely, but kept it to himself. If everything else went according to Bercoutte, Longman wouldn't be around very much longer to annoy him. "Don't worry. I've got everything under control." He hung up abruptly.

The best move for Maiden appeared to be getting down to College Street and as far away from Longman as possible.

As usual, Sergeant Overman was waiting in front of the lifts in the small foyer for anyone important. He stepped forward quickly when Maiden emerged.

"There you are. You had us worried again. Can't you turn up for these things a little earlier than sixty seconds beforehand? Shit, what's that you're wearing?"

Maiden kept his temper. Here, he was a stranger in a strange land and he couldn't afford to upset the sergeant who could provide a rough or smooth passage through these press conferences.

"There's plenty of time. Anyway, it's not my fault no bastard tells me about the damned things until the last minute. Don't worry, I've got a suit coming."

"Where the hell is it? We've got three television crews here this morning."

"Martin is trying to get it pressed for me. He should be here any minute. You haven't got any of the morning papers handy, have you?"

Apparently Janet Brown's suggestion wasn't unusual, because Overman pointed to a door and said, "On my desk in there. I've highlighted in green a couple of things we want to play down—just don't comment on them. The rest you can feed to the press in any way you feel fit." Overman glanced at his watch. "You've got about ten minutes. Do you want a coffee?"

"That would save my life. Strong, white with two."

"OK. You'll be in the big room today. Those bloody TV crews take up too much space."

Overman disappeared in the direction of the kitchen. Maiden threaded his way through an increasing crowd in the corridor to Overman's office and slipped inside. The article on Vicki Colonel's abduction was front page news with an editorial comment promised inside. Maiden was beginning to read the latter when he heard someone come into the room behind him. He turned, expecting to see the sergeant with his coffee, but it was Bercoutte.

"Come and see me after the conference," he said briefly. He stayed long enough only for Maiden to nod he understood before he vanished.

Overman came in, holding out a steaming cup. "You're getting popular," he said wryly.

"I could do without the bloody politics, while I'm trying to track down a damned psycho. Longman almost told me directly this morning my investigating this on my own was a waste of time and I should step down and request a task-force. That bastard can't wait for me to fall flat on my face."

Maiden guessed correctly that Overman was well versed in the political manoeuvring within the department. The sergeant was an unofficial link between the higher ranking officers in College Street and the rest of the police force.

"I wouldn't worry too much about Longman, if I were you—unless you do fall flat on your face. Then they'll probably let him chew you to pieces. Mind you, if manpower wasn't such a problem we'd probably *have* a dedicated taskforce on this case by now. As it is, the canvassing you've been requesting has drawn a lot of grumblings."

"What the hell am I supposed to do? Go knocking on the doors myself?"

"No, you're supposed to narrow down the amount of doors you need knocked," Overman smiled. "Now, are you going to be all right in this conference?"

"I suppose so."

Overman reached past him and picked up a sheet of paper from his desk, handing it to Maiden. "Here's an official statement describing the armed hold-up and abduction last night. Read this aloud word for word and answer any questions. Try avoiding any of those things I marked in green in the newspaper—did you get to read it?" Maiden nodded, glancing over the statement. Overman put his finger near the bottom of the page. "Those names I've pencilled there are journos who'll probably try to get their teeth into a bit of sensationalism and nag at you to say something stupid. They're all wearing name tags. Don't stress yourself out about it though, because if you don't give them anything crazy, they'll make something up anyway."

Maiden nodded again nervously. Creane poked his head inside the office. "I'm looking for—oh, there you are." He handed over the suit, freshly pressed and covered with plastic on a wire coathanger.

"Thanks, Martin."

With the three of them in the small office in wasn't easy for Maiden to change his clothes. Finally he shrugged into the jacket, adjusted his tie without the benefit of a mirror, then looked at Overman.

"OK?"

"You'll have to do. Let's go."

The three of them walked down the corridor to a set of double doors. Maiden's nerves started to build up significantly and he was feeling more like a criminal going to his execution than a policeman. He took some deep breaths and reminded himself it wasn't such a big deal. The television people might use fifteen seconds of footage at the most. It was more important that he concentrate on the information he was handing out—and getting that right—than on how he looked or sounded for a television audience.

As the doors opened, the rumble of conversation inside the room died momentarily, then there was a rustle of papers and equipment being readied as Maiden stepped onto a raised platform. Mini arclights on cameras flared into life, making him squint. He stopped himself from holding up a warding hand.

He cleared his throat and said, "Good morning, everyone." There was a mutter of replies. Cameras clicked, whirred and flashed. Tape recorders were set in motion.

Maiden concentrated on his task so much he was unaware of time passing. He carefully read out the official version of the armed hold-up, then fielded questions with bland, often non-commital replies that frustrated some of the journalists to the point where they began to drift out of the room. Others fired queries at him which were designed to provoke a more sensational response, but Maiden always took a moment to think before replying and the ploys didn't work. He neither confirmed nor denied whether the department regarded the armed hold-up and the mutilations as having been carried out by the same person, although he had to concede Howard's threat to cut his captive up. Maiden had to admit Howard and his hostage had disappeared and no-one knew where to start looking. Apart from this, Maiden made it clear he wasn't giving away any secrets—and he managed to keep hidden the fact that they had no secrets to reveal.

There was an interruption when Bennett's photograph of Vicki Colonel arrived and the cameras took close-ups. Vicki's good looks sparked a murmur around the room, but Maiden ignored it. Without realising it, he was presenting the perfect picture of a police force too busy trying to solve crimes to be giving the media any more material than was due. It was lucky someone had thought of calling him out to the hold-up scene, otherwise Maiden would have been badly underinformed about the crime. A small voice in his mind wondered whether Longman didn't know he had been at the garage last night and that his performance at the press conference was expected to discredit him. Almost by accident he was keeping one step ahead of his adversarial superior.

He was surprised when he felt a hand on his shoulder and Overman's whisper, "That'll do. Wind it up."

Maiden abruptly thanked them all for coming. There was an unhappy pause before everyone in the room began to leave. Overman spoke quietly again.

"Well done. That was so uninformative it wouldn't even rate any space on the news, if it wasn't for the girl's photo. We should get you to do these things more often."

"Like hell," Maiden said over his shoulder as he watched the crowd file past him through the door. Overman patted his back and slipped away. Creane was close by and Maiden caught his eye.

"I'm starving," he told him. "But I've got to see someone here first. Want to meet in the cafeteria for breakfast and we'll plan the day? I shouldn't be long."

"Signing autographs?" Creane asked. He was through the door before Maiden could think of a suitable rebuke.

A minute later Maiden was knocking gently on Bercoutte's door. Mary wasn't at her desk. A muffled voice told him to come in. Bercoutte was writing, and looked up at Maiden without bothering to put down his pen.

"What's happening?" he asked shortly.

"I'm getting no support from Longman at all. Do you want to hear about it?"

"Not really. Is it stopping you from doing the job?"

Maiden thought for a moment. "No. He's shooting at me personally, not the investigation."

"What about the hold-up last night? Did we miss a chance at your perpetrator?"

Maiden shook his head. "I don't think so. We don't know much about either side, but at the moment I can't see the two being connected. The mutilations are being done by a psycho of some description—they've got to be. But it's a *slick* psycho. Last night was an armed hold-up that went wrong and now that guy's got himself an attractive hostage. It's a different story altogether."

"We can't ignore it though, can we? There *may* be a connection."

"Only because the bandit himself has claimed an association, but as soon as I can definitely separate the two investigations, I will." After Creane's earlier suggestion about the search for Howlett's car, Maiden wasn't about to do anything of the sort, but he wouldn't tell Bercoutte that.

"Are you handling the load?"

Maiden felt one of his flashes of anger. "That's what

Longman's asking. I'll tell you if things get too much. I'm damned if I'll be telling Longman."

"OK, calm down. Do you need any more help?" The way Bercoutte asked this made it plain he didn't particularly want to offer any.

"No, not yet. As long as I can get the usual resources for canvassing, forensic and computers, if I need it. I don't need anyone closer yet. Overman said there was some grumbling about the manpower I was using up, but it got results. We found out the last victim was a consistent gambler and not always in his office, where everyone expected him to be. It adds an important piece to the puzzle."

"Just try to keep the requests to a minimum, will you? Bennett in Penrith has got half the damned police force looking for that girl's car. I've told him to keep you informed about everything because of the chance you're both looking for the same person, but apart from that leave him alone and stick to your own investigation."

"Bennett's got a job in front of him," Maiden said. "There's only about a million cars answering that description in Sydney. He might have a better chance of someone recognising the girl from the news. She's a real beauty queen."

"So I saw. It's a damned pity, isn't it?" Bercoutte was keeping his expression carefully neutral.

"It might keep her alive," Maiden replied.

"It might just have got her kidnapped, too. Still, let's hope for the best. Stay in contact with me directly. I don't want to have to ask Longman about your progress."

This was an almost ridiculous order, considering Bercoutte's seniority and position. His desire to avoid a confrontation with a subordinate because of in-house politics was absurd. Maiden resisted an urge to shake his head in despair, simply nodding his understanding. His instincts suggested, too, there might be more to this situation than was presently obvious. If it were possible, he might have to be even *more* careful. It wasn't unknown for the careers of people like Maiden to be burned to fuel the aspirations of more senior officers. People like Bercoutte, for instance.

Chapter Fifteen

Vicki had stopped herself watching the green LED readout of the dashboard clock. It had only made her terrifying situation drag by more slowly. Howard's inane questions added to her fear. A wrong answer might send him into a rage. Sometimes she found herself wishing he would do just that. Then she could start screaming and that might bring help. But softly, politely, he kept asking trite, naive things about her home, parents and her work at the garage. He didn't ask any more about her boyfriend—a mythical figure of perfect manhood Vicki invented on the spur of the moment to convince Howard she couldn't possibly be lured into doing anything with another man, no matter what. She didn't know if her story was going to make any difference.

In some ways Howard was like a teenager on his first date, searching for a topic of conversation that would find favour with his new girl. He spoke in whispers. Her answers were short and monosyllabic. Vicki didn't want to talk, but she was also afraid not to. At one point Howard mentioned a girl called Fiona. It gave Vicki a flicker of hope that he might have some moral obligations to another woman and that these might make her safer. Then Howard told her that Fiona "wouldn't fuck him" and Vicki's fear doubled. It was the way he said it. Suddenly it sounded more like he had bad sexual problems, and that was terrifying.

She just wanted to get out of the car and run away, and she constantly wondered what he would do if she asked to be let out to go to the bathroom. For the moment, she couldn't find the courage to try it. Making a bolt for safety was out of the question with the shotgun cradled ready on his lap. The canvas bag with its unsatisfactory takings from the garage cash register was beneath his legs. So she lay in the seat next to him and stared up at the car's roof lining while she answered his questions.

Howard's unwashed stench filled the car, making her feel ill. Finally, during one of the silences, she asked timidly, "Can I open the window a little? It's getting very stuffy in here and I feel a bit—a bit sick."

Out of the corner of her eye she saw his knuckles whiten on the shotgun. He took a moment to answer. "Only a bit," he said.

Vicki reached forward and wound the handle until a small gap appeared at the top of the glass. She didn't dare take it any further. It didn't help remove the sour odours and she longed to put her face to the gap and take deep, cleansing breaths, but she knew Howard would stop her rising from her prone position. It probably wouldn't have made her any more visible to anyone outside, because the windows were heavily misted with condensation caused by the two warm bodies inside the car on a cold night, but Howard wouldn't consider that.

Vicki closed her eyes and found herself trying to will the fresh air down towards her face. A wash of light swept over the car.

"Shit," Howard said, trying to shrink down further. "Close the window—and keep down."

"Who is it?" Vicki asked, torn between hope and fear of what Howard might do.

"How the hell would I know?" he hissed.

Vicki flinched at his tone.

The light lingered on the car. Howard tugged at Vicki's sleeve and put his finger to his lips. The childish gesture was made shocking by the fierce threat in his eyes. The two of them lay motionless and listened. There was the sound of a door slamming and footsteps crunching. The other car's motor was still running. A muttered curse came through the glass.

Howard breathed, "We must be in his parking space." His hand slid to the trigger of the shotgun. "I wonder how keen he is to get it back?"

Vicki was dreading the sudden blurred outline of someone trying to look inside the car. Should she scream? It might save someone's life.

Then she might lose her own.

The footsteps crunched some more. Vicki thought they were moving away and again experienced conflicting emotions—relief that there wasn't going to be a confrontation, mixed with despair at a lost opportunity. They heard a car door close and the vehicle parking somewhere else. The last sound was a curse thrown towards Vicki's car as the driver walked past on his way to his flat.

"Good choice," Howard said, running his hand meaningfully down the stock of his shotgun.

"How—how much longer are we going to stay here?"

"I don't know."

"Are you going to let me go?"

"I don't know."

"You don't need me anymore, do you?"

Howard's face was blank as he replied, "Need you for what?"

"For a hostage. That's what I am, aren't I?"

"I don't need any hostage to keep ahead of these bastards. I might use you for something else."

His calm words caused a sickening ball of ice in Vicki's stomach. She didn't want to ask him what he meant, being deadly afraid of the answer. She pulled her legs up underneath the steering wheel and onto the seat, curling herself into a ball and turning her back to Howard.

The constant fear was exhausting and after a long silence, incredibly, Vicki fell into a disturbed sleep. She moved and twitched, her mind teasing her with frightening images of Howard touching her, pressing against her, forcing himself on top of her. His eyes were always staring with that strange, blank expression which scared her more than any display of anger.

She had only been asleep for a few minutes when something warned her Howard's stare was real. Vicki jerked as she woke, desperately turning her head to see his over her shoulder.

He was looking at her with an intense, unmoving stare and one of his hands reached towards her.

"Don't move," he told her softly. He pushed his hand between her body and under her arm, searching for her breast. He felt around inexpertly until he finally cupped it. Howard's sour breath spilled over Vicki now. His finger and thumb pinched at her, trying to feel the nipple through the layers of her sweater, shirt and thin bra.

"Please don't," Vicki moaned, fighting back sobs.

"I can do what I want," he whispered, still pinching and squeezing. "You'd better do what I want, if you want to see your fancy boyfriend again."

She started to cry softly and tightened the curl of her body. With a snarl of annoyance he pulled his hand away.

"Have you got any tools?" he asked, so unexpectedly that Vicki didn't answer him. She hardly understood the question, her focus still on trying to deny him the vulnerable parts of her body. Now he used his fingers to prod her hard, making her gasp with pain. "I'm asking you something! Have you got any bloody tools in this heap of shit?"

She shook her head without looking at him. "I don't

know," she said miserably. "I wouldn't know how to use them, anyway."

He stared out the windscreen, breathing heavily. After a while he said, "I'm going to get out of the car and go around the back. These Japanese things have always got a kit in the back and I'm going to find it. Don't even think about trying to run away, hear me? I'll catch you, and you're not going to like what I'll do to you for trying to get away."

Vicki had her lips close to the fabric of the seat. "I won't try," she said into the material, which was damp with her tears.

He leaned across her and took the keys from the ignition, then reached above his head and found the internal light for the car, sliding the switch so it wouldn't come on. He opened the door slowly, ready to close it again if he'd turned the lightswitch the wrong way, but the car stayed dark and Howard was able to slip out unseen. Vicki listened to him fumbling the car keys in the lock, then heard the squeak of the boot being opened.

Howard could see faintly from the wash of some nearby security lights. They also revealed him, but he wasn't too worried, unless the flat dweller who'd recently arrived home decided to come out and challenge him. He was more concerned with someone spotting Vicki in the car. An attractive girl would look so out of place with someone like himself that suspicions were bound to be raised.

The first thing he did was drop the shotgun into the boot, concealing it. He inspected the inside of the cavity, running his hands around it, hoping to discover a plastic roll of tools. After a minute he'd had no success and was getting frustrated, when he spotted a small compartment set into the side. Opening this he found a pair of pliers, a reversable screwdriver and some spanners all neatly clipped to the compartment's cover. With a grunt of triumph he took the screwdriver.

He quickly removed the registration plates from the car,

and put them carefully into the boot so they didn't clang noisily together. He risked moving some distance away from Vicki as he scanned the plates of the other vehicles close by. He let out his breath with a hiss when he saw some interstate plates only two cars away. Their different colouring would be a bonus, helping to turn away searching eyes from Vicki's car. Keeping one eye on the Mazda and listening for the sound of Vicki's door opening, Howard removed these registration plates and reinstalled them on Vicki's car. Tossing the screwdriver into the boot, he retrieved the shotgun, closed the lid and got back into the passenger seat.

"Come on," he said, giving her a shove with his fist, then opening his fingers to reveal the car keys. "Get up. We're moving again."

Vicki ignored the keys as she painfully uncurled herself, twisting around under the steering wheel. Howard shook the keys angrily and she took them, careful to avoid touching his hand and grasping only the keys. In a numb daze she did as she was told automatically, her face blank. She started the car, turned the windscreen wipers on and waited while they wiped away the condensation on the outside of the glass. She switched the interior demister on full, the fan making a soft roar.

"For Christ's sake, get going," Howard snapped, craning his neck to watch the flats. It was possible the person who used the parking space might be foolish enough to come back out to air his grievance when he heard the motor start. People could be stupid like that, Howard knew. Things like allotted parking spaces could be the most important thing in the world to them. He wouldn't hesitate to gun the man down, but at the same time he wanted to avoid gunfire which would immediately bring a dragnet of police into the area.

Vicki put the car into reverse, checked the rear-view mirror and began winding her window down.

"What the fuck do you think you're doing?" he said,

gripping her upper arm and digging his fingers into the flesh. Vicki let out a small squeal and tried to jerk away.

"I can't see through the back window," she told him, startled out of her near-stupor.

"Don't try anything, I'm telling you."

"I'm not, honest."

"Then get us out of the car park. Head for the main roads."

This was easier said than done after Howard's haphazard escape route and the aimless searching for a block of flats with clear parking space. Vicki drove in one direction and tried not to backtrack in case it angered Howard. He didn't give any directions, but she could see him beginning to fidget impatiently with the shotgun by the time a major road sign directed them towards a freeway access ramp. Vicki allowed herself a moment to close her eyes with relief.

"Will this take us to Waterloo?" Howard asked, breaking the silence.

"It—it can," Vicki said, thinking furiously. "Not directly, though."

"That's where we're going. I want you to take us there."

On the move, Vicki temporarily felt a little safer. The drive towards Waterloo would take time, at least. Time that might let her think of a way out.

"I'm going to duck down again," Howard told her. "Don't forget I've still got the shotgun. If you do anything to attract any attention, like speeding or anything, the last thing I do before they catch us will be to kill you, understand? I've got nothing to lose. If they want to put me in jail, I don't give a shit if they put me in there for a hundred years. I'll escape or kill myself anyway. I don't care, OK?"

Vicki believed him. Despite her terror, in their conversations so far she had come to realise Howard was a dangerously simple human being, uneducated and naturally unintelligent. Vicki told herself to regard Howard as little more than a vicious animal. When she let her mind stray to her own chances of survival, the hopelessness of her situation struck her with a crippling despair. She had to force herself to concentrate on driving the Mazda.

"Tell me if any police cars come near," Howard said after a minute. His seat was back in the reclining position again, the shotgun pointed at her.

Vicki nodded. But as Howard couldn't see out of the car she wasn't going to warn him if a patrol car came close. In that moment she also decided there wasn't going to be another situation like the one at the garage. She would do anything—anything, as long as it meant she wouldn't be alone like this with her captor. If a police car stopped them and Howard fought back, she was going to struggle, no matter the result.

It was well after four o'clock in the morning by the time Vicki told him they'd arrived in Waterloo. When she told Howard where they were he edged himself further up in the seat and peered warily over the dashboard. He didn't say anything for some time, silently watching the lights of the buildings slide past, until he finally said, "Turn to the right somewhere around here. Make it soon," he added, warningly.

Vicki complied, turning into a side street. Immediately, he told her to park the car. She pulled up against the kerb, but left the engine running.

"Kill it," he said. "Leave the keys in the ignition and get out of the car. Don't think about running."

"Leave the keys?" she asked timidly. "Someone might steal it . . ." her voice trailed away as she thought Howard might consider she was insulting him, suggesting he lived in a bad part of town.

"That's the idea, you stupid bitch," he said flatly. "We've got to walk from here on."

He tucked the shotgun into the canvas bag in such a way that he could easily put his hand inside and fire the weapon. He made sure Vicki was aware of this, giving her

a meaningful look. Then he looked around them for anyone who might be a threat. There were no pedestrians in
sight. Traffic on the main road behind them was sporadic.
He motioned for Vicki to leave the car, and got out himself
at the same time, not dropping his guard for a moment. He
gestured for her to join him at the front of the vehicle.

"We're going to walk along here side by side," he told
her, nodding at the footpath. His breath clouded in the
cold, silhouetted against the glare of a distant streetlight.
"We're going to walk just normal-like, like we're together.
If we meet anyone on the way, keep your head down and
don't look at them. And if they get cocky and start talking,
leave it to me. Now, let's move." He put a hand on Vicki's
shoulder and gave her a push. She hurried to start walking,
using the haste to pull away from his touch. Several metres
down the footpath Vicki threw a glance over her shoulder
at her car.

"Forget it," Howard told her unkindly. "By dawn it will
be gone. You can get a new one on insurance," he added
with a bark of laughter.

Dawn might have already been close. Vicki couldn't tell
if the faint glow in the sky was a reflection of the city lights
or the sunrise beginning. Given a choice, she would never
have ventured into this part of the city on foot—especially
at this time. Vicki and Howard moved through the streets,
taking several turns which quickly disoriented her and left
the main road behind. She felt like every step was taking
her deeper into a foreign, dangerous land.

The high-rise buildings loomed out of the twilight. They
looked grey and prison-like. Howard steered Vicki towards
the closest one. They kept close to the walls, out of sight
from anybody who might be on the balconies and looking
down into the car park. No-one ran into them. The foyer
was bare concrete, the walls and floor heavily stained.
Graffiti covered everything, too. There was a smell of
garbage coming from close by. The place made Vicki cringe
with fear and disgust.

The lift was already on the ground floor. Despite the hour, Howard was relieved they hadn't met anybody. He didn't know if anyone would have challenged him, but they would certainly remember the strikingly attractive girl with him and the fact she appeared frightened by everything around her. He had no doubt Vicki's face would soon be in the papers and on television, probably with some sort of reward for any information about her whereabouts. They would remember her then—and who she was with.

His luck held. No-one was waiting for the lift on his eighth floor and nobody emerged from their doors as he pushed Vicki ahead of him towards his flat. He pulled a single key from the pocket of his jeans, reached past Vicki to unlock and open the door, then shoved her inside. She stumbled forward and stopped, afraid of tripping on something in the gloom. Behind her, Howard ran his hand over the wall until he found the lightswitch and turned it on.

Vicki was appalled at what the light revealed. The stench of rotting garbage in one corner made her almost gag.

"Sit on the beanbag," he told her, putting the canvas bag on the small table. Vicki lowered herself into it. The beanbag lacked beans and the vinyl pushed up around her shoulders bringing with it a waft of dried sweat. She put a hand over her mouth as casually as she could and breathed through it, trying to filter the smells.

Howard took the shotgun from the bag and placed it deliberately on the table in front of him. He began pulling the money out in untidy bundles and dropping it on the table, scratching around the bottom of the bag for the coins and using them to weigh down the notes. Satisfied he had got it all out of the bag, he began to painstakingly count the money. He was slow. Vicki watched his lips silently mouthing figures as he separated everything into different piles. The higher the piles got, the more the frown on Howard's face deepened. When everything was sorted he wiped a hand over his face, sighed in exasperation and started counting again. Vicki stayed silent. Then Howard tried a third time.

Suddenly he turned to her. "Why the fuck am I bothering?" he said, startling her. "You know how much is here, don't you?"

"No—no, not exactly," she stammered. No matter what he said, he frightened her.

He stood, picked up the shotgun and gestured for her to take his place on the seat. "You count it," he said. "Tell me exactly how much is there. Don't try to trick me, either. I've already counted it myself, remember."

Vicki struggled out of the beanbag and took a seat at the table. Howard had sorted out the different denominations of notes and coins, so it only took her a minute to check each pile and calculate the total.

"Four hundred and thirty-two dollars, fifty cents," she told him.

Howard couldn't believe she had counted it so quickly. "Check it again," he said, narrowing his eyes suspiciously.

She did, doing it even faster this time. "It's the same," she said.

He stared at her, anger flickering through his eyes. "You're a smart bitch, aren't you?"

A voice inside her head screamed at her to be very careful. She forced herself to look at him calmly. "No, it's just that I count money all day."

"That's how much I counted, too. I'm not fucking stupid, you know."

"I know. It's always a good idea to have someone check for you, though."

"Do you think I'm stupid?" The shotgun lifted slightly.

Vicki tried hard not to look at it, or his finger on the trigger. "Why should I?" she said quickly. "I don't know you. I don't even know your name."

This bewildered him slightly. "It's Howard," he said eventually, then added sternly, "Just Howard. That's all you need to know."

"Howard," she repeated. "I haven't met a Howard before."

There was a taut silence. Through her fear Vicki was managing to keep a thread of common sense connected to her instincts for survival. Each time she adapted to her new situation, like getting taken hostage, then the long wait in the car and now being in this disgusting flat, Vicki told herself to get *thinking*. As much as she wanted to simply succumb to her fear and curl up into a terrified ball on the floor, shutting everything out, she knew that wasn't going to get her home alive. Escaping on her own seemed impossible right now, but she had to believe there was a chance. And to have that chance, Vicki needed to stay alive and mobile.

She knew it was vital Howard come to like her. The thought made her cringe—his very appearance scared Vicki and his unwashed smell made her feel sick. She remembered his hand groping awkwardly at her breast and suppressed a shudder. He was looking at her strangely now, confused by her comment about his name and what it represented—a small, but willing, invitation to start a conversation.

"I don't like my name," he said. "It's not normal, like everyone else's."

"Yes, it is. Lots of people are called Howard." Vicki winced at her own contradiction, adding quickly, "I just haven't met any before, that's all."

Suspicion was back in his eyes again. "So, what's your name?"

"Vicki, Vicki Colonel."

"Vicki," he nodded, openly looking her up and down. "You look like a Vicki, with all your blonde hair and good looks and everything."

There was another silence. A fresh, choking fear had come with his lustful appraisal of her body. Making her terror worse, Vicki recognised the sexual craving in Howard didn't stem from any experience of making love with women. Right now he wouldn't be imagining taking her clothes off and taking her into his bed for normal sex. She believed Howard could just snap and try to take her like an animal, ripping her clothing and raping her at any moment.

She broke the silence, desperate to change the subject. "Can I have a drink of water?"

Howard nodded and stepped back and watched as Vicki stood and went to the sink. Strewn across the benchtop was a collection of plates, cups, knives and forks. All were caked with food scraps or drink. One of the cups was half-filled with a scum of greenish stuff, making Vicki's stomach turn when she saw it. She twisted the tap and let the cold water run for a few seconds, then cupped her hand under the flow and drank straight from the tap.

"I'm going to have to tie you up," Howard told her as she came away from the sink, wiping her mouth on her shirt sleeve. She froze in mid-action and stared fearfully at him. "I'm going out and I can't lock you in here."

Vicki couldn't stop herself. "Can't you just let me go? You're home safe now. You don't need me."

"How the hell could you know why I need you?" he asked coldly.

"I—I just thought . . ." She steeled herself and asked, "You're not going to hurt me, are you? Like you told that guard, about cutting my . . ." She couldn't finish.

But Howard was already ignoring her, rummaging inside the canvas bag. He produced a roll of wide black tape. "Go into the bedroom. I'll use this."

Vicki's knees weakened. "I need to use the toilet," she said desperately.

Howard jerked his head at another door. "OK, go in there first."

The toilet was in the same filthy condition as the rest of the flat. A magazine with torn pages was obviously the paper she was supposed to use. Vicki closed the door, grateful for the small barrier it provided, pulled down her jeans and panties, and squatted over the bowl. She stared at the door as she did, expecting Howard to burst it open so he could see her undressed. The fear of this made it hard for her to start urinating. When she finally did, Vicki felt such a feeling of release that tears came to her eyes. It was as if her whole body had been tense for so long that to allow one part of it to relax triggered a chain reaction that would send her into a collapse, sobbing to the floor. She fought back the tears. An idea came to her out of nowhere to stay locked in the toilet, where Howard couldn't get her. But there was no lock and he would have probably broken down the door anyway. He would be angry too, and Vicki didn't want that. Reluctantly she finished, dressed herself, and flushed the toilet. Howard was waiting expectantly outside.

"In here," he said, gesturing to the bedroom.

At least there were no food scraps in here, but the room still stank of dirty bed linen, soiled clothes and other odours Vicki didn't recognise. The large blood stain next to the bed, where Howard had hacked off Decker's fingers, had, luckily for Vicki's peace of mind, darkened to an un-recognisable colour. There was another strange, musty smell closer to the bed, too, where Howard had mastur-bated onto the sheets several times. It was on these he or-dered Vicki to lie now, on her side and facing the wall with her hands behind her back. She did as she was told, the foulness of the linen filling her senses.

There was a ripping sound as Howard unravelled the tape. First he wound it tight around her ankles, the tape sticking to the denim of her jeans. Then he did her wrists, the adhesive pulling at the fine hairs on her forearms. She felt her head lift as Howard tied a filthy singlet over her mouth for a gag. The material forced itself between her teeth and pressed against her tongue. It tasted disgusting and Vicki nearly vomited.

Howard stepped back and examined his work. Satisfied, he said, "I'm going out, now. Don't try anything. No-one will hear you, anyway. Not that anyone in this building will give a shit, anyway."

Vicki didn't move, but lay there willing him to go away, her back still to Howard. She jumped when he touched her again. This time, without warning, he pushed his hand down the front of her shirt and forced his fingers under her bra until he was touching her nipple. Vicki tried to scream, the sound muffled by the gag, and began twisting violently against her bonds as she attempted to roll on her stomach to protect herself.

Howard pulled his hand away. It took a moment for Vicki to realise he had stopped trying to touch her. Oddly, he whispered, "I'm not fucking stupid, you know." Then turned and walked from the room, slamming the door behind him.

Vicki lay frozen, terrified by what had happened. When she heard the front door closing, only then did she allow herself, one unwilling muscle after another, to unwind.

She closed her eyes and began to pray, something she wasn't used to doing, and the words in her head sounded jumbled and meaningless. She doubted any God would answer them. And she let her tears flow now, rolling down her face to soak the sheets, mingling with Howard's sweat and semen—and Decker's dried blood.

Chapter Sixteen

Maiden arrived at the restaurant first. There was only one other couple in the room and he felt self-conscious sitting by himself, an opened bottle of red wine in front of him. Letting the wine breathe, he began examining the menu, but couldn't concentrate. His eyes kept wandering to the door, waiting for Janet Brown to come through it.

Fifteen minutes later she did, walking cautiously in and scanning the restaurant for him. She caught his eye and smiled, waving to an approaching waiter that she knew where to sit.

"Sorry I'm late," she said, a little breathless. "I'll give you one guess what held me up."

"A flat tyre?" Maiden asked, innocently.

"Nothing so simple." She fumbled in her handbag. "I really should start preparing to leave work about two hours before I actually need to go. That way I might have a chance of getting out on time!" Now she looked around. "Can we smoke in here?"

Maiden hadn't been comfortable about lighting a ciga-rette, but now he looked around, too. There were no forbidding signs. He spotted an ashtray on a nearby table and retrieved it.

"Want one of these?" she offered her pack. Maiden took one.

He was nervous about this dinner and what, exactly, it might turn into. Brown seemed completely relaxed and far from her stiff, professional persona.

"I'm glad you brought the wine," she said, nodding at the bottle. "I was going to buy some, but I figured that would add another minute or so to my being late, and I was sure you wouldn't miss out such an important detail," she finished with a smile.

"Of course not. First thing I thought of." Maiden filled two glasses and lifted his in a toast, but he was at a loss what to propose.

"Here's to time off work," he managed awkwardly. "We should have more of it."

"I agree." Brown touched her glass to his. "Mind you, if you're like me, you've only got yourself to blame for not having the wit to say 'enough is enough' and get out of the place at a decent hour."

Maiden nodded. "To be honest, we have got a man-power problem. That's the reason I'm still doing my investigation with only Martin to help me. Otherwise, we'd probably have a big taskforce to deal with it."

"Surely you've got more than one person to help you by now?"

"Oh, I must have had thirty guys out there canvassing the clubs and bars the other night, but they weren't permanently attached to my investigation and somebody would have been counting every minute they were out, ready to snatch them back the moment they decided I was wasting time."

"Did the canvassing do any good?"

"Yes, as a matter of fact. Normally we *do* end up wasting a lot of hours, but this time we came up with something worthwhile. It was about Howlett." Maiden paused and saw Brown nod, acknowledging she knew which victim he was talking about. "It seems he was diddling his company with an overtime scam. Nothing huge—he was keeping himself on the books when he was actually in a bar down the street playing the poker machines. Not a big deal really, but it helped answer a few of our questions."

"It must be fascinating, piecing together a criminal investigation like this," she said.

"Bloody frustrating, normally. Your department is probably the best shot we get at working out the details."

Brown let out a rueful laugh. "My department is often too tied up providing evidence for cases that are already solved. Like trying to identify blood and hair samples to convict killers who are already pleading guilty and looking to deal with the prosecution for a lesser charge. It's crazy, when investigations like your own get lost in the mess."

Maiden smiled. "No-one ever tries to tell us the system runs smoothly."

They began studying the menu. There was the usual choice of vindaloos and curries. Maiden didn't think it would make much difference what he ordered—it would all taste the same—but he didn't say so. Coming here had been his idea, after all. A minute later the waiter returned to take their orders. They both decided on soup, a main dish and a bowl of boiled rice to share between them. The waiter drifted away again.

"How about this abduction thing?" she asked quietly. During the day it had gained momentum in the press. Vicki Colonel and her captor had become the subjects of a "massive" police search, according to the media. What the police had so far managed to conceal was that the entire city was under scrutiny, because they had absolutely no idea where to search. They didn't have the identity of the gunman, either.

"Nothing to do with me," Maiden said. "That press conference this morning was just bullshit by my boss, Longman. He'll do anything to discredit me at the moment. It should have been handled by someone from the Penrith CIB. It was on their turf."

"But didn't the guy say he would cut the girl up, like he did the others?"

"Sure, but I figure it was just a threat he pulled out of his hat. He reads the newspapers, that's all. Most people agree with me, now they've been given a few hours to think about it. The sort of person I'm looking for has to be too clever to stuff around with armed hold-ups that go wrong." Maiden took a sip of his wine and decided he had time for another cigarette. He held the packet towards Brown. "I should be grateful. This guy's taking the heat off me for a while. Nobody cares about mutilated body parts being left behind in lifts, while there's a pretty young girl being held hostage by a vicious gunman." Maiden imitated the dramatic tones of a television newsreporter.

However, Brown didn't smile. "I suppose so," she said, watching a tendril of smoke curl away from the tip of her cigarette. She frowned, "But somebody has been abducted in your case, too. In fact, we know they've been killed, for God's sake. At least that girl is probably still alive. Yours is a murder case."

"It's still old news already," Maiden said. "Unless we get some sort of a breakthrough, my investigation will slip backwards through the newspapers every day, until by the end of the week it will hardly rate a paragraph or maybe ten seconds on the television. That's the way it works. This abduction, if it isn't resolved, will keep the press howling for days."

"It sounds like you've been through it all before."

"I haven't been in front of the cameras like this before, but I've been a part of it many times." Maiden suddenly shrugged it off. "What should I care? It's only when the newspapers start interfering with an investigation that we have a problem. That's not happening at the moment."

"What is happening? Are you getting close to making an arrest?"

Maiden laughed humourlessly. "Are you kidding? I can tell you I haven't got a bloody clue who's doing these things. Don't let that get around, though," he added, only half joking. It wasn't quite true. Maiden still had his theory that a woman, or someone who looked like a woman, was involved in trapping the victims. He didn't mention it, because Brown was the examining forensic expert in the investigations and Maiden would have preferred she find her own evidence of a female presence, without his suggesting she look for it.

"And is Longman going to succeed in getting you off the case? I mean, can he use your lack of success so far to get you kicked off?"

Maiden shook his head. "I very much doubt it." He quickly explained Bercoutte's support.

Then he decided it was time for a change of subject. He always talked about work, because he rarely mixed socially with anyone except police. Brown was an opportunity to discuss something different. "So, how's the new house coming along?"

She took his cue. "Oh, I'm slowly turning it into a home. It takes time."

They talked for a while about houses they had each lived in before. The conversation inevitably turned to past relationships. Maiden didn't mind. He wasn't embarrassed about being divorced twice. Philosophically, he would admit marriage seemed to be a part of life he just couldn't get right. This was something he told Brown, who understood. Whenever she mentioned her dead husband, David, she spoke in hushed, saddened tones. Maiden resisted the urge to feel sorry for her. He knew she wouldn't like that.

The food arrived and it was good. Again, there were moments that struck Maiden as intimate, such as sharing the bowl of rice and making sure he refilled her wine glass before the waiter got there first. He believed Brown, too, was feeling a building of sexual tension, but neither of them quite knew what to do about it. A dessert followed—a simple ice cream with topping. Maiden didn't really want it, but it provided an excuse for them to stay at the table. Next he took a gamble and, despite the restaurant being unlicensed, asked the waiter if there was a bottle of red wine that a previous customer may have left behind. The waiter nodded knowingly and produced a passable Hermitage. Brown watched it all with undisguised amusement.

"What a carry-on," she said, after the waiter was gone.

"These things have to be done properly," Maiden said, feigning seriousness.

"And how are we both supposed to drive home, since we'll have drunk two bottles of red wine between us?"

"Personally, if I feel too drunk to drive, I'll take a taxi and walk back here in the morning to get my car. It'll do me good. It's not far anyway."

"And am I expected to do the same?"

"If you decide to drive home, I promise I'll close my policeman's eyes until you've gone around the corner."

Brown laughed and held her glass towards him. "I won't break any laws, just in case I can't trust you."

During their meal the restaurant had filled with people, but they had been slowly drifting away, leaving Maiden and Brown once again with only one other couple occupying a table. After a while the waiter dropped an account on their table. Other restaurant staff began to meaningfully clean up around them, but Maiden steadfastly ignored it all until the second bottle of wine was empty. Brown tapped the label of the bottle with her fingernail.

"We've run out of excuses not to go home," she said.

"I guess so," he agreed with a wry look.

"Can we share a taxi?"

He thought about it. "Sure. We're going in the same direction and my place is not long after yours. It's certainly not worth two taxis."

They split the bill in half and left the money on the table. At the reception area Maiden asked someone to call a taxi.

"Do you want to wait outside?" Brown asked him. "I wouldn't mind the fresh air."

"OK. I'll pollute your fresh air with another cigarette."

The cool night air was like a slap in the face for the both of them, flushed from the hot Indian food and red wine. Standing on the footpath Maiden thrust his hands deep into his jacket pockets. Brown did the same. For a moment neither said anything, and watched the traffic go past.

"Are you going to have that cigarette?" she asked quietly.

He nodded and pulled them from his pocket. "Do you want one?"

"Yes, please. That's enough fresh air."

When Maiden held his lighter to the tip of her cigarette he found himself being subjected, for the first time that night, to one of her unwavering, no-nonsense stares. Surprisingly, it unsettled him.

"Anything wrong?" he asked, before he could stop himself.

She hesitated only momentarily, before answering boldly, "Do you want to come home with me tonight?"

Maiden was totally taken aback. "I—I'm not really built to sleep on couches," he said, indicating his big frame.

"You know I'm not inviting you to sleep on the couch," she replied mildly. "I'll be honest with you. I haven't had a man in my bed for a long time. Not since my husband died. It's been too long, really." She reached forward and touched his arm. "I like you, John. And I feel you and I could probably spend a night together and not do too much damage, if you know what I mean. I hope you're not offended by the idea, and I'm sorry if I'm not being particularly romantic or anything."

Maiden was struggling for the right words. He was attracted to her, but that was exactly what Brown was saying she didn't want. As far as he could understand, she merely wanted a night of uncomplicated sex.

Stalling, he said, "We've drunk a couple of bottles of

wine, remember. Are you sure you know what you're saying?"

"Are you saying no?"

"No—not at all. I just don't want you doing something you'll regret in the morning." Inwardly, he winced at the tired cliché. Over her shoulder he saw a taxi turning into the narrow car park.

"I know exactly what I'm doing," she said firmly. "Which is why I asked you not to read too much into it. We're two mature, consenting adults who seem to get on well together." Her manner softened and she moved closer to him, ignoring the noise of the taxi pulling up beside them. "I just want to spend a night with someone I like—and someone I think I can trust not to get out of control."

"We hardly know each other," he reminded her with a wry grin.

"But we'll have fun getting more acquainted," she returned his smile.

This was a totally different woman than the one he had first met in her office little more than a week before. But Maiden wasn't complaining. He hesitated only a moment longer, hoping to score a few points of dignity back for the male species, before he made a grand gesture towards the rear of the taxi.

"You have a deal," he said, sounding more in control than he really was.

In the back of the taxi Brown sat leaning against him without actually snuggling close. They stayed quiet during the ride. Maiden's nerves were jumping with anticipation and he tried hard not to show it. While he watched the streetlights slide past the window a thought intruded into his mind.

Here I am going to spend the night with a beautiful woman, while somewhere else in this same city a terrified teenage girl is being held captive, maybe even raped, by an armed gunman. She may even be dead—or worse, better off dead.

Rather than feel any guilt grow, Maiden had to fight off a

flare of anger. It wasn't fair that his work should invade his every private moment, too. He devoted too much of his life to his job already. No-one could ever accuse him of not doing his share and more, so he was entitled to make to-night his night. There was nothing he could do to help Vicki Colonel right now, anyway. It wasn't even really his investigation.

Brown spoke quietly to the taxi driver, breaking Maiden out of his thoughts. "It's the next house on the left." The driver flicked a glance at her in the mirror. Brown put her lips close to Maiden's cheek and whispered, "I'm getting a little low on cash. Have you got enough to cover this fare?"

"No problem," he said, rising awkwardly from the seat to get his wallet from a back pocket. The taxi pulled to a halt as he got it free.

Complaining about the cold, Brown scurried out of the taxi to her front door, at the same time digging keys from her handbag. The door opened easily and, leading the way inside, she asked Maiden over her shoulder, "Want a hot drink?"

"It might help to warm up a bit," he said, a shiver in his voice.

"Good idea. Do you want to go in the lounge and turn on the heater? I'll make us a couple of hot chocolates."

Maiden offered to help half-heartedly, but she said no and pushed him gently towards the lounge. He turned on the main lights, but used them only long enough to locate the switch for the table lamp. He flicked on the electric heater and waited for the first glow of red to make sure it was working, then took his jacket off and sat in a single lounge chair. After a moment he kicked his shoes off and stretched his legs towards the heater, grateful for the warmth on his feet. He could hear Brown rattling crockery in the kitchen and he smiled to himself self-consciously. Looking around, he saw Brown apparently wasn't too concerned with personal touches. There were no pictures of her family, her deceased husband or anyone close. He no-

ticed something framed, but it was leaning on the wall in
the shadow of the fireplace with its backing towards him.
Without thinking he reached out and tipped it backwards
so he could see the picture. Instead, he saw it was a docu-
ment composed of old-fashioned, florid writing. It took
him a moment to understand it was something to do with
Brown's doctorate, but it was made out to what he guessed
was her maiden name—Janet Susan Feitler.

"Snooping around?" Brown asked him, coming into the
room with a mug of hot chocolate in each hand.

"Sorry," he said, putting the certificate gently back
against the wall. "I didn't realise it was something personal.
I thought it was painting of some sort and I was checking
out your taste. I wouldn't have looked, if I'd known."

She hesitated a fraction before handing Maiden his
drink and then curling up on the lounge opposite. "It's not
a big deal. It's not even official, just a decorative copy of
the real thing that took my fancy at the time. Funny, but I
don't like it anymore. I wouldn't dare hang it in my office."

"Feitler—your maiden name? Were your parents Ger-
man or something?"

Brown shook her head. "Swedish. They came to Australia because they believed Hitler would eventually take
all of Europe and they didn't want to leave their escape until too late. In the end they were wrong, of course, but they
didn't go back."

"They must have been difficult times," Maiden murmured, sipping his chocolate.

"Yes, I suppose so. Are you OK?"

"OK?"

"You look uncomfortable."

Maiden decided to be honest. "No, I'm just not used to
doing things this way."

"Have you changed your mind?" she asked gently.

"No, not at all. It feels funny not to be—" His voice
trailed off, uncertain.

"Playing the games?"

"That's a good way to describe it. It feels funny not to be going through all the motions and playing the games."

"We shouldn't have to at this point in our lives, don't you think?"

Maiden agreed with a small incline of his head. "I said it felt funny. I didn't say I don't like it."

Brown deliberately changed the subject, asking what he thought of the restaurant meal. They talked about this and other trivial things for about ten minutes, then Brown put her empty cup on the floor.

"Ready for bed?"

Maiden did the same. "Sure."

"Don't worry about the cups. I'll get them in the morning." She rose and went to the heater, flicking it off, then turned off the lamp, too. In the darkness Maiden saw her extending a hand towards him and he took it. "Come on," she said.

Brown led him across the hallway into her bedroom. She didn't turn the light on, but streetlight coming through parted curtains filled the room with a silvery glow. The place smelled of womanly things, like perfume and make-up. The double bed had a thick, lacey eiderdown and a mound of pillows. Brown turned to Maiden and pulled him close a moment, kissing him on the lips too suddenly for him to have a chance to respond properly.

"I'm going to the bathroom," she said. "Why don't you get undressed and warm the bed? It's less romantic, but more practical," she added with a low chuckle. She slipped away before he answered.

Alone, Maiden stripped naked. He draped his clothes over a chair, aware he might have to wear them again the next day. The sheets were cool as he crawled between them. The mattress was alarmingly soft and sank under his weight. He lay on his back and stared at the ceiling, listening for sounds of Brown returning. It wasn't long before he heard a toilet flush and her feet padding softly along the hallway into the bedroom. Propped by the pillows, he watched her come in.

She wore a towelling robe. As she came close to the bed Brown let it fall carelessly to the floor, the faint light revealing her body. Her breasts were firm with dark nipples jutting forward. A narrow waist curved out to full hips and muscled, shapely thighs. Maiden couldn't stop himself staring hungrily at the triangle of dark hair between her legs. Brown hurriedly got into bed, shivering with the cold and immediately pressed herself on top of him, rubbing her groin against his erection, which had grown in anticipation. She began kissing his face and lips, and nipped gently at his neck while she curled her fingers into the hair on his chest and tugged at it. Maiden ran his hands up and down her back, reaching further to cup her buttocks and sometimes spread them, probing with his fingers and making her groan softly. She opened her legs further, inviting him to do it more.

He held her in place and slid down the bed underneath her, kissing her breasts, moving down her stomach and further. Brown found herself suspended above him, feeling the heat of his excited breathing on the insides of her thighs. On an impulse she whispered, "Wait," and throwing the covers aside quickly turned around so she could lower her mouth to him at the same time. They stayed like this for a long time, keeping each other at a peak of arousal, until Brown suddenly needed to have him inside her. She changed positions again, straddling him and slowly coming down on top of him. She moaned and whispered meaningless things, lost in her pleasure, and when she had him all the way in she began to rock back and forth, slowly at first, but with increasing fervour.

Maiden was trying to control himself, but was losing the fight. "I won't last long like this," he told her breathlessly.

"It doesn't matter," she replied quickly, gasping in time to her rocking.

Moments later, and too soon for his liking, Maiden orgasmed. Instead of disappointing her, feeling him burst inside her took Brown further and she briefly, but mercilessly, rode him hard, coming to a climax herself. For long seconds she was locked into a posture of ecstasy, then she collapsed forward and lay her head on his chest. Maiden wrapped his arms around her tightly, feeling the warmth of her flesh. It was Brown who eventually spoke first.

"I think I needed that," she said quietly and wonderingly.

They silently stroked each other for a while, then started to make love again. This time they took it slowly and afterwards Maiden felt completely exhausted, but sexually satiated. But when he lay next to Brown in what he thought was a comfortable silence he sensed tension in her.

"Hey, are you all right?" he whispered.

"I'm fine." She didn't sound it.

"Do you want me to leave now?"

"No, of course not. Don't be silly."

Maiden was puzzled and not thinking clearly. Against his better judgement he persisted, "I see there's a spare room here. Have you got a bed in it? I could sleep the rest of the night there, if you like." As he said it, Maiden knew he would rather catch a cab home.

Brown took a long time to answer. "That's my son Jeremy's room."

Maiden stiffened before he realised whoever she was talking about couldn't be in there now. "Your son?" he asked carefully. He did some rapid calculations. Going by what he knew or heard about Janet Brown and her marriage, any children couldn't be in their teenage years yet. Where was her son now?

"Don't worry, he's not here."

"I wasn't thinking that," he said hurriedly. "But where is he?"

"In hospital—he lives in a hospital. A special one, as

they say," she added with bitterness, guessing his next question. "I can't afford the treatment or the specialist doctors without earning a salary, so I can't afford the time to keep him at home either. Not on my own, without David . . ." her voice drifted away for a moment. "He comes home here most weekends." She hesitated again and her manner softened. "Look, it's my problem and nothing you should be concerned about. But I would feel very bad, if someone—a complete stranger—were to sleep in there. Especially after this—us. It would be like betraying him, and David, too."

"It's OK," Maiden stroked her hair. "I understand."

But she went on hurriedly, "And that's why I'm a bit funny now. It's guilt, I guess. I don't want you to go home, even if you feel a bit uncomfortable. It's a bridge I have to cross and you're helping me cross it."

In answer, Maiden kissed the top of her head. He waited a few minutes, looking up at the dim ceiling, then although he was loath to break the mood he said, "We're both falling asleep and we need to set an alarm clock. Have you got one?"

He was pleased to hear her quietly chuckle and reply, "A very loud one with a bell, which is why it's under the bed. It's not so painful that way. Is six o'clock all right?"

He feigned grumpiness. "It'll kill me, but it's not like we have a choice, is it?"

Maiden awoke thirsty from the red wine. It was still half-dark and he figured it must be close to five o'clock in the morning. He looked at Brown, who lay over one of his arms. He had no choice but to disturb her as he extricated himself.

"What's up?" she asked, sleepily.

"I'm just going to get a drink from the kitchen."

"Water in the fridge," she muttered, falling back to sleep immediately.

Maiden walked naked through the house, the early

morning chill bringing goosebumps up all over him. The cold water in the fridge was in a plastic jug and, after making sure Brown hadn't woken and followed him, he quickly drank straight from this. The cold getting to him, he was going to go right back to the bed, but he saw her telephone on the wall and a guilty impulse made him go over and pick up the receiver. He punched in his own number and waited impatiently, dancing about to beat the chill, until his answering machine clicked in. Once the recorded message finished Maiden quickly dialled another four digits, commanding the machine to replay any messages he had received. There was only one, but at the first sound of Martin Creane's voice he was instantly wide awake.

At first Creane had expected Maiden was at home with the answering machine on. He had called, "John! John? Answer the bloody phone. It's me, Martin." After a brief exasperated silence the recorded voice went on, "OK, so you're not at home. As soon as you are, contact me through Despatch, understand? We've found Howlett's Commodore, and guess what's in the boot?" As an afterthought he added, "Ah, it's four-thirty in the morning—so where the hell are you?"

"Damn," Maiden muttered, thumbing down the cradle button to break the connection. He put a call through to Despatch and after quietly speaking to the officer on duty he dropped the receiver down gently. He quickly went back into the bedroom, shook Brown awake and explained what had happened. She sat up in bed sleepily and pulled the covers up to her neck.

"So, what are you going to do?" she asked, yawning.

"I'll get a taxi back to the car."

"Do you want a cup of coffee or something?"

"No, you stay in bed. I'll just slip outside."

"OK," she agreed without any regret, snuggling down again. She lay so she could watch him get dressed, but was quickly asleep once again.

Maiden pulled his clothes on hurriedly, made sure he had everything and got his shoes from the loungeroom. Next he called a cab and slipped back into the bedroom on his way to the front door. He kissed Brown on the only part he could see above the eiderdown—her forehead. "I'll call you later," he said. She didn't answer.

He let himself out of the house quietly and stood in the cold, his first cigarette between his lips, and his hands in his pockets. After a few minutes the taxi hadn't arrived and Maiden was regretting not having made a coffee to drink while he waited out there. Then the taxi arrived and Maiden gratefully got into its warmth. As it pulled away from the kerb he watched Janet Brown's house disappear.

This wasn't exactly the "morning after" he had been hoping for.

Chapter Seventeen

Howard had wanted a drink, and he knew where to get one. There were two hotels in his part of town which opened at six o'clock in the morning to cater for shift workers. And he had a pocketful of money.

He'd had half an hour to brood on the front step of the bar, before opening time. He thought about Vicki Colonel. His hostage both excited and worried him. To have someone like her he could touch, feel—do what he liked with—gave him such a sense of power. He was going to have sex with her, and soon. Howard had only denied himself so far because he wanted to make sure everything was right. He wanted it to happen on his bed, like so many of his fantasies, and where it would perversely taunt Decker's ghost. Howard needed to feel safe too, which was why he took Vicki home and didn't try to rape her in the car. And he needed some liquor in him, so he wouldn't disgrace himself. Even though she was his captive and Howard knew—but wasn't yet ready to consider—he would probably have to kill Vicki when he was finished with her, he still wanted to display his sexual prowess. He wanted her to respect

him. He didn't want to orgasm too quickly. He believed alcohol would help him there.

His worry came from the stress of keeping her in the
flat. Despite all his precautions, there was always a risk
that she might escape. The police would already be searching for her—and him—with a greater effort than they
would devote to an armed robber, at least. And at home he
would have to constantly watch her, or keep her bound up,
in case she managed to attack him.

Howard was slowly coming to the conclusion that he
would have his fun with Vicki Colonel, then get rid of her.
As he sat on the front step of the hotel he calmly considered exactly what he might do with her body, or parts of it.

A newsagency delivery van halted briefly in front of him
and the driver, after giving Howard a suspicious look,
dumped a bundle of newspapers on the pavement. When
the van had driven away, Howard immediately examined
them all eagerly. He swelled with pride when he saw each
edition featured his armed hold-up and abduction on the
front page. One of them showed a large photograph of the
garage itself with police barricades and tape crisscrossing
the scene. Howard was reading the article, struggling
through the words and mouthing them as he read, when
the hotel door behind him abruptly opened.

An hour later Howard was quite drunk. Three other
people had been in the bar, all of them in soiled overalls
and familiar with each other. None of them bothered to
speak to Howard, who sat on his own and stared into his
drinks. He looked sullen and unapproachable, but inside
Howard was very satisfied with himself. An early morning
talk show muttered from a television in one corner. Someone on the screen said "Vicki Colonel" and Howard twisted
around to see John Maiden addressing the press conference. As Maiden went through the details and answered
questions Howard studied him. By the time the brief news
coverage ended Howard decided the big detective wasn't
someone he would give a moment's chance, if they met.

He would shoot him on the spot. A picture of Vicki came on and one of the overalled men grunted his appreciation, giving Howard a further surge of satisfaction.

He figured it was time he went home. Howard had felt like telling these men the beautiful girl on the television was waiting for him, but he stopped himself, knowing it was the one pleasure he would have to forgo. Anything else was his to do—and take. Especially Vicki Colonel.

He gave the barman twenty dollars for a six-pack of beers and told him to keep the change. Howard was feeling good. Things were going his way again.

He had found her exactly as he'd left her, lying on her side and facing the wall.

"I'm famous," he announced to her back, slurring his words a little.

Vicki's fear doubled when she heard his drunkenness. She closed her eyes, squeezing tears onto her cheeks.

"You're famous, too," he said, waving one of the beers expansively in the air. "But it's not your fault, so it doesn't count." When Vicki failed to respond he leaned forward and pulled her onto her back, where she lay awkwardly with her hands bound behind her. He stared down and a leering smile crossed his face. "Some guys at the bar reckon you're a little beauty queen. I'll bet they'd like to see what I'm going to see."

Swaying, he raised the beer to his lips and tipped his head back, emptying the bottle. Vicki watched in terror as his Adam's apple bobbed obscenely. She knew each time he swallowed brought her rape a moment closer. Howard finished the beer and deliberately dropped it on the floor.

"Don't fight me," he told her in a husky voice. "If you fight me and make it hard for me, I'll hurt you, understand?" Vicki could only look at him with wide frightened eyes.

Howard reached down to her and wrenched open the top button of her jeans, separating the zip as well and exposing the top of her panties. Vicki tried to scream through the gag and roll away from him. A stinging slap came to the side of her face, which made her head ring. She stopped struggling and froze.

"Don't fight me," he repeated in a hiss, putting his face close to hers, his foul breath washing over her.

He went back to her jeans, tugging them down to her taped ankles and dragging her panties halfway. Next he pulled these down all the way, tearing the thin fabric. Vicki clamped her legs together, but he stood for a moment and stared open-mouthed at the pubic hair visible at the top of her thighs. Then Howard moved again suddenly, making her flinch. He pushed and ripped upwards at her sweater and shirt, then her bra, until all three were bundled underneath her arms and around her neck, exposing her breasts. Vicki was naked except for the clothing bunched around her upper body and ankles. She was sobbing and finding it hard to breathe. Her eyes were closed again and she was praying.

"Open your legs," he told her, his breath coming in harsh gasps of excitement. Vicki didn't move. Another slap, harder this time, and delivered to her thigh made her scream again into the gag. When he put a hand to her knee and pulled her legs apart, she let him.

He stood back from the bed and began undoing his jeans, his shaking hands fumbling with his belt buckle. Unconsciously, Vicki closed her legs again, but Howard was too busy undressing. He fought with his jeans for a full minute, snarling at the delay as he tried first to pull them over his boots, then having to sit on the floor and reverse half his efforts and remove his footwear, before finally getting the jeans off. He wore no underpants. Howard came back to the bed. Something whispered in his mind and he took his singlet off, too—he'd remembered that's how lovers made love. Naked. He didn't give Vicki a warning this time, and slapped her thigh again.

"Spread your damned legs."

She did as she was told, but Howard was disturbed that her ankles were still bound together. He began hauling at her jeans to remove them, ripping the tape before he could free her legs and pull the jeans completely off. He deliberately grasped each of Vicki's ankles and spread them to both edges of the bed. Then he knelt between her legs. Vicki took one look at him, before turning her face away in horror. His erect penis was just as soiled as the rest of him. A sour stench came from his groin. A blankness of shock threatened to take over her mind. Only the adrenalin of fear stopped it. Vicki fixed her eyes on a speck on the wall in front of her face and waited for Howard's weight to come down on her.

After too many long seconds, it hadn't happened.

"What the fuck is *this*?" she heard Howard snarl incredulously.

Without taking her eyes away from the wall Vicki forced herself to listen. Something was wrong.

"What the fuck is this?" Howard repeated, his voice rising.

Slowly Vicki turned her head to face him. Howard was still kneeling between her legs. He was staring down at her crotch, a look of total disbelief on his face. Vicki didn't understand. She suppressed a germ of hope, because hope was impossible. Yet something had stopped him. Could it be Howard was such a virgin he hadn't seen a naked woman before? Was it possible he didn't know what to expect—and now had no idea what to do?

Howard darted his hand forward and touched her, probing and running his fingers roughly through her pubic hair and making her jerk violently. Trembling, he held his fingers up in front of Vicki's eyes for her to see. There were traces of blood on them.

She couldn't see it, but there was also blood smeared over the insides of her thighs.

"Are you on the fucking rag?" he asked, angrily. "Are you?"

He looked so furious Vicki tried to answer, but the gagging singlet stopped her. He reached forward and pulled it over her head, wrenching her neck. In the movement his bare chest came close to her face. His body odour was thick and overpowering. He went back to his kneeling position and glared at her, waiting for an answer.

"It's—it's my period," she whispered, fearfully. "It must have started." Vicki tried to think through her numb confusion, but couldn't remember whether or not her period was due.

"You *bitch*!" Howard said, still staring at her crotch.

A realisation was dawning on Vicki—a true ray of hope that might be worth grasping for. Howard was an ugly animal who had no qualms about stealing, killing and raping, but through ignorance, or maybe even superstition, he baulked at interfering sexually with a woman having her period. She fought against the fog of shock which had started to overtake her mind when being raped had seemed imminent. She needed all her wits. With desperation gnawing at her, Vicki gambled Howard was truly sexually naive and ignorant.

"You—you shouldn't touch me again," she breathed, terrified that any word she uttered might send him into a murderous rage. "Not with the blood. You might get infected," she added, before she could stop herself. It might be taking things too far.

"Infected?" He changed his angry glare back to her face. "With what? Have you got fucking AIDS?"

"No, no, I've got a type of—" Vicki thought frantically for something appropriate, "Hepatitis. A mild strain of hepatitis."

"Hepatitis? I've heard of that." Howard's expression altered from anger to a puzzled frown, then back to anger again. "So you could make me sick? You're fucking useless to me!"

"No! Not at all," Vicki said urgently, knowing she was buying time, as long as he didn't kill her first. "It's only unsafe while I'm bleeding—during my period, that's all."

"How long's that?" He looked at her suspiciously. She could see he was deciding whether to let her live

"Four or five days, maybe a week at the most. I'll need some tampons, to keep myself clean."

Howard turned his face away in a gesture of disbelief. "You want me to go out and buy you some fucking tampons?"

"Please, it's very important. Otherwise I might infect myself. I—I need to stay clean. Then you can—do anything you want."

Vicki was actually thinking the opposite. Her bleeding sometimes only lasted three days. She thought that if she quickly used four or five tampons, then hid them somewhere in the room, she could reinsert an old one when her period finished and trick Howard into believing otherwise for perhaps up to a week. It would be a risk to her own health, but better than rape. And anything could happen in a week. "Please, Howard," she said again, calling him by his name for the first time.

He moved so quickly she only had time for a short, choked scream. Howard threw himself on top of Vicki, using his weight and hips to keep her legs spread. Like a lover he smothered her and put his cheek to hers. Vicki turned her head away desperately. Her arms—still pinned behind her back—hurt badly. She thought with an awful misery her gamble had failed—he was going to rape her anyway, and she waited to feel his penis probing at her. But Howard was only rubbing himself against her lower abdomen, jerking frantically and spasmodically and making grunting noises in her ear. He ignored her breasts. He had lost control of himself, but he wasn't going near her bleeding. Only seconds elapsed, before she felt a wide smear of hot semen over her stomach, squashed between their two bodies. Bile rose in her throat and she only just managed to swallow it again. Howard lay still on top of her, breathing in gasps.

Then, without another word he rolled off and got to his

feet. With angry moves he gathered his clothing and boots and stalked from the room, slamming the door closed.

Vicki turned onto her side to take the weight off her arms. A trickle of semen ran across her stomach onto the filthy sheets. She told herself not to cry, over and over again, but it was hard not to. She had bought herself time and maybe her life. She had won, with a little help from Mother Nature. There was still hope.

With single-mindedness Howard dressed and quietly let himself out the door. He walked down to the Vietnamese supermarket, scanned the shelves until he saw a product with "tampon" written on it, and took it to the check-out. He glared at the wizened owner, daring him to comment. The Vietnamese man kept his face inscrutable, while he took Howard's money.

Back at the flat Howard walked unannounced into the bedroom. He had a knife in one hand and a plastic bag in the other. Vicki looked up at him fearfully. He stepped up to the bed and grabbed her upper arm, flipping her over onto her stomach. She felt the cold steel of the knife run over her buttocks and between them. The tip of the blade paused between her legs. Howard pulled the knife away and inspected the smear of menstrual blood on it. Then with quick movements he used the knife to slash through the tape binding her arms. Next he tipped the contents of the bag onto her back. It was the packet of tampons.

"This better not last too long," he said, and left the room.

Chapter Eighteen

The traffic leading to the airport got steadily worse, puzzling Maiden. As far as he knew there were the usual morning flights scheduled, but nothing to create this sort of snarl so early in the day. There were no arriving dignitaries or celebrities who might attract a crowd.

"What the hell is this?" he growled as the lane he was in ground to a halt once more.

Five minutes later he crawled through an intersection where the lights had been turned off and a uniformed policeman was directing the traffic. Uncaring about the barrage of car horns he instantly caused, Maiden stopped beside the policeman, leaned out the window and shouted his identification, before asking, "What the hell's happened? Has there been an accident up ahead?"

The policeman wore the expression of a man who'd already had enough of abusive drivers and people deliberately trying to run over his toes. He scowled at the line of cars behind Maiden, as if his look might stop the people leaning angrily on their horns. He yelled above the noise,

"Another fucking flash protest about the new runway. They're picketing both the airport terminals."

"Shit, that's where I'm trying to go!"

"You might be better off walking, sir," the policeman said. "It only gets worse from here. The bastards have managed to stuff up everything. Can you keep it moving?" he added wearily.

Maiden gave him a wave and eased his car away. It was only a matter of metres, before he was back against the rear bumper of the car in front. "Jesus Christ, why today?" he asked aloud. The traffic policeman was right—it would have been faster for Maiden to get out and walk, but he was still a long way from the airport. He endured the slow crawl for another five minutes and his frustration was reaching boiling point when he noticed flashing blue lights in his rear-view mirror. In the distance a police car was making its way cautiously up the wrong side of the road. Maiden made a decision, gunned his motor and swung the Ford in a tight U-turn. With a grinding bump he parked over the kerbing on the opposite side of the road, got out of the car and locked the doors, then stood in the centre of the road. Ignoring the curious stares of the drivers still caught in the traffic jam, he watched the blue lights getting closer. Maiden had his identification ready.

Three vehicles, two of them vans filled with men to do picket duty, approached. Holding his ID high above his head Maiden stepped out in front of the marked car escorting them. As the driver pulled to a halt Maiden ran forward to his window.

"Are you guys going to the airport?" Maiden asked, urgently.

"Who isn't?" the driver replied, glancing at Maiden's ID. "They want us at the international terminal."

"Anywhere close will do me. We've got a homicide in one of the car parks there. Can you give me a lift?"

The driver looked doubtful, but said, "Sure, squeeze in."

Maiden got in the back where two burly constables were

already sitting. With three big men it was a tight squeeze, but at least they were moving at a reasonable pace towards the airport. Everyone in the car began exchanging picket-line stories, and Maiden briefly explained the homicide he was investigating, making it clear he couldn't discuss it further. Close to the airport the car moved slowly through a crowd of protesters, most of whom were waving placards and chanting, so didn't hear the car coming up behind them. The police driver continuously pressed his horn, but it made little impression and the protesters only moved aside reluctantly. Often someone would bend down and peer into the rear seat, hoping to see somebody important or an official they could harass. The policemen glared back and Maiden fought the urge to wind his window down and punch each face as it appeared.

Eventually the driver said, "Bugger this," and turned on the siren for a few seconds. The effect on the people close by was spectacular, the strident noise scattering them against each other like startled birds.

"Don't stampede 'em," one of the constables next to Maiden said, with a grin.

"Stupid bastards," the driver replied over his shoulder. "Worse than sheep."

He used the siren again several times and they made better progress through the crowd to reach the terminal. A line of policemen cordoned off the building, only allowing people with airline tickets through. Maiden thanked the driver for the lift and pushed his way through the crowd in the other direction, heading for the car parks. Soon he was away from the terminal and the roads leading to it, and it was easier to move. He found the open air, long-term car park and climbed up onto the back of a pick-up truck, using the extra height to scan the area. He saw a gathering of police cars and the colourful fluttering of the crime scene tape on the opposite side of the large block. A few minutes later, out of breath from the quick walk and annoyed at having to zig-zag through the sea of parked cars, Maiden finally stepped under the tape and into a crowd of policemen, forensic officers and photographers. Central to them all was a brown Commodore sedan with its boot open. Creane was standing next to it and, seeing Maiden arrive, waved him over.

"There you are. Have a nice drive?"

"Very funny," Maiden grunted. He needed a moment to adjust his thinking to the job at hand, then looked into the boot. "What have we got?" He glared angrily up at a passing aeroplane with its shattering roar.

Creane raised his voice to a shout. "Mr. Howlett, at a guess—or what's left of him. He was strangled, from the looks of it. And he's minus an arm, of course."

Howlett's body was crammed into the boot in a fetal position, his feet towards the back seat and his head and shoulders to the rear. He was lying on his side, with the severed stump of his missing arm beneath him. It gave Maiden the strange impression the corpse was somehow reaching through the bottom of the car.

"Have you touched anything? Moved anything?"

"Of course not. We were waiting for you." The mild, mocking rebuke was obvious in Creane's voice.

Maiden looked at him. "Aren't I allowed to have a private life? Do I have to stay at home, in case you try to call me?"

"No, of course not," Creane said with a small smile. "I just didn't think you were the social type, staying out until after four in the morning."

"How do you know I wasn't home? Maybe I was in bed and I didn't want to answer the damned phone for a change."

"Uh-huh," Creane's smile widened.

"I don't think it's appropriate for you to look so bloody cheerful at a homicide scene, Detective Constable Creane."

"I'm just enjoying my work, sir. So anyway, who was she? Anyone I might bump into?"

"You are getting bloody cocky, aren't you? It's none of your damned business."

"So it *was* somebody?"

"Are we investigating a homicide, or swapping screw stories here? Give it a break, OK? Has everyone done their business? Photographers, the forensic people?"

Creane became serious again. "As much as they want to, before we start moving things."

"Good, because that's what I want to do. Let's pull him out of there and have a closer look."

Creane turned and called out, "OK, everyone, we want to remove the body from the car."

A plastic sheet was produced and laid out on the asphalt. Four men, including Maiden and Creane, gathered close around the car and started hauling the corpse from the confines of the boot. Rigor mortis was present in the body and it needed a disrespectful amount of tugging and twisting before they got Howlett's remains out of the vehicle and onto the ground, with the severed stump uppermost. This produced a flurry of activity from the small group of journalists who had either somehow defeated the traffic jam and made it to the crime scene or diverted themselves from covering the airport demonstration. Flashbulbs flared from beyond the barrier tape. Maiden bent down, deliberately obscuring the body from the press and with a pen touched some massive bruising around the corpse's neck.

"This guy was strangled, all right." He put the pen away and used his hands, holding them in a fan shape above the body, to demonstrate. "By someone with very big, strong hands."

Creane noted Maiden's own hands would fit that description, but didn't mention this. "Why do you say that?" he asked instead.

"Because most people who strangle somebody don't know what they're doing. They are in a fit of anger, or something like that. Still, it's almost natural for them to concentrate their strength on the soft windpipe in the throat and that's where a majority of the bruising should show. Even a trained soldier who keeps his head and kills like this methodically would focus on the larynx or thereabouts. They know pressing on the back of the neck is a waste of effort and time. But look at this guy," Maiden nodded down at the corpse. "The bruising around the neck is nearly uniform. Something wrapped around it and squeezed, crushing everything. That takes a hell of a lot of strength."

"Could they have used a rope, or a garotting wire?"

"The bruising is too wide. In fact, you can almost pick out the finger marks anyway. No, the killer was a big, strong man who used his hands." Maiden stared at Creane. "Remind you of anyone?"

"There's absolutely no motive. No connection at all," Creane reminded him quietly. "For either of them."

"Maybe they're both a lot damned smarter than we credit them for. If there is a woman involved, she's pretty enough to do it. She attracts them, and he kills them."

Maiden was keeping his voice low, so Creane asked quietly, "You still haven't run this idea past anyone else, have you?"

"No, but it's nearly time to, I think. I don't want to get it into the papers, though."

Other policemen and the forensic experts were now closing in around the corpse too, gathering evidence and taking photographs from every conceivable angle. Some were examining the floor of the car's boot, looking for clues. Creane crouched down next to Maiden and stared thoughtfully at the body, while Maiden searched the dead man's pockets.

"Tell me," Creane said, casually. "If you were going to chop off someone's arm, where would you start?"

Before he could reply Maiden was handed Howlett's wallet, found in the boot beneath the corpse. After looking through it he silently showed Creane the driver's licence, then he tossed it to a constable who was bagging material evidence. "I call that good enough to tag him a Mr. Gregory Howlett," he said, and turned back to Creane. "I don't know—the shoulder I suppose."

"Yes, but where on the shoulder?"

"How the hell would I know?" Maiden looked at the severed stump and shrugged.

"Exactly. Personally, I'd probably hack around like a drunken butcher and make a right mess, before I managed to cut the bloody thing off. I'm no doctor, but this looks quite neat, don't you think?"

Maiden was slow to answer. "You're suggesting again this has been done by someone with a knowledge of human anatomy. Like a doctor."

"It could still be one of Longman's medical students, without the prank angle. It doesn't have to be someone with a complete medical training. In fact, I did a year myself, before I dropped out." He pointed at the corpse. "I know that much . . . sort of."

Maiden frowned, hiding his surprise. "So it could be a nurse, or for that matter, a mortician or a chiropractor—anyone with *any* sort of medical training. Maybe even a university drop-out like you. Hell, it could even be someone who takes the time to look at the coloured pictures of the human body in any decent encyclopedia. We've already decided this person must have at least average to high intelligence, which cancels out our armed robber. How much brains would it take to figure out how to cut off a human arm if you knew you were going to do it and prepared yourself?"

Creane gestured helplessly. "OK, scratch the doctor theory."

"No." Maiden said, standing and patting Creane briefly on the back. "It's good thinking. Keep it to yourself, though. I'd prefer Forensic to come up with that suggestion by themselves. Don't go putting any ideas into their heads."

One of the constables searching the boot of the car cursed and said, "Shit, this is a *note!*"

He immediately had everyone's attention as he turned from the vehicle, gingerly holding a piece of paper by one corner. The note was stained by blood that had been running freely over the bottom of the boot. The paper fluttered in the breeze.

Maiden snapped, "Be careful! Don't lose it, for God's sake!"

The constable solved the problem by offering it to Maiden, who held it by a different corner. He turned the paper so he could read it. The writing was large, but neat, written in thick marking pen. Maiden was about to read it aloud to everyone who had gathered around quickly, but he turned and pointed with his free hand at the journalists waiting beyond the tape.

"No way!" he called loudly to their expectant faces. "We might have a copycat killer with a young girl as hostage right now. The contents of this note could help us separate the two investigations. If this note gets in the press, I'll personally arrest the bastard responsible for putting it in print."

The journalists looked collectively disappointed. Regardless, the detective lowered his voice so only those close could hear him.

"OK, it says, 'They cut us to pieces like dogs fighting over scraps. They ruin our lives and leave us with nothing. Now it is their turn. The greedy and the cruel. Maybe they will learn that the names in their ledgers are real people living real lives.'"

There was a silence, until Creane said, "You've got to be bloody joking. Howlett sent someone bankrupt, so they killed him for it?"

"Not Howlett," Maiden said, quietly. He stood still, thinking hard, then he motioned for the constable with the evidence bags to take the note. "Howlett's company, I would say. Someone has taken revenge on his employers by killing a person who works for them. Howlett just happened to be the poor bastard they targeted."

"But—what about the others?"

"Others?"

"The finger, and the hand."

Maiden began absently, his mind working furiously, "It will be the same. All we have to do is find someone in their company records who dealt with all three businesses and we'll narrow down our search."

Something in Maiden's tone made Creane wary when he asked, "So, isn't that good? Won't that help us a lot?"

"Do you think so? Have you got any idea how many people a company like Howlett's has represented for over, say, the last five years? Thousands, probably. And that's only individual accounts. We could be looking for someone who was associated through a company, then a *subsidiary*, and whose name doesn't actually appear on the books." He waved towards the constable, who was giving the note close attention. "That note is a clue, but a bloody small one. The person who wrote it knows full well they'll get their message across with only minimum risk."

"Are you going to give it to the press? That's who it's aimed for, isn't it?"

"I might have to, otherwise I could be accused of not warning the business community of the potential threat," Maiden said bitterly. "No," he decided. "We'll hold it."

Creane shook his head in wonder. "So, it's all about a personal vendetta against businesses who've sent someone broke. It's a hell of a way to get back at them." He began ticking points off his fingers. "What have we got so far? Accountants, now with Howlett, Dawes was a software company and the finger came from—what?"

"He worked for a debt collection agency."

"Well, that and accountants certainly fits into a group that a failed businessman may want to take revenge against. But what about the software company?"

"Could be just a creditor—and don't forget, I haven't

dismissed the possibility that's a different case. Peter Dawes's angelic friends might have taken a leaf out of this guy's book." Maiden nodded down a at Howlett.

"Maybe they did this one, too? That big bastard looked capable of anything."

"But why kill somebody else? At least we have a vague motive for killing the flatmate."

"They liked the thrill? It happens, doesn't it?"

"God forbid," Maiden muttered. "Before you know it, we'll have people copying the bloody copycat killers." He was half-serious.

Creane stayed silent while a stretcher arrived to take away Howlett's corpse. Another plastic sheet was draped over the corpse to hide it from the journalists' prying eyes. He waited until the stretcher was on the way to an un-marked van, then asked, "So, if that isn't the case and we're dealing with one killer I guess the question is, how far does he want to go?"

"How many people does it take to make a business fail? The killer could have had a hundred creditors by the end, and he's pissed off with all of them. And that doesn't in-clude the court system or anyone else who served him a summons, wrote a nasty letter, or came in contact in *any* way with the company. Shit, he might even be blaming the country, the government and everything else and wind up killing a politician. When you think about it, we have the potential here for one hell of a serial killer, Martin."

Creane's flippant manner had changed to sombre thought. "What do we do next?"

Maiden held his hands up in surrender, but said, "Work out what *he's* going to do next. In the meantime we'd bet-ter start a more detailed search of all these companies' rec-ords—who they dealt with and in particular people who had bad debts. I'm betting that will be an enormous bloody list and God knows when we'll get a chance to look at it. Still, we can't ignore the possibility of a match-up clue. I wonder if we can get some help with that?" he mused, looking doubtful. Then his face turned grim. "And I think we should pay another visit to Mr. Fischer."

Maiden rapped hard on the door of the flat. When no-one answered within a few seconds he did it again, harder. "Tom Fischer?" he called loudly. "It's Detective Senior Sergeant John Maiden and Detective Constable Martin Creane. We want to speak with you, now."

Nobody answered, but Maiden gave Creane a knowing look when they heard someone moving around inside. There was a rattle of a deadlock and the door eased back. Jennifer Musgrave peered through the crack.

"What the hell do you want?" she asked, her voice dull from sleep. "Tom isn't bloody here—he's at work."

"Then we'll talk to you," Maiden said unkindly. "Are you going to let us in?" From the tone of his voice, she didn't have a choice. Jennifer moved reluctantly aside and swung the door open.

"Come right in," she said sarcastically.

Inside the flat it was gloomy and smelled of stale, smoke-filled air. Jennifer walked away from them towards the kitchen sink. She wore only a very short towelling robe. Creane raised his eyes at her legs and exchanged a look with Maiden, who kept his expression impassive.

"Had a late night, Jennifer?" Maiden asked. She was filling a kettle, moving slowly. "Was Tom with you? We'd like to know what you were both doing last night."

"What the hell for?"

"Because we want to know."

"I can't believe this shit," she told them, her face twisting. "Tom's best friend is missing and you guys think he's been killed, and you come around here hassling *us*. Shouldn't you be out somewhere, looking for him?"

"Tom's best friend?" Maiden sounded surprised. "I got the impression you were glad to get rid of him."

"You know what we meant," she said. "Shit, we didn't want the guy dead, for Christ's sake."

"We haven't said he's dead."

Jennifer looked at him in disgust. "Don't bother with those games. I don't know if he's dead or alive, or what." She pulled a cup down from the cupboard, gave it a wipe with the bottom of her robe, giving the two men a glimpse of white upper thigh, and dropped it onto the bench. She searched around for coffee.

"So, where were you last night?" Maiden asked again.

"Out. Nightclubbing."

"Both of you?"

"What do you think?"

"Where did you go?"

"How the hell am I supposed to remember?" Jennifer threw her hands up in the air, then stood still, unwillingly giving it some thought. She rattled off the names of several clubs.

"Anyone you know see you there? People who can vouch for you?"

"Who? People *you'll* believe? I doubt it. What's this all about anyway? Have you found Peter?"

Maiden looked amused. "I was wondering when you'd get around to asking. You're not exactly frantic about him, are you?"

"That's my business," she said sullenly, keeping her eyes on spooning coffee into the cup.

Surprising Maiden, Creane asked from where he was crouched in front of a bookcase, "Who's the one studying medicine? You?"

Several thick volumes were crammed into the shelf. She looked at him and said, "They're my sister's. I'm looking after them." Jennifer dismissed them with a wave. "She's overseas for a year."

Creane picked a magazine from a pile. "I suppose this is more your sort of material?" It was a soft-porn magazine of poor quality. Jennifer stared at him without answering, an odd look on her face. Creane had a hunch and flicked through the pages. He found pictures of her near the centre, and recognised the furniture in the background. He showed it briefly to Maiden and asked her, "Is this the sort of photographic shop Tom works in?"

"It's a real job," she said defensively. "He's allowed to use the stuff after hours for his own work. Nothing illegal about that."

"When's he coming home?" Maiden asked her. Creane was looking through another magazine.

"He'll be late. I really don't know when," she shrugged.

"*Real* late, after you call him about us coming back, right?"

"Shit, what do you expect?"

"John," Creane said softly. Without letting her see, he showed Maiden another series of photos. This time Jennifer performed a striptease. She started out in a nurse's uniform and finished completely naked.

"Hey," she said loudly. "If you're going to get off on that, go and buy your own fucking copies. That's how it's supposed to work, you know. We're all trying to make a living here."

Maiden tapped the page with his hand. "What did Peter Dawes think of all this?"

Jennifer laughed cruelly. "Spun him out. He thought we'd all get arrested or something. Still, he got to see me naked and that started all the trouble."

"How much trouble?"

"I told you—don't make a big deal out of it."

Maiden took the magazine and walked back to the bookcase, throwing it onto the pile. Creane moved toward Maiden, out of earshot of the girl, and they whispered together.

"What do you think?" he asked Maiden.

"She's got us fucked, Martin. She can say they were all over town last night until dawn and we can't dispute it. The meathead boyfriend will be told to say the same thing, no matter what they were doing. We're wasting our time."

Creane frowned, puzzled. "So, what did you expect?"

"Not as much as we got. I wonder how far she likes to take playing nurse? Something's wrong here, Martin. I can smell it."

"What do we do?"

Maiden looked grim. "Nothing. She's *still* got us fucked. Let's get out of here."

Chapter Nineteen

The investigation was stepped up, with more manpower, time and resources. Maiden managed to delegate a lot of it, keeping himself at the "sharp" end of tracking the killer.

Howlett's car and the corpse inside it could have provided the best clues yet for Maiden to draw closer to his quarry. But the reality was exactly how he'd explained it to Martin Creane. Leaving a body to be eventually discovered by the police, alone with a note, was a deliberate move on the part of the killer and Maiden soon confirmed he wasn't any wiser than the murderer wanted him to be. The day of the discovery was filled with exhaustive procedure which couldn't be ignored, despite the fact Maiden knew it would provide little new evidence. Fingerprinting Howlett's car and all the nearby vehicles only produced a mountain of samples, most of which would eventually prove unidentifiable, unknown or belonging to a vehicle's innocent owners. Tracing the owners was a difficult process in itself. They were tracked down through vehicle registrations, then travel plans and frustrating phone calls to businesses, tourist resorts and convention centres all over the country to ask for a fingerprint—something many people didn't care for—and to check whether by chance they had seen the driver of a brown Holden Commodore parked adjacent to their own vehicle.

At the end of the day Maiden was physically and mentally exhausted. He pushed himself to make one more phone call and only just managed to stay civil. Then he found himself dialling Janet Brown's office number. She answered after one ring.

"Hi," Maiden said softly, so other detectives near his desk couldn't eavesdrop. "I just wanted to call and say thanks for last night, and see if you're OK."

"I'm fine," she replied. "And there's no need to thank me."

"Maybe we should thank each other."

"Something like that."

Before he could stop himself Maiden said, "What are you doing this evening? I've had a pig of a day and I wouldn't mind a few drinks and a bit of company."

There was the smallest trace of coolness in Brown's reply. "Seeing each other two nights in a row doesn't exactly fit with what we were trying to do last night. And I'm really tired. I need an early night and a good sleep."

Maiden felt foolish and angry with himself. "You're right," he said, tightly. "Like I said, I've had a bad day. I shouldn't have called."

A pause on the other end had him expecting another rebuff, but Brown lifted his spirits by saying softly, "Look, don't get me wrong. I really enjoyed last night and I'd like to do it again sometime soon. But not tonight. I wouldn't be good company." Another pause, and she added, "Call me tomorrow, when you have a chance. Maybe we can do something on the weekend."

"That sounds good," he said. "I've got to go." Maiden said goodbye and broke the connection hurriedly, as if making sure Brown didn't have an opportunity to withdraw her invitation to call the next day. He stared at the phone for a moment.

"I'm getting worse than a bloody teenager," he told himself.

Chapter Twenty

Julie MacQuarrie and Susan Easton enjoyed their Wednesday nights together. For a start, it was overtime their employers gladly paid. Even better, once the eight partners of the law firm had finished their weekly meeting and moved to a Japanese restaurant ten minutes away, the two girls were allowed to enjoy a bottle of wine between them, while they tidied up the week's business, typed up the minutes of the meeting and set themselves ready for the new week. Lawson and Bates arranged their working schedules beginning from Thursday through to Wednesday. This otherwise tedious part of the girls' jobs was made much more tolerable by the relaxed atmosphere of after-hours work.

For several years it had only been Julie who stayed behind, but in the last month Susan had been asked to do the same, because increasing business had taken Wednesday night's work beyond needing just one person. Normally they each had an office and served as secretaries to four partners each, but on these nights Julie swapped to one of the partner's desks so she could gossip with Susan through the doorway.

It was after nine o'clock and the partners had left for the restaurant fifteen minutes earlier.

"How much further have you got to go?" Susan called, pausing to refill her wine glass.

From the next office Julie replied, "Nearly at the end of the minutes and that's it. How about you?"

"I've got miles to go on the Horden contract. If you want to go home, don't stick around on my account. It's getting pretty late."

"I've still got a few things to do. I haven't shredded the expiries yet."

The law firm occupied one floor of a twelve-storey building and space in their offices was at a premium. The partners were fastidious about dead files that, legally, had reached an expiry date and no longer needed to be kept. Every week these were found and shredded and the large plastic bags of wastepaper were taken to the recycling bin behind the building.

Julie finished typing up the minutes, checked her work, then printed it out. Topping up her glass of wine as she passed Susan's desk, she went to the main laser printer and waited until she was satisfied it was working properly. Next she walked to the staffroom where the shredder was installed. It was a noisy machine and this room was the furthest from the partners' offices. A pile of manila folders was stacked on a table. Julie started the shredder and began feeding the old papers in, mindful that her fingers didn't go into the rotating blades. Just the thought of it made her shudder every time she used the machine. The plastic bag below was bulging with waste and Julie had to squash it a couple of times to make enough room for tonight's files. When they were all shredded she took the bag out, tied it with a plastic tie, and headed for the rear door and the service lift which ran down the back of the building.

She paused before going out and yelled down the hallway, "Can I lock the saferoom?"

There was a moment of silence, then Susan called back, "Yes. I haven't got anything that needs to go in there."

The saferoom was a walk-in safe with a solid steel door and combination lock. It was back down towards the staffroom and Julie decided to close it on her return journey. She let herself out the door and went down a narrow corridor to the service lift.

This part of the building was a warren of spartan passageways, never intended to be seen by the public and used mainly by the cleaning staff, so they could go about their business during the day unnoticed. When Julie stepped into the elevator it greeted her with its familiar smell of detergents and disinfectants. Carrying the bulky, but lightweight, bag of shredded paper was easy. She pressed the button for the ground floor.

From the service lift to the outside was only a few steps through a fire exit, then a double door with emergency bars to open it. Julie backed into the door and shoved the bar with her rump, bursting the doors open with a clatter. The paper recycling bin was just outside.

It was a hopper bin, designed to be loaded when full onto the back of a truck and replaced with an empty unit. The whole thing attached to a hydraulic ram operated by a single green button. All Julie had to do was throw her plastic bag into the maw of the compressor and, if she wished, press the button for the ram. It returned automatically to its starting position afterwards. Usually, you could see if the mouth of the compressor was filled with enough cardboard boxes and paper to warrant starting the ram. Julie, uncomfortable with such a large mechanical device, never pressed the button.

Normally, she would have been outside the building for under thirty seconds. Doing this chore at night didn't scare her, despite the lack of lighting and shadows around the bin. It was familiar ground and the back of the building wasn't the sort of place people would hang out. At worse, a street drunk might think it a suitable spot to spend the night, but there was little in the way of shelter and in her seven years working for the law firm Julie had never encountered anyone except employees from other companies who shared the bin.

She walked confidently up to the compressor and tossed the plastic bag in, playfully flipping it in a high arc. The wine was having its effect. She glanced towards the alleyway beyond and marvelled, as she always did, at just how the trucks were able to negotiate the narrow space, turn around and retrieve the bin. She had seen it once, the truck huffing and wheezing its brakes as it laboured through a tight turn, making her think of some enormous animal forced into servitude. Julie turned from the compressor and looked towards the welcoming light of the service entrance.

Someone stepped in between, cutting her off. The silhouette was slim. Julie, with her heart suddenly in her mouth, thought it was a street kid.

"Excuse me, but what are you doing here?" she asked in a shaky voice supposed to be authoritative. "This is private property."

A flicker of movement in front of her eyes happened too fast for Julie to even cry out. It was a large hand clamping over her mouth. A palm pressed against the side of her head and she was shoved violently sideways. Her temple struck the steel of the recycling bin hard, causing a moment of exploding lights in Julie's head. A second time rendered her unconscious. A third, and Julie MacQuarrie was dying.

Technically, she wasn't dead when they laid her down on the cold concrete, but Julie was beyond comprehending. The knife came out and slit the waistband of Julie's designer suit skirt. Another flick of the sharp blade and her panties were removed along with her stockings, the nylon tearing easily. They pushed her blouse and jacket upwards and out of the way.

"Pull her legs apart," the woman commanded softly.

He hesitated, mesmerised by the white flesh and dark triangle of pubic hair, then reached forward, grabbing Julie's thighs and spreading her legs.

She did the work this time, running the knife from deep into the V of the crotch in a shallow curve to the top of the hip, almost following the bikini line Julie had tried so hard to keep in the summer months. In the dim light the blood looked black, spilling out over the pale flesh. She did the cut several times, slicing deeper each time. The steel could be heard grating over bone as it touched the hip and pelvis.

"Turn her over," she said, moving back to give him room. He did it easily, untroubled by the weight of Julie's corpse. This time she cut between the buttocks. Again, it took several passes of the knife until she was satisfied.

"Pull hard and it should come away," she told him, stepping back again. He moved his grip to below the knee, then pulled and twisted the limb at the same time. The hip joint came out of the socket with a soft popping noise. It took only a few seconds to cut the remaining muscle and sinew still attached to the torso. The severed leg was put into a green garbage bag.

"We can throw her into the recycling bin."

Julie's body landed on the paper with a gentle rustling sound. She weighed even less, missing one of her legs.

Susan was typing madly, not caring about any mistakes she might make because the software programme would fix them faster than she could. She felt guilty, knowing Julie wouldn't leave her to finish alone and she was keeping her from going home. She kept one ear open for the sound of Julie returning from downstairs, ready to call her apologies and say she wouldn't be long. She was so absorbed in trying to get her work done that she was thankful rather than concerned that Julie took longer than usual for the trip to the paper recycling bin. Every second before her friend got back counted towards her getting the contract typed and them being able to go home.

Echoing through the corridor, she heard the back door open.

"I'm nearly done, Julie," she called desperately, finding an extra spurt of speed in her flying fingers. "If you haven't closed the safe yet, I've remembered there is something I could lock away, but it doesn't matter if you have."

There was no answer. Susan didn't worry. Julie would probably have moved back towards the staffroom, in which case she wouldn't have heard anything she said. To confirm this, she heard the hollow thud of the safe door closing.

The contract would take only minutes to finish and less to print out. And four hours' overtime, at their rate of pay, wasn't to be sneezed at.

Susan guessed Julie wouldn't be complaining.

Ten minutes after Susan heard Julie return from downstairs, the truck collecting the recycling bin arrived noisily in the alleyway. The driver was too busy turning his vehicle in the narrow confines to notice the red slick of blood near the bin. He was an old hand at the job and was quick to load the bin. A quarter of an hour later he was at the processing plant.

Harold Betterman nurtured a hate for most of his fellow humans. It had grown over the years to become a deep-set thing. He hated them because they made his job so bad.

He was responsible for watching the unloading shute when the trucks delivered the recyclable material, using their tippers to spew the contents of the bins into Harold's section—a ten metre long area of flat, shaking aluminium tray which spread the rubbish and gave him the chance to see anything foreign in it before it was processed.

The trouble was, it wasn't just the occasional soft drink can or bottle. People threw anything into the paper hoppers to save themselves the trouble of finding the correct bin. Harold spent all his shift desperately grabbing out all manner of garbage. People were lazy pigs, as far as he was concerned. Paper was paper, cardboard was cardboard—it was that easy. You'd think people could understand that. But he ended up fishing out food scraps, beer cans, bottles and all sorts of filth from his ten metres of responsibility. He had even rescued a litter of kittens once. That had got him into the local newspaper. Harold doubted there was any sort of garbage he hadn't raked out of the recycled paper hoppers at one time or another. He often told himself he'd seen just about every form of human waste try to slip past his vigilant eyes. People were just too damned lazy and didn't care about workers like him.

But he wasn't prepared for Julie MacQuarrie's body to come tumbling out of the back of the latest truck.

Chapter Twenty-one

Maiden was trying to convince Bercoutte's night-time counterpart, a man called Atkinson, to break every rule in the book. Instead of calling down the usual crime-response teams and flooding the alleyway with uniformed police, forensics, and detectives, Maiden wanted to keep them all away. He wanted Atkinson to give him men for a stake-out around the law firm's office block. But Atkinson didn't like jeopardising his own career, just because the day shift couldn't finish their business when they were supposed to—murder or no murder. Maiden was growing angrier on Creane's mobile phone as he drove one-handed through the city centre.

"Listen," he said to Atkinson, at the same time looking at Creane in the passenger seat and giving him a frustrated shake of his head. "We've got a victim already identified. Her colleague started screaming to the police she was missing at the same time the garbage company told us they had a corpse in one of their bins. It's pure luck they emptied the damn thing what must have been only minutes after she was dumped in there. But there's *no report of the sev-*

ered leg, yet. We got the other girl out of the office with a minimum of fuss and maybe we got away with it. There's a bloody good chance the killer's still planning to plant the thing in the building somewhere. All I want is surveillance until the morning and I need people to do it."

He paused, listening for a moment. "I know it's a long shot. The killer is probably scared off and miles away by now and the leg's in the harbour, but you never know. He might just take a risk and still put it under our noses." Maiden fell silent again. Creane could hear the squawking of Atkinson coming from the receiver. Maiden sighed and said with heavy sarcasm, "Thank you, sir. I appreciate that. Yes, I will take full responsibility."

He gave the mobile to Creane saying, "How do you turn this bloody thing off?"

Creane obliged and put it down. "See?" he said. "Handy little things. You should get one. I've only had it since this morning and I've been using it all day."

"It's just a bloody toy," Maiden grunted.

"A handy toy, though. What did Atkinson say?"

"He's going to give us a team, though he isn't happy about it. Reckons he had a drug bust scheduled for five a.m. and it's going to make him a hero. A drug bust, for Christ's sake! I could give him one of those every fucking night, if that's what he wants. I wonder sometimes if we're all on the same side," Maiden ended savagely, then added, "it's bad enough I've got to put up with Longman during the day."

"Do you really think someone's still going to try and plant the severed leg somewhere? Why hasn't it been done already?"

"I don't know—but it *hasn't* been done. That's the important point. We've had some bloody good luck tonight so far."

"I hope this is worth it," Creane said quietly, wondering if Julie MacQuarrie would agree about Maiden's "good luck." "This is so far off proper procedure it's crazy. If the press get hold of it, we'll all be out of a job. We should be in there with a forensic team and the whole works, by now. It's a crime scene, remember? That alleyway should be sealed off at least." He shook his head and repeated, "We'll both get fired in the morning. It'll be the happiest day of Longman's career."

"Look, if the girl's body was in there it would be impossible, you're right. But it's ten kilometres away in a paper recycling factory. Standard procedure can go to hell for a few hours."

Five minutes later Maiden pulled the car to a halt half a block from the law offices. Nearby a garish neon advertised a brand of business equipment. Maiden explained, "Atkinson said his men would meet us here. They'd better not be long. Every minute counts."

Creane stared through the windscreen at the distant building. "Do you want me to go up there now?"

"Yeah, you should. Cover that back alley and be bloody careful until I get there. I'll spread everyone else around the building so that nothing can squeak through, then I'll come and join you. Somebody is supposed to be bringing one of the business partners to let us back into the offices. We'll be going in the back way, where you'll be, so don't shoot us."

Creane nodded and got out of the car.

Maiden stayed where he was and watched the traffic flowing by, the headlights glaring at him. This was a busy city street and it was just after ten-thirty—it would be a few hours yet before the traffic lessened appreciably. But all the buildings around were either office blocks or related businesses selling office equipment and there were no bars or restaurants, so pedestrians were almost nonexistent at this time of night. Right now Maiden couldn't see a single person walking anywhere apart from Creane, disappearing into the distance.

Maiden started thinking about what he hoped would happen next. A human leg was a bulky package. *Am I really hoping somebody will be strolling down the footpath with a long, strangely wrapped bundle over their shoulder?* It would be heavy, too, but Maiden remembered the bruising on Greg Howlett's neck and decided the leg's weight wouldn't be a problem. Their killer was a strong man. Why the limb hadn't already been placed somewhere was the real mystery. It was, after all, the main object of the killing. Or had the killer been disturbed? The service lift should have been an obvious choice. Easy to get to and consistent with the killer's methods. Yet, when two constables and a plain-clothes detective picked up Susan Easton and hurried her away, they checked both the service lift and the internal lifts as well and found nothing. It didn't make sense.

The alternatives were clear and might mean Maiden was wasting everyone's time and risking the wrath of Longman in the morning. Either the killer had been scared off and the leg wasn't going to be placed anywhere, or the target building wasn't the law offices. In which case, Maiden was looking at an impossible choice of hundreds of offices within the city centre. He would be better off going home to bed and waiting to hear who got a nasty surprise in the morning.

"No, damn it, this has got to be better than lying in bed," he told himself.

Any further doubts were interrupted by three pairs of bright headlights pulling in behind him one after the other. Maiden got out of his car and walked to the first vehicle. Two vaguely familiar faces peered out at him from the front seat. Three more men sat in the back. Doors on all the vehicles opened and detectives dressed for the cold gathered on the footpath. There was a lot of foot-stamping and blowing into chilled hands. Nearly all of them lit up cigarettes. Maiden did a quick head count and asked them all to come close.

He explained what had happened and what he wanted them to do. Most of the detectives had done this many times before. The men knew they were probably facing hours standing in the cold and dark. They accepted their assignment with mute resignation.

Pocket-sized radios were distributed, one to each pair of men and one for Maiden himself. After making sure everyone knew their place and stressing how dangerous the killer might be, Maiden sent them on their way. The detectives spread out from the footpath in different directions, leaving behind a nervous, bespectacled man standing alone.

Maiden said, "Mr. Lawson, thank you for helping us like this. It could make all the difference."

Lawson spoke hesitantly. Maiden guessed he was still in shock and overwhelmed by events. "If it helps to catch whoever did this terrible thing, of course I'll do anything I can."

"Can you let us into your offices from the service entrance?"

"I have a key, yes."

Nodding, Maiden took Lawson's arm and led him to the alleyway, passing the two detectives posted at the opening. It was over a hundred metres from the street entrance to the area where the recycling bin was kept, with the alley running past the rear of several other buildings. Each property had some sort of caged yard or fenced section for holding rubbish bins and providing a service entrance. The alley was rich with sour garbage odours. Sections of the asphalt had filthy puddles from cleaners hosing out bins. Maiden had to squint to see them in the dim light. The recycling bin, he figured, must be a communal arrangement between all of the properties. He asked Lawson.

"We all share the cost," he replied. He looked uncomfortable in the dark alleyway and was watching the shadows anxiously.

The recycling bin hadn't been replaced with an empty one, on Maiden's request. Maiden could see the black square hole of the electrical compressor. Pieces of wastepaper were stuck inside, while others were pinned against the wire netting.

"Martin?" he called cautiously, making Lawson jump. "It's me."

Creane stepped out from behind the compressor and briefly flashed a small penlight towards him. As Maiden got closer he directed the beam to the ground. "Don't step in this puddle," Creane warned. "It's blood—litres of it. This must be where the leg was cut off. Christ, John, this is crazy. We should have a bloody army of people here looking for evidence. There's been a homicide right where we're standing."

Maiden warned him with a look towards Lawson, but it was lost in the dark. He motioned for the solicitor to stay back a moment and went to Creane. "Where'd you get the torch?" he asked. "What are you, a bloody boy scout?"

"It was a present," Creane said, snapping the beam off. "I carry it with me all the time, now. It's a handy thing."

Maiden growled, "And that telephone isn't going to start ringing at the wrong moment, is it?"

"No, I've turned it off," Creane replied patiently. "OK, what do we do now? While I still have a career, that is."

Maiden looked beyond the cage of the compressing ram. The alley continued to the street on the opposite side of the block. "I've got people at either end of the alley, some out the front and a few walking the street. It's possible the killer could come back into the alley from another of these buildings, so I want you to keep an eye on things here. I'll get Lawson to give me a look inside his offices, then I'll come and keep you company."

"Thanks," Creane said dryly, with visions of Maiden raiding the coffee machines and lingering in the warm building.

"Don't worry. I won't be long." He handed Creane the radio. "Scream into this, if you need help."

Lawson had kept his distance, eyeing the ominous puddle. Now Maiden steered him carefully around it, asking him not to touch anything as Lawson unconsciously stretched a supporting hand towards the ramming mechanism. At the back of the building beside the fire-escape door was a smaller security entrance. Lawson used a key and took Maiden inside. They headed for the lift.

"Don't touch anything," Maiden repeated as they stood in the service lift for the ride up. He was carefully looking at every square centimetre of the lift's interior. He couldn't see anything—not a scratch or dent from a struggle inside the elevator. Certainly, there wasn't any blood where the severed leg might have been carried inside.

All the lights were on inside the law firm's offices. The place had the air of someone having left in a hurry. Desk lamps were still switched on, computer monitors glowed with programmes running. Maiden did a slow tour of the rooms, followed by Lawson answering questions. Maiden tipped back the wine bottle and looked at the label.

"Would the girls have been drunk?"

"One bottle between them, and they were regular drinkers," Lawson replied. "I doubt it."

"Was it normal for one of them to go downstairs to the bin at this time of night?"

"Julie worked here for a long time. I'm sure she would have done it. Maybe she'd done it too many times and got careless. It is a back alley, after all. God knows who could be lurking down there."

Maiden stared at the solicitor. Lawson looked pale and shaken. "Exactly," he said. "Perhaps you should change your office procedure?"

The accusation was lost on the solicitor. "My office is through here. Would you like a drink?"

"No, no thank you," Maiden shook his head, but trailed Lawson through the door anyway.

It was obviously a senior partner's office, lushly appointed and clear of paperwork and clutter. A wide wooden desk dominated one end of the room and an expensive leather sofa ran along another wall. Lawson went to a cupboard and opened the door, revealing a shelf of liquor, red wines and a selection of glasses. A small bar refrigerator filled the lower half. Taking down a tumbler, Lawson used fumbling fingers to drop in several cubes of ice and poured in a generous slug of Scotch. Maiden could almost taste the drink and was tempted to change his mind.

"What do I have to do now?" Lawson asked.

"Tell me if there's anything unusual in these offices at the moment. Like furniture that's been moved—things like that."

Lawson didn't bother to do another examination of the rooms. "There's nothing," he said immediately. "I've already told all this to the uniformed policemen. Usually when I come in at night or I'm the first in in the morning the lights are all out and everything is turned off, but that's all."

It was the answer Maiden expected. He was just going through the motions. "If you don't object to leaving us in charge here, you are quite free to go home now, Mr. Lawson. There's really nothing you can do."

"I would only stay awake all night. I might as well stay here. I'm a bachelor," he added a little self-consciously. "I live alone. Perhaps I can get some work done, though God knows I don't feel like it."

Maiden suspected the bottle of Scotch was the greatest incentive Lawson had. He nodded and said, "If I could have the key you used for the downstairs security door, I'll come back regularly to check on things."

Lawson took the key from his key ring and handed it over. "Why are you watching the office anyway? Why do you think the killer will come back?"

It hadn't occurred to Maiden that Lawson didn't know of the girl's amputated leg or that it might be placed somewhere in the building.

He lied smoothly, "It's very common for criminals of this

kind to return to the scene of the crime, just so they can witness the panic and trouble they cause. Sometimes they think it will help them figure out if we have any clues about their identity."

Lawson accepted this without question. He had finished his drink and was looking towards the bottle, but he seemed concerned about refilling his glass in front of Maiden.

"I'll be going back downstairs," Maiden said. "I'll be back soon."

He didn't leave the offices straightaway, but detoured with a quick search of all the adjoining offices and passageways. He didn't really expect to see anything—he would have heard about it from the uniformed men anyway.

On the lift ride down Maiden was regretting bringing in the solicitor to reopen the offices. It had achieved almost nothing and now he had someone else to worry about. Still, the whole operation would have felt incomplete without access to the building itself and Lawson, intercepted just in time as he came out of the Japanese restaurant, had been the quickest and simplest method.

The whole business, from Susan Easton calling the police only minutes after Harold Betterman saw Julie Mac-Quarrie's corpse fall from the waste bin, through to the present moment, had been as unconventional as it could be when it came to doing things the correct way—the police way. Maiden had broken more rules in the last few hours than during his whole career. Still, his instincts were telling him he was going to be breaking a few more yet to catch this killer, because the killer wasn't exactly playing within the rules either.

Back outside, he stood in the darkness near the ramming machinery and listened carefully, wondering which way Creane would have gone. He heard the soft crackling of a radio and he walked in that direction. A shadow detached itself from a wall.

"John?" It was Creane.

"I heard that radio from a mile off."

"It's the first time the thing has made a noise. I didn't know it was so loud."

"What's the problem?"

"Nothing. Just everybody checking everybody else."

"OK."

Maiden joined Creane in the shadows, leaning back against damp bricks.

"How long are we going to give this?"

"Until first light, I guess. I can't imagine anybody dropping off a whole human leg in broad daylight."

Creane twisted his watch around until he caught some light on it. "Shit, it's only midnight now. Dawn must be six hours away!"

"Welcome to the police force."

"Thanks to you it's probably my last day in it."

"I'll tell Longman the whole thing was my idea."

"Well, it *was*."

They fell silent and watched the dark buildings around them. After ten minutes they moved to a different location and did the same thing again. It was a tedious routine that soon had both men thinking they were wasting their time, but neither said this aloud. Maiden didn't want to split up to cover more ground. They were dealing with a killer who, by all indications, wasn't somebody he would want to face alone.

After an hour they were already feeling disappointed and going through the motions with Maiden suppressing a bitterness about things not working out better. Everything up until then had seemed like good fortune presenting them with a chance. Now it appeared to be an empty opportunity. Maiden was silently ruing their efforts when Creane touched his arm.

"Look," he whispered and pointed. At the rear of a nearby building, moving with obvious caution, a man in a long overcoat walked towards the law firm's office block.

"Jesus," Maiden breathed. "Give me the radio, quick!"

Turning his back to the stranger Maiden tried to bury his face in his own jacket, speaking in urgent whispers into the radio. He didn't give anyone a chance to acknowledge, afraid even the smallest crackle of an electronic voice might echo along the alleyway and alert their target. He could only hope everyone else was still alert and had understood his instructions.

"John, we'll lose sight of him, if we don't start moving," Creane said anxiously.

"I know, I know," Maiden was stuffing the radio into his pocket. "Come on."

They walked with care, keeping away from any areas of light and ready to instantly press themselves into hiding if it appeared their target might turn around to check behind him. They didn't have to get close just yet. The two detectives from the opposite end of the alley would be closing in, too.

When the overcoated man reached the rear of the law firm's building he stopped and looked about uncertainly. Maiden and Creane immediately shrank back against a fence. Maiden put his face close to Creane's ear.

"He's confused about the missing bin. I'll bet that's got the bastard worried. He wasn't expecting that."

"But he isn't carrying anything. Where's the leg?"

"He probably stashed it somewhere. Maybe he got scared and dumped it quickly. Christ, we didn't think to do a search of the waste bins or anywhere like that. Now he's come back to finish the job properly."

"This is crazy."

"No, Martin, this is a godsend. We've got this bastard cold." Maiden stopped and made a grunt of satisfaction as they saw the man go through the gate into the small fenced area behind the building. "Come on, let's see if we can trap him in there while we can."

They pushed themselves away from the shadows. The distinctive rattle of an empty drink can being kicked along the alleyway came from the distance. Maiden cursed and froze. "Those useless pricks," he hissed.

The man in the overcoat froze too, standing like a startled animal as he searched the darkness for who had caused the noise. It wasn't hard to see, in that instant, the silhouette of one of the other detectives flicker across a pool of light.

The man broke and ran, crashing into the fence as he tried to get through the gate in a rush. He turned away from the noise and started to bolt down the alleyway—directly towards Maiden and Creane.

Maiden tugged the radio from his pocket, snapping into it, "He's running! Moving towards Phillip Street."

The two detectives only had to wait for the man to run into their arms, but with his senses heightened by fear he saw the menacing shapes now in front of him. His running wavered as he saw the trap and he veered off to one side and tried to wrench open a gate to another small service area. The fencing shook as the gate refused to yield. A moment later he was desperately climbing the wire.

Maiden and Creane were already running, with Creane calling out a warning for him to stop. As they got closer Maiden saw there was a narrow gap between the two buildings, somewhere their quarry might be able to slip through to the street beyond. Maiden cursed and ran harder. Creane pulled ahead of him, but neither detective reached the fencing before the man toppled over the upper wire and fell to the concrete. Scrambling to his feet he disappeared into the shadowed gap. Creane lithely vaulted to the top of the fence and dropped to the other side. His coat caught, but he uncaringly ripped it away. Maiden was attempting to climb the fence with less alacrity, the wiring sagging under his extra weight.

Creane followed the man into the gap. He nearly fell as the concrete ended abruptly and there was a small drop to bare dirt. The place smelled damp and unclean. The gap between the buildings was less than two metres wide and it was completely black. Up ahead a column of light showed him where the gap ended at the street, but the light was too high up. There was some sort of solid barrier at the end that their fugitive would have to climb.

If he was still running.

The place could be a perfect trap. Creane couldn't see in front of him at all and he slowed, afraid he might crash into something. He knew the man they were chasing might now have turned like a cornered animal and be waiting to strike in the darkness. Creane remembered the small torch he had in his pocket, but decided not to use it. It would only show the man how close he was getting. Then he heard a scuffling sound in front of him.

The man was still trying to escape—not lying in wait. Behind him Creane heard Maiden enter the gap.

"Martin, have you got him?" Maiden's voice echoed down the walls.

Creane started running blindly through the narrow space. With every footfall he expected to crash headlong into an obstacle. The light in front of him got closer and he still hadn't seen the silhouette of anyone trying to scale the barrier. Then there was a clanging of metal and Creane knew his target was trying to climb the corrugated iron sheeting blocking the end.

He also knew he would get there before the man got over the top.

"Stop right now!" he called breathlessly. A head popped up above the barrier and there was the sound of feet scrabbling to grip onto the iron sheeting.

A second later Creane was there, reaching up as the other man was about to sling one leg over the top. The overcoat gave him plenty to grab onto and the man was off-balance. Creane hauled hard and with a cry of fear the man tumbled backwards towards him. Creane avoided the falling body and dropped onto his captive, who was now yelling with the pain of his fall. The darkness was complete at the base of the iron sheeting and Creane had to blindly grab for anything to suppress the man's struggling. He was grateful to have Maiden come in beside him and join the scuffle. The weight of two policemen convinced the man to stop fighting and he went limp.

"Please I didn't do anything." The voice was pleading and not the voice of the strong, brutal killer the detectives expected. The man's body was surprisingly small, too. Without the darkness Creane might have easily held him alone. The man had a sour, unwashed smell.

"Just shut up," Maiden panted. He was pulling a set of handcuffs from his jacket and in the darkness searched the confusion of limbs for the right ones to cuff. Now Creane produced his torch. The narrow beam shone on the white, frightened face of a young man. He blinked owlishly at the light.

"Let's get him back to the alley," Maiden grunted, reaching down to lift the youth roughly to his feet. Creane went first, using his torch to guide their way. Maiden followed, sandwiching their stumbling captive between them. Up ahead the other two detectives called anxiously into the gap and Creane answered, reassuring them. It reminded Maiden of the radio and he used it first to notify the men working for him that a capture had been successfully achieved, then he put in a call to Despatch informing them what had happened. With a sense of relief Maiden requested the crime-response to now move in. All the time the youth kept repeating his innocence and confusion over why they had chased him.

Back in the service area at the rear of the building Maiden waited until a patrol car with a pair of bolt cutters arrived, instead of climbing the fence and having to man-handle their captive over the wire. Maiden used the opportunity to body-search the man.

As he ran his hands through the youth's clothing he took a closer look. Creane obliged by running his torchlight over him again. The man was in his early twenties, pale and sick looking. The clothes were the cast-off rags of a street-dweller. It didn't feel good and Maiden was angrily already beginning to think they had the wrong man. Still, it was too early to make any rush judgements.

"You're in a lot of trouble, son," he muttered, still out of breath from the chase. He began searching the pockets of the overcoat. "What's your name?"

"Darren," the man answered, meekly turning so Maiden could easily reach his other pockets. His voice quavered.

"Darren? Darren who?"

"Darren Gallery. Look—what's this for? What have I done?"

"You tell us," Creane put in harshly. "What are you doing back here? Why did you start running when you saw us?" Behind them the alley was washed by a glare of light as a patrol car entered. It made the youth's face appear even whiter and showed the dark smudges of illness under his eyes.

"I—I know I'm not allowed in that place."

"What place?"

"Where they keep the paper and stuff." Gallery looked desperately in turn at the two detectives. "But it's dry and clean. No-one else knows about it, I think."

It took a moment for either Maiden or Creane to understand. Creane asked, surprised, "You mean you *sleep* in there?"

"Not every night. I got other places, too," Gallery shrugged defensively. "Sometimes there's not much paper in there, but when it's full it's like a big, soft bed. Now they've taken it away," he added sadly, looking past them towards the ramming mechanism.

The radio hooked to Maiden's lapel had been squawking incessantly for the past few minutes, but it was only now he realised it was his own name being called. He snapped an acknowledgement, his disappointment about the youth showing.

The metallic voice of Despatch told him, "We've got a guy on the phone called Lawson who's asking for you. He sounds hysterical and didn't make much sense, but we worked out he knows you're just outside. What do you want us to do? Send a car?"

Maiden gave Creane a look and breathed, "Goddamn," before replying, "no, I'll handle it."

A policeman from the patrol car was about to cut the chain locking the gate. Maiden told him to hurry and the moment the chain parted between the bolt cutter's jaws he pushed his way through, shoving Gallery in front of him at a gathering of men on the other side. Maiden snapped, "Look after this fool. Come on, Martin. You two constables follow us!"

The alleyway was filling with back up cars and a van with a team to seal off the crime scene. Headlights glared and blue lights flashed, reflecting off the close buildings. Maiden weaved his way through quickly, with Creane and the puzzled constables following close behind. Several people were already starting work around the recycling dock, cordoning off the bloody pool, but no-one was inside the service area of the building. Maiden was searching his pockets for the back entrance key, finding it just as they reached the door. Neither detective said anything until the four of them were squeezed inside the service lift and riding upwards. Unfamiliar with the place, Creane was looking around as Maiden had done.

He asked, "What do you think's happened?"

"I've got a bloody good guess," Maiden replied grimly.

In Lawson's offices he didn't hesitate, but strode briskly through to the solicitor's own room. There they found Lawson sitting at his desk. A near-empty Scotch bottle was in front of him. Lawson lifted his head to look at the detectives as they entered. His expression was dull and shocked.

"There's something in the safe," he told them hoarsely. "I opened it to get some files—and found it."

Maiden swore and immediately ducked back out of the office again with Creane hurrying behind. In his haste

Maiden took several wrong turns before he found the safe. The door was open revealing a large walk-in style cupboard. A fluorescent light brightly illuminated the space.

On the narrow floorspace between the tiers of shelving was Julie MacQuarrie's severed leg.

Maiden stared at it for a long time, then closed his eyes wearily and leaned back against the doorframe. "Fuck it, it was here all the time," he said.

"No-one would have thought of looking in the safe," Creane told him quietly. "You wouldn't expect the killer to have had the combination anyway. Shit, it must have been the *killer* who the other secretary heard close it, not the victim. I guess she's lucky to be alive."

Maiden looked at him, his face was blank, not registering Creane's attempt to console him. "Is there a note? Can you see one?"

Creane pushed past him and went over for a closer inspection. He leaned over the top of the leg so he could look around it without disturbing it. "I don't think so," he decided.

"No," Maiden said, sighing and slowly shaking off his mood. "But it doesn't really need one, does it?"

Chapter Twenty-two

The note was Vicki's idea.

Howard was checking on her regularly, giving him the excuse to stand in the doorway of the bedroom and stare hungrily at her while he tried to make conversation. His awkward attempts at talking only increased Vicki's stress, because she didn't want to reject him any more than she had to, but the topics were always naive or childish and it was difficult for her to keep up a pretence of interest. He hadn't mentioned the girl called Fiona again and that made Vicki feel worse. Howard was obviously more interested in who he had now. Fiona—whoever she was—was forgotten.

Vicki realised Howard was on an emotional tightrope, treading a fine line between treating her with a kindness as if he were an aspiring young lover, and succumbing to the black, angry moods where he could abuse her any way he wanted. He desperately wanted to have sex with her—it wouldn't be rape in Howard's mind. Vicki could see the pent-up frustration in his face and in his trembling fingers, and the way he blatantly touched her private parts whenever he was taping her up before he left the flat. Every time Howard needed to go out, he would make Vicki lie on her stomach and tape her arms behind her and her feet together. Then he would indulge himself for a short while, pushing his hands beneath her body to cup her breasts and squeeze her nipples. Sometimes he stroked her buttocks and let his fingers probe between her legs. She was always fully dressed and he did these things through her clothing, as if Howard used the materials of her jeans and sweater to protect him from the tainting he believed her menstruating threatened. When he returned from wherever he had been, Howard would release her, then stand in the doorway and chat while Vicki stayed on the bed, as if none of the binding or physical abuse had ever occurred. Vicki would dazedly try to recover, after sitting or lying taped up on the filthy sheets sometimes for hours. She was losing track of time, but could tell by the night sky outside that Howard's absences began in the evening and ended in the early hours of the morning. He came back smelling of liquor. Once, she caught the faint whiff of perfume.

"How much money are you asking for me?" she asked once, after he untied her. It was incredibly difficult for Vicki to speak to him normally after being trussed and touched, then left for however long he wished. But she knew it was the only way she might survive this nightmare. Vicki had to respond to him as if his actions were perfectly all right. She looked for a positive side to everything. At least these were moments of comparative safety, tied up but knowing he must be out of the flat. It gave her time to think with lessened fear and to tell herself over and over again her ordeal would end.

"Money?" he asked, looking at her warily.

He had brought her a bottle of Coke. Oddly, it was something he did every time he went out and Vicki always drank it gratefully, because she didn't want to drink the water from the tap if she could avoid it.

And she was collecting the bottles.

She opened a bottle now, using the moment to judge how receptive Howard might be. "Aren't you asking for a ransom? Isn't that why you took me?" She watched his eyes go dull as Howard slowly processed the idea.

"How much do you think you're worth?" he asked carefully.

"I don't know." Vicki was about to mention a million dollars, because it was such a magical figure, but decided at the last moment that something more realistic would be better. "My parents aren't rich, but I suppose their house is worth about a hundred thousand dollars," Vicki said even though she had no idea of the value of her parents' home. "I guess the bank would lend them that much."

"A hundred thousand?" The idea struck home, then he looked at her suspiciously. "Why the fuck are you being so helpful?"

Vicki kept her voice calm. "Because I know it's what you're going to do. I just want to go home. If you ask for something they can't give you, I don't know what's going to happen to me. I just want to go *home*, OK?"

A flicker of what might have been hurt crossed Howard's face and Vicki inwardly tensed herself for an attack, thinking she had gone too far. But he relaxed. "OK, I'll ask for that much," he said. "I've been thinking about it. I was going to write them a note today."

"Please, let me write it." Again a frown of suspicion came to Howard's face and Vicki quickly went on, "My parents know my handwriting. It will let them know I'm still OK. They may not pay the money, if they're not certain I'm . . . all right." She nearly said "alive," but stopped herself again. Vicki couldn't bring herself to say aloud anything to suggest Howard might be going to kill her.

He was nodding jerkily now, already accepting this idea as his own. "OK, we need some paper and a pen," he said, looking around. But from his expression she could see he didn't have either in the flat. Vicki wouldn't have been surprised if Howard couldn't write a word. "I'll send it to your house tomorrow."

The fear of Howard knowing where she lived chilled Vicki. Common sense told her that if she survived, Howard wouldn't be spending the rest of his life safely locked in jail. He would be released eventually. Visions of him returning years later to haunt her made her say quickly, "No, you should send it to a newspaper. They will take more notice of it and they'll want to believe it's genuine."

Unintentionally, Vicki touched on a chord in Howard's sense of importance. His obsession with getting newspaper coverage was stronger than ever. Now he was staring at her in a strange way and Vicki again feared she had gone too far, or that Howard detected she had other ideas in mind. In fact, he was considering whether a note to a major newspaper would have more impact if he included one of Vicki's fingers with it.

"I'll have to get some paper," he said absently. "I have to go out."

Vicki knew what that meant. He left the room and returned moments later with the adhesive tape. There was no point in protesting. Vicki rolled over onto her stomach and presented her hands behind her back. There was a ripping sound and she felt the tape being wrapped around her wrists. The skin there was raw now. All the fine hairs on her forearms had been pulled out. Next he did her ankles, pulling her legs together and running the tape over her clothing. Then Vicki tensed herself for the inevitable.

She tried not to flinch too much at his first touch. Howard thrust his hand between her legs and was groping inexpertly at her groin. Then he withdrew it and pushed under the waistband of her jeans and underwear so his palm felt the bare skin of her buttocks. This was the first time since his attempted rape that Howard dared to go beyond the perceived safety of her clothing and Vicki began to panic.

In desperation she breathed, "Be careful," and he instantly pulled his hand away again. She didn't look up at him, but she could hear his breathing coming in short, excited gasps.

There was a silence, then he told her, "I'll be back soon." And left the room abruptly.

Vicki wasn't surprised when Howard returned sooner than usual. He carried a six-pack of beers in one hand, a Coke in the other and a paper bag was tucked under his arm. Putting everything down he tore the tape off Vicki, then tossed her the bag. After massaging her wrists for a moment she looked inside it. There was a cheap writing pad, a pen and some envelopes. The envelopes were much bigger than required for the paper, but she didn't comment.

"Start writing," he told her. He sat on the bed near her and twisted the top off one of the beers.

"But . . . but what do you want me to write?"

"Tell them who you are and how you got here," he said confidently. Howard had been thinking about this while he was out. "Then tell them I want a hundred thousand dollars in used cash for your safe return, or I'm going to kill you." At Vicki's alarmed gasp he looked at her and added, "I won't do it. But they have to know I'm serious."

Vicki was terrified at the total lack of conviction and compassion in his voice. Hiding her fear she opened the writing pad and balanced it on her knees. The pen shook as she started the first sentence and after a few words Vicki swore as best she could and tore the page away, screwing it into a ball and tossing it towards a corner of the room. She started again, writing more carefully. It took some time before she was finished.

"What do you want them to do with the money?" Vicki asked.

There was another silence, longer this time and filled with tension. Finally, Howard said angrily, "I don't know. I can't think of a way they can pay without them following me, or tracking me down."

The expression on his face of frustration and anger was becoming familiar to Vicki and she knew he was close to breaking point. "You'll think of a way," she said hurriedly.

"Damned right, I will," he replied, grating his words, but he fell silent again and stared moodily at the floor. He startled Vicki by fixing her with a glare and asking, "Are you still bleeding?"

"What? . . . Of course. It's only been a day since I started," she said, suddenly frightened again.

"Show me."

"What?"

"*Show* me. I don't trust you."

"Please, it's always at least four or five days—"

"Show me, I said!"

Looking into his eyes Vicki believed this had nothing to do with trusting or believing her. This was about paying her back. Howard was making up ground he felt he had lost by not having a complete plan and displaying a lack of intelligence that Vicki possessed simply by being able to write the letter for him. Now he wanted to reassert his power over her and hurt Vicki some way to drive the point home.

Luckily for her state of mind, Vicki didn't know that in one of their most recent bar-room conversations, Fiona had answered Howard's awkward enquiry about feminine hygiene by telling him that she rarely bled for more than two days.

Her humiliation and fear were so intense it locked a pain in her chest as she slowly unfastened her jeans and first pulled them, then her panties, down her legs to her knees. The writing pad and pen slipped away and fell down between the bed and the wall, but she made no attempt to stop them. She could feel Howard's eyes staring down at her nakedness. It was almost as bad as his touching her. With shaking fingers Vicki removed the tampon and held it up for him to see. It was bloody and needed changing, but she wouldn't do it now in front of him. Vicki already had two other soiled tampons hidden under the bed and she wanted to keep this one, too.

"See?" she said miserably. "I told you."

Howard didn't reply. He left the bed, but only to stand next to it, facing her. Vicki bent her head and concentrated on replacing the tampon. As she finished she heard a rustle of clothing and, dreading what she would see, looked up.

He was now masturbating directly in front of her face. Howard wore a tight grimace, as if in pain, his eyes only slits as he stared at Vicki's groin. His putrid smell wafted over her.

"Oh, *please*," she whispered, turning her head away and praying he wouldn't demand she do something for him.

But he was orgasming after only seconds, some of the warm semen splashing down onto Vicki's exposed skin. She pressed herself against the wall to get away. Howard didn't notice. He was panting, his eyes closed now.

When he recovered Howard dressed himself quickly. He looked defiant, yet with a trace of shame, and didn't say another word. He picked up the remains of the six-pack and left the room, slamming the door behind him.

Vicki didn't move for a long time, leaning her face on the cold wall and putting the flats of her palms against it, as if this were comforting contact with the only friend in the world she had. Finally, she moved to the bottom of the bed and used a portion of the sheet there to clean herself, then pulled her jeans back on. She kept her tears back.

Things had, in fact, gone OK.

Vicki now had a pen and paper—more than the screwed-up page she had been hoping for. The only window in the room could be opened less than ten centimetres, not enough for the most determined suicide to jump to their death.

But more than enough for an empty Coke bottle, with a note, to be dropped outside.

* * *

In the lounge room Howard couldn't understand the feelings of burning embarrassment and inadequacy filling him. He kept telling himself it didn't matter. The girl was there for him to do with what he wished. It wasn't like Fiona, who told him what to do. Vicki was *his*.

But the feelings didn't go away.

He drank three more of the beers and came to a decision.

When the girl's bleeding stopped he would have sex with her as many times as he wanted. It would happen non-stop, night and day, until he was sick of her and didn't need her around any more.

Then he would kill her and use parts of her body to convince someone to pay the ransom. Small parts, so they wouldn't know she was dead. Maybe bigger parts later, just to stick the knife in and show them who was boss. The newspapers would be full of it.

And besides, he could always get another girl with the next job. It had been easy enough this time.

Chapter Twenty-three

Maiden was angry. The failure to produce anything positive from his attempts to trap Julie MacQuarrie's killer left him wide open to criticism from people like Longman, and he didn't think they would let the chance go by. So now he was waiting at his desk, expecting the axe to fall at any moment. His anger stemmed mostly from everyone else's willingness to condemn what he had done—not that he particularly cared what anyone else thought. It was the *attitude* he hated. No-one wanted to recognise he had tried something different to break a stalemate, when standard procedures had been getting them nowhere. There was only condemnation.

To make matters worse the press were starting to pay a lot of unhelpful attention to the case. Someone had leaked the contents of the note found on Greg Howlett's body and the media grabbed at the implications wholeheartedly. The morning editions were screaming large headlines about the serial killer now "stalking corporate Sydney." Anyone, they claimed, who was a white-collar worker was at risk, but particularly those people involved in debt-collecting, legal services, accountancy and bankruptcy. Maiden had to agree that was just about correct. It was also exactly what the killer was probably trying to achieve—panic and fear within the business community. But more than anything, he only really cared about receiving a flood of bogus letters and notes all claiming to be authored by the killer. It was the last thing he needed.

He had sent Creane off to question Susan Easton again. It was tempting to go along too, if only to see the reaction on the woman's face when she was told the killer had been in the office with her for a short while. Otherwise, he didn't expect Creane would achieve much at all, but this way Maiden would probably screen him from most of the repercussions that would fly about the failed operation. It was only a matter of when, finally, Longman tired of letting him stew.

The telephone rang. Maiden took a deep breath, re-minded himself once more not to tell Longman to shove his job, and picked up the receiver. He was surprised and even a little annoyed to hear it was only the sergeant at the reception desk downstairs.

"We have got somebody here who claims he could help your investigation, sir," the sergeant told him for-mally.

"Who? How do they know me?"

"He doesn't. He just reckons he has some information on the girl who was found in the rubbish bin. That is still your investigation, isn't it, sir?"

It was probably an innocent question, but Maiden fig-ured that even the desk sergeant held the opinion he had blown procedure so badly it was likely he was no longer on the job. "Yes, it's still mine," he said, wearily. "I'll come down and see if he's worth interviewing."

Maiden pulled his jacket from the back of his seat, put it on and left the office. The lift took him straight to the main foyer. It was just past midday and the place was busy. Because he was tired, the crowd of people irritated Maiden. He had gotten home from the crime scene at Lawson's offices after three o'clock, then got less than four hours' uneasy sleep, which wasn't enough. The desk sergeant saw him coming and nodded at a dishevelled man sitting apprehensively on a bench. Maiden went straight over. As he got close he saw the man was wearing a uniform of some sort.

"I'm Detective Senior Sergeant Maiden," he said, startling the man into standing. "You have something you can tell us?"

"Paul . . . Paul Jones." Jones looked uncertain whether he should be offering a handshake. "I heard on the radio news this morning they found a girl's body in a rubbish bin."

"It was a paper recycling bin actually, but what about it?"

Jones's gaze flickered nervously at the people all around, prompting Maiden to add resignedly, "OK, follow me."

He took him through to an interview room and seated the man at the bare wooden table. Maiden walked impatiently around him. "This can be completely off the record, if you want. You won't get into any trouble, as long as you haven't done anything yourself."

Turning his eyes up to Maiden, Jones hesitated before saying, "Well, I think I seen another one."

Maiden's gut tightened, but he kept his face neutral. "Another what?"

"Another body, in a bin I mean. That's what I do— empty rubbish bins." Jones put a finger on one of his uniform badges and Maiden recognised the name of a waste disposal company.

"Why didn't you tell us this before?"

Jones said defensively and quickly, "Hey, I see a lot of funny things come out of people's rubbish. If I reported everything, I'd be talking to you guys every day. And besides, I wasn't sure what I seen, but when I heard the news this morning, I figured you might want to know, just in case." He shrugged, "Anything could help, like."

Maiden knew exactly what the man's attitude would have been. He wouldn't have wanted to get involved. Rather than letting his annoyance show, which it was threatening to do, Maiden told himself to be grateful Jones had decided eventually to come forward.

"So where would this bin be now? Do you think the body will still be in it?"

Jones looked puzzled. "I was *emptying* it. That's when I think I saw it. I got this mirror see, that lets me watch what's going in the back. It could have been one of them blow-up dolls for all I know, that someone's chucked out. It was only a sort of shape I saw, just for a moment. Whatever it was, it'd be buried down the landfill site by now."

In Maiden's mind pieces were clicking dramatically into place. Jones was talking about the fingerless corpse found at the landfill site. He asked absently, as he thought over all the possibilities, "Can you tell me the address this bin was sited at?"

"No," Jones admitted, then went on before Maiden could react, "But I could show you on a map. I'm not good on street names and such, but I could find the place on a map."

"That's good enough. OK, come this way." Maiden tapped him on the shoulder, impatient to get Jones on his feet and out of the room. In the Despatch room Jones stared wide-eyed at the row of telephone and radio operators, while Maiden pulled him across to a large detailed map of the city on the wall.

"Was it somewhere around here?" Maiden asked him. "In the central business district?"

"No, it was out Waterloo way."

This disappointed Maiden, but he didn't let it show. He

waited patiently while Jones studied the map, then traced a route with his finger. He tapped a portion of it.

Jones asked, "Is that where the big McDonald's is? With all the different drive-throughs?"

Maiden looked at the map over Jones's shoulder and considered the question. "Yes," he said, finally.

Jones moved his finger to the left. "Then it was in that street there. The bin belonged to the first set of flats in that road."

Maiden noted the name of the street, then put his hand on Jones's shoulder. "Thank you. What you've told me is going to be very useful indeed, but I still need you to write it down as an official statement." Jones looked worried. Maiden told him, "It's only a formality as far as you're concerned. You'll probably never hear about the matter again. I'll get a sergeant to help you with it now, because I'm going to get to work on it right away."

Maiden walked away abruptly, heading back to his desk, leaving Jones looking confused and still anxious. Maiden needed to think—and to think hard. He now believed there *was* a connection between his investigation and the fingerless corpse found on the landfill site, but he had no real evidence to back that up. It was only a hunch.

He was only just beginning to put the pieces together when his phone rang. Maiden snarled a curse and picked it up. He suddenly remembered Longman was waiting for a chance to rebuke him. It was the last thing Maiden wanted to deal with now.

But it was Janet Brown. "Are you trying to send me enough work, so I can't leave this place at night?" she asked, teasing gently.

Maiden, expecting Longman's acid tones, had to readjust his thoughts. "No, of course not. I'd be much happier if both of us had nothing to do at all. Why, have you got some news for me?"

"Nothing that you don't already know or might have guessed." There was a pause. "OK, listen to this. The murdered girl died of massive head injuries. Blood and hair samples taken from the steel of the bin suggest her head was bashed against it several times and that's what killed her. Also, we've compared the wound where her leg was removed to the stump of the limb found in the office safe and can confidently say it's her leg," Brown finished. Maiden couldn't tell if she was being serious.

"Well, thank Heaven for small mercies," he said in a similar tone. "Otherwise I'd be out there looking for another one-legged corpse and a severed leg without an owner."

"You can thank modern forensic science."

"OK, thank you."

Brown hesitated, before saying, "Look, I feel bad about not letting you come over the other night. I really was tired. I didn't say no for . . . other reasons."

"I know," he lied, feeling his heart skip a beat. "I didn't take any offence, if that's what you're worried about."

"Good. I'd like to meet you for a drink after work and maybe make it up to you. By buying you a drink, I mean," she added, self-consciously. "It would make me feel better, at least."

"I'd like that," Maiden said, his gut twisting with disappointment. "But I might have a break in my investigation and I want to follow it up. I don't know how long it's going to take me. I might let you down."

There was a silence as they both struggled for a solution.

"Is it a good break?" she asked to fill the gap.

"I really don't know. I'm waiting for Martin to come back and we'll get right onto it." Thinking of Creane gave Maiden an idea. "Hey, Martin's got a mobile phone. Maybe we can arrange a time and a place, then I can call you, if it looks like I'm going to get caught up?"

"That sounds like it would work. I can always have a few drinks on my own, if I know you're only going to be a bit late."

"If you're lucky, you might get picked up by some handsome bachelor," Maiden joked, aware that it was a real possibility.

"I'll wear my Black Widow uniform. That should keep them away."

He smiled. "Maybe I should just make sure I get there first."

"That sounds even better."

Maiden suggested a bar and a time. She agreed and said goodbye.

He went to hang up his own telephone, then changed his mind and left the phone off the hook. He didn't want any more calls to disturb him.

It took him a while to clear his mind of memories and visions of his night with Janet Brown, but when Maiden finally devoted his whole attention to the problem at hand, he became totally absorbed.

In truth, nothing fitted. The landfill corpse had too many things going against it to suggest it was part of Maiden's investigation. He was the wrong sort of victim too, for a start. He was a tough young hooligan in jeans and a singlet, not the white-collar workers the killer had targeted so far. Also, he had been killed by a shotgun, while Maiden now had two victims confirmed as killed by sheer brute strength. While he had no identification at all, his clothes, haircut and tattoos were a good indication he lived rough.

However, Maiden was considering a theory that his serial killer might have had a trial run. Perhaps the killer wanted to test his own resolve and see if he was capable of murder and getting away with it. And to see if he had the courage to mutilate his victims afterwards.

It would explain several things. First, the use of an industrial bin to dispose of the body. Rather than being a coincidence, it wasn't unusual for a killer to employ a successful method more than once. Chopping the fingers off might have been an attempt merely to prove he could do it. Many people who kill possess no stomach for cutting up the corpse afterwards. As for the landfill victim being of the wrong type, it made sense that someone who wanted to practice a particular method of killing it might begin in a location where their activities may more easily go unnoticed. Even the shotgun could have been an experiment proving too noisy and therefore abandoned as a bad idea, or perhaps the tougher youth prompted a harder approach and use of the shotgun, while the filing clerks and female secretaries of the CBD needed nothing more than two strong hands as murder weapons.

This was the last piece of the puzzle Maiden was building in his mind. The killer he was searching for *was* the murder weapon—and little else. It wasn't someone capable of masterminding the campaign of terror in the CBD. That had to be someone else's idea. Someone who, when they wanted a person dead and torn apart, were wielding this killer as a weapon just as sure as if the knife were in their own hands.

Maiden realised it could all be possible, or that he might be painting himself a scenario that would take him even further from finding his killer, but he had no choice about that. Whatever the result, Maiden believed there was nothing to rule out positively the landfill corpse as part of his own investigation anymore. Having a closer look might give him the break he needed.

"Photographs," he muttered to himself, recovering the phone. He remembered asking for shots of the corpse to be circulated around the CBD and inner-city police stations in the hope someone would recognise them. Maiden wanted some copies for himself now, but it took some fast talking to arrange it. The photographic department was always busy and didn't like interruptions to its schedule, but in the end Maiden got more than he'd hoped for. The technician working at that time offered to run off copies of the pictures straightaway, as long as Maiden didn't mind a lack of quality. His equipment wasn't set up for it. Maiden happily agreed and said he would be down soon to pick them up.

At that moment Creane walked up to his desk and sat tiredly on its edge.

"That was a complete waste of time," he announced. "Apart from scaring the hell out of the poor woman, when I told her the killer was actually in the office with her. She didn't see a thing and she thinks she *may* have heard something—but won't commit herself. It was just a noise, like a door closing, anyway."

"It doesn't surprise me," Maiden said casually. "Never mind, we have a better goose to chase."

"Really? What?"

Maiden explained the story given to him by the rubbish truck driver. Creane wasn't enthusiastic or holding much store in Maiden's hunches.

He said, "We already dismissed that killing as not being part of our case. Knowing where the body came from doesn't change things much."

"What about the use of the industrial bin?"

"Big deal. It's a pretty obvious place to hide a body, if you ask me."

"OK, how about this?" Maiden went into details about his theory of the killer being only an accomplice for a more intelligent, motivated person, and that perhaps the landfill corpse was the result of a practice run by the killer. Now Creane was more impressed, but still had his doubts.

"It all sounds good, John. But are you sure you're not seeing too much in all of this? You haven't got a hell of a lot of hard evidence to tie all of this together."

Maiden gave Creane a knowing look. He said, "Following long-shot ideas like this one right through is the difference between a good detective and a rule-book fool like Longman. You have to look at all the possibilities, especially when nothing else is working for you, which is where *we're* at, at the moment."

Creane indulged him with an agreeing nod, but couldn't resist asking, "Then how come he's in his office over there as your boss, and you're only a floor detective?"

Maiden stood and patted his pockets, making sure he had everything. He said gruffly, "Because I can't suck like Longman, that's why. And while we're on the subject of that bastard, he hasn't called to abuse me for last night. All of a sudden I don't feel like waiting around for it. I've got some photos being run off downstairs. Let's sign out a car and do a run down to Waterloo. Maybe we can jag an ID on this landfill corpse. It's better than sitting around here doing nothing."

"Suits me," Creane shrugged.

Maiden led the way. As they passed the glassed-in cubicle at the end of the room he saw Longman, who was on the telephone, notice them passing. He tried to finish his call quickly, half-standing behind his desk.

"Come on," Maiden said, darting out the door.

They detoured into the photography department. Here they had to wait ten minutes in a tiny reception area for the promised copies. The detectives helped themselves at a café bar and sat down in silence, nursing the plastic cups in front of them. The technician emerged, carrying photographs and dabbing at them with paper towelling.

"They're OK," he admitted "but not the best. The paper is too big and you've lost a bit of definition. Still, they're usable." He dropped them on a low coffee table in front of Maiden.

The pictures showed their subject exactly. The corpse looked like a dead person who had been found on a rubbish dump, cleaned up and had his eyes propped open for the photograph. There was no mistaking the dull, dead expression. Normally, such pictures were reproduced in a smaller scale and the deathly appearance wasn't so marked.

"They'll do fine," Maiden said, scooping them up and putting them in an envelope.

* * *

They started on the main road, taking the pictures into every grocery store, liquor outlet and petrol station they came across. This part of Waterloo was old, many of the buildings near-derelict. Rather than splitting up, Maiden and Creane kept together. It meant one detective could show the photos and ask the questions while the other watched for any suspicious reactions. In the first few hours they covered a lot of ground, but drew a blank everywhere.

It wasn't until the late afternoon that a barman finally thought he had seen the man drinking in his bar, but couldn't be sure. He had no idea of the dead man's name.

"Look on the bright side," Maiden said to Creane as they left the bar. "At least we might have wandered into this guy's own territory."

Neither of the detectives saw the look given them by a slim, drug-ravaged woman who had slipped into the toilets when they first walked in and watched through a crack in the doorway until they left.

Outside on the footpath Creane agreed wryly, "Yeah, but we're still only looking for a victim, remember? We want the killer." Gazing around him at the people passing by, he focused on a group of youths with torn leather jackets and faded jeans, and thought half the local population would qualify.

It seemed Maiden's optimism was premature. They ran into another succession of blank looks and shaking heads whenever they produced the photographs. Undoubtedly some of the people were turning defensive and sullen when they realised they were talking to policemen and this began to anger Creane. He started thinking they were wasting their time and he said so out loud.

"What else do you expect?" Maiden told him. "We can't give in yet. We're not going to achieve anything if we don't try, are we?"

But he was getting disheartened himself. It came almost as a shock when the wizened Vietnamese owner of a small grocery and milk bar stared at the photograph a long time, then nodded.

"He not been in here for a while," he said, gravely.

"What?" Maiden asked, the two detectives coming to life. "You know him?"

"He come in here and eat." The owner shrugged, a habitual gesture, and waved at the café tables. "And he buy, but he always buy junk. Nothing good."

"Do you know his name?"

"No, why should I?"

Creane moved closer and asked, "Have you ever delivered groceries to his home? Do you know his address?"

"No, I don't deliver," the shop owner shook his head. He repeated, "He don't come in here for a while."

"Damn it," Maiden said quietly, turning to Creane. "We're getting closer, but there's still hundreds of flats and houses in this area. He could have lived anywhere."

"Maybe if we mark down the hotel and this place, we can write out a search grid that's not so big?" Creane suggested.

The man was still looking at the photograph as if it meant something more to him. Off-handedly, not worrying if the detectives were listening, he said, "His friend still come here. He only buy junk, too."

That caught both the detectives' attention. Trying not to intimidate the shop owner, Maiden asked, "Are you telling me this man had a friend, and he still comes shopping here?"

"Sometimes."

"When? How often? Every day?"

"Two days—maybe three. Who knows?"

"What sort of junk does he buy?" Creane was thinking they might be able to narrow down their man to a particular habit, which could limit the amount of stores they needed to watch.

To answer the shop owner shuffled out from behind his counter and beckoned them to follow him to the grocery shelves. As he moved among the racks of goods he pointed at different items and said, "This, and this." They were mainly potato chips, chocolates and cheese biscuits. Nothing to make him out of the ordinary. Disappointed, Maiden and Creane let him finish. Then he got to the hygiene section and took down a packet, showing it to them.

It was a packet of tampons.

"The other day he buy these, but I don't know why. No woman would ever want to live with him. He should buy soap!" he added with a curl of his lip. "He smells very bad. He *always* smells very bad."

A memory slammed into Maiden's head. One of the security guards at the petrol station armed hold-up had said exactly the same thing. Stunned he turned to Creane. "*Jesus Christ*," he whispered. "Do you know who he's talking about? *This* is the guy who's holding the girl hostage! It *has* to be!"

They hurried back to the car, but Maiden surprised Creane by stopping him from driving away.

"Wait, Martin. We have to think about what we have here and what we're going to do about it."

Creane took his hands from the ignition keys and looked at him. Maiden was counting the facts off on his fingers.

"The landfill corpse was killed by a shotgun, and we know this guy definitely has a shotgun, right? The corpse's fingers were cut off, and the bandit said as he left that he would cut the girl up like he did the others, if anyone tried to follow him. What if he was talking about the landfill body? He cut his *friend* up. And now *here* we have some guy who is apparently ugly as a pig and smells like shit— just like those security men said—who suddenly needs to buy tampons. For who, Martin? I say he's our man. He had a fall-out with his mate, topped him with the shotgun and chopped his fingers off for God knows what reason, then he went out to do a job on his own that went badly wrong and he ends up with a hostage. The girl's period starts while he's holding her and from some twisted sense of compassion he buys her some tampons. What do you think?"

"It'd be thin, if it wasn't for that smell factor," Creane said, staring through the windscreen as he thought. "And maybe the bit about chopping people up. But otherwise, yes, I think he's got the girl. This is the guy, all right."

"We have to get a team together to start doorknocking all the high-rise flats in this area. But we do it very quietly. Two guys to a team in plain clothes and doing it casual. We don't want to flush this bastard out and let him get away again. There can be a backup team with firepower around the corner, just in case."

Creane shook his head. "Hey, hold on a second—get a team together? *Another* team? After last night, you'll be lucky if they give you a retired drug dog."

"Very funny, Martin. This is a lot stronger. Besides, I don't want to deal with bloody Longman. I'll go straight past him and ask Bercoutte to OK it. I'll call Despatch and try to get a message to him to stick around." Maiden snatched the radio microphone from its holder on the dashboard. "What's the time?"

Creane checked his watch. "Just before six-thirty."

"Damn! Lend me your mobile phone, will you?"

"I thought you didn't like them? You said it was a toy—"

"Just give me the bloody phone!"

Creane handed it over. He kept a smile off his face when Maiden had to ask for instructions on how to use it. He punched in the number and waited, then lowered his voice as a connection was made. Creane started the car and pulled away from the kerb, but he was listening with great interest.

"Hi," Maiden said quietly into the phone, then scowled

at Creane as the younger detective's eyebrows went up at Maiden's tone.

"Where are you?" Janet Brown asked.

"I'd say I'm caught up for another hour. Do you still want to do it, or do you want to make it another time?"

"I can easily work here for another hour or so. Why don't we make it eight o'clock instead? Same place?"

"That's a deal," Maiden said. "I've got to go. Big Ears is listening."

He turned off the phone and went straight back to the radio, before Creane could comment. His request to speak to Bercoutte caused some confusion and took over five minutes to be answered.

"Mr. Bercoutte is in a meeting and says he'll be here when you get in," the radio finally told them.

"Good," Maiden nodded grimly.

Creane said, glancing at him, "Did I hear you tell someone we're only going to be an hour? Do you really think we're going to get organised, find this guy and bring him down that fast?"

"Hell, we won't be knocking on any doors tonight, Martin. Every second door we knock upon tonight will have some bastard flushing drugs or whatever down the toilet and we'll start a wildfire of panic that our target is bound to hear. Worse, he might kill the girl and try to run on his own." Maiden was convincing himself as he explained. "No, we need to wait until the morning, when at least some of the people will be at work and only the bad guys are home to answer the door. Besides, I don't want to give this guy any darkness to slip away in. I want all the advantages on my side."

"But that means you're gambling the girl will survive another night."

"I know. Actually, I'm gambling that somebody who buys their hostage tampons doesn't plan to kill her anyway."

* * *

Bercoutte was waiting in his office. If Creane was surprised that Maiden had the influence to bypass Longman this way he managed to hide it. After a perfunctory greeting Bercoutte ignored the younger detective.

"John, I spent half my day doing damage control for you," Bercoutte said, acidly. "What the hell did you think you were doing last night? You must have broken every rule that's ever been bloody written."

"Last night was worth a try," Maiden told him stubbornly. "OK, it didn't work, but it was still worth a try."

Bercoutte stared at him, then sighed and let his anger drain away. "All right, I suppose we were getting nowhere. But we've got some cleaning up to do. I hope you appreciate it. Now, what's this all about?"

Maiden explained what they had found out that afternoon. Bercoutte listened patiently, nodding occasionally at some of the details. When Maiden finished, Bercoutte stared at the desk in front of him for a while. "OK," he said, finally. "I think you're right. The bandit with his hostage must be living in a high-rise flat somewhere close. But how the hell are you going to find them?"

"Let me form some teams, two men each in plain clothes, and we'll start doorknocking. We'll keep it quiet, not something that will scare the entire neighbourhood. A massive doorknock in an area like that will only flush him out and he'll slip through our fingers again. Give all the teams a picture of the landfill corpse and see if we can't stumble across a neighbour or somebody who'll show us the right door. From what the Vietnamese guy was telling us, this guy won't have many friends. He's a real prick and most people would love to point the finger."

Bercoutte was looking doubtful. "You can't rely on that."

"No, I'm hoping we'll actually knock on his door sometime. We've got a bloody good description. We should have a State Protection Group waiting around the corner, just in case."

"After last night, giving you any *more* people is not going to be easy," Bercoutte said dryly. "You've already got more research staff than I have and they're achieving nothing. We need some results first. Who was originally chasing this hostage?"

"A detective called Bennett, in Penrith."

"Well, surely he's already got a sizeable team together? Why don't you arrange to do this with him? It makes sense and I don't care who works in whose area of operations. Let them argue about it later."

Maiden had already thought of this idea, but it needed someone with Bercoutte's seniority to make it happen. "I'm sure he'd be interested," he said. "I can give him a call straightaway."

"Good. I'll take care of the official side of things."

The meeting was over, but Creane didn't realise. He was taken by surprise when Maiden abruptly turned and headed for the door. But as the two detectives were leaving Bercoutte called after them, "And John, for Christ's sake make this one work. We need a win."

Maiden paused long enough to nod, then slipped through the doorway with Creane following.

Out in the hallway Creane crowded close to him as they walked. "How come you get to just walk into Bercoutte's office and demand things?"

"It's not quite like that, Martin."

"Yeah? It looks pretty good to me. No wonder you don't give a shit about Longman. Does he know about it?"

"No, and he'd better not find out," Maiden added warningly.

"Of course not. Where are we going, anyway?"

"We call Bennett and work out a plan for tomorrow morning. Then we get the hell out of here, because tomorrow's going to be a big day."

Creane looked pointedly at his watch. "And you've only

got—what? Half an hour, before you're supposed to meet someone?"

"That's none of your business."

Creane grinned. "Can I come, too?"

"No."

Chapter Twenty-four

Even though he expected her, Maiden was relieved to see Janet Brown still waiting for him. The bar was a private, low-ceilinged place with expensive prices and an up-market reputation.

"You made it," she smiled up at him.

"I left a few criminals running around free, but they can wait until tomorrow. Do you want a fresh drink?"

"Please."

He returned with the drinks and sat on the opposite side of the table. Brown leaned over to him.

"So, you've been having a successful day?"

"Better than some."

"Well, come on. Tell me about it."

"I thought you didn't like talking about work?"

"And I told you I didn't like talking about *my* work. I'm really interested in what you have to do."

"OK, I forgot," he conceded with a smile. Maiden made sure no-one nearby was listening. "Well, you know about the armed hold-up that turned into a hostage thing?" Brown nodded, her face full of interest. "It looks like we've got his location narrowed down to a few square kilometres. Tomorrow we're all going to turn into Avon ladies and start knocking on doors. Hopefully, we'll find him."

Brown frowned at him. "But what's that got to do with your investigation? I thought you said there was a break on your side of things?"

"I think there *is* a connection. Remember the corpse they found at the landfill site? The one with all its fingers chopped off? I'm betting it was some sort of trial run by our killer, which is why most of the details didn't fit."

She looked doubtful. "So you think the man who held up the petrol station and took the girl hostage is also your serial killer?"

Maiden hesitated before he replied. Her direct question, without his weave of coincidental evidence around it, was harder to answer. On the face of it, it was very unlikely the bandit with his hostage was the same person plaguing the inner city with severed human limbs. His theory that the killer was only an accomplice to someone else's larger plan still made the most sense, but with Brown putting it so simply, saying it aloud, caused doubt to creep in.

For one thing, the armed robber—if nothing else—had been a little *busy* lately to have a second career as a serial killer.

"I think so," he said finally.

"You *think so*? I don't understand."

Maiden was staring into his drink now, his mind filling again with all sorts of different theories. It was all getting too confusing. Brown was looking at him expectantly. He said, "OK, I'm *thinking* maybe this guy does all the dirty work? That would make sense. Someone else—somebody a damn sight smarter—is dropping the fingers and hands in the elevators." He paused, his imagination racing. "After all, I haven't given any more thought to the woman I think is involved."

Brown leaned even closer. "Woman? What woman?" Maiden was aware of her lips only a breath away from his own. "We think—well, that is I think, and Martin agrees with me—that there's an attractive woman somewhere who is luring the victims away to be killed without risk. The first few victims, at least. These were guys who acted out of character. They went out on the town, but on nights they wouldn't normally go out, so it was probably to meet someone new or different. Everything seems to point to a good-looking woman."

Brown looked amused and asked, "Isn't that a little old-fashioned and sexist?"

"It's not exactly a novel concept. It's been done before."

"What about last night's victim? It was a woman."

"She didn't have to be lured anywhere. She walked all by herself straight into a place perfect to get herself killed."

"OK. Do you have any idea who this woman is, or where she comes from?"

Maiden made a snorting noise and finally took a sip of his drink. "It's only a theory and no-one except you and Martin knows about it. Even if I was sure she existed, I wouldn't have a bloody clue where to start looking for her." He had an idea and looked at Brown differently. "You're a smart woman—and this person I'm theorising about has to be clever, too. Where do you think I might find her?"

Brown was startled and drew back, then she laughed and said, "I don't know. Let me think about it a moment. Have you got a cigarette? I'm out and haven't got change for the machine." She seemed pleased Maiden had asked her to be involved in his deadly puzzle. He found his cigarettes and flipped out one for each of them, then offered his lighter. Brown took an appreciative lungful of smoke and speared it at the ceiling.

She said, "She must be pretty and young enough to attract these junior clerks, right? But she must also be rich, or she wouldn't have this armed hold-up guy working for her." Brown waved her hand, dismissing her own thinking.

"But then, he wouldn't have to go out doing armed hold-ups, would he?"

"She could be paying him with sex," Maiden said, interested. "Maybe he's a relative doing it for love and he still needs his own crime to get money." He took his own thoughts further. "Perhaps he's out of control and wasn't supposed to go out robbing petrol stations—that could make the relative idea even better. It would explain how the connections are sneaking through, when they shouldn't be. Someone who is being paid, one way or another, isn't as likely to be allowed any mistakes. Relatives or lovers often do things of their own accord, wanting to prove they are just as smart as the person planning everything. In fact, if my idea of that landfill body being a trial run is correct, I wouldn't be surprised if it wasn't supposed to happen at all. I wonder if the person behind it all knows about it?"

Brown was looking at him, admiration plain in her eyes. "I think you must be a good detective," she said, softly.

Maiden smiled wryly. "You think so? Then I should tell you I haven't got an ounce of real evidence to back all this theorising up. It's all just hunches and feelings on my part. Not exactly your forensic science."

"Are your feelings normally correct?"

Something in the way she said this changed the whole tone of the conversation. Maiden stared into her eyes and saw the invitation, causing a swell of feeling inside his chest. There was a silence between them, which Maiden broke by asking gently, "Do you want to stay here? Or we can find somewhere to eat, if you like."

"I'm not hungry. Why don't we pick up a bottle of wine and go back to my place? We both need to relax, and I can rustle up a snack, if we need it."

"That sounds great," he said, reaching over the table to touch her hand.

* * *

Later, as they made love in her bed, Maiden felt a new passion coming from Brown. Before, the sex had been two consenting adults satisfying each other, doing things they knew to cause pleasure and, in some way, revelling in a close personal contact that came without commitment.

Now Brown stroked and caressed Maiden with a different feeling. She whispered his name and pressed her body against his with an urgency, as if she wanted every part of herself to be touching him in the same moment. Through his passion Maiden heard faint alarm bells. Without his expecting it—although he couldn't deny it was what he wanted—things were fast moving towards a changed relationship. It was the suddenness which worried him. It hinted at an instability in Brown that he wouldn't have thought possible, considering the serious, no-nonsense woman he had first met in her office.

But these could also be, Maiden knew, the sort of imagined fears which led to him losing two marriages. Instead, perhaps he should have accepted her new tenderness without doubts. She was obviously someone who didn't give affection away easily. He should return it and see where their feelings took them. Worrying about it would only ruin things right from the start.

The conflicting emotions arose again when it came time for Maiden to leave. He wanted to stay the night, but he needed a change of clothes for the morning and, more importantly, wanted to be near his own telephone. If anything happened during the night which might alter the course of action for the next day, Maiden wanted to know about it. He could have called The Rocks and given them Brown's number, but it would have added one more link to the communication chain that could fail. Besides, it didn't seem like the right thing to do—growing relationship or otherwise.

When Maiden explained to her in the darkness why he was leaving, Brown nodded sleepily and murmured she understood. Still, as he let himself out into the cold night,

Maiden couldn't help feeling he was doing something wrong and selfish. That perhaps he should stay until daylight.

At the same time he hated the personal complications too, and wondered if he really wanted them after all.

Chapter Twenty-five

Bennett surprised Maiden with a group of a dozen detectives. It was more than he'd hoped for. Each man was dressed casually, wearing jeans and running shoes. All of them also wore a loose, bulky jacket of some sort allowing them to conceal their weapons and radios. They met at eight o'clock in the morning in the car park of the McDonald's outlet. The car park was already well patronised by people buying breakfast in the store and the fourteen men standing in a group, dressed as they were, could have been any manner of businessmen gathering for a day's excursion.

Maiden and Bennett had decided on a format for the search during their telephone conversation the previous night. Because the team was comprised mainly of Bennett's men, Maiden let Bennett bring everyone together in an empty parking space and brief them on what was going to be done. He explained that each team of two was to be given specific streets or blocks of flats to canvass. Every door was to be knocked on and the slightest hint of suspicious behaviour was to be noted, but *not* acted upon unless it was absolutely necessary. Instead, surveillance would be stepped up and the State Protection Group, stationed even less conspicuously in an unmarked van at the back of a nearby garage, would carry out any required raids.

When he had finished detailing everything, Bennett turned to Maiden. "Have you got anything you want to say, John?"

Maiden nodded and stepped forward. The dozen unfamiliar faces regarded him carefully. He was an unknown.

"I'll start by admitting we have a lot of ground to cover and we'll probably all end the day pissed off and with sore feet. We could be back here tomorrow and even the next day, who knows."

Maiden stopped and cleared his throat. "But—if we do get lucky, here's what you need to know. We have a good idea of who we hope to find," he began, now speaking slowly and clearly. "In fact, you guys have probably got a better picture than Martin and myself, because you've been looking for him harder. He's obviously armed with a shotgun and dangerous. We have no name. New evidence that came to us yesterday strongly suggests this guy killed his partner with the shotgun and dumped the body in a waste bin, so he is not scared to pull a trigger. Martin and I are here with you, because we believe the target may have something to do with the recent killings and mutilations in the inner-city area. Some of our evidence there tells us this person is strong—and I mean *very* strong."

Maiden paused to let this sink in a moment. He already had their undivided attention, but unexpectedly associating the armed robber with the serial murders had them all suddenly more tense. "We are talking about an almost freakish strength which may not be apparent. If you have an opportunity to bring this man down physically, think twice about it. I don't care how good you all think you may be, this person is going to be hard to handle. You'll get hurt." Maiden jabbed his finger at them to emphasise.

"Now, let's not beat around the bush. His hostage is an

attractive young female who's probably had a rough time. So no-one's going to burst into tears if you use a bullet to slow this prick down. Obviously, I don't want him dead, because there are a few matters I would like to clear up, but I strongly recommend you use your weapons to convince him to co-operate. I doubt he is going to respect any physical show of strength. Of course, most of all, the safety of the hostage is paramount. No heroics, if you please. We have the State Protection Group team standing by for that sort of shit." Maiden could see his hard words had unsettled the men a little. These days, policemen had to work in an unfriendly environment filled with enquiries over shootings and public outcry when even violent criminals were shot during pitched gunbattle. And they faced the outrageous spectre of law-breakers bringing assault charges against their arresting officers.

Maiden softened his manner. "OK, I know it can be bloody hard, but do your best. When we start, don't just throw yourselves at it, by the way. Take it easy and grab a coffee or something. Try to get a vibe for the area you're working in, first." He finished lightly, "In other words, try not to look like a bunch of policemen."

This brought a rumble of laughter. It was a standard joke—not too far from the truth—that despite all the changes in fashions and style, members of the force always managed to stand out in a crowd as policemen, no matter what clothes they wore or how they cut their hair.

"OK, guys," Bennett announced, breaking them up. "Let's get going. Don't forget, hourly checks into Despatch and a personal check-in with either myself or Detective Senior Sargeant Maiden when you've finished your allotted area. We may have somewhere else for you to look."

Maiden and Creane started with a high-rise building. They went to the top—the tenth floor—planning to work their way down. The first door to open for them—the third they knocked on—gave a taste of what they would probably get all day.

It was answered by an overweight youth wearing jeans and a black T-shirt with a heavy-metal motif flaking off it. His eyes were red-rimmed and his slack face was pale and looked unclean. His hair was clipped close to the scalp. A cigarette hung from his lips. Behind him in the flat, music blared at a distorted volume from a cheap stereo.

"Yes?" he asked insolently, his voice rough. The odour of foul breath washed over Maiden, who had taken the lead. The detective hated the youth on sight and wanted to arrest him for something—anything—just so he could have the pleasure of throwing the man into a cell.

"We're police officers," Maiden said. He was slightly mollified by the look of panic crossing the youth's face. "We are looking for somebody."

"It can't be me. I haven't done anything."

"No, of course not," Maiden said dryly. "We want you to look at—"

"Have you got any ID?" the youth interrupted, regaining his insolence.

Creane began pulling out his wallet, but Maiden was fixing the youth with a hard stare. "Yes," he said sharply. "But if you have any doubts, we can take you down to the station and have everyone identified *officially*. Mind you, it could take all day. Do you want to sit around The Rocks police station for a few hours? You'd have to stay until everything was absolutely fucking clear—"

"OK, OK," the youth held up a hand. "Just asking. I mean, it's not safe to open your door these days, is it?"

Maiden shook his head in disgust and turned away. "Show him the picture, Martin," he growled, spreading his hands on the balcony railing and looking down on the untidy sprawl of the suburb around them. He used the moment to calm himself, only half listening to Creane's questions behind him.

"Do you know this guy?" Creane said, taking the photograph from an envelope. The youth looked at it, but Creane could already tell the answer was going to be no, regardless of his recognising it or not.

"Never seen him," he replied shortly.

"Are you sure?"

"Yeah. What'd he do?"

"He died," Creane said, pulling the photograph out of his hands. "Thanks. That's all."

Without a word the youth stepped back and closed the door in Creane's face, slamming it just hard enough to register a protest.

After a moment Creane sighed. "Well, that's a good start."

"Get used to it," Maiden told him, heading for the next door. "Who do you think lives in these places? The royal family?"

But it wasn't that bad. As they worked their way along the doors Creane was intrigued by the completely different situations they encountered from one home to the next. One flat could be clean and carefully tended with its tenants trying to make the best of what could only be described as difficult conditions—the small, cramped living spaces with little room to breathe. Opening the next door could reveal the exact opposite. Perhaps a group of youths sharing the flat and not caring about cleaning up or opening the windows to remove the stale smells. Not all the doors answered to the detectives' knocking. Some flats, they suspected, were occupied but the people ignored the visitors. Creane noted the numbers of any flats that didn't answer. If their searching brought no results, somebody would have to come back and try these places at another time.

It took them three hours to completely cover the first building. Over half the flats responded and their owners at least looked at the photograph though many were obviously never going to help in any way. Nobody recognised the dead face in the picture. Every hour Maiden used the radio to confirm with Despatch they were still OK, and twice he called Bennett to see if anyone in their teams had any progress at all. The answer there was no, too.

It was near midday when, back on the ground floor, Maiden pointed at a small corner shop across the street.

"Let's grab some lunch."

The shop was crammed with small goods, magazines and newspapers. All it had to offer in the way of food was meat pies that had been sitting in the warmer for several days. Wincing at the taste and texture, Maiden stood outside and ate one as he waited for Creane, who was still inside using the opportunity to show the picture. He appeared moments later carrying a pie smothered in red sauce and hugging the envelope of photographs under his arm.

"No luck," he said.

"Surprise me."

"What next?"

"That one, I guess. While my legs are still holding up."

It was another high-rise, dwarfing another close beside it.

"Why don't we go for the smaller one?" Creane complained.

"I hate this too, Martin. But we may as well get it over and done with. The more we do, the less I'm going to feel like doing the larger places. That's why I try to do them first."

"But he might be living in one of the smaller ones. That way, you might never have to climb through all the bigger buildings."

"Except that Murphy's Law exists for us, too," Maiden said, tossing half his pie into a rubbish bin. "Believe me, if we find this guy, he'll be at the top of the tallest building and in the very last place we look."

"Then why don't we go there first?"

"We are."

* * *

The next building proved to be just as fruitless as the first. The two detectives both began getting irritable and short-tempered as each door they knocked on brought them the same response. They became resigned to being answered with a shake of the head or blank looks when the photograph was shown. No better news came from the other teams.

By the time they'd finished the high-rise it was after four o'clock in the afternoon. Disheartened and weary, their legs aching from what felt like endless flights of stairs—it never seemed worthwhile to take the lift only one floor—Maiden and Creane stood on a small patch of struggling lawn and looked up at the building they had just covered. The structure was L-shaped with two wings. Several faces stared back down at them. Some people regarded the policemen's visit as a novelty worth observing and neighbours had gathered on their balconies and watched Maiden and Creane's progress across the distance on the opposite wing.

"We're entertaining them," Creane muttered, darkly.

"Of course. There's nothing better to see than a couple of coppers getting nowhere." Maiden turned away and started walking back towards their car parked on the street opposite the building's car park.

"Have we finished for the day?" Creane asked in surprise, hurrying after him.

Maiden took a moment to answer, then said tiredly, "I don't know. Let's check in with the others and see what Bennett thinks. I don't want to give up, but I'm sick to death of knocking on bloody doors and having people freak when they hear who we are."

Crossing the asphalt of the car park Creane nodded towards the smaller high-rise shadowed by the one they had just left. They were looking at the back of it—a sheer wall of concrete broken only by rows of small windows. The balconies and doors of the flats would be on the other side and, as far as Creane could see, there was only one wing. "That one's only small. It won't take us too long."

Maiden flicked a glance over his shoulder. "Maybe we can do some of these houses instead," he said, dismissing the building. "There's no bloody stairs then. But let's see what Bennett's got to say, first."

His hand was on the doorhandle of the car when there came the distinctive, but far-off sound of smashing glass. It was explosive, like something had been dropped from a height. Instinctively, both men looked towards the noise. It seemed to come from the smaller building. None of the windows they could see appeared broken.

But Maiden saw something that made him say softly, "Get in the car, Martin. Get in like nothing's happened."

Creane obeyed, asking as he moved, "Why? What's the matter?"

"Just get in."

Sitting in the front seat they had to lean forward and peer up through the windscreen to see the building properly. "Look about eight or nine storeys up," Maiden explained. "And about three windows in from the right. See it?"

"There's someone at the window," Creane said, after a moment. "Is that it? So what? People have been gawking at us all day."

All they could see was a white blob that could be someone's face framed in the small opening. There was no way to determine whether the face was male or female. Creane was unimpressed, but there was something about the face that struck a note in Maiden's mind. There was a movement at the window and a small object appeared, then dropped. An empty bottle glittered gaily in the afternoon sunshine as it fell, then smashed spectacularly when it hit the ground.

"Should we go up there and arrest them for littering?" Creane asked. "Maybe they want us to come close enough, so they can drop one of those on our heads."

"I certainly want to go up there and knock on that door, even if we don't do any others today," Maiden told him, sounding tense. "But not from here. Drive around the block and park somewhere else. If that's who I think it is, I don't want to get her hopes up and cause her to act foolishly."

While Creane nervously started the car, Maiden tried to count the floors and windows of the high-rise, calculating exactly which flat the window should belong to. A few minutes later Creane pulled into the kerb on the opposite side of the building. They got out and walked calmly towards the lift alcove.

"You think it's Vicki Colonel, trying to signal us," Creane said quietly.

"That's right, Martin."

"Then shouldn't we be calling the State Protection Group?"

"Let's just knock on the door first—see who's home."

Chapter Twenty-six

Vicki's spirits had been getting low. She felt dirty and unwell, though part of that was her own fault. She didn't want to shower. At first Vicki hadn't wanted to risk taking her clothes off, fearing what might go through Howard's mind if he knew she was on the other side of the bathroom door naked. Worse still, he might insist on watching her bathe. Also, she wanted to be unclean in the slim hope Howard would find her less attractive. However, judging by his own personal hygiene standards that was never going to happen. Howard hadn't even questioned her own lack of wanting to bathe. He appeared to accept it as perfectly normal. All during her ordeal Vicki was only washing her hands. These brief visits to the bathroom revealed only one filthy towel and no soap.

Now she stayed in a self-imposed imprisonment in the bedroom. Howard as usual was in the main room watching the indecipherable television. Once he allowed her to join him, but Vicki soon learned this could be worse than being locked up. Even though the television was almost unwatchable, the sputtering sounds of advertisements and programmes brought memories of home and normality. Whenever the picture flickered somewhere close to clarity, the smiling faces of people in commercials—happy and doing everyday things—only reminded Vicki of her situation. The craving for everything to be as it should, instead of this constant terror, could build up in Vicki's chest like a physical block that choked her.

And Howard might start his inane questions again, as if she were a visiting friend and could walk out the door any time. Vicki even thought about doing that. There was a moment when everything seemed so strangely normal that she wondered if she *could* simply leave the flat. Would Howard stop her? Perhaps his madness would let her leave.

But the moment had passed and Vicki didn't find the courage.

So it was better for her to keep using her menstruation as an excuse for feeling tired and needing to sleep. Vicki would stay in the bedroom and close the door against the sound of the television, but rather than lying down she would pace the room, or alternate between sitting, lying and pacing. She was a caged animal with nowhere to run.

Often she would stand close to the window, leaning her forehead against the cool glass and stare down at the impossible freedom below. The nearby high-rise with its car park wasn't a pretty sight, but Vicki would have given almost anything to be able to walk across that open asphalt on her own.

Almost anything.

She knew what Howard wanted from her most of all. The ransom idea hadn't been mentioned again. It was only sex. Vicki sometimes wondered what he would do, if she offered him consenting intercourse. Would he let her go afterward? Could she make a deal? She couldn't tell, and the odds were stacked against her anyway. There was no reason to believe Howard would honour any deals and he was still only waiting until her period finished. Then he would take her as he pleased. It was only while he couldn't have sex with Vicki, through his own ignorance of menstruation, that her survival was guaranteed. Her hopes of escaping the living nightmare were getting less as this deception was becoming harder to maintain. Her bleeding was definitely nearly over and she was constantly using soiled tampons now, in case Howard demanded another examination. Vicki was beginning to lose faith she would come out of this alive.

Then, late in an afternoon, she saw the two men crossing the car park.

Something about them made Vicki's breath catch in her throat. From what she could see, they were dressed casually like anyone else who might live in these buildings, but something didn't fit. The clothes and bulky jackets looked too neat, or the men appeared somehow out-of-character. And the car they were walking towards was a modern vehicle in too good condition to have been parked in this part of the city every night.

Vicki didn't know who the men were, but she sensed they were outsiders. Insurance men or health inspectors— people who dressed as they were did so in an attempt not to be so conspicuous in a place they didn't belong. It didn't matter. With little time to act Vicki desperately decided it was worth trying to attract their attention.

The only thing was, she wasn't prepared. Vicki had the Coke bottles, and the paper and pen, but she hadn't written a note ready to drop out the window in case Howard found it. Now she didn't have time.

She grabbed one of the empty bottles, flipped it through the small opening of the window and waited, breathing aloud a prayer. She had no idea what was directly below her. For all Vicki knew there could be long grass which would cushion the falling bottle and prevent it smashing.

The sound of the exploding glass below frightened her. It was louder than she expected and suddenly there was the fear of the people living below coming to investigate. Howard would be able to keep them scared beyond the door, no doubt. Then she would have to face his anger.

The men had reached the car in the same moment the bottle smashed. She couldn't tell if their hesitation was because of it, or if they were simply discussing something over the roof of the vehicle. Vicki's heart came into her mouth, when she became certain they were looking towards the building.

"Please, *please* come over this way," she whispered. If the men walked over to investigate, Vicki would have the time to write a note and put it in the next bottle.

But they opened their car doors and got inside.

"Oh *no!*" Vicki cried. The car didn't move. The men were sitting inside it, but not driving away. Were they trying to make up their minds? Frantically, she snatched up another bottle and threw it out. She flinched at the sound of it smashing and expected Howard to come bursting angrily through the door.

Pressing her face against the window again Vicki held her breath, staring out the window and willing the men to get back out of the car.

But the car started moving, pulling away from the kerb and disappearing up the street.

Vicki couldn't stop herself from breaking into uncontrollable sobs. She didn't care now that Howard might come in to find out what was wrong—if he heard—though Vicki would have become instantly terrified if he had. Lying face down on the bed she buried her face in the stinking bedclothes and cried so hard her chest hurt.

When Howard heard a knock on the front door he was surprised, but not too alarmed. He felt secure in the anonymity of high-rise living and didn't consider for a moment it could be someone who was a danger to him. Still, he arose quickly and darted into the bedroom. Vicki had her face pressed into the bedding and didn't move. He wasn't sure she was even awake.

"Don't make a fucking sound," he told her in a low, menacing voice.

Vicki didn't move. She hadn't heard the knock on the door and was only concerned, at this moment, that he not see her tearstreaked face. She expected to feel him begin taping her up and was surprised to hear Howard leave the bedroom.

Howard opened the door as the knocking came again. The sight of two serious-faced men, rather than a neighbour, startled Howard and he struggled to hide it. "Yeah?" he asked, keeping the door open only enough to accommodate his own body.

Maiden said quickly, holding up his identification, "Good afternoon, sir. We're looking for someone we think lives in this area." Taking the envelope of photographs from Creane, he pulled one out and showed it to Howard, who was blinking in surprise and trying to remember where he'd seen Maiden before. "Do you know this man?"

Maiden was instantly edgy at the sight of Howard, a youth fitting the Vietnamese shop owner's description, and he was ready for anything. He knew his approach was blunt and he should be more careful, but it was too late now.

"Who are you?" Howard asked, without looking at the picture.

Maiden held up his ID again. "We're police officers. This guy is wanted for questioning as a witness, that's all. But he's proving a little hard to find." The lie didn't come easily, especially as Maiden was aware the man in the photograph didn't appear very available—he looked quite dead.

Howard dropped his eyes to the picture and saw Decker's corpse staring back at him. The effect was unnerving and he took a fraction too long to reply.

"Never saw him," he said, shortly.

"Are you sure?" Creane asked.

Howard looked at the younger detective and saw the mistrust in his expression. "I keep to myself, OK? I don't get around much."

"That's fine," Maiden said gently, taking the photograph back. "Thank you, we won't waste any more of your time."

He turned away, fixing Creane with a meaningful stare, and started walking back towards the lift alcove. Creane gave Howard a nod and hurried after Maiden, but he was listening for the sound of the door closing again. It didn't come until both detectives were out of sight and in front of the lift doors.

"Jesus," Creane said, as soon as he could. "I don't believe you've walked away from that! Did you see that guy? He looked bloody close to our description."

"More than that," Maiden said quickly, pulling the radio from his jacket and using his free hand to summon the lift. "Did you smell the bastard? He stank to high heaven. The smell coming from the flat nearly made me vomit."

"So you think he's the one? Why didn't we rush him?" Creane was speaking urgently, excited by the prospect of action.

"Take it easy, Martin," Maiden said, stepping into the lift. "Let's do it properly."

They travelled to the ground floor, where Maiden called Bennett. They could tell over the radio the other detective's voice was enthusiastic, but also guarded.

"Are you sure, John?"

"As sure as I can be. This guy rates enough to be worth a raid. He looks right, and the picture rattled him bad. He smells like shit, too."

"He smells?"

Maiden realised it was something he hadn't mentioned that morning, when he addressed the gathered detectives. "Believe me, it means something. I want to do this right. Get the State Protection Group in here—the works."

Bennett sounded dismayed. "Hell, I stood them down

not five minutes ago. They've been on standby for hours and they needed a break. I was just about to call and warn you. They'll be on their way back to the Police Centre by now."

Maiden was shocked. "Then for Christ's sake, call them back."

"It's probably too late, John."

"Try!"

Snapping the radio off Maiden looked up at the building above them. Creane was watching him worriedly. Maiden said, "What a fuck up. We can't do it on our own, Martin. We might get her killed. We might have to put this under surveillance and wait until tomorrow."

Back inside the flat Howard was deeply troubled. Seeing the picture of Decker's corpse had thrown him. He'd never expected to see that face again. When you put things into rubbish bins they are supposed to disappear forever.

Even bodies.

He had to decide what to do. If the police could stumble across his front door once, they might do it again and the next time he might not be doing such an innocent thing as watching television. The girl could have been in the room with him! The policeman's face still nagged at him, too. But Howard couldn't remember why.

Howard had the urge to do something straightaway. He was badly disturbed by the close call. But he knew that to react without thinking, especially at this time of day and with the two policemen still somewhere close by, might see him rush into a mistake. Howard believed he was too smart to do something that stupid. Decker had always called him stupid for one reason or another, but Howard wasn't like that. And Decker was the one who was dead, not him.

He ripped a warm beer from the six-pack on the floor. It was a deliberate move to create time. Howard intended to think about what to do, and that meant he was going to drink a beer or two and see what solutions he could come up with. One of his odd blackouts was threatening on the edge of his mind, but Howard pushed it away. This wasn't the time to retreat into the safety of those dark, silent corners inside his head.

He glugged the beer down fast, nervousness making his hands tremble.

He came to one decision. The girl had to go. She was too dangerous to keep around now.

He thought about her. Seeing her naked was the epitome of his fantasies and he desperately wanted to have sex with her. It was a physical craving torturing him. Only a complexity of adolescent taboos and ignorance had held him back before. Now, mixing with a fear of some failing in his own sexual performance, even with a helpless hostage, it all began to boil over in his mind.

Howard made up his mind there was one thing he was going to have, regardless of the consequences. He would have Vicki Colonel. Then he would kill her.

Tossing the beer bottle heedlessly into the corner, he went to the canvas bag and took out the machete. He was carrying this in front of him when he walked boldly into the bedroom.

Vicki had rolled over onto her back, listening for sounds from the rest of the flat. Through her despair, puzzlement was pulling at her mind. Howard's command not to make a sound and his abrupt exit from the room had confused her and Vicki dreaded she'd missed a vital opportunity. When Howard reappeared in the room she stared wide-eyed at the machete.

"Get your clothes off," he told her. Vicki saw he was wound up to near breaking point. It took her a moment to understand.

"But I . . . I'm still bleeding. You can't—"

"I don't fucking *care* anymore."

Her mind started going blank with shock at this sudden attack. She tried to stop him, the acid taste of fear coming into her mouth as she said, "You . . . you might get ill or something."

"I told you, I don't *care!*" Suddenly he was shouting into Vicki's face.

She drew backwards in panic and whispered, tears filling her eyes, "Please, don't make me do it."

Vicki had no idea what had caused Howard's change of behaviour. His demeanour was terrifying now, his eyes wild and almost bulging. He didn't realise he was waving the machete crazily in the air in front of her.

His face ugly, he snarled, "We're going to do it, and you're going to *enjoy* it. Do you understand, you bitch? I'm going to be the best fuck you've ever had."

"*Please*, Howard, it can't be like that. It doesn't work like that."

He leaned angrily forward, venom and madness in every word. "I'm not waiting anymore. I don't want to hear any of this shit. I'll cut you with this, somewhere it won't matter to me, if you don't make me feel good. I'll cut your leg or your arm—I don't care." He lashed out with his free hand and slapped at her, but it was his left hand and the blow wasn't strong. Still, Vicki screamed as it stung her face.

"Get undressed," he said, harshly.

Vicki sat on the bed, her knees drawn up and hugging herself. There was only one way for her to survive now, but accepting her fate was hard. Slowly, she began pulling her sweatshirt off.

"Come on!" Howard snapped. He reached forward, grasping the bottom of her sweatshirt and pulling too, hauling it roughly over her head and taking her blouse with it. He threw these aside and quickly did the same with her bra, gripping it by the back strap and dragging it off her. Vicki began sobbing and tried to cover her breasts with her arms.

"Do the rest," he told her, staring hungrily. "Do the rest *now*." When Vicki didn't move he put the edge of the machete against her upper arm. Instantly she screamed again and pushed it away, then started undoing her jeans before he could think again about cutting her somewhere. As soon as she had unfastened the button and drawn the zipper down Howard dropped the machete and began dragging her jeans off. He pulled so hard he lifted Vicki off the bed. One of her ankles twisted hard and she cried out with pain as he ripped her jeans away, clawing her shoes off with them. Her panties were already down around her knees. He tore these off with one hand.

Completely naked apart from her white socks, she cowered away from him on the bed. Howard lashed out again, slapping her hard on the thigh.

"Lie still!" he said. "Do it *right*." When Vicki didn't respond he slapped her again, this time finding her buttock, then again in the same place. She cried out both times. "I told you, lie down *properly*!" he shouted.

Vicki straightened her legs and slowly eased herself onto her back. Closing her eyes she began silently praying this would end—any way. Even being killed would be better than this. Unconsciously she was covering her breasts with one arm and between her legs with her other hand. Howard pulled her hand away and told her to keep them at her sides. She could feel the tears pouring down her cheeks.

"Take it out. Take that thing out." he said.

She had forgotten all about the tampon. With trembling fingers she reached down and took it out. She prayed the sight of it might change Howard's mind, but he struck her hand, making her drop it. He grabbed her ankles and pulled her legs apart.

"Wait," he said, his voice tremoring, not with anger now, but excitement.

Vicki kept her eyes closed and tried to shut her mind to what was happening, but that was impossible. She heard every sound and pictured it just as clearly as if she were watching. Howard was hastily tearing his own clothes off. The stink of his body odour getting stronger, worsened by the sourness of his groin. The bed creaked and Howard's weight was on top of her. The stench of him was overpowering. He began thrusting himself inexpertly, probing at her. Then started grunting, as if in pain.

Someone knocked on the front door again. Harder this time.

Howard froze. Vicki opened her eyes and saw the look of disbelief on his face. The knocking came harder now, enough to rattle the door in its frame.

Vicki couldn't stop herself. All her caution and instincts for survival left her and she screamed, *"For God's sake help me! He's going to kill me!"*

They had three of the State Protection Group team on each side of the door, waiting to burst through. The rest were spread along the balcony. Maiden was doing the knocking, hoping the youth would open up again. When he heard the scream Maiden immediately put his shoulder to the door. "Help me," he snapped at the nearest SPG member. Together they tried to break it down. It wasn't going to be easy and there wasn't much room to get a run at the door. Maiden knew each time the door failed to break inwards gave the youth inside more time to arm himself.

"You fucking bitch!" Howard yelled, jumping off the bed and flinging a punch at Vicki's head. She put her arms up in time and caught the blow, but it still hurt and she squealed. She waited for the next and it took her a second to realise it wasn't going to come. Howard was ignoring her now. He yanked open the cupboard door and reached onto the highest shelf, bringing down the sawn-off shotgun. He cocked it and held it one-handed, then leaned over and snatched a handful of Vicki's hair, hauling her to her feet. He released her for a moment, grabbing the machete, then stood behind her and wrapped his arm over her shoulder. The blade of the knife was pressed against her throat and Vicki was trapped in front of him as a human shield.

Howard didn't care they were both still naked. Cursing continuously, he dragged her from the room into the lounge so they were facing the front door, which was shaking to repeated blows from the outside. The wood around the jam was splintering.

With the next crash the door flew open, bringing Maiden and the SPG officer falling in with it.

"*Hold it!*" Howard screamed at them, waving the shotgun at the two of them. "Stay back or I'll kill her."

Maiden was trying to stop his forward momentum, his balance teetering. The SPG officer had automatically rolled away to one side at the sight of the shotgun. Now everybody froze, including the policemen outside who could see through the doorway. Howard's eyes were crazed and he was moving the shotgun frantically. Maiden expected the blast of its muzzle any moment.

"You all stay fucking *back*!" Howard said. "I'll cut this bitch's head off if you come any nearer. You can lose the guns, too."

Maiden had his revolver, while the SPG officer had a compact automatic rifle. Neither of them dropped their weapons. Instead, Maiden held up his free hand slowly and said, "Take it easy. Don't hurt the girl and everything will turn out all right." Maiden wasn't sure Vicki hadn't been hurt already. Her naked, dirty appearance had shocked him.

Howard's insane stare locked on him. "Hey—I'm making the rules here, OK? Come any nearer and she's *dead*. I don't give a fuck about myself. I'll go down fighting you bastards. I told you to drop the fucking gun!"

"No-one has to get hurt," Maiden told him, still holding his gun. He would achieve nothing by relinquishing his weapon and removing himself as a potential threat to the gunman. Taking his cue from Maiden, the SPG officer did the same. Maiden went on smoothly, "Guarantee the girl's safety and you could come out of this a lot better than you're probably thinking. We're only talking about kidnapping here. Think about that. Even kidnappers don't spend the rest of their lives in jail." He turned his eyes to Vicki Colonel, who was staring at him with a helpless, pleading look. "Has he hurt you, Vicki? You *are* Vicki Colonel, aren't you?"

She nodded shakily and whispered, "Yes."

"Has he hurt you, Vicki?"

Vicki thought of all the torment she had been through. Howard touching her body and the near-rape that had just occurred. She was about to try and say something—anything—which might tell this policemen of the many ways Howard had hurt her. She didn't want Howard to ever get out of jail. As she opened her mouth Vicki realised the reply Maiden wanted.

"No," she told them haltingly, understanding just in time. "No, he hasn't hurt me. He's been treating me . . . very well."

"That's good," Maiden said, looking at Howard again. Behind him he could hear members of the State Protection Group keeping spectators clear. "That's good for you. Let the girl go and you'll come out of this OK."

Howard only tightened his grip on Vicki, making her gasp as the machete pressed harder against her throat. "I'm not interested in any of this shit. I don't want to hear any talking. I want out of here, and she's coming with me. That's my fucking *guarantee*."

Maiden's stare turned hard. He said harshly, "Look, my friend. There's no way you'll be able to get out of here without us knowing where you're going. You can try all the tricks in the world—make any demand you want—but we'll still know where you are. It's never going to get better than it is now, do you understand? Make it harder for us, and it will go harder for you, when the time comes."

"You're damned right I can make any demands I want." Howard's eyes were flicking constantly now between Maiden, the SPG man still prone inside the room and the faces at the door. "I'm getting out of here and you fuckers are going to help me do it. And you won't be following me, understand? If I even *think* you're following me, I'll start throwing this bitch's fingers out the car window until you back off—and I won't stop when I run out of fingers."

Creane was speaking quietly from somewhere behind Maiden. "John, you can back off. A hostage negotiator is on the way. Ten minutes, tops."

Maiden ignored him. Backing off now would give the youth an opportunity to turn the shotgun on the girl or even himself. He didn't want either.

Vicki asked in a trembling whisper, "Please, don't let him take me with him. I don't want to go. I . . . I couldn't stand it."

"Shut the fuck up!" Howard snapped into the side of her face, jerking the machete and making Vicki cry out again.

"Calm down, just calm down," Maiden said, holding his hand up again. "Why don't you tell us what you want? Let's try and figure something out."

The blank look coming over Howard's face told Maiden the youth had no idea how he was going to extricate himself from this situation. His awkward silence threatened to burst into ugly, frustrated anger.

Then a completely different, strange expression came over the gunman's face.

Vicki knew one thing—she wasn't going anywhere with Howard. The idea of returning to being alone as his hostage was unbearable, even if what the policeman said about always knowing their whereabouts was true. Vicki couldn't have stood the torment all over again and knew that, given the opportunity, her rape would be the first thing on Howard's mind. Vicki was prepared to get hurt and even die, rather than be taken away by Howard.

She managed to realise two other things through her fear.

The machete was blunt. Even though Howard was pressing it hard against the soft flesh of her throat, Vicki hadn't felt the sharp, slicing pain of her skin being cut. She figured that any attempt to break away might result in her getting hurt, but the injuries wouldn't be fatal. In fact, the way Howard held her meant the blade was touching the side of her throat, not the larynx, and if she twisted the right way it would put the blade towards the back of her neck. Any struggle, however brief, could give the policemen time to capture Howard. Vicki was desperately willing to be wounded for the sake of that chance.

The last, most vital piece of information, came from her fingertips. Howard's strong grip from behind and across her shoulders was forcing Vicki's arms to her sides. Much as she wanted to cover herself, any attempt to do this only made Howard increase his hold. Her nakedness was exposed for everyone to see and amid her terror Vicki also burned with shame.

But Howard was naked, too. Vicki's fingertips were involuntarily brushing against matted, tightly curled, pubic hair. She had been revolted by his touch from the moment he first handled her and her reaction, even now, was to shrink her fingers away. But now she told herself things were different. His most vulnerable part was within her reach.

The change in Howard's expression came when he felt the soft touch of Vicki's fingers curling gently around his penis. It was the sensation of his dreams, one he'd never experienced in reality. Not even the prostitute had handled him like this. It was a sensually shocking moment for Howard, and Vicki's fondling caress felt so profoundly sexually exquisite, he was instantly stunned and absorbed in the sensation. Even when her hand moved in a stroking motion up to his testicles Howard still could only marvel at the feeling, finally, of a woman's fingers playing with his genitals.

Too late he understood the threat as she cupped his testicles. And squeezed so hard her fingernails met her palm, utterly crushing the soft sac and cutting into the flesh of his balls.

Howard screamed inhumanly and his knees sagged. With a cry of her own Vicki lunged away from him, breaking his grip and feeling the machete blade draw across the side of her neck in a stinging flash of agony. Howard was falling to the floor, but kept the shotgun barrel up and with a tortured mask of hate filling his face he swung his aim towards Vicki.

Maiden had his weapon aimed, but before he could pull the trigger there was the shattering noise of gunfire inside the small flat. He knew it wasn't him, and he could see it wasn't Howard's shotgun either. He vaguely registered the redness of Howard's head exploding like a burst melon. Maiden threw himself at Vicki instead, bringing her crashing to the floor. He smothered her body with his own and held her down, his face pressed against the back of her head. He could feel her hair against his cheek.

For an eternity he waited for more gunfire. It didn't come.

His ears were ringing. A long moment passed. Someone slapped his shoulder and said faintly, "It's over, John. He's dead."

Maiden felt the girl squirming beneath him. He rolled his weight away and she put her head up, looking around dazedly. Vicki caught sight of Howard and screamed. Maiden quickly gathered Vicki to him, put his arms around her and pressed her face into his jacket so she couldn't see.

The bullet, fired by the SPG officer, had struck one eye and exited, taking most of the back of Howard's head with it. A gore of tissue and blood covered the wall behind the corpse.

Maiden hugged Vicki hard and hoped she recognised his touch was from someone who was helping her, not hurting her. He put his lips down to her hair and told her, "It's OK, now. It's all over. You're going to be OK." She was crying uncontrollably into his chest. A trickle of blood rolled down her shoulder blade from the cut on her neck.

Maiden looked up and caught the eye of the SPG officer who was about to inspect Howard's body.

"Forget that prick," he said, snapping. "Find this girl a blanket, for Christ's sake."

The State Protection Group had their own paramedic crew following up. A medical blanket came within seconds and an ambulance was on its way. Maiden stayed where he was, holding Vicki in the blanket and using his body to shield her from both Howard's corpse and the open doorway. Soon she started murmuring for her clothes, but Maiden gently told her she was better off staying as she was and, though he understood why she wanted to dress herself, the blanket was warm and clean, while her clothes would be filthy. Vicki would be better off never wearing or seeing those clothes again. She was completely safe among the policemen and her dignity was totally covered by the blanket.

Maiden was only being half-sincere. He was also interested in keeping the girl's clothes inside the flat, where any forensic evidence would remain untainted. If she were to wear them in the ambulance and through the hospital, it would infect the clothes with a hundred extra elements the forensic people would need to discount.

More police arrived, including a female officer who took charge of Vicki. They made sure a free passage was cleared all the way from the flat's front door to the ambulance below, including securing the lift. Only then, away from the prying eyes of the neighbours, did they put Vicki on a stretcher and wheel her away. Her shock from the gunfire and seeing Howard killed was changing to relief at being safe. She even managed a weak, grateful smile at Maiden, who snatched at the opportunity to ask Vicki if Howard had ever mentioned another woman—someone who he'd been seeing and spending time with.

"Only someone called Fiona," she told him in a whisper, looking up at him from the stretcher as he walked beside it. "But I never saw her. I don't even know if she's real."

Maiden squeezed her hand to thank her, hiding his own disappointment. He'd been hoping for more.

Over the next half-hour the State Protection Group were replaced by the usual crowd of crime-scene experts. Maiden and Creane moved among them, examining things for themselves.

"How the hell can anyone live this way?" Creane asked, after he disturbed the top layer of a pile of rubbish and caused a waft of rotting stench.

"He's sick in the head. An antisocial misfit or animal of some kind," Maiden said, bending down to look in the cupboards. "The experts will tell you all about it, if you give a shit. Personally, I don't. I say he's just another freak." He moved aside to let a photographer take a picture.

"I can see that. Do you think he's *our* freak, though?"

"I don't know, Martin," Maiden said, with a sigh that also said he wasn't hopeful. "There's something wrong. Something that doesn't fit."

Creane gingerly inspected the filthy plates on the sink. "How could anyone ally themselves with a disgusting pig like this guy? How could they stand to deal with him? I mean, it's not just this dirty living. I'm saying he can't be entirely sane. Maybe Vicki Colonel's right and this Fiona person is a figment of Howard's imagination. A sick fantasy?"

Maiden was nodding. "I guess that's what I don't like about it, too. He strikes me as a loner, at least since he killed his partner. God knows, they may even have had a disagreement over his personal habits and this one got to the shotgun first. We can't entirely discount the existence of this Fiona. Even worse, we have to look for her, which is a waste of time with Howard no longer a threat."

"So, what if she doesn't exist? What about the coincidences between this case and the serial murders? Is that what they are? Only coincidence?"

"Maybe—probably, at this point. We're going to be working our butts off to figure it out one way or the other."

Maiden gestured at the corpse, now covered by a plastic sheet. "Especially now our best witness has half his brains painted all over the wallpaper."

"Damned shame," Creane said, without much sincerity.

"Crap, Martin. Apart from a few unanswered questions, I'd say we got the best result. I'm sure Vicki Colonel would, too." Maiden walked off towards the bedroom, adding over his shoulder, "Beats putting the prick in jail for a few years."

That evening Maiden went straight home and stayed there, having a few quiet beers before falling asleep early. He was physically and emotionally exhausted. He didn't want to call Janet Brown. There was a relationship growing between them and now that he was confident something was happening, he didn't want to rush things. He wanted to get to know her better before things got much further, despite her surprising affection of the previous night. But tonight he was too tired for playing those sorts of mind-games. And besides, he told himself, it did some good not to chase a woman too hard. Often, the best thing to do in a new relationship was nothing at all.

Anyway, the following day would probably have them seeing a lot of each other, going over the forensic details of the gunman's flat, clothing and weapons.

Chapter Twenty-seven

Geoff Parsons had time to watch the late news on a portable television. What he saw made him feel much better. The CBD, it appeared, was safe again.

He owned a printing company specialising in letterheads, business cards and the like. Every evening he worked late, which was why he spoiled himself with the portable set. He could watch his favourite shows while he was occupied with menial tasks such as packaging orders to be sent away the following day. He always finished, like tonight, by backing up all his files on the accounts computer. It took time, because Parsons allocated the less demanding work of the day-to-day office bookkeeping to one of his older machines. This computer should have long since been upgraded along with the rest, a fact he reminded himself of each time he had to sit and wait for the back-ups to be completed. Still, it gave him time to see the late news bulletins. The rest of the staff had long since gone home. Fridays were the only exception from this routine, when he tried not to work so late and they all usually had a few drinks together while the computer clunked and ticked away at its work. Today wasn't a Friday.

The news report pleasing him was an account of a late-afternoon police raid on a high-rise flat. An attractive young girl, taken hostage days earlier during an armed hold-up, had been rescued safely and her captor killed during the raid. Parsons smiled about the strong speculation by the television reporter the dead gunman had also been responsible for the spate of serial killings and mutilations in the CBD. Police were refusing to comment officially (and at this moment the reporter allowed himself a small, knowing smile), but comments made by the gunman during his escape from the hold-up and threats to chop the girl's fingers off suggested obvious conclusions.

The report went on with footage of the high-rise, an ambulance arriving at a hospital and a single stretcher being rushed inside, and the usual shot-from-a-distance coverage of a corpse being removed from the building.

Parsons's attention was pulled away from the television when a beep from the computer announced the back-up was finished. He sighed with satisfaction at another day's work done. He liked to do much of it himself. It saved paying overtime and gave him peace of mind the job was being done properly. He leaned forward and snapped the television off. It was time to go home. Tonight, it seemed, he needn't worry about any serial killer stalking him in the street.

He did a leisurely walk around the offices, making sure nothing was left turned on wasting precious electricity. Then Parsons put on his jacket, made sure he had his wallet, house keys and the return ticket he needed to catch the train to Bondi Junction. He picked up his briefcase and finally began flicking off all but one of the lights. He was comfortable in the near-darkness. He knew the office like the back of his hand.

He moved into the reception foyer and through the double glass doors, which he locked behind himself, and into the lift lobby. There were only two lifts in this twelve-storey building and at this time of night he was probably the only person left in the place. He pressed the button summoning a lift, fully expecting one to arrive within a minute.

So it puzzled him when, after several minutes, neither of the lifts had appeared. Parsons stepped back and looked to the indicators above the doors. Both lifts were still on the ground floor.

"Damn," he said, aloud. He figured they had to be stuck in some way. Perhaps they were being cleaned? He was on the sixth floor, so it wasn't a big deal to walk down the emergency stairs instead.

Parsons went through the fire-escape door. The concrete stairwell wasn't well lit with only spaced footlights high-lighting the steps. He listened to the echoes of his own footfalls as he descended the first flight. A solid clunk from above of the door closing behind him reminded Parsons he needed the security card in his wallet to retrace his steps now. It was the only way to reopen the emergency door from this side.

He realised with a start he was thinking like this because the dim stairwell frightened him a little and he considered going back and trying the lifts again.

"Don't be bloody stupid," he told himself. "It's going to take all of about sixty seconds to go down these stairs and I'm out of here. I'm sure the bogey man has got better places to be—"

He stopped in mid-step, because beneath his own talk-ing he thought he heard a noise coming from somewhere below. A scraping sound, like someone shuffling their feet. He listened some more, holding his breath, but didn't hear it again.

"Now you *are* being a damned fool," he muttered. He started down again, reaching the next landing before an-other sound stopped him again. At least Parsons *thought* he heard another noise. This time it sounded like a single sniff, or smothered sneeze.

Why the hell would anyone be hanging around in this stairwell, at this time of night?

More nervous with every passing second, Parsons tried to tell himself it must be—if it was anyone at all—another late worker using the stairs to smoke a cigarette. It happened all the time during the day. Almost all the offices in this building were smoke-free. He thought again about turning around and going back upstairs. He could use his security card to get back inside the foyer and see if the lifts were working. But he might be waiting a long time and still end up having to go down the stairs, if the lifts were being serviced.

Before he could stop himself, he called out, "Hello? Is that someone down there?" Immediately he felt silly. He'd sounded like a frightened child and whoever was down there was probably having a great laugh at his expense right now.

But no sounds of laughter came floating up from the lower levels. No noises came up at all.

"Well, that answers *that* question," Parsons said with a shaky relief, aware he was trying to convince himself. He began descending again, thinking he had been in the stairwell a ridiculous length of time now. If he had just walked down the stairs normally, instead of hearing imaginary monsters with every step, he would have been out on the street by now.

This time it was definitely a smothered cough.

Someone, somewhere on the flights below, had put their hand over their mouth before they coughed.

Parsons stopped once more with the noise. "Look, who is that down there?" he called, trying to instill some authority in his voice, but to him it only sounded like he was getting frightened—which he was. He glanced over his shoulder at the stairs ascending behind him. It was very tempting now to turn around and go back to the foyer. He could only try his own level, because of the security card system. But what if the lifts refused to work at all once he got up there? Was he going to have to spend the night in his office, too scared to go home, because some street bum was sheltering in the emergency stairwell?

"Damn it, let's try and see who the hell it is," he said, gripping his briefcase harder and wondering how it rated as a weapon. Could you bludgeon someone with a cheap plastic briefcase full of papers and an empty lunchbox? Once again he began descending the stairs, but rather than watching where he was putting his feet, Parsons tried to see around the approaching corners and into the shadows.

Another cough from below made him falter, but he kept going.

"This is private property, whoever it is down there," he said loudly, now attempting to sound angry. "I hope you have a damned good reason for being here!"

With only one flight to go Parsons saw the shadows moving below. This time he did stop.

"Who *is* that?" he snapped.

The movement stilled for a moment, then began again. Someone stepped out from beneath the last flight and turned to stare up the stairs.

"*Dear God,*" Parsons breathed. "Who—" But the rest of his words locked in his throat, caught by cold terror.

It was a man with the hulking, massive shoulders and squat figure of an athlete, his whole body tensed and ready to hurl itself up the stairs at his next adversary. But this wasn't to be a game. This was no innocent, playing-field competition. Parsons realised he was staring into the face of a hunter. Dark eyes were fixed upon his with a single-minded intensity.

The eyes of someone who intended to kill.

Parsons said shakily, "Hey pal, I don't think you should be in here. Are you OK—like, are you lost or something?"

A soft voice murmured from the shadows and the man nodded. Reaching out for the handrail, he showed how large his hands were. Something about the purpose with which he began climbing, his gaze never leaving Parsons's face, was as terrifying as the murderous expression in those eyes.

"You . . . you can't come up here." Parsons held his hand up. "There's nowhere to go anyway. Only the roof. All the other doors are locked."

His words were ignored. The man continued to climb. With only a few steps to go Parsons's nerve broke and he spun around, quickly retreating halfway to the next landing. He paused to see if this had any effect, but it hadn't. Steadfastly pursuing, the man merely followed Parsons's progress with his eyes as he kept climbing.

With stubborn disbelief that the worst could be happening, Parsons pointed his finger and said shakily, "Look, I don't know what sort of game you think you're playing— but I don't have to damned well play it! You're wasting your time and mine, and I've got a good mind to call the police about this. This might be your idea of some kind of fun—" Parsons had to break off and retreat again up to the next landing. The man might have been deaf, for all the reaction he showed to Parsons's anger. He continued to climb at a steady rate, his face upturned to watch Parsons all the time.

"Damn you!" Parsons snapped from the next landing, turning to face his pursuer from a moment. "I'm going back to my offices where you can't follow me, unless you have a security card," he added with a shallow triumph. "Then I'll call the police and tell them to clear you and your friends out of this building. You'll be lucky if you don't spend a night in jail. I don't care if you're drugged or drunk and somebody's putting you up to this—" Again Parsons had to forgo the rest of his threat, because he needed to back up the steps some more.

This time he didn't stop, hurrying up the stairs. He was alarmed to hear a hissed encouragement coming from the bottom of the stairs and his follower's footsteps quickened to match his own. Parsons's terror became uncontrollable as he understood he was truly being stalked. Frantic, he tried to speed his ascent and tripped, nearly sending himself sprawling. Half the problem was he only had one hand, the other still gripping the briefcase. He thought about abandoning it and, instead, an idea came to him. Hastily he leaned out over the handrail and looked down. The man was only two flights below and moving fast. Parsons lifted the briefcase above his head and hurled it. Too late he realised it was an impossible target and he should have waited until his pursuer appeared at the bottom of his own flight. The briefcase bounced spectacularly off a handrail, then ricocheted between the concrete stairs for several levels before disappearing out of sight.

Parsons let out a yelp of fear when he realised how this small pause had allowed the gap to close. He started running awkwardly up the stairs again, dragging at the wallet in his jacket pocket as he went. There was only one flight to go, but Parsons figured with a sickening feeling that he now didn't have the time to use his card. The system required a few seconds to read it, ask for a PIN number, then unlock the door. Those few seconds would be too long. His attacker would be upon him.

Blindly running straight past his own level—his only opportunity to leave the stairwell into a place no-one could follow—Parsons knew his sole choice was the roof. He had no idea what was up there. Once, a long time ago, he had peeked out the door on a cold, blustery day and seen an uninviting expanse of unpainted concrete surrounded by a grey skyline. Parsons had no experience of heights other than the complete safety of an office window and he had decided on that occasion it wasn't a good day to find out how he handled them. Embarrassed at his own timidity, he'd backed off and returned to the office.

Now he wished he'd looked more closely. What was up there? Somewhere he could hide? In a flash of optimism Parsons wondered if the lifts themselves might go to the roof. Maybe there was a serviceman's level that would let him summon the lift. A wild plan formed in Parsons's panicking mind. He could blockade the top door of the stairwell, at least long enough for the lift to arrive and whisk him safely downwards.

Then he thought hysterically, *We'll see how fast the prick can run down stairs then! Not fast enough, I'll fucking bet.*

His moment of defiance vanished. Parsons was only one level away from the roof exit. He could hear the grunting, almost animal noises now being made by the man chasing him as he laboured up the steps. Other strange sounds puzzled Parsons until he realised he was making them himself. These were small squeals of fear which might have been screams, had he not been so breathless from running up the stairs.

He burst through the doorway into an eerie, chilly night. The eeriness came from the flickering coloured light of nearby rooftop signs. One erected on an opposite building was so close he could hear its electrical buzz. It washed the roof with a strange blue haze. Parsons whirled around and slammed the door shut behind him. With a groan of fear and frustration he saw there was no way to lock it. Searching around him in the bad lighting revealed nothing at all he might use to jam the door or render the handle unusable. Parsons leaned his weight against the door, concentrating most of his strength on the lever mechanism itself, hoping to prevent his pursuer from unlatching the lock. He waited for the first indication someone was trying to come through.

"Dear God, someone help me. Why is this happening to me?" he whispered wretchedly. Then Parsons remembered he was out in the open and nothing prevented him from yelling his lungs out for help.

"Someone help me! I'm being—being attacked. Somebody's trying to kill me!"

There was a thud against the other side of the door as someone tried to open it and met the unexpected resistance. Parsons cried out with fear. The lever started twisting in his grip and he put all his strength into his wrists to prevent it moving. Slowly, inexorably, he began losing the contest. When it was fully depressed the door was pushed outwards. Once, Parsons got the purchase to close it again, but the second time a thick arm and shoulder squeezed itself into the gap. A large hand groped for him and managed to grip the lapel of his jacket.

With a hoarse cry of horror Parsons gave up the struggle with the door and fell away, tearing his jacket off and slipping away from the man who emerged from the stairway reaching for a better hold on him. In the blue light of the neon Parsons saw the man's face was still impassive—a mindless machine intent on its purpose of capturing him.

"Leave me alone! Get away from me!" Stumbling, Parsons ran for the square structure housing the lift shaft headgear in the centre of the roof. He could see it didn't have access to the lifts themselves, but there was a door marked 'No Entry' and he was desperate to try anything.

It was locked.

Looking over his shoulder as he hauled uselessly at the door, he could see he had time to check the rest of the structure. Parsons ran around it in a sideways, crab-like motion, praying as he reached each corner the next side would reveal an escape route. He found nothing but blank concrete. By the time he returned to the door his attacker was only metres away, crossing the roof towards him with the casualness of someone who knows their prey is cornered.

"Who the *fuck* are you?" Parsons screamed, backing away towards the opposite edge of the building. Another desperate idea came to him and he turned and ran to the edge. A small wall pressed into his stomach as he looked over the side. The dizzying sight of the street twelve storeys below seemed to try and suck him over and Parsons tumbled backwards hastily. Scrambling to his feet, he rushed over to the next face of the building and looked again. Then the next, and the next. Each time the man chasing him altered his course and made sure Parsons didn't have a clear run back to the stairwell. And unlike every movie he had ever seen, the building didn't have an adjacent roof Parsons might courageously leap over to and escape.

His pursuer was closing the gap. Parsons dodged to one side and managed to elude a grasping hand, but it forced him into a corner. He wasn't going to last much longer. In desperation he went to the edge again and leaned out.

"For God's sake, somebody help me!" he screamed down at the passing traffic. Uncaring or oblivious, the cars and trucks continued their ant-like progression without stopping on account of Parsons's screams in the night. Too late, he twisted back around to see the man upon him.

Incredibly strong hands gripped Parsons around the neck and began to squeeze. He fought back, punching and trying to knee his opponent in the lower body, but his strength ebbed with the pain and shock of strangulation. Dimly he realised he was being held over the edge of the building and half his own efforts were devoted to stopping himself from being thrown over the side, rather than fighting back. The coloured lights of the neons began to spin in his vision, then blur. A tremendous pain in his lungs, from a lack of oxygen, took the last fight out of him. Like a drowning man seeing his life flash before his eyes, the last thing Parsons saw was a faltering image of the television news reporter's knowing smile as he told his viewers a serial killer was probably dead, gunned down that afternoon.

She had come out of the stairwell door during the last minute of his pursuit. She saw Parsons killed, half his body dangling over the drop as he flailed uselessly at his attacker. Then the body was lowered gently to the concrete.

"Is it over?" she asked softly, walking over.

Crouched over the corpse he looked over his shoulder and nodded once.

"Good." She reached out and stroked his cheek lovingly. "I have your reward in the car. As soon as we're done here, you can have it."

His eyes sparkled at her with gleeful anticipation and she roughed his close-cropped hair.

Dropping beside Parsons's body she murmured, "This is better. The stairs would have been good, but out here is better." She had a canvas satchel over her shoulder. From this she took out a pair of scissors and she began deftly cutting away the collar and much of the upper part of Parsons's shirt. His tie she simply sliced through and tossed aside. With his neck and breast exposed, she replaced the scissors with a surgical scalpel.

"Tip his head back, like when I give you a shave."

He obliged, putting one of his large hands behind Parsons's neck and lifting. On her knees and bending low to see, she placed the scalpel under one ear and made a deep, deliberate cut under Parsons's throat all the way across to his other ear. The skin parted easily and blood welled out in a flood. Unperturbed, she repeated the cut, slicing further through muscle and the windpipe. When the blood pooled too much under Parsons's head and threatened to run onto her clothing, she said, "Move him this way, out of the blood."

He did as he was told, hauling the body a metre. Two more cuts at the front satisfied her. She felt the scalpel grate against the bone of Parsons's vertebrae. "Turn him over," she said. He rolled Parsons onto his front.

From the street below came the sound of a police siren and she stiffened, listening intently. The siren quickly faded into the distance again. Satisfied, she went back to her task. Now she was cutting above the nape of the neck, but below the base of Parsons's skull. She only wanted the head, not any part of his neck. The head was the message—nothing else.

When everything was severed, Parsons's head literally rolled away from his body, the vertebrae providing no resistance once she quickly ran the blade around the highest joint.

"Leave him," she said. "This is as good a place as any." She was taking a plastic bag from her satchel. Gripping Parsons's head by the hair, she carefully put it inside the plastic and twisted the bag to seal it. The shape of Parsons's face, clear against the thin material, spun grotesquely in the air.

"Come on," she said, rising to her feet. "Let's put this away where it belongs and I'll take you back."

Soon afterwards the two of them were sitting in her car and it was time to give him his reward. It was all he ever needed to do anything she asked. It worried her sometimes that he could be so single-minded.

Reaching behind the seat she brought out a small plastic-wrapped box. She gave it to him and he peered eagerly at the box, trying to see the illustration in the poor light.

"Don't open it until you're back at the home," she told him sternly, getting a disappointed look in return.

Chapter Twenty-eight

Maiden was sitting in Janet Brown's office. She had just returned with a morning cup of coffee for each of them. He had gone there straight from his home, rather than going to The Rocks first.

"We've had people working on some of this stuff all night. I hope you're grateful." Her voice was coolly professional. Maiden didn't know if it was because of the circumstances, or that he was in trouble for not calling her the night before.

"Of course." He tried a smile.

"It's bad news. I think it is, anyway."

There was a pause and he allowed himself a disappointed shrug. "Try me."

"I even checked it myself, first thing this morning. I took that damned finger out again and had another look. I don't know how many times I've examined the thing, looking for something different. Then I checked the severed hand and the woman's leg, too. I believe they all tell me the same thing—there's no way any of those amputations were performed with that machete. The cuts were too clean. Nothing was hacked off."

"Damn," Maiden said softly, thinking. "It would have made things a hell of a lot easier. Now we have to find the real weapon, too. Anything else?"

"There's no evidence of his bad hygiene on the severed limbs or the two corpses we have. Admittedly, the woman spent enough time in a recycling bin to be properly ruled out, but the corpse in the boot of the car might have given trace elements of the disgusting mess the killer lived in— and I mean trace. It was always a long shot, but worth looking for."

"I guess we can stop calling him the killer, right? You don't think he did the mutilations." Maiden snorted his frustration. "At least I don't feel so bad about not looking hard for Fiona, whoever the hell she was. In fact, I'll call off the search for her completely for the moment. I don't need anybody wasting their time right now."

Brown gave him a sympathetic look. "He probably killed his flatmate, remember. Maybe she can tell you something about it."

"Maybe, but to be honest I don't really give a shit about that. It's old news and nothing to do with this investigation."

Brown clicked her tongue in mock disapproval.

"OK, I know," he said, sighing. "Any more news?"

"Nothing you want to hear. We'll keep working on it, but I'm sure everything we turn up will only put another nail in the coffin of your theory Howard Quentin was the serial killer."

"Howard Quentin," Maiden rolled the name over his tongue. "Sounds like a college professor, not a vicious criminal."

"He was a bad one, by all accounts. Have you questioned the girl?"

"Later today."

"She must be a mess."

"Actually, I've heard she's a bit of a tough cookie. Kept her wits about her and her hopes up, too. Often that's the hardest thing of all to do when you're a hostage."

Brown only nodded at this, watching him expectantly. There was an awkward silence.

"Look," he said uneasily. "I suppose I should have called you last night, but I was pretty burned out."

Her gaze didn't alter from a steady examination of him. "John, you don't have to say things like that. I like you a lot—and that's not something I say easily to a man. I enjoy your company and respect you. We seem to have a mutual attraction, but we're a long way from either of us having to explain what we do every hour of the day. You don't have to call me every night. In fact, I think I might even resent it if you did."

He wondered if he should be so forthright back, but decided he had enough to worry about. Maiden accepted the status quo gratefully. The details could be thrashed out later.

"I'm glad of that. Sorry I asked. I've had a few things on my mind and I'm not thinking well."

She smiled, a genuine look of sympathy. "I think I'll forgive you."

The telephone rang, a perfect interruption. Brown only listened briefly, before handing the receiver to Maiden. "It's for you."

He took it, nodding his thanks. "John Maiden," he said into it.

"John, it's Martin." There was the smallest pause, but something in Creane's voice stopped Maiden from interjecting. There was a tremor in it. "We've got a whole head this time, John. A severed head sitting in a fucking lift."

Shocked, Maiden whispered, "Christ almighty . . . where? And where are you?"

Creane told him the address and added, "I'm just about to leave The Rocks."

"Pick me up on the way. I'll leave my car here."

He put the phone down and in answer to Brown's questioning stare explained quickly what had happened.

"God," she said quietly. "I guess you definitely have your answer on Howard Quentin."

Maiden was already halfway out the door.

The mass of police, ambulance and news media vehicles around the twelve-storey building was causing a traffic hazard. Maiden was angry when Creane had to park their car some distance away. Walking up to the coloured tape sealing off the footpath in front of the building's entrance, they needed to push through a crowd of curious onlookers and press photographers. Some of them took pictures of the two detectives as they passed, the flashbulbs flaring in Maiden's scowling face. It was relief to pass underneath the tape and into the relatively clear area beyond. A cordon of police officers was only letting through those people that could convince them they were employed inside the offices.

Maiden went straight inside. In the ground foyer area screens had been taken from one of the offices to block off the elevator alcove. More coloured tape made sure that only those people who really needed to view the grisly evidence could pass through.

Maiden shouldered an official photographer aside and looked into the lift. "Jesus Christ," he muttered thickly, after gazing a moment.

The head was placed in the centre of the lift, a wide stain of blood spread around it. Because of the way the victim had been decapitated, the head was tilted back slightly. The open eyes seemed to stare imploringly up at Maiden, like a man about to disappear into quicksand. Creane edged in behind him and swore under his breath at the sight.

Creane said, "Look at the mirror."

One side wall of the lift was a full-length mirror. Words

had been finger-painted in the victim's blood, but it hadn't worked well and the writing was barely legible. "I should cut the head off all the greedy and the cruel."

"What the hell's that supposed to mean?" Creane asked. He looked slightly sick.

"Same as the note in the car at the airport," Maiden reminded him grimly. "Normally we could confidently say we're dealing with the same killer, but since the press got hold of the contents of that note we can't be absolutely certain."

"Surely it's got to be the same person."

"I agree. I'm just being bloody-minded. Do we have an ID?" he asked loudly, a general question for everyone.

A constable nearby replied, "The woman who found him is in shock and has already been taken to hospital. She and a co-worker are the only ones who've seen the body. The co-worker thinks it's a guy who owns a printing business on the fifth floor."

"A *printing* business?"

Another detective, in charge of the crime scene until Maiden's arrival, reached over and tugged on his sleeve. "John, we've already found the rest of him. On the roof."

Maiden looked at him, surprised. "That's good. Quick work, too. Who thought of looking up there first?"

"No-one," the detective admitted reluctantly. "One of the news helicopters saw it as they were passing overhead. They probably got plenty of footage of the poor bastard before they bothered to tell us."

Maiden bit back a curse. It couldn't be helped. The police response team would have been systematically searching the building for the rest of the body, probably working from the ground floor up. There would have been no reason to move straight to the roof.

"Let's go and take a look," he said, nodding at the free elevator.

The morning air was clear and cold with a breeze to make everyone on the roof hunch into their jackets. Another large group of people had gathered around a bloody bundle near the edge of the roof. Photographs were being taken. A helicopter was passing close overhead and Maiden glared at it, as if that might make it go away. As they drew close to the corpse someone was flipping through a wallet taken from the dead man's clothing. The policeman handed the open wallet to Maiden.

"This confirms the ID," he said, nodding a greeting at the same time. "His name is Parsons and he runs a printing firm based in this building."

Maiden didn't bother to examine the body himself. "Do we know cause of death?"

"There's no gunshot or knife wounds, apart from the obvious," the policeman gestured at the gored stump of the corpse's neck. "Nothing on the head itself, either."

"Pathology will find strangulation, no doubt," Maiden told him. He stepped away and did a slow search of the surrounding buildings. Many of them were higher than the one they were standing on and had office windows overlooking the rooftop. "We need to do a canvass of these neighbouring buildings," he said, pointing. "For a start, we can concentrate only on the offices facing this rooftop and on a level high enough to see across or down."

It wasn't an order, but more Maiden thinking aloud. Only Creane answered.

"So, what are you going to do? Call in to Longman and ask him for *more* manpower?"

Maiden stood silently, making decisions. Finally he said, "We'd better go back to The Rocks and find out if I'm still running this show. It's getting too big, especially with the press coverage this one will get. We have to taskforce it now. I wouldn't be surprised if they put somebody over the top of me."

"Do you think Longman will take it himself?"

"God forbid. I think I'd resign before I had to act as a damned dogsbody to Longman. We'd better pull in Fischer and his girlfriend, too. We've got to make sure about those

two. I'm through with playing games with them. This poor
bastard was strangled by a gorilla and Paul Fischer fits the
bill. I don't care that we haven't got a motive. Maybe he'll
just tell us why, if we ask him the right way."

Creane was worried. Maiden seemed to be losing control. Arresting people without a good reason was the best
way to ruin a case. "But John, wait a minute. You've got
nothing to charge them with."

"Then we'll just charge 'em with the first thing they deny
doing. They'll mention something, don't worry."

This time no-one answered the door. Maiden had a search
warrant and he brandished it in front of Creane's face before he put his shoulder solidly to the panelling. The door
buckled and nearly opened the first time. Once more, and
it burst inward.

Maiden shouted, "Tom Fischer? Jennifer Musgrave? It's
the police! Don't try anything stupid." Both the men had
their weapons drawn and waited tensely in the gloom of
the lounge. No-one came out of the rooms.

"Shit," Maiden spat, lowering his weapon. "Where the
hell are they?"

"Should we try and fix the door?" Creane fingered the
splintered wood. "Try again later?"

"Very fucking funny, Martin—" Maiden stopped. Something struck him as wrong.

Creane had the same feeling. "The magazines are gone,"
he said absently. "In fact, it seems like a lot of stuff is missing. Have they made a run for it?"

"No," Maiden said heavily. He walked over to a drawer,
which was half-open. "I think they've had some visitors before we got here."

"Who?" Creane looked tense again, raising his weapon
slightly and glancing at the door.

"Us, Martin," Maiden said, despairingly. "Bloody *us*. This
place has been picked clean for evidence."

Creane took a moment to understand. "What?"

"They've been *raided*, Martin." Though he looked angry, Maiden playfully waggled his fingers in the air. "Whisked away by a bunch of bloody coppers."

Creane dropped a report sheet on Maiden's desk.

"You wouldn't believe it. Fischer was sending drug packages all over the damned country, using his company's packaging and logo—he even paid the postage out of their petty cash. And the clever bastard always included some family snapshots. The chemical smells from the photographic prints hid any other odours."

"Jesus, I told you something was wrong." Maiden didn't bother reading the report. He felt bad.

"It gives them a great alibi for our latest killing," Creane said wryly. "They've both been in the Day Street station holding cells for the last twenty-four hours. Alibis don't come any better than that."

"I'm so glad you're impressed, Martin. Have you got any bright ideas to replace the only decent suspects we had—not that they were much, anyway." Maiden rubbed a tired hand over his face.

"I've got one hunch. Want to hear it?"

Maiden looked up at him. "Is it good?"

"You can't hear it yet. Maybe soon."

"Tell me when. I'm busy trying to work out a way to keep Longman off my back."

Chapter Twenty-nine

A small taskforce of twenty junior detectives and uniformed policemen was formed to work on nothing except the serial killings. These detectives were separate from any normal uniformed officers who could be drafted temporarily for canvassing work at any time. As the senior detective, Maiden still remained in charge, but he couldn't shake the feeling it wasn't going to last. He suspected he might even be being set up as a scapegoat for the lack of progress in tracking down the killer. The only thing keeping his professional head above water was probably his success in finding Howard Quentin and the safe recovery of Vicki Colonel. Once the plaudits for that operation faded to silence, Maiden expected to feel the axe fall on his own neck.

He set the taskforce onto the canvassing, but stayed at The Rocks himself and began re-evaluating all the evidence they already had. Maiden had to redirect his thinking, now that Howard and all his potential involvement in the case could be discounted, along with Paul Fischer and Jennifer Musgrave. It was deeply frustrating and disappointing for

Maiden to admit that he was back to square one. They had almost no idea of who might be doing the killing, apart from the strong possibility the killer's name might be a common debtor to all the customer databases for each company where an employee had been a victim. These lists were still enormous and, as he already knew, there was no guarantee the name they needed wasn't hidden within a registered business title and not noticeable as common to the others.

Maiden studied a map and looked for a clue in the locations where severed limbs had been placed. Nothing was obvious. He went completely over all the forensic evidence, but there was nothing to hint at the killer's identity there, either. The only solid information they had now was positive matches for all the body parts with known corpses or missing persons. It wasn't enough.

Maiden got tired and annoyed after going over the same scant evidence time and again, and coming up with nothing new. By the early afternoon he was considering going out to check on Creane and his canvassing, just to get out of the office for a while and clear his mind, but Creane surprised him by appearing next to his desk and dropping a list in front of him.

Maiden raised his eyebrows. "What's this? Success?"

"Nothing to do with the canvassing. I had an idea and checked it out before I came back to see you about it. That's it." He nodded down at the paper.

"What is it?" Maiden glanced at the list. It had about thirty names and business titles on it.

"This morning's victim, Parsons, owned a printing firm. Nothing else, right? He just did stuff like business cards, letterheads—that sort of thing. I couldn't figure out what this guy might have done that would piss someone off enough to warrant having his head hacked off. So I went through his records and got a few names of people he dealt with. I went and saw them, asked what they thought of Parsons and how he treated them." Creane had, as usual, perched himself on the edge of Maiden's desk. He paused and looked at Maiden, who rolled his hand in the air to tell Creane to keeping talking.

"OK, Martin, I don't need that stupid look on your face to be aware you've done something clever. Just spit it out."

"Apparantly Parsons was a good businessman, but pretty tough with his debtors. Like, if you were overdue a few days paying the bill he wasn't backwards about calling up and reminding you himself. He upset a few people and lost some accounts, but it looks like he had very few bad debts."

Maiden didn't look impressed, but accepted that it was better than nothing. Better than anything he had come up with after a day's brainstorming all the available evidence. "So you're saying our killer is someone who didn't pay his bills—we know that. Parsons's business was one of the companies who was getting no money, so Parsons called him up to give him a reminder and pissed our killer off so much, he put Parsons on the list of people for special treatment."

"I can be a little more specific than that," Creane said, nodding at the list. "These are all the people or companies that have gone through bankruptcy proceedings in the last three years and have Parsons named as a creditor against them. Anybody who went down the financial drain and filed for bankruptcy, and had Parsons put his name forward as being owed money, are on that list. I reckon if we do the same with all the other victims' companies' and only compare those names who have *declared themselves bankrupts*, we must be looking at much smaller lists, right? I mean, the note next to Howlett's body said the killer had been ruined, but I figure it might mean the whole way, like officially bankrupt."

Maiden was angry at himself. "Of course! Why the hell didn't we think of this before?" He paused and offered his own excuse. "I only thought they meant financially ruined—dead broke or desperate, who knows? Not officially *bankrupt*. How bloody stupid am I?"

Creane shrugged. "I didn't give it much thought, either. In fact, I've been avoiding those lists because it seemed like such an enormous task. I've always hoped we'd get a break in the case some other way before we had to tackle a mountain of paperwork."

"Then we're both bloody fools. This is good work, Martin. Well done. I want you to do the same with the other company lists—and do it yourself. I don't want to waste time waiting for it to run through the system."

"No problem," Creane grinned, pleased with himself. He stood up from the desk and was about to move away, but stopped and leaned over and tapped the list in front of Maiden. "Those two names I've marked are the two that Parsons actually initiated bankruptcy proceedings against. In other words, he's the one who pulled the rug out from underneath them and made everyone else follow."

"Even better," Maiden said, grudgingly conceding again that Creane had done some smart thinking. "I'll start digging around these first. Look for the same with the other companies."

"I was going to." Creane left in search of a spare computer terminal.

Maiden looked down at the list, but his mind was elsewhere as he was already trying to think further ahead. However, one of the names Creane had marked leapt out of the page at him.

Feitler.

Janet Brown's maiden name.

Completely unbidden, a memory swept into Maiden's head, startling him. It was something Creane had said at the airport when they were examining Howlett's body: *"I'm no doctor, but this looks quite neat, don't you think?"*

Janet Brown was a doctor. And an attractive woman.

"Don't be so bloody stupid," Maiden told himself qui-

etly, but he was shaken. It wasn't just the coincidence or
Brown's uncommon maiden name showing up on the list.
It was one of Maiden's hunches coming hot and strong—
and unwelcome.

He went back to the print-outs of all the victims' companies dealings. These were complete, not the narrowed-
down listing of bankrupts Creane was putting together. It
didn't matter. Maiden was only looking for one unusual
name.

It didn't show up on any of the other lists. However,
there were plenty of Browns.

*What was the name of her husband? She had said it once—
what was it?*

David.

He went back to the lists and tried again. All except one
listed a D. Brown in their databases as a past customer.

"This is crazy," Maiden muttered, but an unmistakable
cold feeling settled in the pit of his stomach.

He needed to check this one out for himself. It had to be
a crazy coincidence and Maiden figured he was just tired
enough to let his own imagination run wild, that was all.
The reality was he couldn't allow a whisper of this to get to
anyone else, because any hint of Brown being a suspect in
any investigation—regardless of it being coincidental and
no matter how major or trivial—could stick to her for the
rest of her professional life, especially if the killer was
never caught.

As impossible as it seemed, at the moment Janet Brown
would be considered an outside-chance suspect, at least as
an accessory to murder. For her sake and Maiden's too, he
had to squash that chance as quickly as possible, before
someone else noticed her association with the company
lists.

He suddenly thought, *But no-one else knows her maiden
name. Maybe I could just forget it.*

That wasn't good enough. But it gave him better odds

nobody would see the connection before he had managed to discredit it.

The Rocks had a small department dealing with white-collar crime. They were part of the fraud squad, but specialised in such things as computer hacking, tracking down bogus company fronts and any other investigations that required working among the paperwork maze of the corporate world. They had originally supplied the lists Maiden was using now and were still working on them, but he wanted to talk directly and discreetly with the department's head, a studious-looking man called Gould.

Gould's eyes were glued to a computer terminal when Maiden walked up behind him. Without turning his head, he said, "Sorry John, but everything's tied up completely for the rest of today and half of tomorrow. I just sent your partner away to do his own digging. I suppose he came crying to you?"

"No, Bob," Maiden said easily, aware that Gould was someone who needed handling gently. "He'll cope on his own somehow. Actually, I've just got a few quick questions for you that won't need any of your electronic wizardry."

With a sigh Gould pulled back from the computer terminal and looked at Maiden. "OK, ask away."

"We've been looking for a common name among those lists you got for us and I think I might have found one. But there's a snag. It's a maiden name."

"You mean, a suspect's wife's maiden name?"

"Exactly."

"So?"

"Well, how easy is it to do that? Register a business, say, in your wife's maiden name?"

"Very . . . and quite common. Some people do it for tax purposes, because they call their marriage a business partnership and reap certain tax benefits. It's sort of a way of proving to the tax guys that the wife is an active part of the business, not just a deduction. Pointless really, but lots of

people are paranoid about the taxation department."
Gould shrugged. "Sometimes they do it for completely different reasons, like they're in financial trouble and can't get
credit under their own married name, but the maiden
name looks clean."

"So there's every chance these names are connected?
There is no system or law in place to prevent him using her
maiden name?"

Gould shrugged again. "What do you want to hear?
How common are the names?"

Maiden hesitated. "Fairly common," he lied.

"Then that's the only odds you need to worry about.
Otherwise it's standard practice to do it. Actually, you
maybe shouldn't even bother to ask the businessman, but
his accountant instead. The business guy might be a
dumb-as-dogshit truck driver, but it's the sort of thing an
accountant would do, almost without checking with his
client, if you know what I mean."

Maiden was already nodding and moving away.
"Thanks, Bob. That's all I needed to know." He waved
wearily.

"Hope I helped."

Maiden went back to his desk. One possibility was ruled
out, or rather one chance at dismissing Janet Brown was
closed to him. The next thing he wanted to check was going to be a little more difficult.

Creane caught him staring moodily at the list.

"Having second thoughts? You don't look too happy."

Maiden looked up guiltily. "No, just doing some thinking."

"Seen the newspapers?"

"No, why? Are they going to lynch us?"

"Probably. No, actually I was referring more to the near-
hysteria they're starting to encourage. All of a sudden our
killer is the biggest news again—and I mean big. There's
reports of after-hours overtime falling to almost nothing.

Nobody wants to be caught working late. In fact, they're even suggesting no-one should ride in a lift alone."

"For Christ's sake, nobody's been *killed* in a lift."

"Try telling that to the newspapers."

"Sensationalist bastards."

"They're making you a household name. You read 'Detective Senior Sergeant John Maiden' in just about every paragraph."

"How the hell can that be? I haven't talked to anyone! It's the last bloody thing I want to do."

"Then obviously someone's sticking your name against any press releases or information that's coming out of this building. You did the original press conferences, remember?"

"How can I forget?" Maiden glared along the room towards Longman's glass cubicle.

Creane followed his line of sight. "You think it's him?"

"I think I'm getting set up to take the heat, put it that way." Maiden let his anger boil for a moment longer, then pushed it away with a wave. "Look Martin, I want you to do something for me."

Creane knew something was wrong by his tone. "Sure," he said carefully. "What?"

"Remember you once talked about these amputations being really neat, like they were done by a doctor? We were at the airport car park."

"You were hoping Forensic would pick that up themselves."

"That's right, and they haven't."

"So you want me to go and ask them?" Creane was puzzled. "Why don't you just call Janet Brown? You guys seem to get on pretty well."

"That's part of the problem," Maiden said, trying to keep his tone easy. "I'm concerned she's the one who's made the mistake. That she hasn't seen the possibility of a trained hand doing the cutting."

After a pause, Creane said, "I don't get it. Since when did criticising anyone worry you?"

"Since now. I figure the best way to do this is for you to go down there and ask one of her assistants about it. Pretend you want to check something trivial—something that doesn't need her authority and so asking one of the assistants won't matter. You could just about grab the first person you see through the door. They're all bloody experts down there. Just ask 'em."

Creane frowned. "This sounds like a lot of fooling around, when a phone call from you would answer the question in five seconds flat."

Maiden took a deep breath and silently cursed Creane's inquisitiveness. "Martin, let's say I've been . . . spending some time with Janet Brown. *That's* why I can't go down there myself, because she'll undoubtedly want to help me out, no matter how small the query. I can hardly telephone them and ask for 'anyone but Janet Brown.' And obviously it would be a little difficult for me to question her ability at the moment."

Creane's puzzlement turned to barely concealed humour. "Ah, I see the problem—"

"No, you don't," Maiden cut him off. "But I'd appreciate it, if you could do this for me. Perhaps there's some simple medical bullshit we don't know about which means *we're* wrong and they are right."

"OK," Creane said, quiet now as he saw Maiden was seriously concerned. "Do I need to ask about all the pieces?"

"No, just one will do. The hand at least, perhaps."

"How about I ask if the victim was left or right handed, then slip in the question about the medical skills?"

"Good thinking. That's innocent enough."

"Where will you be?"

"Here. I've still got that canvassing to run and I've got a few other things I need to check out."

Creane nodded. "I'll call you from Surry Hills, with whatever I find out. Then I'll head back to the canvassing myself."

Maiden watched him go, then returned to brooding over the list. Finally an idea occurred to him and he picked up the phone.

It took several calls, all of which needed time after he insisted on an answer immediately, requiring people to retrieve files and read aloud the contents. Faxes were being sent too, but Maiden only needed these for confirmation—he wanted to actually hear the information now.

Eventually he got what he wanted to know. David Brown died in a car accident. Nothing unusual, just another tragedy for everyone involved, but otherwise something that didn't even rate newspaper space on the day. Brown had filed for bankruptcy only a week before and could have been depressed and maybe suicidal, but the circumstances of the accident didn't suggest it was a deliberate attempt to kill himself.

A trip to the fax machine gave him some of the documents he'd requested. One of them was a listing of Brown's business interests, but behind the corporate listings and legal jargon it was difficult to understand exactly what David Brown made his fortune in or what took it away again. Maiden thought about going back to see Bob Gould and asking him to decipher it, but he decided he'd pushed his luck there far enough.

Going back to his desk once more, Maiden got the distinct impression he was running around in pointless circles. No sooner had he sat down when his telephone rang. It was Bercoutte.

"John, I want you to come down and see me. Are you free?" Of course, Maiden didn't really have a choice. It took him ten minutes to get to College Street.

Bercoutte was sitting behind his desk, and motioned for Maiden to close the door behind him. "What can you tell me about this morning?" he asked without any greeting.

Maiden explained everything, adding at the end,

"They've given me a taskforce team of twenty. They're canvassing the area right now. I'm hoping someone saw *something* on the roof."

"I gave you that team, John. You'd better do something with them pretty damned smartly, too. People are beginning to scream for our blood."

Maiden said tightly, "If you don't think I'm doing the best we can, feel free to replace me. I'm sure there's some who would like to see it."

Bercoutte looked irritated. "Replacing you will achieve absolutely nothing except delay while a senior officer gets brought up to speed on the investigation. But I'm warning you. This thing is getting so big and starting to involve so many people that soon *politically* I might have to appoint an overall commander of the taskforce. You don't have enough seniority to be handling so many staff."

Maiden felt his anger building again and answered glibly, "So, promote me. Would that solve your problem?"

"I want you to solve the *case*, John," Bercoutte snapped back. "For God's sake, have you got any credible suspects yet?"

"Not really," Maiden lied. "But we've come up with an idea which will narrow down the field a lot. A couple more days might bring a result. It takes time flogging through these fucking computer lists of could-bes. But it's all we have." He rubbed at his face tiredly. "There's nothing coming off the streets—no criminal connections or associations with previous killings. As far as we can tell, this is a normal, innocent person who's gone out of their mind and is now killing other normal, innocent people."

"What, completely random?"

"No," Maiden said. "That's one thing I'm certain of now. The killer is picking the victims well beforehand and studying them—discovering times and places where they are vulnerable and can be hit without interference."

"What about that gunman and his hostage? No connection?"

Maiden shook his head. "I thought there was, but it turned out to be coincidence."

"Well, it was good work," Bercoutte said grudgingly. "In fact, it's saved your skin temporarily, otherwise this conversation would have been taking place yesterday morning and I wouldn't be able to give you any rope." He fell silent and picked up a paper from his desk while he considered Maiden's position. After a moment he said, "I'll give you until Monday, John. If you don't come up with something significant by then, I'll have to put a fresh mind onto the investigation."

This was a polite way of saying Maiden would have someone appointed over the top of him and his career could be damaged through the perceived failure—and seriously, if someone like Longman wanted to take advantage of it.

Maiden asked acidly, "And what about your grand plans of easing Longman into obscurity?"

"Then it won't happen," Bercoutte said shortly, staring at him. Maiden knew the responsibility was being placed squarely on his shoulders. Not trusting himself to say any more he gave Bercoutte a curt nod and left the room.

Back at The Rocks, Sayers caught Maiden's eye. As Maiden negotiated the desks scattered around the room, he tried to clear his mind of the anger and frustration Bercoutte had sown.

Sayers was annoyingly cheerful. "How's it all going, John? Creane just tried to call you. He's left his mobile number to call him back straightaway. I've written it on your desk,"

Maiden thanked him and put a call through. The ringing tone was answered quickly by Creane.

"Hello?"

"Martin, it's me."

"Hang on a second," Creane said, his voice made tinny by the mobile. "I haven't got a good signal. I'll step out-side." There was a wait of nearly a minute with the only noises being muted footsteps and doors opening or clos-ing. "That's better. I'm outside Surry Hills."

"What have you found out, anything?"

"I got looked after by a bright young spark who couldn't stop himself voicing his opinion. A real smartarse, but it sounds like he knows what he's talking about. We looked at the woman's leg, too. The head's in another laboratory and Janet Brown's checking over that one herself." He paused. "She'll probably hear about my visit and what I was asking. Sorry."

"I'll worry about that when it happens," Maiden said. "Maybe we can use it as an excuse—that she wasn't avail-able when you got there." He was tense, anxious to hear what Creane had found out. "So, what's the story?"

"This guy reckons it's definite. Whoever took off the wrist and leg knew exactly what they were doing. They weren't trying to save any lives or anything, but the skills are undoubtedly there. The limbs were cut off by the fastest and most expedient method by someone who knew how to do it. They knew what to cut and where."

"So we can start looking for someone who's bankrupt *and* with a medical background."

"It whittles down the field," Creane said enthusiastically.

"Yeah," Maiden nodded into the phone, trying to sound the same. His bad feelings were returning strongly.

"What do you want me to do?"

"I need to make some more calls now. Can you get over to the canvassing and check them out? Have a closer look at Parsons's business records, too. He would have the smallest database of them all anyway. Look for the medical connection."

"OK, I'm on my way. I'll call again later."

Creane hung up, keen to get moving and continue the chase.

Maiden dialled Janet Brown's office number expecting to get a secretary or answering machine. He wasn't prepared to hear her own voice reply.

"Janet Brown." There was a silence while Maiden composed his thoughts and she asked, "Hello? Who's there?"

"Janet—ah sorry, Janet. It's me, John."

"You're quick. I only just stepped out of the lab. I haven't written down the results from the tape yet."

It took a moment for Maiden to realise she was talking about her examination of the severed head. "No, actually that's not what I'm calling about."

"Oh?"

"I wanted to see you. Talk to you."

She sounded annoyed. "This is not the best of times to ask. I've just been studying a decapitated head, for goodness sake."

"I know, I'm sorry. But it's important . . . very important."

This made her pause. "What's it about?"

"Not on the phone. I want to come over tonight."

"You can't. Not tonight." She answered so quickly, almost panicking, that Maiden was surprised.

"I don't think this can wait, Janet. Whatever it is you've got planned, you'd better find time for me."

"Is this about us? You and me?"

"No."

This silence was longer. So long, in fact, Maiden thought the connection might have been broken. He was about to say something when Brown replied, "All right. Come over after nine o'clock. I'll be back home by then."

"OK," Maiden said, relieved. He wanted to lighten the mood, hating the facts that had brought him to this. "Don't get too worried," he said. "I'm sure we'll work it out in no time."

"Work *what* out?"

He regretted it. "Janet . . . tonight, OK? And don't worry."

"What do you expect me to do?" she said curtly.

Maiden tried to think of something calming, but heard the clunk of the telephone being slammed down.

Chapter Thirty

Maiden could have done a lot of things at this point. He had a good theory, something more definite than he'd had since the very beginning of the investigation. All the paperwork was in front of him. With the priority the case had finally been granted he could ask for anything and get a result within minutes.

But instead, he brooded around the office and fooled with details that didn't matter. Eventually he realised he was presenting a prime target for Longman and he didn't have the stomach for any confrontations like that, especially with Bercoutte close to pulling his support out from underneath him. Finally he told Sayers he was going out to interview some people and he would take a beeper with him.

As soon as he was outside Maiden turned the device off.

It was late afternoon and soon the rush hour traffic would begin to build. Maiden intended to find a drink in a bar close by, but changed his mind and headed for his car instead. He could drop into a bar nearer home. Somewhere the traffic wouldn't matter.

He was only killing time, and he had a lot to kill until nine o'clock.

Twenty minutes later he was sipping on a light beer and trying to run over the details of the investigation in his mind. A jukebox nearby kept playing all the wrong sorts of music, annoying him. A group of office workers bunched around a table fed a continuous stream of coins into the machine, repeating the same songs and greeting each with a raucous attempt to sing the opening lyrics. The workers looked drunk enough to have been there since lunch and Maiden had an urge to go over to them, show his ID and suggest none of them should drive home. It wasn't because he cared about their potential drunk-driving. He merely wanted to spoil their mood. The cheerfulness filling their corner of the bar seemed unfair, because Maiden didn't feel very happy at all.

"Why am I thinking the worst?" he asked himself aloud, earning a puzzled, enquiring look from the barman. To cover himself Maiden flicked his finger at the nearly empty glass in front of him, then drained it while the barman got him another.

Like I told her on the phone, we'll clear this up in no time. Trouble is, she's going to get damned upset that I thought it worthwhile to ask her at all.

He changed his thinking to exactly how he was going to broach the subject with Brown, but the jukebox and rowdy office workers still bugged him.

Maiden downed the second beer fast. Suddenly he didn't want to be in the bar. Everyone and everything was vexing him and he would do something stupid if he didn't get out. He strode quickly back out to his car, got in and started driving home. It was as good a place as any to waste more time. He still had no idea what he was going to say to Janet Brown.

Almost without realising it, he drove straight past the turn-off to his own home and kept going. Maiden was going to cruise past Brown's house and have a look. Just to satisfy his curiosity.

Turning into her street he slowed right down, ready to change the manoeuvre into an escaping U-turn if Brown was out in her front yard. The closer he got to her driveway, the more convinced he became she wasn't home at all. Her car wasn't there. A quick look at his watch reminded Maiden he was outside of his normal time-frame. Brown would still be at work . . . just. He wondered if she was coming home first, before she went out to wherever she was going. And where was she going, exactly?

For Christ's sake, Maiden told himself. *She had a life before I came along. It's Friday night. She's probably meeting someone for a few drinks after work.*

This didn't ring true in his mind, probably because he'd got the impression over the telephone that getting home by nine o'clock needed an effort on her part. That didn't sound like social drinks. Worse still, Maiden had to admit to the pang of jealousy he felt over the image of Brown spending time and having drinks with someone else, rather than himself.

He pulled the car to a halt outside her house.

What am I going to look for? I've been inside the place! What am I going to see now that I won't see tonight?

He had to have a look anyway.

Maiden felt self-conscious going through the gate. He knocked on the front door twice and gave plenty of time for anyone to respond. Nothing happened. He went back into the yard and moved towards the rear of the house. He had to be careful he didn't start some sort of incident. Normally, if a neighbour were to question what he was doing Maiden would have no problems pushing his ID in their face and telling them to mind their own business. But somebody could be calling the police already and he hadn't allowed for that by giving the local police station his name and the address he was going to look at, because he'd never intended to do this. Then Maiden admitted to himself perhaps he *had*, ever since the moment he left his desk looking for a drink, knowing Brown wouldn't be home.

Whatever his true intentions, it was too late now.

The back yard was overgrown and untidy, but then he didn't pick Brown as the greenfingers type. She was hardly at home during daylight hours, anyway. The rear of the house was an open laundry. The door to the kitchen was locked. Standing on tiptoes next to the laundry windows, Maiden tried to look inside the kitchen. It was hard to see anything in the shadows. Only a little light was coming in from the afternoon sky outside. All he could see were familiar shapes of things he recognised from his visits. Nothing unusual. He went back out and went to the other side of the house. Here, there were two windows and he had to think for a moment what they could be. One, he realised quickly, was the bathroom. Frosted glass and a lace curtain made it pointless to try looking through. The other, Maiden decided, had to be the spare bedroom that Brown wouldn't let him inside.

Why? Because it was her son's room. Her child who needed "special" attention. Janet never mentioned what, exactly, was wrong.

The curtains here were drawn, too. Only the smallest chink was left between them. Expecting any moment to hear the indignant call of a neighbour, Maiden put his face to the glass and tried to look with one eye through the gap. He could see nothing at first, but he persevered, waiting for his sight to get used to the darkness inside. He was rewarded eventually with a strange outline suspended in front of him. Puzzled, he stared at it. That didn't help, so he deliberately looked to another part of the room and tried using his peripheral vision. Suddenly Maiden knew what it was.

He could see part of a model aeroplane, hanging by a thin thread from the ceiling.

That made sense and confirmed Maiden's own guess at

how old this child should be. Disappointed he'd found
nothing better, he dropped away from the window.

The sound of a car pulling into the street alarmed him.
He ducked against the house, knowing in the same moment it was a silly thing to do if it was Janet Brown. His
own car was parked out the front. How was he going to explain why he was snooping around her house? The approaching car swept past before he thought of an answer.

"Damn it, get the hell out of here," he told himself. Not
surprisingly, he had achieved nothing and for all he knew
one of the neighbours *had* seen him and was waiting for
Brown's return to tell her. She'd probably recognise him
from a description and he would have to explain himself
that night.

He felt nervous all the way back to the car and during
the half-minute he needed to drive out of her street. Only
then did Maiden feel safe from discovery, and foolish about
his actions.

By the time he returned at nine o'clock that night Maiden
was utterly confused and feeling exhausted. He had been
home and tried to put everything out of his mind until
he'd talked to Brown. Watching television seemed like a
good idea, but a news update had Parsons's killing as the
lead story and the reporters milked every drop of horror
out of the story. A thought slammed into Maiden's head.

*I'm actually thinking Janet is a party to this, somehow. Am I
going mad? Do I believe she's capable of strangling someone,
then mutilating the body?*

For the first time, Maiden saw a hole in the fabric of his
fears. Janet Brown was obviously *physically* incapable of
the sort of strength evident in the strangulation of at least
one victim, Greg Howlett. Maiden had seen the bruising
himself in the airport car park. Of course, the presence of
an accomplice had always been likely. In fact the emphasis
in Maiden's theories had been the reverse—that an attractive female was luring victims to the motivated male killer.

Not the *woman* having a motive to kill and using a male accomplice.

Sitting in the solitude of his lounge room with only the chattering television for company, his thoughts had turned once again into a turmoil of confusion and indecision. He should have been helping Creane. He should have been back at The Rocks trying to solve the crimes before Bercoutte had him replaced. He should have been working hard and damning any stupid emotions stopping him from achieving results.

Instead, he sat at home and waited until a few minutes before nine, when it was time to drive back to Brown's house.

Janet Brown answered the door dressed in the thick towelling robe, which dwarfed her. Hugging herself against the cold air from outside she quickly stepped aside.

"Come in," she said, shortly.

"Hi," he said, squeezing past. She didn't seem open to a greeting kiss, so he didn't try. He went straight into the lounge and sat down. The overhead light was on, brightly defusing any intimacy. The electric bar heater glowed in the fireplace. Following him into the room, Brown eased herself onto the lounge opposite and looked at him coolly.

"OK, so what's all this about?"

"Look, sorry about all the alarmist stuff, but it isn't something I wanted to talk to you about over the telephone."

"Are you saying it's not that important after all?"

"No, not at all."

Brown tucked her legs underneath herself. Maiden couldn't help looking at a glimpse of thigh the movement offered. If she noticed, Brown ignored it. She told him sharply, "John, I don't like being treated like this. If I say it's a bad night for you to come around, I mean it. I don't appreciate you convincing me otherwise, unless it's damn well worth it."

Maiden told her flatly, "Of course I think it's worth it!

I'm not making some story up, just so I can come to see you. It's about my investigation."

There was a silence and Brown's expression hardened more. "This is about *work*?"

"If you like. The problem is your name—your husband's name—has come up as a common factor in all of the victims' histories. He dealt with each of the companies they worked for." Out in the open, it didn't sound worth all the anxiety he'd suffered and Maiden felt bad.

There was another brief silence. Her anger hadn't abated. "I don't understand what you're telling me."

Maiden wanted to keep it professional. He didn't like this, or the way she was looking at him. Seeing her upset only made him want to get the issue out of the way even more quickly. It was hard for him to explain patiently.

"Listen, Janet. We've been comparing lists of all the people who had dealings with each company—the companies the victims were employed by. It's been a massive job, until Martin came up with the idea of looking only at clients who have declared themselves bankrupt. There was a reference to bankruptcy on a note we found with one of the victims, but I didn't take it literally. Now we have, and the lists are much smaller. Your husband's name has come up in each list as common in all except one. That one has your maiden name." This was a lie, because there was one company that had neither her maiden nor married name listed. Right now, it was a minor point.

Brown raised her eyebrows. "My maiden name?"

"Feitler." He nodded down at the framed certificate still leaning against the wall. "I remembered it from seeing that."

The look on Brown's face had slowly changed from irritation and barely concealed anger to one of mild shock. "What the hell are you saying?" she whispered.

Suddenly Maiden felt sorry for her. He wanted to go over and take her in his arms. He pushed the urge down. "Very soon, Janet, the system will spit you out as a suspect.

Do you understand? . . . A *suspect*. We need to knock that possibility on the head straightaway, before someone starts making trouble."

"You mean find me an alibi?"

"Something like that."

Her voice rose. "For a spate of *serial murders*, for God's sake?"

"I just need you to account for your time."

"But that's *crazy!* Insane!" She was starting to break now, sitting up anxiously in her chair.

Maiden spread his hands. "It's the system, Janet. Nothing else. That's what I'm trying to explain!" Maiden felt trapped and useless. "Common sense will prevail, I promise you. But the system will initially produce your husband's name—and therefore *your* name—as a suspect."

"So, do *you* think I've been going around strangling people and cutting them up?"

"No, of course not! Why do you think I'm here now, instead of arresting you?"

This got through to her. Brown collapsed back into her seat and put a hand over her face. Maiden didn't have the courage to say anything. Finally she spoke through her fingers.

"This can't be as bad as it sounds," she said quietly. "All I have to do is prove my innocence and that will be the end of it, right? I mean, I had nothing to do with David's business. I don't even know who or what he dealt with."

"It should be very simple," Maiden said, trying to sound confident. "It'll be easy. Look, I'm not here because I think you might be a serial killer, for God's sake. That's ridiculous. I'm concerned about your professional standing. Something like this could damage your career, if it gets out at all. You know how bloody computers will bring out anything for the rest of your damn life if it goes on record. We need to bury it *before* it can go on any record and before anybody starts asking stupid questions."

"Like who?"

"*Anybody*, Janet! They're talking about more and more people being attached to this case. I'm losing control. In fact, if I don't come up with some answers by Monday, Bercoutte will fire me."

Brown pinched the bridge of her nose with her fingers. She stayed like that for a while, then asked, "So, what do I have to do?"

"We'll work out your alibis. Let *me* dismiss you as a suspect, while I'm still running the case. In fact, I'm the only one who knows your connection so far." Maiden paused, had a thought and shrugged. "Hell, I'm the only one who knows your maiden name, too, for that matter."

She looked at him. He was surprised by the return of her anger. She said harshly, "So without your prying and taking advantage of our relationship, this situation probably wouldn't be happening now?"

"No, nothing like that at all!" Maiden said, wearily. After a moment he shrugged. "OK, maybe it would have taken longer to emerge, but it would come out eventually."

"How can you be sure? Wouldn't it be easier for you to forget you know my maiden name?"

Despite his feelings for her and knowing this must all be a shock, Maiden couldn't help feeling a flash of his own anger. "For Christ's sake, Janet! I can't deliberately ignore evidence! If they found out, then eventually you'd still end up in the clear and *my* career would be down the tubes instead. Believe me, the best way is to clear your name now."

"But how could they know you've ignored anything?"

"Because I *won't* take the risk."

"All right, all right," she held her hand up. "Don't get mad."

"I'm not mad . . . just worried. If I didn't have these feelings for you, I'd be hauling you down to The Rocks right now and forcing you to explain where you were on about five separate occasions."

She looked at him oddly and her voice softened. "What feelings, John?"

He hesitated, thrown into unfamiliar territory. "You know what I'm talking about," he said, trying to return her intense look. "We've been getting on pretty well—you and I. We seem to click, or something. I like that—I like *you*."

She surprised him with a twisted smile. "This has got to be the craziest conversation I've had in years. First you accuse me of multiple murders, and now you're telling me you are attracted to me."

"It is pretty wild," Maiden agreed, trying to smile back. There was another uncomfortable silence between them. He used it to force himself to become hard again. The real business wasn't finished with.

He said, "Look, let's work out these alibis together and that'll be the end of it. Tomorrow I can tell everything to Martin, clear your name at the same time, and then I can get on with the job of finding the real killer before Bercoutte assigns me to professional death and obscurity."

"Oh John, not now, surely?"

"Not now?"

"I mean, do we have to work them out tonight?"

"I told you, I have to talk to Martin in the morning. I don't want to take the risk of any delays."

She looked at him helplessly. "You expect me to remember where I was on some night—what, two or three weeks ago? God, my mind's doing a million miles an hour. I can't think straight."

"You have to, Janet," he said softly. "We can't afford to wait. Someone could be going over the case right now and stumble over your husband's name."

"Then stay the night here, John," she said, leaning forward invitingly. "We can get up really early in the morning and do it then. Everything always seems better in the morning. I'll be able to remember more after a good night's sleep."

Maiden was taken by surprise and hesitated. He'd expected to be thrown out into the street. He asked, puzzled, "Are you sure?"

"I'm sure." Brown was ashamed. "Look, I realise now you came here tonight to help me. I reacted very badly and I'm sorry."

"Well—that's OK. Of course it's OK. I don't blame you."

"Then, will you stay?"

Brown looked lost and vulnerable, all the fight and anger beaten out of her. Maiden pointed a finger and said with mock severity, "Only if you *promise* to get up early enough for us to have a talk. I need some places, times and especially people who can vouch for you."

"It shouldn't be a problem, John," she said, smiling gratefully. "I'll bet I was at work every time."

"That would be great, just great."

"Just great," she murmured. She got up from her chair and walked to the doorway. There was a click and the room went dark, lit only by the red glow of the electric fire. Brown came back and stood in front of Maiden, staring down at him.

"I need you," she said and slid the gown off her shoulders, letting it drop completely to the floor. She wore nothing underneath.

Maiden's mouth went dry. "You don't have to do this," he said huskily.

"I know. I'm not doing it because I think I have to. I'm doing it because I *want* to." She reached down and took one of his hands, placing it on her mat of pubic hair.

There was an instant when he didn't know what he should do. Then he was overcome with wanting her. Maiden leaned forward and put his other hand on her buttocks, pulling her onto him. They fell together. It was awkward, the two of them on the lounge, but for the moment neither of them cared. Maiden kissed her stomach and breasts, while Brown concentrated on undoing his tie, shirt buttons and trousers. The romance suffered as he needed to struggle from his clothing, but she only laughed softly at his efforts and tried to help. Finally, both of them naked, the caressing and lovemaking became more serious.

"Let's get comfortable," Brown murmured with warm breath into his ear. He allowed her to move away and expected to be led into the bedroom, but instead she pulled him down onto the floor in front of the fire. "I've always wanted to do this," she said.

"No real log fire or even a rug?" he asked, smiling down as he pushed her onto her back.

"You can't have everything."

She spread her legs and wrapped them around him, trapping Maiden. Then, reaching down she guided him inside her, gasping with the sensation. He tried to be gentle, thinking she wouldn't be ready, but he was wrong. They stayed like that, Maiden keeping his weight off her with his elbows and moving slowly in and out. Brown began to groan, more loudly with each time he thrust against her. He could see her clearly now in the red electric firelight, her mouth open, but her eyes closed with pleasure. After some minutes she went still and stared up at him.

"Please," she said, asking him to get off, but not refusing him. She pushed at his chest with her fingertips and he pulled away gently. As soon as she was free Brown rolled over and got to her hands and knees, presenting herself to him that way. "Please, I like it this way," she whispered again over her shoulder to him.

Maiden obliged, moving in behind her. This time she called out loudly with pleasure as he entered her, then she repeated the cry again and again, each time more forcibly, as his own excitement rushed him and Maiden bucked against her. He felt his orgasm approaching undeniably and fought it, trying to wait for her. He told himself to think of anything except the naked, writhing woman in front of him and what they were doing together. He turned his face aside so he couldn't see her and looked to the wall.

And saw the monstrous shadow flicker across it.

He twisted desperately away from Brown, hurting her, and threw a protective arm up in the same moment a pair of huge white hands grappled for his throat. Brown scrambled aside as Maiden fell backwards. Now *he* had someone strong and heavy forcing themselves down on top of him, kneeling on him.

He found himself staring into the wide, dumb face of a freakish boy. Maiden's arm, locked into a struggle to keep his hands from closing around his neck, trembled with the effort. The boy was trapping his other arm with his knee, like a wrestler.

"Janet, for God's sake call him off!" Maiden yelled, knowing instinctively she was a part of this. She had control.

Brown's face appeared next to her son's. She stared impassively down at Maiden. "I think this is a better way," she said calmly. She moved out of Maiden's sight. He couldn't know she was sitting to one side on the floor with her legs open again, stimulating herself with her fingers at the sight of her son Jeremy attacking a man.

Only Jeremy's eyes showed any expression as he bore down mercilessly on Maiden, who was weakening fast. The boy was bewildered. He hadn't encountered so much resistance before. He hadn't fought anyone of Maiden's strength. Unheeded, a single line of drool fell onto Maiden's face as the boy tried to concentrate. Looking for more purchase, Jeremy moved his legs, momentarily freeing Maiden's other arm.

Maiden recognised the chance—and the heat of the electric fire on that side of his body. Losing precious millimetres in the fight to keep Jeremy from his throat, he focused instead on groping for the fire. He burnt his fingers locating it, then grasped the metal casing from behind, feeling more heat through his palm.

Praying the cord would reach, he pushed the heater hard into Jeremy's thigh.

With an inhuman scream the boy toppled off Maiden. The stench of singed hair and burned flesh filled the air. Brown was suddenly screaming too, panicking at seeing her son release Maiden. Jeremy rolled around in the middle of the room, clutching at his leg and screeching with agony. Crawling on his hands and knees, Maiden moved close to the boy and watched intently, choosing his moment.

He smashed his fist into Jeremy's face with all his strength—once, twice, then struck him hard in the stomach. The screaming changed to a whooping choke, so Maiden punched him in the face again. He felt bones crushing under his knuckles.

Brown launched herself onto Maiden's back, scratching at him anywhere she could reach. Maiden easily shrugged her off by pushing himself to his feet. When she rose from the floor to come at him, he slapped her viciously, cutting off her own banshee noise and sending her reeling across the room. Remorselessly he followed, hitting her twice more until she crumpled back to the floor and cowered away from him. Blood poured from her face and down her breasts. Maiden spun around, expecting Jeremy to be recovering, but the boy was curled into a whimpering ball where he fell, still grabbing uselessly at the large, blistering burn on his leg.

Maiden was stunned, trying to come to terms with what happened. He looked at Jeremy in disbelief. Janet Brown's child was pitiably deformed in many ways, but nature had compensated with immensely powerful arms and shoulders. Maiden dimly realised he had been lucky to escape them. He saw Brown moving and he quickly positioned himself so he could guard himself against both of them. She was looking up at him with tear-filled eyes. A welt was already rising on her cheek. Blood, black in the light of the heater, ran over her lips and chin, coating her teeth.

Maiden said to her hoarsely, pointing a shaking finger at Jeremy, "Who is he? Who is this poor bastard? You've trained him to kill like some fucking wild dog, haven't you?"

Brown spat blood from her mouth and said with a

painful, wretched slowness, "You know who he is. He's my son."

Maiden stared at her incredulously. The room started to spin and he needed a conscious effort to stop it. In his whirling vision he saw the white of a telephone and began stumbling towards it, but as he fumbled the receiver off the base Brown cried out in horror and started to crawl towards him.

"Stay back," he snarled at her, raising his fist.

"No . . . *no*," she shook her head and cowered, droplets of blood flying. "Please!"

Maiden edged away, taking the phone with him, realising she wasn't about to attack him, but wanted something else. Without getting off the floor, Brown cautiously reached up and snatched an address book off the small table. She began frantically flipping through the pages. Blood dripped onto the paper.

"Here," she said desperately, her words muffled by swelling lips. "Please, *here*." She held the book up at Maiden. "It's his hospital. They'll come and look after him—after Jeremy. They know he can be bad and they won't ask any questions. Please, just tell them he attacked you—nothing else. For his sake, *please*."

"Don't be stupid!" Maiden snapped, the words catching in his throat. "What sort of fool do you think I am?" The room was still spinning and his scalp ached dully. He realised Brown must have got one good blow to the back of his head before he threw her off.

"Please, John! *Please*. What about you and me?"

"You and me? *Us*?" His voice echoed painfully in his skull.

Brown was on her knees in front of him, still holding up the address book. A trickle of blood ran down to her groin as she looked at him beseechingly. "It's all over, John," she said urgently, dropping into a whisper. "Parsons was the last one. I can't do it anymore. I don't *want* to. Something's snapped inside me and I'm finished with it. It's like that

Janet Brown who was so full of hate is dead now, just like David is dead. I could start again—you and me."

Maiden couldn't believe what he was hearing.

Adding to his injuries was an ache in his heart.

"You lying bitch! You don't even *like* me!" he said, croaking with emotion. "You only wanted to know how my investigation was going. You were *fucking* me, so you could find out if I was going to *catch* you."

"No!" Brown shuffled towards him. "At first—yes. But not now. Now I'm falling in love with you!"

"No, you're insane," Maiden told her, staring down. But an insane thought of his own crept into his mind as he looked at her nakedness.

Even bruised and bloodied, he still wanted her. The truth shocked him.

Brown was imploring him. "John, don't call the police. Just call his hospital. Everything will be all right, I swear to you on his *life!*" She threw her hand out towards Jeremy, whose whimpering was getting quieter. "The killing's stopped, I swear it. I don't even know who did those terrible things. I don't think it was me, honest to God. It wasn't *me!*" she finished despairingly, touching her breast with her hand. She raised the address book again.

"Please, John. Call his hospital. They'll send an ambulance."

The handwritten telephone number swam in front of Maiden's eyes. He had been meaning to call The Rocks direct, rather than the emergency triple-O. He'd wanted the aftermath to happen among people he knew. Now the two numbers mixed together in his head. He shook it to clear the confusion and his eyesight focused momentarily to show him Janet Brown, begging at his feet.

He had to decide what meant more to him—how much *she* meant to him. What was possible—and what was impossible. And what was right.

He tried to dial by holding the phone in one hand and the receiver in the other, his free finger stabbing at the buttons, but he couldn't do it. He had to put the telephone back onto the table to steady it so he wouldn't make a mistake with the dialling. He knew he wouldn't be able to do it twice.

Chapter Thirty-one

She had always been an extraordinarily beautiful girl. Here, there was no late blossoming or ugly duckling transforming into a swan, but a truly pretty girl who became an attractive teenager and then a beautiful woman.

On the outside.

On the inside she had been irreparably disfigured when her father raped her at the age of fourteen—and planted his seed. She ran away from home and took her pregnancy to its full term. She didn't blame the child within her. It would be just another victim, like herself, and somebody to be pitied, not hated. She wouldn't compound the crime by killing the fetus in her womb.

She might have changed her mind, had she known just how much pity the living infant would deserve. It was obvious at birth the damage that had been wrought by the mingling of forbidden genes. The child was severely disabled, and as he was delivered one of the nurses let out an involuntary cry of dismay. The mother suppressed her own horror and hate at a world that had dealt her another cruel blow. She channelled her emotions back into a new determination. A resolve to survive this and to love and raise her child as well.

Pieces of the girl's mind were already coming apart, but they were subtle mechanisms always hidden or ignored, because of her smiling beauty.

The damaged child went into a special home and his mother went back to school. She wanted to study medicine, so that at some time in the future she could care for her son at home. It was her dream—the first dream she'd allowed herself for a long time—to earn a doctorate in medicine, a good income and a fine home where she might care for her child. Maybe even a man too, but her brief experience of men created an extra mental block.

Some years passed, then the very worst thing to happen to this woman occurred.

Her dream came true.

The man was the gentlest human being she had ever met. He treated her with a kindness she hadn't known before. He asked for nothing in return, knowing that eventually his efforts would be rewarded. It took an age for her to have the courage to admit she might have fallen in love, especially with all her other ambitions within reach. It seemed foolish to jeopardise them all for such a trite emotion as love, but the feelings grew despite herself. It took even longer for her to accept him and allow herself to trust another person completely. It needed years for her to take him to the special home and introduce him to her son.

The man wasn't shocked or horrified at the sight of the disfigured child. Instead, he sat and talked to the boy as if he were an old friend.

They married and, soon afterwards, it seemed the dream had come true. The impossible had happened. Even the ruined parts of her psyche began to heal and be pushed to the unreachable, buried corners of her mind.

But nothing lasts forever.

He was a successful businessman. Her husband was recognised and prosperous because of one brilliant idea.

That idea sustained him for years, but one day when he made a single mistake, the corporate wolves began to close their jaws around his throat and, sensing an easy kill, it began a series of events that would lead not only to the death of a career, a business and a woman's dream but, among others, also to the death of a man called Parsons on the roof of his own office block.

Her husband was the gentlest human being she had ever met. He didn't know how to fight the vicious lawyers, accountants and debtors who had convinced themselves he was a man about to fall and therefore they should grab their pound of flesh before the meal was all gone. They wore him down mercilessly, like hunting animals running their prey into the ground.

He was killed when his car drove straight through a stop sign and was crushed under a semitrailer carrying concrete railway sleepers.

It was an accident, officially. But the woman, her dream shattered, knew it was no accident. Her husband had driven through that stop sign because his mind had been filled with torment and stress. Worry. Intense anxiety over what the future held for him, his wife and her handicapped son.

The corporate wolves had killed him, just as surely as if they had been behind the wheel themselves and waited for the semitrailer to come along.

That was when the broken parts of her mind suddenly found a new dominance. They had been set free to damn her after the rape, then festered for too long beneath her determination to succeed in a new life, before finally being suppressed by good fortune and the love of her husband. But in truth they had always been there, alive and awaiting their chance to ruin her, ever since the night she had closed her eyes to the sight of her father's ecstatic face poised above her own as he pushed himself between her legs, telling her in excited gasps it was his *right*.

His right.

She knew about rights, now. She always had. And she believed the corporate wolves never had a *right* to hound her husband to his death, picking his life and career to pieces like carrion birds sharing a corpse. Pulling him apart piece by piece.

Which was how she arrived at the idea of teaching them all a lesson. Giving them a taste of what it was like to have your dreams destroyed, leaving behind only pieces. Human pieces, to force the lesson home.

Perhaps the lessons might make them think twice before believing ten bankrupt cents on the dollar was worth more than the value of a human life.

FAMILY INHERITANCE
DEBORAH LeBLANC

The dark, impenetrable bayous of Louisiana are filled with secrets that can never be revealed and mysterious forces that can never be understood. Jessica LeJeune left Louisiana, but she brought some of those mysterious forces with her—and now she's being called back home to her Cajun roots to confront a destiny she could not escape and a curse she might not survive.

Jessica's younger brother, Todd, has descended into a world of madness. His shattered mind is now the plaything of an unimaginable evil. But Jessica is not alone in her battle to save her brother's soul. For deep in the misty bayous, in an isolated wooden shack, lives the person who is their only hope....

- -

JAMES A. MOORE

POSSESSIONS

Chris Corin has the unshakable feeling that he's being followed. And he's right. But he doesn't know what's after him, what waits in the shadows. He doesn't know that what his late mother left him in her will is the source of inconceivable power. Power that something hideous wants very badly indeed.

By the time Chris realizes what's happening it may already be too late. Who would believe him? Who could imagine the otherworldly forces that will stop at nothing to possess what Chris has? No, Chris will have to confront the darkness that has crept into his life, threatening his very sanity. And unless he can convince someone that he's not crazy, he'll have to confront it alone.

FEARS
UNNAMED
TIM LEBBON

Tim Lebbon has burst upon the scene and established himself as one of the best horror writers at work today. He is the winner of numerous awards, including a Bram Stoker Award, critics have raved about his work, and fans have eagerly embraced him as a contemporary master of the macabre.

Perhaps nowhere are the reasons for his popularity more evident than in this collection of four of his most chilling novellas. Two of these dark gems received British Fantasy Awards, and another was written specifically for this book and has never previously been published. These terrifying tales form a window into a world of horrors that, once experienced, can never be forgotten.

DARK UNIVERSE
WILLIAM F. NOLAN

Welcome to William F. Nolan's *Dark Universe*, a universe of horror, suspense and mystery. For the past fifty years William F. Nolan has been writing in each of these worlds—and compiling a legendary body of work that is unsurpassed in quality, style . . . and the sheer ability to send chills down the spines of readers. At long last, this volume collects many of Nolan's finest stories, selected from his entire career. These are unforgettable tales guaranteed to frighten, surprise, delight and even shock readers who like to explore the shadows and who aren't afraid of the dark.
